DANGER'S KISS

PRAISE FOR CHRISTINE MICHELS'

DANGER'S KISS

"With the publication of DANGER'S KISS, Christine Michels proves that she is a versatile talent who can write a compelling tale of romantic suspense that leaves readers breathlessly anticipating what comes next. There is an intriguing secondary character named Stone whose story begs to be told."

— *Affaire de Coeur*

"There's suspense as well as [ ] romantic involvement in this imaginative story, which goes behind the friendly façade to uncover dark small-town secrets."

— *Verne Clemence, The Star Phoenix Newspaper*

"DANGER'S KISS is a thought-provoking statement about the serious and compelling problem of serial killers in our society. It offers some insight as to why they exist, and points a blood drenched finger at the major role that society plays in helping to create them... DANGER'S KISS is a roller coaster ride through the depths of emotional despair and terror. This spicy, nail-biting thriller will have readers thinking twice about the boy next door."

—*Gothic Journal*

"One surprise after another keeps this story moving rapidly. I sat on the edge of my seat, riveted by this unfolding story of pain, love and insanity. The real life characters, tension building suspense, intense passion, and dynamic climax make this fantastic read one to savor long after the last page is turned."

— *Rendezvous*

DANGER'S KISS

When you feel Danger's kiss
upon your spine.
Don't look back.
For you'll soon be mine.

The macabre poem was the first clue Kim Tannas had that her life was in jeopardy, but it was far from the last.

When Kim Tannas returns to the small town of Lillooet Creek, she finds herself the target of terrifying threats. Desperate to escape from a deranged serial killer, she turns to three people for help—three people whose secrets might place her in deadly jeopardy:

VAUGHN GARRETT—The handsome sheriff quickly learns all about Kim's past, but he hides from her a dark and painful childhood.

LIZ MURPHY—Mysteriously drawn to Lillooet Creek, the psychic discovers a link to the town that will forever change her life.

SPECIAL AGENT STONE—Stern and forbidding, the FBI agent relishes investigating crimes almost as much as the murderer enjoys committing them.

Drawn into a tangled web of danger and desire, Kim doesn't know whom she can trust. But time is running out, and before long, she might feel the fatal touch of danger's kiss.

"Christine Michels has penned a suspense packed romance with just enough twists and turns to keep the reader jumping. . . and completely engrossed. A real page turner!"

— The Talisman

"DANGER'S KISS is hard to put down. It's a romance with all the elements of a fast-paced and absorbing mystery thriller plus added spice as the heroine finds herself in the handsome sheriff's arms."

— Paperback Forum

"Christine Michels weaves the elements of mystery and romance together with such intrigue that the reader is drawn into the desperate race to solve the murders of Lillooet Creek. The reader is warned to lock her doors and windows when reading this wonderfully scary but entertaining tale of murder and romance."

—GEnie Romance Exchange

Follow Christine on Twitter:
@CMichelsAuthor

~~~

Or "Like" Christine on Facebook at:
http://www.facebook.com/Michels.Christine

DANGER'S KISS

CHRISTINE MICHELS

DEDICATION

This one is dedicated to the readers who have written me letters and email correspondence over the years letting me know how much they enjoyed my work. "Thank you."

ACKNOWLEGEMENTS

I would like to express my gratitude to the following people for their help in making this novel a reality.

To Sheriff William A. Logan of Chehalis, WA, who so generously answered all of my questions.

To the staff of the Lloydminster Public Library for their support in finding the research material I needed.

And to Bernice and Esther for their critiquing ability.

Thank you all.

The responsibility for any failings this novel may have, naturally, rests with me.

PROLOGUE

Only the flickering light of the television battled the darkness of the room. Shadows leapt and capered over the walls and furniture like living things. His eyes glinted in the dimness as he watched them. Then slowly he reached up to take hold of the switch on the lamp. "Boo," he said softly as he turned it. The shadows disappeared. He smiled and ran his hand gently over the fraying binding of the book in his lap, letting it fall open. Removing the braid of rich, golden-blonde hair he'd used as a bookmark, he lowered his eyes to the page.

Of all the poems she had forced him to read over the years, only a few had achieved any significance. This one, by John Donne was his favorite. It seemed so pure and simple. Yet each time he read it he discovered hidden nuances, elusive meanings he'd misinterpreted. He read it again.

The Funeral
by John Donne 1573 - 1631
Whoever comes to shroud me, do not harm
Nor question much
That subtle wreath of hair about mine arm;

The mystery, the sign you must not touch,
For 'tis my outward soul,
Viceroy to that which, unto heav'n being gone,
Will leave this to control
And keep these limbs, her provinces, from dissolution.

For if the sinewy thread my brain lets fall
Through every part
Can tie those parts, and make me one of all,
Those hairs, which upward grew, and strength and
    art
Have from a better brain,
Can better do't: except she meant that I
By this should know my pain,
As prisoners then are manacled, when they're
    condemn'd to die.

Whate'er she meant by 't, bury it with me,
For since I am
Love's martyr, it might breed idolatry
If into other hands these reliques came.
As 'twas humility
T' afford to it all that a soul can do,
So 'tis some bravery
That, since you would have none of me, I bury some of
    you.

    Finished reading, he turned off the lamp to reflect. He liked the darkness; it blanketed him, isolating him from distraction, allowing him to see things more clearly. He replayed the words of the poem in his mind from memory. Had he gleaned all there was to learn from it?

    He ran the long braid of hair through his hands as he considered. Its texture distracted him. How warm and alive it felt where it had been cradled within his palm; how cool and lifeless where it had been exposed to the freshness of the air. He raised it to his face, felt the satin caress against his cheek. It still carried her scent. Clean, like spring flowers. Ah, Candace. In the end, she had understood and accepted her punishment. And he ... he had felt liberated.

The formidable coiled tension he'd lived with for as long as he could remember had relaxed its hold for a time, and he'd felt the tranquility bestowed by retribution. But the pressure, the urgency, was building again, like a reptilian monster in his gut. His fists clenched on the binding of the book in his lap; his knuckles whitened. Then, forcing his hands to relax, he smiled. Patience.

An image from the glowing television in the dark-ened room caught his eye. A beautiful brunette cavorted on a sunny beach, reminding him of another woman. The monster stirred in its sleep and the muscles of his flat stomach clenched. Soon.

CHAPTER 1

*E*very man she had ever loved had been murdered. Kim faced the sudden realization grimly. How was that for being jinxed? Driving instinctively, she maneuvered her small red Ford Focus around another series of curves in the mountain road.

When she was 13, her father had been robbed and stabbed to death while closing their small Lillooet Creek service station for the night. His killer had never been caught. Two years ago she had lost her husband Ken to a bullet when, as a Seattle police officer, he'd been called to a domestic disturbance. His killer had blown his own brains out before he could be taken into custody. And now her cousin Trent, a native of Lillooet Creek, had been murdered. His killer was still at large.

A fresh spate of grief clawed at her throat but she swallowed, choking it back. She had done her grieving for Trent. After receiving the news, she'd closeted herself in her bedroom and cried until there were no tissue's left in the box. Until her eyes had been swollen shut and her nose had been nothing more than a red blotch in the center of her puffy face. Until the enormous cloud of anguish had been reduced to a small, cold knot in the pit of her stomach. Now, she took refuge in action.

Shortly, she would arrive in Lillooet Creek. Trent's funeral was tomorrow. This afternoon, the first thing she planned to do was check in with local law enforcement. She didn't trust small town sheriff's departments, not since her father's killer had escaped justice.

Clenching her teeth to control a sudden rush of guilt and anger, she pressed down on the accelerator a little. Trent had been killed in the same town as her father. The same damn department was in charge of the investigation. That didn't bode well. But this time the killer would be caught. Kim had made a promise to herself. . . and to the spirit of her dead cousin.

Completely oblivious to the incredible mountain scenery, she whipped around another curve in the road and slammed on the brakes. Shaking her head, she grimaced. She would love to get hold of the state highway planner—or whoever it was—who had economized on highway signs announcing Lillooet Creek's proximity. Unless you were familiar with the road and paying attention to natural landmarks, that last curve always caught you by surprise. Then, to compound the stupidity, the town planners had decided to place an enormous "Welcome to Lillooet Creek" carving right there, smack dab at the end of the road where it branched into three segments—two streets that entered Lillooet Creek and a third that took a hairpin loop to continue on up the mountain.

Whenever she came to Lillooet Creek, which wasn't any more often than necessary, Kim avoided as much of the town as possible. In the 17 years since she and her mother had moved away, she'd been back a few times to visit her relatives. But the closeness she'd been able to maintain with her aunt and cousins over those years had been due in large part to the fact that one or the other of them had visited her frequently at her home in Seattle. Kim was reasonably certain that their almost monthly visits were precipitated in part by their understanding of her feelings concerning the town. Her sentiments would have been obvious to anybody, for, when she did visit Lillooet Creek, it was rare indeed that she ventured from her aunt's home onto the streets of the town.

She wouldn't admit, even to herself, the reason for this. She'd convinced herself that she hated the town. But the simple fact was that, every time she walked the streets of Lillooet Creek, she had to face a thousand memories of her father. Those memories inevitably triggered the painful emotions linked to that horrible night when she was 13 and had witnessed her father's death. That's all there was left of that night—*emotions*. Not even two years of therapy and hypnosis had been able to dredge up the memory of the events of that night. And then came the guilt. Why? Why couldn't she remember? Why had she allowed her father's killer to escape unpunished?

Had she only been older at the time, perhaps things would have been different. Perhaps she would have retained a memory of that night. Perhaps she would have been able to tell the investigators something. Perhaps she could have done something to ensure that the sheriff's department had not given up so easily.

Now, turning left onto Lone Pine Road because it would allow her to avoid Main Street and much of the town proper, Kim crossed the bridge and entered the town. She had proceeded just one block, and was in the process of continuing through the intersection when a horn basted. A flat-bed lumber truck shot toward her, ignoring the stop sign. She slammed on the brakes. With her heart in her throat, she came to a stop a mere foot from the truck which halted in the center of the intersection. It was one of the small fleet of trucks owned by Carter's Lumber. What the hell had the driver been doing?

As her attention shifted from the vehicle to its driver, she forgot her anger. She had never seen such strange eyes—cold, pale green, celery-colored eyes. The driver sat with his left elbow protruding from the open side window as though he hadn't a care in the world, staring at her for an eternity. Then, without the slightest change in expression, he turned away, put the truck in gear and proceeded on. Kimberley expelled the breath she'd unconsciously been holding. That was one man she certainly wouldn't want to meet in a dark alley.

Kim depressed the accelerator and proceeded down the road. The county court house, which housed the sheriff's department, was two blocks north on Jackson Avenue. Coming to a stop in front of the large brick building, she took a deep breath before getting out of the car and walking boldly up the cement walk.

As she opened the door and entered, she bumped into a woman whom she'd last seen at least ten years ago while visiting her Aunt Vivian. "Aunt Willie!" she exclaimed as she sidestepped to move out of the doorway. How could the woman age a decade without changing one iota?

"How are you?" Kim extended her hand in greeting and felt it swallowed by the enormous, calloused grasp of the tallest, most muscular woman she had ever known. Willie wore a man's red plaid shirt and denim jeans. Her white hair was pulled into a no-nonsense braid that hung over one shoulder, almost reaching her waist. Despite Willie's not unattractive facial features, Kim didn't think she'd ever seen a more mannish woman. And yet, incongruously, Willie's fingernails and toenails were polished a bright shade of burgundy.

Aunt Willie looked down at her with her clear green eyes and frowned slightly. "You're that Clayton girl, aren't you? Kimberley, isn't it?"

Kim smiled. "That's right. Only it's Kimberley Tannas now. I didn't think you'd remember me."

"I never forget a face, child."

Aunt Willie was really no relative at all. Somehow

through the years, Wilma Nielsen had become Aunt Willie to virtually the entire populace of the town. She sobered now as she looked at Kim. "It's a shame it took such sad circumstances to bring you home. I know how close you were to Trent and Deirdre. I'm real sorry."

Kim felt the smile tremble a bit on her lips and she avoided Aunt Willie's eyes. God, she hated sympathy. It always brought tears too near the surface. "Me, too."

"Well I got to be going. I'm on the way to the creek to do a little fishing." Opening the door, Willie stepped out of the office and into a pair of rubber boots that had been left sitting beside the step. "I'll see you tomorrow, child."

Kim nodded. "See you."

Aunt Willie grasped a fishing rod that had been left leaning against the side of the building, extracted a ball cap from the pocket of her jeans and pulled it firmly down over her head before walking down the sidewalk. Willie might be an eccentric and often brusque woman, but for someone well into her sixties, she was one of the most vital and energetic people Kim knew. Kim admired her.

Turning away, Kim cast a glance around the sheriff's department main office. A deputy watched her with a vigilant brown-eyed gaze from his position near a small table containing coffee supplies. He had apparently been preparing a cup for himself when she'd entered. Despite his striking bodybuilder's physique, he wasn't a very attractive man. His nose and cheekbones showed signs of being broken; his features were harsh and angular. He reminded Kimberley of one of those brainless gorilla types you saw as bodyguards in the movies. Then, abruptly, he smiled. The expression performed a miracle.

"Hi," he said. "I'm Deputy Lewis. Can I help you?"

She smiled. "Yes. I was wondering if the sheriff is in?"

He looked toward a closed door off to his right. "I'm

not certain. I just returned myself." He noted the entrance of a pretty dark-haired woman. "Here's Melissa now. I'm sure she'll be able to help you." Without another word, he turned and disappeared through a doorway.

The woman, Melissa, took one look at her, seated herself behind the reception desk and proceeded to smile up at her in a peculiarly expectant manner. Kim checked her name plate: *Melissa Adams*. Why was Melissa looking at her that way? She looked vaguely familiar, but. . . Melissa? Kim frowned. "Did you used to be Melissa Johnson?"

"I'll be damned. You remembered."

"It took me a moment. You've changed some from the girl in pigtails. But I couldn't ever forget completely. We got into more trouble together that last summer. . . ." She trailed off as she remembered why their brief but tumultuous friendship had been cut short. She wondered what paths her life might have taken if her father hadn't been killed. "Well," she said, forcing a smile. "Who is this Adams character? I don't remember any Adams."

"You wouldn't. Curt moved into town about nine years ago. Came to fill an opening for a dentist."

Kim grimaced. "I hate dentists."

"Yeah," Melissa's expression said she commiserated with the problem. Then she suddenly smiled again. "But he leaves the drills and needles at the office when he comes home." Melissa's expression sobered. "I'm really sorry about Trent, Kim. Everyone is."

"Thanks." Kim avoided Melissa's eyes, looking instead at a picture hanging on the wall behind her. It was a scenic view of a tropical beach. "Actually that's why I'm here. Is the sheriff in?"

"You're in luck. He just got back a few minutes ago." Kim followed her gaze to the closed office door. It was just opening. "Here he is now."

Following her gaze, Kim felt as though she'd been

kicked in the gut. Her stomach curdled with the force of her instant dislike. She stopped breathing. Only her heart, pounding frantically in her ears, continued to mark the passage of seconds. Kim watched the man walk from his office to the coffeepot that sat on a nearby table. He possessed the same indefinable quality that actors used to portray with such mesmerizing effect on old Western movies. This was the sheriff who could step into the saloon and, without saying a word, silence every blustering bully, gunslinger and gambler in the place. He wasn't that tall. Close to six feet, maybe, but certainly not over. Yet he had "presence", an aura of command and confidence that Kim had never seen anywhere other than on the screen. It was a quality she had always admired. Until now.

Because, in addition to that indefinable quality that she called "presence", the sheriff was one of the handsomest men she had ever seen. So much like another man she had known that they could have been brothers. She felt she already knew him. He would be arrogant and self-centered—so self-centered that he would be oblivious to the actuality that other people had feelings.

She was transported back in time—back 14 years to a high school gym where a naive 16-year-old girl had been taken in by a male just like him. Gage Linson had been younger—an 18-year-old high school jock. But like Gage, this sheriff wore his extraordinarily handsome looks like a license to use and manipulate. He would be the kind of man who thought that good looks and practiced charm could compensate for a lack of substance in character.

"Sheriff," Melissa called to him. "Kimberley Clayton is here to see you."

"Tannas," Kim snapped without meaning to. She swallowed and moderated her tone. "Kimberley Tannas."

"Kimberley Tannas," Melissa enunciated her name clearly as the sheriff strode toward them. "This is Sheriff Garrett."

All the emotional shields that Kimberley had developed to protect herself from men like Gage Linson slammed into place. She was determined not to notice the way the forest green shirt of his uniform fit his wide shoulders and thick biceps as though it had been tailored exclusively for him. Or the way the loose-fitting tan trousers pulled taut over powerful thighs as he walked toward her. Or the way strong, even, white teeth flashed in a smile calculated to cause heart palpitations when he stopped in front of her.

"Ms. Tannas." Sheriff Garrett extended his lean, tanned hand in greeting, and Kim forced herself to take it, briefly.

She felt as though her entire face had been injected with Novocain. "Sheriff," she said through wooden lips as she nodded in greeting. "May I speak with you a moment please?"

He frowned slightly. "Certainly. Come into my office." Grasping her elbow, he guided her.

"Have a seat." He indicated a brown vinyl chair sitting in front of his desk as he closed the door. Kim sat and watched him as he walked around the desk to seat himself in his high-backed office chair. He wore his uniform like a man who felt he'd earned it and the respect that went along with it. Kim thought he'd probably managed to win the election primarily on charisma. His sort practically oozed the stuff.

"What can I do for you, Ms. Tannas?" he asked as he leaned back in his chair and linked his fingers behind his head—the posture of a male confident of his superiority.

"I want to know exactly what you're doing to apprehend my cousin's murderer, Sheriff Garrett." The statement emerged in a dictatorial tone that Kim would have called back if she could. Despite her dislike for

Garrett, and all men like him, she had no desire to antagonize the man; she needed to be able to communicate with him.

Garrett stared at her. His strange gold eyes hardened. "You want . . ." his voice trailed off and he cleared his throat before squaring his broad, intimidating shoulders and leaning forward to place his arms on the desk in front of him. "I see." He paused and the silence stretched between them. Kim refused to attempt to fill it. "Let me assure you, Kimberley," he said, finally, "that everything that can be done is being done."

"*What* is being done, Sheriff? Do you have any suspects? Have you found any witnesses?"

"Ms. Tannas, I resent your attitude. You may rest assured that this department is doing everything that can be done to resolve this case. There is nothing you need to worry your pretty head about." The response seemed to be a calculated declaration of war.

Kim's backbone took on an extra measure of steel. "And I resent your condescending attitude, Sheriff. I am perfectly capable of understanding the particulars of homicide investigation."

"Unfortunately I have neither the time nor the inclination to instruct you in those particulars, Ms. Tannas."

Kim tensed and mastered the urge to enter the verbal fray with no holds barred. Instinct told her that such tactics would gain her nothing. She forced a smile and tried to inject a note of conciliation into her tone. "Sheriff, my concern is that another killer does not escape justice in this town because of−" Oh, hell. She'd been about to say because of the ineptitude of small town law enforcement and politics. Another remark not exactly likely to encourage a spirit of cooperation. She formulated a less inflammatory conclusion to her sentence. "Because of a lack of communication between the townspeople and the sheriff's department."

When he spoke, he chose to ignore that part of her

statement anyway. "What other killer are you talking about?"

"The one who murdered my father seventeen years ago."

He nodded as he considered her thoughtfully with watchful amber eyes. "Kimberley Clayton," he said as though he was musing to himself. "Ah, yes. I remember."

Kim frowned slightly. He remembered? How? Who the hell was he? Why didn't she remember him? She raked her mind for a memory associated with the name Garrett and came up empty. Damn!

"I'm pleased I was able to jog your memory," Kim said with an edge of sarcasm, forgetting, once again, to censor her tongue. "Now, if you'll just answer my question?" Kim raised an eyebrow expectantly. "I don't want to monopolize your valuable time. Once you've brought me up to date, I'll simply check in with you occasionally to make certain you . . . um, keep the case at the top of the list."

The gall of the woman was incredible. Garrett cleared his throat and wished he'd listened to his instincts. When he'd first turned around to see her standing in his outer office, he'd felt an instant shock of recognition; not for her—although, after hearing her name, he remembered seeing her occasionally years ago—but rather for her type.

Every honey-blonde hair on her head had been pulled into a tight French braid that broadcast assurance and self-confidence. She wore a slim-fitting black skirt and black pumps with heels that had to be at least three inches high. He surmised that this was an effort to compensate for nature's lack of generosity in the height department. Even with the pumps, he was certain she was no more than five foot five or six. And despite the loose-fitting cut of her red blazer, he could tell that her spine was arrow-straight. She had stood there, facing him squarely, her weight evenly distributed on both feet, a portfolio-style briefcase hanging from a strap over her left shoulder. This was a lady who wanted—no *demanded*—to be taken seriously, a cast iron bitch.

But despite the past experience which had enabled him to categorize her, Garrett had taken one look at those big smoky-blue eyes set in a face made exotic by a subtle slant of cheekbones and had ignored his instincts.

He considered those liquid eyes again now, remembered the elegant curve of those magnificent legs in black hose, and fascination soared within him. Damn, he was a real sucker for punishment. It was a good thing she was married. That put her securely off-limits. He pitied the man who'd married her. Garrett cleared his throat again as he forced himself to focus on the conversation. What had she said? Oh yeah. "I will tell you this much, Ms. Tannas. My men and I have questioned virtually everyone in town. Nobody saw anything. We have no suspects at this time."

"In other words, you have nothing."

"We know a little more than we did a few days ago. But there is no conclusive evidence."

"I see." Kim rose and paced back and forth a couple of times. Then, apparently deciding there was nothing more to be said, she stopped in front of his desk and looked down at him. "Well, Sheriff Garrett, I thank you for so generously sharing your time. I'll be in touch. . . regularly."

Garrett tensed at her sarcasm, then cursed himself silently for letting her get to him. "Let me suggest that the next time you want to speak with me, you do it by phone."

"I fully intend to, Sheriff."

"Good. I'd hate for this town to suffer the trauma of another homicide so soon. Justifiable or not."

Kim stared at him coldly. "Is that a threat, Sheriff?"

He bared his teeth. "Good-bye, Kimberley."

She left his office, leaving the door open behind her. Garrett watched her walk away—he'd always been a sucker for a well-shaped behind, and Kimberley Tannas had a particularly nice one—and shook his head. There went one vote he would never get. He had not handled the encounter with his usual finesse at all. He was typically adept at soothing the concerns of citizens. But something about Ms. Tannas seemed to bring out the worst in him.

* * *

As Kim left the sheriff's office and drove up the hillside to her aunt's home where it overlooked the town, she massaged her aching temples with one hand. She knew she had been incredibly rude, but she had found over the years that rudeness seemed to be her instinctive self-defense against the machismo male. She had difficulty controlling it. That type of man brought out the worst in her. Her cousin Deirdre's husband, Kyle Ward, affected her the same way. They had learned to tolerate each other for Deirdre's sake. In the last few days, she had even managed to appreciate his existence in an abstracted way.

Kyle had actually surprised Kim by taking charge and making all the arrangements for Trent's funeral. She hadn't thought he would be able to pull himself out of his self-absorption long enough. Then again, he managed his own reasonably successful men's clothing store, so she guessed he wasn't incompetent. And he'd really had little choice. Immobilized by grief, her Aunt Vivian and her cousin, Deirdre, always the fragile sort, had been incapable of coping with the details of the arrangements. And Kim had been unable to get away from her own small craft boutique in Seattle. Her partner, Kathy, had inconveniently chosen that particular time to be on vacation in California. It had taken Kim an entire day just to track her down. When she reached her, they'd discussed closing the store for a couple of days, but this was their busy season so Kathy had decided to cut her holiday short by a week and return to manage the boutique.

Kim turned into her aunt's long, wide driveway and pulled her car over next to the old garage. This place never changed. It was more home to her than any other place since her father's death. She wished she could transplant it—complete with loved ones—to another town. One nearer Seattle. One that wasn't overflowing with painful memories. One that wasn't Lillooet Creek.

* * *

The night had passed slowly. The funeral service even more slowly. Oh, God, poor Trent. The smell of freshly turned soil, damp from the previous night's rain, invaded her senses. Kim separated it from the other scents on the air and blocked it out, concentrating instead on the clean smell of wet pine needles. She closed her eyes to the sight of Trent's newly excavated grave and fought the urge to succumb to renewed sobbing. She wouldn't cry any more, she *wouldn't*. Not in public. Her throat convulsed with the agony of suppression. But she won.

Through swollen eyes, she noticed her Uncle Jake standing across from them, distancing himself. At least he had come alone, she mused. She was almost surprised he had come at all. His relationship with his family hadn't exactly been smooth in the last few years.

Abruptly her cousin, Deirdre, moved ahead. Kim watched as she led Aunt Vivian forward to lay a flower on the casket. She wished her own mother was here. But, remarried now and living in Australia, it simply hadn't been feasible for her to come. In her stead, she'd sent a telegram expressing her condolences.

The sound of loud, heart-rending sobs suddenly echoed through the hazy atmosphere as her aunt was overcome by misery. Kim stepped forward intending to help Deirdre support Aunt Vivian, but was gestured back by Uncle Jake as he moved to assist his ex-wife. It was the first time they had stood together as a family in five years. Kim bowed her head.

Grief radiated from those present, surrounding her like a gray wall. She felt consumed by it, as though it would absorb her into itself. It weighed down her heart like a stone. She looked for something, anything, on which to focus her attention besides that wall of misery.

A single water droplet clung to a blade of grass. She concentrated on it, studying it. It had rained during the night. A gossamer curtain of cloud still hung overhead, subduing the brilliance of the summer sky. Yet as she observed that drop of rain, a single ray of sunlight fought its way through the thin clouds, striking the droplet and transforming it into something beautiful: a tiny, shimmering, fragile gem. For some inexplicable reason, that simple beauty made her feel better.

And then Aunt Viv was at her side again and it was Kim's turn to say farewell to Trent. God, she hated funerals; she hated death. She forced herself to move forward, to place the hot-house daffodil on his casket. Trent had loved daffodils. It seemed silly to say that of a man like Trent, but it was true. He would never have admitted it, of course, but his preference had been obvious. It was always the type of flower he gave to others. He'd never given two hoots about the proper type of flower for a particular occasion; he'd simply given a flower that made him feel happy. He'd placed a special order with a hot-house grower in order to give Kim an enormous bouquet of them for her graduation. She smiled tearfully at the memory.

"Thanks for everything, Cuz," she whispered. "Save a place for me." She was startled by the words. Lord, she hadn't said those words to Trent since the carefree days of their childhood when the three of them—Trent and Deirdre and Kimberley—had gone everywhere together, playing and fighting and caring for each other like siblings. That had all ended when Kim and her mother had moved to Seattle immediately following her father's death.

Paralyzed by memories of the past, of happier times, Kim didn't realize that she was holding up the proceedings until somebody gently coaxed her back to her aunt's side. She grasped Aunt Vivian's arm and, with Deirdre supporting her mother from the other side, they turned and began walking toward the row of parked vehicles. Uncle Jake, having preceded them, was already getting into his car.

Suddenly, the sun came out. A million clinging raindrops began to sparkle. A red squirrel chattered irreverently from the branches of an enormous Douglas fir before dropping onto the arched surface of a white headstone. And people began to speak in respectful murmurs as they moved away from the grave. Life goes on, thought Kim.

"Mrs. Farris."

They had almost reached the car, where Curt Adams, who had served as a pallbearer, waited to drive them home, but the sound of her aunt's name being called halted them. They turned to see a man approaching. It was Sheriff Garrett. Today, as Kim noted the details of his appearance, she saw nothing that would alter her initial impression of the man. He wore a black dress shirt and a silver-gray tie that contrasted perfectly with his pin-striped gray suit. His dark, blonde hair, slightly longish, curled up a bit where it brushed the collar of his suit jacket. The shadow beneath the flesh of his clean-shaven jawline bespoke a beard that would be a number of shades darker than his hair. And he walked with the same bold, confident stride Kim remembered from the previous day. She wondered why he stayed in Lillooet Creek. Surely a man which his striking appearance and undoubtedly predatory character would find the pickings better in a larger center.

"Mrs. Farris," he repeated as he came within speaking distance. "I won't be able to make it up to the house, so I. . . well, I wanted to express my condolences."

Kim noted that his eyes, too, were reddened by grief. That surprised her. He must have known Trent well, yet she couldn't remember Trent ever speaking of him. And she was certain she'd never met him herself. Of course she could count on her fingers the number of times she'd been to Lillooet Creek in the last 17 years. And since she had rarely left the house on those special weekends when she had forced herself to come, she supposed she shouldn't expect to know everyone with whom her cousin had associated.

Aunt Viv grasped Garrett's hand. "Thank you, Vaughn. I appreciate your sympathy." She looked intently into his eyes as she squeezed his hand. "But the best thing you can do for me is to catch his killer. Please? I won't be able to rest until—" her voice broke. "Please?"

Vaughn? That name sounded familiar.

Sheriff Garrett covered Aunt Vivian's clutching fingers with his free hand. "I'll do my best, Mrs. Farris. I promise."

Aunt Viv nodded and attempted a smile before turning away to enter the car. Kim opened the door and waited while Deirdre helped her mother into the car. Then, while Deirdre moved around the vehicle to take the rear seat on the other side, Kim closed the door behind her aunt and reached to open the rear door for herself. Another hand beat her to it. Startled, she looked up, directly into intense golden eyes. Sheriff Garrett opened the door for her. "It's nice to see you again, Kimberley." Kim detected the subtle inflection of sarcasm in the statement, but she doubted that anyone else had picked up on it.

Her face felt so tight and drawn that the effort to stretch her lips into a cool smile would have been agonizing. Kim settled for granting him a regal nod of thanks for his courtesy. She'd be damned if she'd let him get to her. Then, incapable of comment, she entered the car.

As the car pulled away from the cemetery, Kim looked back at the man in the gray suit. Vaughn. Damn, that name was familiar. Suddenly she made the connection. She had known a Vaughn Garrett in grade school. He'd been one of Anna Irving's foster kids. But he'd been a thin, wiry kid with a perpetually short brush-cut, a black leather jacket that everyone was certain he'd stolen, and a chip on his shoulder the size of Washington State. A loner, whom—had Kim thought about it at all—she would have wagered would be spending a good portion of his adult life behind bars. It couldn't be the same guy. People just didn't change that much. Did they? But then, how many Vaughn Garretts could there be in a town this size?

With a mental shrug, Kim dismissed him from her mind and focused instead on how she would manage to get through the hours remaining until she could once again escape the boundaries of Lillooet Creek and return to Seattle.

She hoped Deirdre managed to keep going without breaking down. As children, Kim and Trent had always protected her. Kim studied her now. So far she was doing well, but she still had to get through the rest of the day. Immediately following the service, Kyle had been forced to take their two children home. Deirdre simply wasn't up to meeting the demands of the two preschool youngsters at the moment. And, what with most of the county turning out for the funeral and the remainder extremely leery of the fact that Trent had been murdered, they had been unable to find a sitter.

Home for Deirdre and Kyle was seven or eight miles further up the mountain to Crystal Falls, a small winter resort town. Kim had never been there. One of these times she was really going to have to extend her visit long enough to make the short trip up the mountain to see her cousin's home. It was inconsiderate of her not to, she knew. But whenever she came here, she was so on edge. Her visits were always more obligatory than anything. Besides, with the way she and Kyle felt about each other, she was under the impression that he preferred her to stay away. She wondered if Kyle and the sheriff were friends. They were probably nearly enough alike in character to be twins.

* * *

Elizabeth Murphy sighed as the warm water caressed her aching legs. She had been to a doctor not long ago to complain about the tendency the dratted appendages had to become painful and heavy feeling, but the idiot physician had merely told her to take it easy, keep her feet up, and stop traipsing around the countryside. Ridiculous!

As a travel-writer and photographer, she had finally achieved the level of independence that she'd always desired. She travelled all summer; painted, wrote and sold articles all winter. The perfect life—marred only by the solitary nature of her existence. She fervently wished Walter had lived to enjoy it with her. Instead, just a year after the last of their two children had left home, with retirement looming like a shiny, tinsel-wrapped package on the horizon, he had passed away. It wasn't fair.

She sighed in rapture as the warm water soothed tired muscles. Her budget allowed her to spoil herself one night a week, and tonight was the night. Instead of renting a camping spot and spending the night in the cramped quarters of her converted van, she had reserved a room at the Seattle Sheraton. She contemplated the upcoming night of luxury with an anticipatory smile. Room service. A little television. A soft bed. Almost heaven.

A short time later, still toweling dry her thick black hair, Liz unfolded the copy of the *Seattle Times* she'd picked up before coming up to her room and began scanning the headlines. Almost instantly an article on the lower right-hand corner of the front page caught her eye: *Brutal Slaying in Lillooet Creek*. Her hand froze in mid motion as she stared at the words. Taking a deep breath, she forced herself to read the article.

Stunned by the words of the article and the corresponding images that raced through her mind like the randomly spliced-together frames of a horror film, she set the newspaper aside. Then, suddenly galvanized into action, she rose and raced to the phone. Almost frantic in her haste, she shakily dialed a number. Dear God, let them be home, she prayed. As the phone rang, she took several deep breaths until she was almost certain she could speak normally. She didn't want to alarm anyone. Finally, somebody lifted the receiver on the other end and after anxious seconds that seemed like hours she heard the voice she needed to hear.

"Hello."

"Caroline, it's Mom. I'm in Seattle. How—" her voice cracked and she quickly swallowed to recover. "How are you?"

"Oh, hi, Mom. I'm fine. Everybody here is great."

They discussed the mundane concerns of everyday existence for a few minutes. Liz allowed the normality of the conversation to wash over her like a soothing balm, blunting the sharp taste of fear.

But she had to know for certain. "You're. . . not planning on travelling to Washington State anytime soon are you, Caroline?"

"No. Robert isn't due for holidays for months yet. Why?"

"Oh, no reason. I guess I'll just have to wait to see you when I get back."

One down, one to go, she thought as she replaced the receiver and quickly picked it up again. Chewing her lip, she dialed her son's number. And once again she prayed. God, please let him be home. Her prayer was answered.

"Murphy residence."

"David. It's Mom."

"Mom! Where are you? Is everything okay?" David

was always the more perceptive of her two children. She would have to be careful not to alarm him.

"Everything's fine, dear. I'm in Seattle. How are you? How's the business going?"

"I'm fine. Business is a bit slow, but I'm certain it'll pick up. In tough times, people just don't spend money on computer software."

"Maybe you should use the slow time to take a holiday," Liz suggested. "You never take one when it's busy because you say you can't afford to turn away clients."

"No. Wendy and I talked about it, but she can't take any time off at the hospital right now. Besides, it's not as if I have nothing to do. I'm still working."

Liz closed her eyes and allowed her spine to sag with the weight of her relief. She spoke with David for a few more minutes, promising to let him know more about her plans within the next couple of days. He had no compunction about letting her know that he did not approve of her roaming the length and breadth of the country alone. Liz conceded that it was dangerous. Still, there was little in life that wasn't.

Rising from her spot by the phone, she walked back across the room to stare down at the newspaper. Her mind screamed its warning again. She frowned. Her two children were safe at home. Neither had any intention of visiting Lillooet Creek, or even Washington State for that matter. She frowned in perplexity. Except for rare instances, her psychic impressions had always pertained to people who were linked to her in some way—her family or a close friend. Was there someone in Lillooet Creek that she knew? She closed her eyes in concentration. Was someone she cared for about to die at the hands of a killer?

An image formed in her mind. A mirrored reflection of a hunting knife smeared with blood. Crimson spatters dripped from its razor edge to form the blood red impression of a pair of lips pressed to glass. And beyond the image, the vague reflection of someone silhouetted in the doorway of a darkened room. Liz's face drained of color. She had no choice. Tomorrow, she would head for Lillooet Creek.

CHAPTER 2

I t was after seven o'clock when Vaughn managed to escape his office and head home for dinner. Knowing he wouldn't feel like cooking for himself when he got there, he had stopped at the Chopsticks Restaurant to grab himself a couple of containers of takeout. Now, he struggled to unlock the door to his house while juggling the unwieldy cartons along with a sheaf of papers in file folders. The lock proved stubborn—it was too new—and finally he resorted to holding the papers beneath his chin while balancing his Chinese food on an upraised knee in order to use both hands on the door. He'd bought a briefcase a while back, but he always forgot about the damn thing until he found himself in a situation where it would have proved useful. Like now. The door swung open and he just managed to catch his dinner before it slid off his knee.

Maneuvering his elbow in a manner that allowed him to flip on a light switch without losing his grip on anything, he kicked off his shoes. Glancing into the living room on his right, he checked his phone to see if the voicemail light was flashing. It wasn't, so he walked straight ahead to the kitchen. Bypassing the counter, he went directly to the table in the nook area and set everything down.

Now, all he had to do was make himself a pot of coffee, and he'd be ready. He was going to settle in for the night and go over every piece of information connected with Trent's murder. He was missing something—some connection that pointed to the killer's identity. He knew it as surely as he knew the sun would rise tomorrow. And that knowledge was slowly driving him crazy.

As the coffee maker began to hiss and gurgle, he took a knife and fork from a drawer. Seating himself at the table, he removed the lid from one of the containers and began to fork the beef chop suey into his mouth as he stared thoughtfully at the coffee dribbling into the carafe.

A murder had been committed in his county, in his town, and the victim had been a friend. It was his job to see that the killer did not escape justice, but it was also a personal imperative. For more reasons than one.

Three weeks prior to Trent's death, Vaughn had awakened one morning to find a slightly yellowed newspaper article displayed prominently in the center of his breakfast table. The article had covered the death of a young woman who had been murdered almost a year earlier in Seattle. Her name had been Candace Smyth. Vaughn knew Candace—or rather, had known her. They had even dated once or twice as teenagers. It was the first he'd heard of her death. Candace had never actually lived in Lillooet Creek. She'd merely spent her summers here with her grandmother. When old Mrs. Smyth had passed away, Candace had stopped coming to Lillooet Creek.

It had been the night after finding that newspaper clipping that Vaughn's nightmares had begun again. They'd stopped years ago, shortly after he'd left the foster home provided by Anna Irving. Somehow, the news of Candace's death and the knowledge of the violent manner of her death at the hands of another had triggered their return. Or had the return of the dreams been precipitated by the fact that someone had broken into his home, threatening his sense of security, in order to leave him the yellowed news article? He didn't know.

A couple of times since then, he'd come home and sensed that all was not as he had left it. He could never pinpoint anything awry, but he knew that his personal space had been touched, violated. Then one morning he'd reached into the closet for his denim jacket and realized it was gone.

The coffee stopped dripping and he set his dinner aside as he rose to pour himself a cup. He needed to discover who the hell was invading his life. And why? Absently, he added sugar and milk to his coffee. He hadn't been alone in experiencing that invasion. Trent Farris, too, had experienced it in a different way—a much more terrifying way.

Damn you Trent, why didn't you tell me about the harassment while there was still time to do something?

But Trent had always been independent. He'd thought the break-ins and strange, poetic notes to be the work of bored teenagers. It wasn't until he'd awakened one morning to find his German Shepherd butchered on his back step that he'd reported anything to the sheriff's department. And by then—although they hadn't known it—Trent's own death had been mere hours away. Vaughn had wanted to send a deputy home with him, but Trent had refused. Despite the poems and the phone calls alluding to vengeance, Trent hadn't really believed that an attempt would be made on his life. Vaughn frowned as he recalled the notes. They'd never mentioned what form the retaliation would take. Nor had they revealed the nature of Trent's alleged crime. There had been no way to prepare.

Resuming his seat at the table, Vaughn sipped his coffee. He opened the container of chicken fried rice and decided to finish his dinner before he thought about the case anymore. He was already losing his appetite and he needed the sustenance. It was the first meal he'd had since breakfast, almost 13 hours ago. Leaning forward in his chair, he forced himself to relax as he concentrated entirely on his meal. It was good. But then it was rare indeed when he didn't enjoy Chinese food. That was part of the reason he'd chosen it tonight. He knew he'd need something capable of tempting his appetite.

Although he didn't have time to indulge himself often, Vaughn enjoyed food and loved to cook. His kitchen communicated his desire for a pleasant atmosphere combined with efficiency. The cupboards were oak, each door hand-carved in the relief style, and the countertop was polished granite. In the center of the kitchen, he'd constructed an island with a range inset into its surface. Above it, shiny copper pots and pans hung from open-beams spanning the arched ceiling. The room was bright and roomy and relaxing.

He'd actually built the place when he'd learned that Doreen Hanson, his now ex-woman-friend, was pregnant with his child. But despite her pregnancy, Doreen had declined Vaughn's proposal of marriage. And his son, Landon, had never been in his father's home, never seen the room that had been designed for him. Damn, that hurt.

But what hurt more was the knowledge that he'd been duped. Doreen had never wanted a relationship and, according to her, never would. But she had wanted a child. Without telling Vaughn of her intentions, she had gone off the pill and purposely gotten pregnant. When Vaughn had discovered the pregnancy and proposed marriage, she'd finally told him the truth.

She didn't love him. She thought that she was probably incapable of loving any man. That was why she devoted so much time to her career.

With a calculating attitude that would have shamed

many of the most hardened businesspeople, she had simply chosen him to father her child. Then she had embarked on a campaign to become the type of woman Vaughn would be attracted to. She had used him. Doreen Hanson might be a simple teacher, but there was nothing simple about the woman or her ambitions. Where other people spent their spare time reading novels or watching television, Doreen took correspondence courses, studied the stock market, and monitored her investments in mutual funds.

Vaughn's only consolation for having been chosen to play the role of stud in Doreen's plans was that she had insisted, right from the beginning, that they be discreet. As a result there was no gossip circulating about the two of them, no little old ladies clucking their tongues at him for not doing the right thing by Doreen. No one in town suspected that he was the father of her child. Vaughn visited Landon as often as he could without arousing suspicion, but Doreen's decision had been made. The only concession she'd proposed was in allowing him, as a friend of the family, to be named as Landon's godparent. He supposed could have insisted on DNA testing and then sued for greater access, or even for custody, but he wasn't sure that would be the best thing for the child—especially in a small town where everyone talked about everyone else's business.

He pictured Doreen as he'd last seen her: ash brown hair pulled into a perfect chignon, makeup applied flawlessly, a classy yellow skirt suit that had probably cost her a quarter of her monthly salary hugging her tall, slim figure to perfection. A beautiful lady with the instincts of a black widow spider.

Thinking of Doreen brought to mind an image of Kimberley Tannas. Damn, that woman rubbed him the wrong way. Despite the difference in their coloring, she'd reminded him instantly of Doreen: self-assured posture, confident walk, and don't-mess-with-me expression. The same. But there'd been a difference in the way she'd looked at him. Doreen had usually looked at him as though she was starving and he was the main course. Although it had almost certainly been an act, just part of his seduction, at the time it had flattered and aroused him.

In contrast, Kim had looked at him as though he was something she'd just scraped off the bottom of her shoe—or something she'd like to scrape off her shoe. Either way the look had irritated the hell out of him. He wasn't used to women looking at him like that.

She was a real ball-breaking little bitch. And that was all he needed right now. Another man-eating woman was just what he lacked to make his life really interesting. And what really pissed him off was that he wanted nothing more than to see if he could crack the iceberg shell and find a warm, passionate woman underneath. What the hell was it with him? The challenge? Was he just a sucker for punishment?

Angry with himself and the direction of his thoughts, Vaughn thanked God for the wedding ring on her finger. That was one boundary he would never cross no matter how attracted he was to a woman. He replaced the lids on the containers of food and stalked across the kitchen to place them in the refrigerator.

He almost dropped the cartons. A bright yellow daffodil lay on the top shelf. "Son of a bitch!" Reflexively, he grabbed the flower and pitched it into the garbage.

How the hell was the bastard getting in? He raked his fingers through his hair in agitation. Anger rose in him like a tide, swelling slowly in his chest until he wanted to smash his fists into something just to release the tension. He had just changed all the locks on his doors to double dead-bolts. If the guy had that much practice with B & E, chances were he had a record somewhere. All Vaughn had to do was get a print or two, and he'd have him.

Certain he'd have noticed when he'd opened the

front door if there had been signs of tampering, he swung toward the back door. Bending down he studied it. He could just make out where a small amount of paint had been scraped from the door frame by a pry bar.

"Fuck!" He wanted this asshole. Wanted him so bad that the gnawing hunger ate at him like acid. So far, the guy hadn't made a mistake. But maybe this time. . . Vaughn moved to a corner kitchen cabinet where, after the first time his home had been broken into, he'd begun keeping a small latent-print kit. Sooner or later the creep would make a mistake, and Vaughn intended to catch him when he did.

A few minutes later, when the only prints he'd found had been his own, Vaughn conceded defeat in that regard and returned his attention to the files on the table. Somewhere there had to be something.

He forced himself to look at the pictures of Trent's body. It had been left in a ditch on the edge of town. As soon as Vaughn had seen the ritualistic aspects of the M.O., so similar to the abridged newspaper description of Candace's killing in Seattle, he'd begun to suspect what he might be up against. He'd immediately filled out the necessary forms and reports for the FBI to do a comparative search through the Violent Criminal Apprehension Program more commonly known as VICAP. He hadn't mentioned the newspaper clipping.

They'd gotten back to him within 36 hours to say that the M.O. *did* match that used in the murder of a young woman in Seattle almost a year ago. They didn't provide any definite links to other killings, although there were a couple of possibles.

And Vaughn had known with certainty that he was dealing with a repeat killer. The awareness that this killer had struck in two such diverse locations as Seattle and Lillooet Creek might indicate that he was transient, in which case their chances of catching him would have decreased tremendously. But somehow Vaughn didn't think that was the case. Gut instinct told him that the killer was someone he knew. Someone who knew him. Aware that he was dealing with a situation a little beyond his range of experience, knowing that he needed to get somebody experienced in murder investigation into town, Vaughn had called in help.

Special Agent Stone of the FBI was due to arrive tomorrow. Vaughn looked forward to meeting him. But the killer had played a card that ensured Vaughn would move cautiously even in his communication with Stone.

The murder weapon was his. Even now Vaughn swallowed uncomfortably at the knowledge. But there was no mistake. The carving knife had a very distinctive nick in the handle. He'd put the nick in the handle himself when he'd struck it by accident with a chisel. The knife—actually a good strong-bladed hunting knife—had been one Vaughn had used for carving.

Exactly how had one of his carving knives gotten into the hands of the killer? How could the killer have taken it without there being signs of forced entry to Vaughn's workshop? And why had he left it so prominently positioned on the body? Was it some kind of message? It made Vaughn feel sick, as though he had some culpability in the murder of his friend.

Still, he hadn't put that particular evidence in any of the reports. Had he done the wrong thing? Christ, he just didn't know any more.

His first thought, when he'd recognized it, had been that he was being framed. Was he? There'd been no prints on the knife. Not even his own. It had been wiped clean. Was the killer's harassment of the investigating sheriff merely a gesture? Like thumbing his nose at authority. A catch-me-if-you-can message? Maybe he really wanted to be caught? Vaughn had read a number of accounts that stated that was often the case. Yet somehow his gut told him there was something more here.

He felt as though he was being toyed with, his every

move anticipated. But there was nobody that knew him well enough to do that. Nobody.

His eyes lit on the splash of yellow hanging out of the garbage pail. The daffodil had probably come from Trent's grave. Dammit! His friend was dead and the murderer was playing mind games. He raked his fingers through his hair as he tried to think rationally— Vaughn Garrett, the sheriff, not the friend. What message was the daffodil to convey? Triumph? Which of the mourners had left daffodils? Just the family, he was certain. Vivian Farris, Deirdre Ward and Kimberley Tannas. Perhaps it was meant to impart a message to do with one of the family members.

Once again a picture of Kimberley formed in his mind. Angrily he rose and poured himself a fresh cup of coffee. *Forget her*, he ordered himself as the challenge she represented threatened to shift his thinking away from the task at hand. He sipped the scalding coffee. Might as well take in a good dose of caffeine. He didn't plan on sleeping tonight anyway.

As he turned around, his eyes lit on the polaroid snapshot sitting on top of the fridge. It was of himself and Trent together on a fishing trip last summer. They'd gone with Buck Reece, owner of the local sporting goods store. It had been Buck who'd taken the picture and given it to Trent. The snapshot had been placed on Vaughn's table the morning after Trent's murder, before his body had even been found. Why?

Taking his seat, Vaughn reread the three cryptic, poetic notes. Two of them seemed almost familiar; he'd probably read them himself when he was younger. Setting them aside, he leaned back and began to go over the reports for what seemed like the hundredth time. He didn't care if he had to go over them a thousand times. Somewhere there was a clue to the killer's identity. Vaughn intended to find it if it killed him. Which he sincerely hoped wouldn't be necessary.

* * *

Kim escaped the oppressive confines of the house to sit on the veranda. At periodic intervals, her toes dug into the scuffed, paint-free floorboards to renew the creaking sway of the ancient porch swing as she listened to the muffled cadence of sympathetic voices issuing through the screen door. There were fewer of those voices now. She had noticed a number of vehicles winding their way down the road from Aunt Vivian's to the town below. Aunt Viv's house—an enormous old place with dormer windows, fish scale siding and covered verandas—had been built on a rocky outcropping overlooking the town.

Kim stared down at the village from her vantage point. It hadn't changed much since she was thirteen. There'd been virtually no expansion, just a few new apartment buildings. A couple of the businesses had changed ownership. Marilyn's Beauty Salon was gone. In its place was Phoebe's Hair Design and Tanning Lounge. Despite the name change, the place was still simply referred to as 'the Beauty Salon' in conversation.

Old man Hilliard had finally sold Hilliard's Hardware to a nephew and purchased a condo in Florida. According to Deirdre, the nephew hadn't bothered to change the name of the store even though his name was Maddock rather than Hilliard. The guy wasn't stupid. He obviously knew that in a town like Lillooet Creek, it wouldn't really matter what name was exhibited on the sign. The hardware store had always been called Hilliard's Hardware, and it always would be. There wasn't much sense in wasting money on a new sign.

The tall spire of the Catholic Church steeple glowed white against the purpling sky as it caught the last rays of sunlight. Across the street from the church was the park. She could just barely make out one end of the rectangular outdoor pool that occupied the north side. The remainder of the pool was obscured by the roof of the change house. With a nostalgic smile, she remembered the summer she'd turned thirteen.

She, Deirdre, Melissa, and some girlfriends had decided that the best way to have the pool to themselves on hot summer nights was to sneak out of their beds and meet at the park where they would climb the fence to go skinny-dipping. They'd made a regular habit of it for a couple of weeks until Trent had discovered their secret and blabbed to some of his friends. The night that the boys had crashed their skinny-dipping party was one of the most embarrassing of Kim's life.

Screaming and squealing—as only a gaggle of teenage girls can do—Kim and her friends had jumped into as many of their clothes as they could sort out while fending off the grinning, jeering boys who were attempting to steal what clothing the girls hadn't managed to don. Kim had been unable to find her T-shirt and bra in the melee. She remembered racing home through the back alleys only to find that her bedroom window had been securely locked from the inside. Even now she could recall the sick sensation she'd felt in the pit of her stomach at the realization that her parents knew she had sneaked out and were waiting to intercept her on her return.

Why did it have to happen *that* night? If they'd found her out a couple of days earlier, at least she would have been returning home fully clothed. After an agony of indecision when she'd contemplated a whole gamut of solutions ranging from suicide to running away, she'd finally rung the doorbell and, concealing her immature breasts with her hands, had waited for her parents to let her in. She could laugh at it now, but her embarrassment that night, when she'd seem the expression on her father's face as he opened the door, had been enough to make her contemplate suicide all over again. His initial shock and stern disapproval had eventually become tinged with humor when he'd heard Kim's tale of woe and discerned her complete humiliation. But despite that, she'd been grounded for a month. A whole month of her thirteenth summer had been spent lounging around the house alone. God, it had been horrible. But she'd spent more time with her father that summer than she would have otherwise. And for that she was grateful. Only four months later, he was dead.

A loud meow interrupted her reverie and she looked at the screen door to see her aunt's enormous gray Persian, Charity, staring beseechingly out at her. She returned the cat's stare measure for measure as she considered the idea of getting up, walking to the door, and opening it to let Charity out. Somehow it seemed like the effort would take more energy than she had to spare. The cat's enormous gold eyes continued to watch her unblinkingly, and she was reminded suddenly of another pair of gold eyes.

She still couldn't believe that Sheriff Garrett actually was the Vaughn Garrett of years ago. He'd not only grown into a man who was definitely not the thin, sinewy man she would have envisioned, but the reserved, sulky loner had become the sheriff of Waterford County. It was amazing how much a person could change.

And now, Aunt Vivian shared her rocky vantage point overlooking the town with the sheriff. Apparently, he had purchased a two- or three-acre plot just beyond the stand of fir to the north on which to build his own house. Kim peered in that direction. She thought she could just make out some cedar shakes through the branches of the trees. Gossip divulged that Vaughn Garrett was not only the Waterford County Sheriff, but an accomplished carpenter and wood carver as well. That surprised her. He hadn't looked like the type who would want to work with his hands. Dammit! Why was she thinking about him again? Ah well, tomorrow she'd be seeing the last of this godforsaken town and its too-handsome sheriff for a while.

Although it would continue to be up to her to monitor the progress of the investigation—neither Deirdre nor her Aunt Vivian had the fortitude required to keep people from shunting them aside—she still planned to do it by phone. She would simply call Sheriff Garrett regularly to remind him of the fact that a killer remained on the loose. This time, no one would give up on the investigation prematurely.

The screen door squeaked and Kim turned her head to see Deirdre exiting the house with Charity at her heels. Deirdre smiled tremulously at Kim. "We've got enough food left in there to feed an army. Hardly anyone ate anything. And just about everyone has gone home now."

Kim nodded. "I saw the cars leaving." Charity came over to twine herself around Kim's ankles. Kim leaned forward to thread her fingers through the cat's silky fur as she studied her tall, blonde cousin. Deirdre had always been the beautiful one in the family. She and Kim had similar coloring, but somehow it just all looked better on Deirdre. Deirdre was five foot six while Kim was a mere five feet two and a half. Deirdre's honey blonde hair framed perfectly oval features, while Kim's features leaned slightly toward the oblong. Deirdre had beautiful sapphire-blue eyes, while Kim's were a dark, smoky blue. Deirdre had a soft melodious voice; Kim's was deeper, huskier. Yet despite their differences there had never been any jealousy between them. It was simply accepted that Deirdre was the one with a model's looks and Kim was the one with the brains.

Poor Deirdre couldn't balance a checkbook without becoming frustrated to the point of tears. Tears came easily to Deirdre. Not only could Kim maintain an entire set of business ledgers with no problem if she wanted to—which she seldom did because she hated accounting—but, she rarely cried. Lord, she'd cried more in the last few days than she had since Ken's funeral.

She moved over on the swing and patted the spot next to her. Deirdre silently took the offered seat and stared down at the town as Kim had been doing.

"How's Aunt Viv holding up?" Kim asked.

Deirdre shrugged. "Okay, I guess. She's with Aunt Willie right now. I think that's the best medicine for her at the moment."

Charity abandoned the mindless stroking of Kim's fingers to jump up on the railing of the veranda and lie down in Aunt Viv's planter among scarlet-petaled geraniums. Purring loudly, she eyed both Kim and Deirdre through narrowed golden eyes.

"Aunt Willie sure hasn't changed much."

Deirdre smiled. "Aunt Willie never changes. She's like this town: constant."

Kim nodded. "I was just thinking that time seems almost to have stood still here." She looked at Deirdre. "Aunt Willie's sister died a few years back, didn't she?" Kim frowned. "Wasn't Anna Irving her sister?"

"Mm-hm. It would have been about eight years ago now, I guess. Her house burned to the ground." Deirdre shuddered. "I never liked her much. She had all of Aunt Willie's gruffness and none of her compassion or humor. But, God, what a horrible way to go."

They fell silent for a time, each absorbed in her own thoughts. Then Kim broke the silence briefly. "Uncle Jake didn't come up to the house, did he?"

Deirdre shook her head. "No. He was pretty broken up. I mean Trent was his son, too. But he felt it would be better if he didn't come. I think he was right. It's been five years since he took off with that woman, and Mom was just starting to put her life back together when this happened. The last thing she needs is to be reminded of the pain of their breakup by having him around."

Kim nodded. There were so many different kinds of pain. Some worse than others. But they all hurt; they all required healing time. And some hurts never healed—especially those for which justice was never served.

"God, I can't wait to get away from here." The vehement statement burst from her lips, surprising herself almost as much as it did Deirdre. She responded to the expression in Deirdre's eyes. "I'm sorry. I just hate this town."

"No, you don't," Deirdre argued. "You hate what happened here. You hate the fact that whoever did it got away with it. And you hate that you can't remember. But this town has a lot of good in it, too. Somehow you have to learn to see that again."

"How can you say that?" Kim demanded. "Your own brother was just killed here. And you still think this is a good town? A good place to live? Somehow I don't think Trent would agree with you."

An expression of hurt flared on Deirdre's face, and guilt knifed through Kim. Dammit, she'd done it again. She was always saying insensitive things. "Oh, God, Dee. I'm sorry." She wrapped her arms around her cousin and clung to her. "Go ahead and hit me if it'll make you feel better. I deserve it."

Deirdre sniffed as her hands rubbed Kim's back soothingly. "Oh, you deserve it all right. Unfortunately I've outgrown such childish retaliation. I'll have to think of something more appropriate."

"Okay." Kim released her cousin. "At least I've accomplished one thing."

"What's that."

"You won't be too sorry to see me go home tomorrow morning."

"Ain't that the truth," Deirdre said, mimicking one of Aunt Willie's favorite sayings with a wry twist of her lips as she patted Kim's leg in a manner that belied her words.

They fell silent. Below them the lights of the town began to wink on as evening cloaked the valley. Once again Kim began to feel a darkness blacker than the coming of the night, tainting the picture. Somewhere down there was another murderer. Would he, too, escape justice?

No! He wouldn't. Not this time. She had to believe that.

Deirdre must have sensed the shifting of her mood. "C'mon, Cuz." She grasped Kim's arm. "Let's go in and see if we can't convince Aunt Willie to go home and Mom to go for a rest. Then the two of us will be free to clean up the house a bit before I head home."

* * *

He stood in the shadows at the side of the house, listening. Kim hadn't changed that much over the years. Oh, she was a woman now; back then, she'd been a girl. But he remembered her just the same. He'd never forget even *one* of them. She, too, was on his list.

When he'd first returned, he'd thought that she, like so many of the others, would have to be scratched from his list because they'd moved on. But Providence had intervened. She was here. He would simply move quickly, adjust his schedule to accommodate hers. His first gift must be delivered tonight. He smiled. Then her life would belong to him. He would be forever on her mind. She would know that he, and only he, would choose the time of her death. And if she still left tomorrow morning—well, he knew where she lived now. Seattle wasn't too far away.

He would deliver his first little offering and see what happened. He smiled in the darkness. If there was one thing he'd learned over the years, it was how to be flexible.

The screen door squeaked as the two women went into the house. A squirrel chattered in a nearby tree as it readied itself for the coming night. He moved silently toward the nearby wall of trees. He was already getting some very creative ideas. Of course when creativity failed him he could always fall back on the creative works of others. But he preferred to generate his own work whenever possible. Individual creativity was the hallmark of a true artist. He stopped and stared up at the now silent squirrel as it watched him with beady little eyes. Oh yes, this would be good. Very good. He was certain Kim would appreciate it.

CHAPTER 3

"Well, I think that just about takes care of everything," Deirdre said as she glanced at the clock. It was just after nine o'clock. "I really have to get home to Kyle and the kids."

"Sure, you go ahead." Kim gave the counter one final swipe before hanging the dish cloth. "The dishes are done. Everything is put away. And your mother is either sleeping or doing a good job of faking it."

Deirdre grimaced. "She's probably faking, but I hope she's not. She needs the rest."

"She'll be fine, Dee." Kim had seen the naked concern on Deirdre's face for just a second before she'd masked it. Aunt Viv had had a mild heart attack a couple of years ago, and Deirdre was no doubt worried about the effect of all the stress on her mother.

"I know." She waved her hands expressively. "I know. But sometimes it doesn't matter what you *know*, you know. I just can't help worrying."

"I know."

Deirdre suddenly grinned at the oddness of their conversation. "Well, now that we both *know* so much, maybe you'd better go check the guest room to make sure you have everything you need before I leave." She

55

began gathering her purse and keys together on the counter.

"Deirdre, I'm sure it's fine." Kim gave her an exasperated look. "Go home." Kim retrieved the rings she'd removed while doing dishes and slipped them back onto her fingers.

"Oh, all right. But I want to look in on Mom again anyway. You might as well come with me."

Since the guest room was right next to her aunt's room, Kim was certain she was being maneuvered, but she let it pass.

Deirdre quietly opened the door to her mother's room and stepped inside. Not wanting to intrude, Kim stood in the doorway as Deirdre approached her mother's bed and adjusted the crocheted bedding over her mother's sleeping form. That finished, Deirdre turned and began tiptoeing back to the door.

"Dee, is that you?"

Deirdre stopped, her disappointment obvious on her face. "Mom, I thought you were asleep. You need sleep."

"I know, dear. I think I was asleep. . . for a while. I dozed anyway. Are you going home now?"

"Yes. It's after nine. Kim's planning on getting an early night herself so she can head back to Seattle in the morning."

"All right, dear. Come and kiss me good-bye."

As Deirdre turned to bid her mother good-bye, Kim moved on to her room to give them privacy. The doors in her aunt's house were colonial style in a dark wood that looked like mahogany but since Kim didn't have much actual knowledge of wood, she wouldn't have bet on her assumption. As she opened the door to her room, she half expected it to creak. Her aunt's house was so old it would have seemed appropriate somehow. But the hinges were silent. The room beyond was pitch-black.

Kim reached to her right, groping for a light switch.

A second later the room flooded with light from the bare bulb in the center of the ceiling. She blinked. It must be a hundred watt bulb.

She stepped into the room. It had been a long time since she'd stayed here, but nothing had changed. The hardwood floor still gleamed. A large, dark-blue throw rug lay next to the bed. The room had belonged to Trent before he'd left home ten years ago or more. Aunt Viv had never bothered to take down his football pennants, baseball hats and rock group posters. She'd always said those things were part of what gave the room personality. Kim studied the posters of rock bands with a sense of nostalgia. Aunt Viv was right. It was a comfortable room—a place where somebody had lived.

Her small overnight case waited on the bed to be unpacked. Opening it, Kim removed her brush and comb set and turned to place it on the dresser. She froze.

The squirrel lay in an unnatural position. Blood matted its gray-brown fur. Its forepaws had been positioned to hold a tiny bouquet of flowers.

"Oh, my God!" The words emerged in a barely audible croak. She backed away. Her brush and comb fell from suddenly nerveless fingers to clatter noisily on the floor. Who would do such a thing? Bile rose like acid in her throat and she choked it back. She tried to tear her eyes away from the horrible sight, and couldn't.

A square of white attached to the mirror just above the pitiful creature caught her attention. She was glad to have something less horrible on which to focus her attention. Reluctantly, not wanting to see it but knowing she had to, Kim stepped closer to the dresser again. For the first time in a long time, she blessed her farsightedness. The paper contained a typed message. She could read it from about five feet away, and that was the distance she maintained.

*When you feel Danger's kiss
upon your spine,
Don't look back, for
you'll soon be mine.*

Beneath the macabre little poem was a three-dimensional drawing of a tombstone inscribed with the letters R.I.P.. Numbed by shock, Kim could only stare uncomprehendingly at it. And then realization hit her. Someone wanted to kill her.

"Jesus," she whispered. This wasn't happening! It couldn't be happening. Not to her.

"Kim." Deirdre's voice floated to her from a distance, but she couldn't seem to focus on anything but the horrible message on the dresser. "Kim, is everything all right? I heard something fall. Oh, my God." Kim felt Deirdre's hand take her arm. "Come on, Kim. Come on."

As Deirdre pulled Kim's unresisting form from the room, Aunt Viv's voice emerged from next door. "What is it, Deirdre? Kim? What's the matter?"

But Deirdre was incapable of answering. Her resources, taxed to their limit during the past few days, abandoned her. She simply stood in the hallway wringing her hands. "Oh, my God! He was here, wasn't he? Right here in our house." Then she simply said, "Oh, my God," over and over again as hysterical tears began to track down her cheeks unheeded.

Kim wasn't much better off. After all, she was pretty certain the message had been meant for her. Although she wasn't quite hysterical, she was definitely feeling strangely paralyzed. She couldn't seem to complete a single coherent thought. Instinct was telling her to run. But what was it that she *should* do?

Suddenly Aunt Viv, still tying her robe, joined them in the hallway. Gripping her daughter by the shoulders, she shook her. "Deirdre, stop it this instant. Stop it!"

Deirdre, accustomed to obeying that voice all her life, particularly when it was delivered in *that* tone, managed to suppress her hysteria. "That's better. Now tell me."

Deirdre pointed at the doorway to the guest room. "On the dresser. It's . . . it's . . . . Oh, Mom, he's been here." Her voice rose on the final word and hysteria threatened again. Aunt Viv turned even paler at her daughter's words.

"Deirdre!" Her mother said her name sharply, driving the hysteria back once again. "Go call the sheriff. Now!"

"Yes," Deirdre nodded, wiping at the tears wetting her cheeks. "Okay." Obviously the simple expedient of being given a task had a calming effect.

With Deirdre taken care of, her Aunt Vivian turned to face her niece. Kim automatically moved to block her entrance into the room. She didn't know how much more distress her aunt could take. "You don't need to worry, Kim. I have no desire to see what's in there. Are you all right?"

"I . . . yes, I'm all right. But, I've got to get out of here. Now! Tonight! He's after me now, Aunt Vivian." Kim began to pace the hall as she tried to think.

"Oh Lord, what is this person doing in our lives?"

Kim wasn't certain if the peculiar note in her aunt's tone was brought on by weariness or approaching hysteria, but the realization that her aunt might be beginning to lose her cool, too, gave Kim something to concentrate on besides the hovering specter of a 17 year old fear as it attempted to meld with present terror. She forced the encroaching blackness back behind the wall in her mind.

"Come on, Aunt Vivian," Kim said as she grasped her aunt's arm. "Let's go downstairs to the kitchen and wait for the sheriff."

And once he'd arrived to take things in hand, she was getting the hell out of here. She swallowed an urge to laugh, and then cursed. Here she was anxiously awaiting the arrival of the one man in Lillooet Creek she would prefer never to have to see again.

* * *

Vaughn was deeply involved in going over the medical examiner's report when his cell phone rang, startling him out of his chair. Jerking it out of his pocket and automatically noting the caller's identity, he answered it. "Yeah, Melissa. What is it?"

"I just had a call from Deirdre Ward, Vaughn. Up at the Farris's. She's pretty upset. About all I could make out was something about a dead squirrel on a dresser. Then she just kept saying 'He's been here'. I thought you'd want to know."

"Who's on duty? Cheney?"

"Mm-hm." He heard her click her acrylic nails on the desk. "He's on his way over there now. I called Dr. Harcourt and asked him to head over there, too. It sounded to me like at least one of those ladies is going to need a tranquillizer."

"Good thinking, Mel. Thanks for calling. You know where to find me if you need me?" The question was rhetorical, but Melissa decided to answer.

"Wouldn't be over at the Farris's now, would it, Sheriff?"

Vaughn hung up the phone without responding. Sometimes Melissa Adams had the strangest sense of humor.

He glanced at the papers littering his table and decided that, even though he planned on returning to them shortly, he couldn't leave them as they were. His uninvited guest might choose to return. So, he gathered them up and carried them under his arm as he left the house. After conscientiously locking the door behind him, he strode to the two-tone, brown Bronco sitting in the driveway and set the papers on the seat beside him. As he started the vehicle, he glanced into the rear seat out of habit to ensure that he hadn't forgotten to replace his little black bag after the last time he'd used it.

It was in place. His little black bag was in reality his own special, personally assembled evidence collection kit. Among other things, it contained string, a tape measure, rubber gloves, surgical gloves, evidence tags, paper and plastic evidence bags in various sizes, vials, tweezers, scissors, tongs, a jar of Vicks Vapor-Rub, a jar of aspirin, super glue, and anything else he'd ever had need of or read about that he'd thought might be useful someday.

Putting the Bronco into gear, he swung around the circular drive and, when he reached the street, turned south. The Farris's were his next-door neighbors, so to speak, but they lived a good quarter of a mile away. Just a nice walk, if you weren't in a hurry.

Vaughn pulled into the Farris's drive right behind Doc Harcourt. Ray Cheney's green cruiser was already parked.

"Evening, Sheriff Garrett." Jim Harcourt emerged from his car and waited for Vaughn.

"Dr. Harcourt." Vaughn nodded in greeting. Vaughn and Jim had actually become casual friends a few years ago when Jim had first arrived in Lillooet Creek to replace the retiring Dr. Bowen. Shortly after that, Vaughn had been elected County Sheriff. Jim had fallen into the habit of calling Vaughn, Sheriff Garrett, as a kick, so Vaughn had simply returned the favor. Their excessive formality, usually delivered with a slight humorous quirk to the lips, was a stupid habit, but difficult to break.

"You have any idea what this is about?" They started walking toward the house together.

Vaughn nodded. "Yeah." As he stepped up onto the veranda, Deputy Cheney opened the screen door.

"Am I glad to see you, Doc. The ladies here had quite a scare. I think we're going to need you to calm 'em down enough so's we can get a statement."

"You got it, Ray." The doctor followed Ray into the

house with Vaughn at his heels. Cheney was a big man, slightly over six feet tall, with gray hair and kindly blue eyes. His three kids were grown, and the last one had flown the coop about six years ago. Nearing 50 at the time, Ray and his wife Betty had finally begun to devote some time to enjoying their own lives. Then suddenly, just a couple of years ago Betty had died of breast cancer complications. Ray had seemed kind of lost ever since. He seemed to spend more time at work now than he did anywhere.

Vaughn had only taken a couple of steps into the house when he heard the sobbing coming from the kitchen. "Guess you know where you're needed," he said to the Doc. He turned to Deputy Cheney. "What've we got, Ray?"

"It's upstairs. I'll show you." He began mounting the stairs with Vaughn at his heels. "This guy is one sick son of a bitch. Got a real warped sense of humor."

"Yeah, I know." The grandfather clock in the upstairs hall struck the half hour just as Vaughn and Cheney reached the second floor. Vaughn jumped.

"Something the matter?" Cheney asked.

Vaughn shook his head. "No. I've just always hated those damn clocks. They're noisy."

Cheney made a noncommittal sound in his throat.

Both men stuck their hands into their pockets before entering the upstairs bedroom. "Anything been touched?" Vaughn asked.

Cheney shook his head. "Not a thing. The little lady wouldn't get any closer to it than was necessary to read the note. And, according to her, she can read from quite a distance." He nodded to the case still sitting on the bed. "I'd say she's right though. The message is definitely meant for her. With this being an unused room, he'd have had no reason to leave it in here unless he'd figured out where she'd be sleeping. Course the case on the bed has a name tag on it so it wouldn't have been too hard."

"Right." Vaughn stared around the room thoughtfully. "Any idea how he got in without anybody seeing
him?"

Cheney shrugged, looking extremely uncomfortable
with his thoughts. "There were mourners in and out of
the house all day today. For all we know, he was one of
them."

Vaughn shook his head in disgust. "He picked a
good day, didn't he? It'll be useless trying to isolate any
prints downstairs. We had more than half the town
through here." He paused, his eyes narrowed
thoughtfully. He'd be glad when Special Agent Stone
got here.

"Okay, we'll focus on this room then. If we're lucky
he might have made a mistake this time. Take some
pictures of the room. Then, bag that"—he indicated the
hapless squirrel—"and the note for lab tests. Check
everything for prints. Then I want you to look for
anything that would be out of place in a room that
hasn't been used in a long time."

"Such as?"

Vaughn sighed and raked his fingers through his
hair. "I don't know, Ray. Anything. A hair, a blade of
grass, a chunk of soil. Just something." His eyes raked
the room thoughtfully. Finally, he shrugged. "If you
need anything, my bag is in the Bronco."

"Gotcha. You want me to take the statements first,
or are you going to do it?"

"This isn't going anywhere, so I'll let you talk with
Deirdre and her mother while I talk to Kim. It'll save
time." He was adhering to the guidelines by separating
the women for questioning. It was a well-documented
fact that if witnesses began discussing what they'd seen
or hadn't seen, they'd begin agreeing on details. Often
they didn't agree correctly; the witness with the
strongest personality usually won out. And he knew
which of the three had the strongest personality. In this
instance, separating them probably wouldn't make any

difference since everything had been left exactly as it was for him and Cheney to see, and it was unlikely that any of the women had observed anything suspicious earlier in the day. Still, it was best to stick to procedure.

He had another reason, too, for wanting to speak with Kim himself. He was beginning to get an idea. If the killer wanted her, then maybe they could use that. His instincts told him she wouldn't like the idea. Damn! He didn't like the idea. But there had to be a way to convince her. All she had to do was stay in Lillooet Creek a few days. At most, a couple of weeks. Maybe she could get a leave of absence from her job for a while. He wondered where she worked.

A few minutes later, after administering a shot to Vivian Farris and giving Deirdre a couple of tranquilizers that she could take after she'd driven home, Dr. Harcourt left. Cheney, ensconced in the living room with Deirdre and Vivian Farris, prepared to take their statement. Vaughn led Kim into the kitchen and pulled out a chair for her at the table.

And, as he had on each occasion that he'd met her, despite the circumstances, he noticed her appearance. Lord, she was beautiful. Well, not beautiful exactly, maybe striking was the word. No, that wasn't right either. Whatever the hell it was, he liked it too damn much. And that pissed him off. He didn't want to like anything about her. Her smoky-blue eyes were large and soft, almost innocent. But appearances were deceiving, he reminded himself. And her kissable, coral-tinted lips hinted at a deeply sensual nature. Her husband probably had a perpetual case of frost-bite, Vaughn assured himself.

"All right, Kim. I understand you were the first one to find the little exhibit upstairs?"

"Yes." Her hands were folded on the table before her, the fingers so tightly clenched that the knuckles were white. She toyed with a wedding ring. Damn! He'd forgotten to consider the husband aspect in his plan.

There was no way in hell the man would allow his wife to stay away from home as a lure for a killer. Vaughn realized that, despite consciously knowing that she was married, he still tended to think of her as Kimberley Clayton—the slightly spoiled, somewhat stuck-up, little Miss Perfect he'd been casually aware of in school years ago.

"All right, now. I just need to get a statement from you to file a report. What is your full name?"

"Kimberley Rhae Tannas." She offered the correct spelling. Her voice was low and as thick as honey. It made Vaughn think of dim lighting and rumpled sheets. He shifted uncomfortably. Christ! As if he didn't have enough problems.

"Okay, Kim. I want you to tell me in your own words exactly how you came to find it. Can you do that?"

She swallowed and nodded, glancing at the clock. It was almost eleven. "It was a little after nine-thirty I think. Deirdre was about to head home." Apparently finding it too difficult to remain seated, she rose and began to pace the room as she recounted her story.

As Vaughn listened and jotted down his notes, he watched her stride back and forth. Despite himself, his observer's eye noted everything about her. Actually, she didn't remind him quite as sharply of Doreen now. Doreen wouldn't be caught dead dressed the way Kimberley was at the moment.

He confirmed his earlier observation that she wasn't very tall—probably little more than five foot two or three—as he watched her pace barefoot back and forth across the floor. She'd changed from the black skirt-suit she'd worn at the funeral into faded Levi's that clung to her shapely hips and thighs. A short-sleeved, coral blouse of some soft material, possibly silk, clung to the upper half of her body in all the right places. Her golden-blonde hair was still pulled back from her delicate features into the French-braided style she'd worn earlier, but the look had been softened by a few curling tendrils that had escaped. The softness emphasized the slightly exotic cast of her cheekbones.

Kim's story stumbled to a halt. "That's about it I guess. We just sat here in the kitchen and waited until Deputy Cheney arrived. Oh, yes. Deirdre did say that she plans on taking her mother home with her tonight because she refuses to leave her alone here after what happened. We all kind of want to get out of here as soon as you're finished, Sheriff." She looked rather pointedly at him and, since he wasn't a complete idiot, he read the look but decided to ignore it.

"You're staying with Deirdre tonight, too?"

"No. She doesn't have the room. I'm going home."

He stared at her in surprise. After the stress of a funeral and the shock of the thing left for her upstairs, her plan to drive pitch-black, winding mountain roads struck him as incredibly foolhardy. "Do you really think driving all that way tonight is a good idea? How will your husband feel about it?"

Kim froze. "My husband is dead, Sheriff Garrett," she said. "He was killed two years ago."

Vaughn was stunned by the revelation and ashamed of his almost instantaneous surge of hope for his plan. "Oh, um, I'm sorry. I hadn't heard."

"Forget it."

They were interrupted as Deirdre poked her head around the corner. "Kim, we're finished out here so I'm taking Mom and going home before she collapses on me. Put out a couple of days' worth of food and water for Charity before you leave, okay? And call me tomorrow?"

"Sure, Dee." Deirdre didn't look all that far from collapse herself. "Go home and get some rest."

Deirdre nodded and attempted a smile. "Bye."

"Bye, Cuz." As soon as Deirdre disappeared around the corner, Kim seemed to droop somewhat, as though she'd been putting on a show of strength for her cousin and aunt and now the necessity to maintain the facade was gone. Vaughn watched her as she leaned against the kitchen counter and rubbed her temples. She looked tired. He fought back a surge of compassion.

"Are we just about finished here, Sheriff?"

"Yeah." He closed his notebook and put his pen in his pocket. "How did it happen?"

"How did what happen?"

"Your husband—how was he killed?"

Her lips thinned slightly as she dealt with remembered pain. She eyed the package of cigarettes in his breast pocket. "Could I have one of those?"

"Sure. But I have to warn you they're getting pretty dry. I'm down to about three cigarettes a day and this is the last of the pack."

"If you're quitting smoking, why do you still carry them?"

He shrugged. "Masochistic, I guess. Do you want one?"

Kim hesitated then shook her head. "No, I guess not. I don't smoke; I just figured now might be a good time to give it a try. There are so many things I haven't done yet," she said quietly, as she stared over his shoulder at some point on the wall behind him. Then she seemed to give herself a shake and she focused on him. "You wanted to know what happened to Ken?"

"Yeah," Vaughn answered, "unless you don't want to talk about it."

"No. It's okay." She took a deep breath. "Ken responded to a domestic disturbance. He... he was shot." She flattened her palms against her denim-clad thighs.

"He was a cop?" Vaughn asked. That revelation surprised him.

Kim nodded and turned toward the coffee machine sitting prominently on the counter. "I need a coffee. Would you like a cup, Sheriff?"

Vaughn knew the offer was made out of courtesy

rather than a desire for his company. Although she'd managed to be less rude than she had the other day, Kim's voice continued to crackle with frost when she spoke to him. But he still had to find a way to get her to stay in Lillooet Creek. Besides, some perverse impulse in him wanted to irritate her.

"Thank you, I'd appreciate it. Why don't you call me Vaughn? This is a small town. We don't stand on formality much around here. And people could presume all kinds of peculiar things if we persist in being formal with each other. Besides, it's not as though we're total strangers."

Kim spooned coffee grounds into a filter and placed it in the machine. Turning the tap on to fill the carafe, she spoke over her shoulder to him. "Of course we are. I'd never have recognized you. And even seventeen years ago we barely knew each other." After pouring the water into the already hissing machine, she turned to face him.

"You're right. We are complete strangers. I guess you'd better call me Sheriff Garrett."

Startled somewhat by Garrett's droll concurrence, she couldn't help but smile slightly. "Point taken," she said. "What do you take in your coffee?"

"A little of each, please."

As Kim set two cups on the counter, she considered the change in Sheriff Garrett's appearance. He'd changed from the suit he'd worn this morning into his sheriff's uniform again. The dark green shirt, with its tan accents at the shoulder and pocket, suited his tawny coloring. And Kim couldn't help but notice that his tan trousers, though not worn snugly, nonetheless revealed that he was in good shape—very good shape. But what Kim found most unusual was that in a strange way each outfit suited him equally well. Even the pistol he now wore, butt forward, on his left hip seemed like it belonged there. With some people, you could always tell the type of clothes they were used to wearing because they looked at ease in them. When you saw them wear anything else, they appeared extremely uncomfortable. Garrett didn't appear to be like that. She thought she'd read something about that in a book on body language once, but she couldn't remember what it meant. It was probably something to do with his inherent vanity, she supposed.

As soon as Kim opened the refrigerator door to remove some milk, Charity came running into the room, her tail held high like a flag as she yowled to announce her hungry presence.

"That cat must have radar," Vaughn said. He had a smooth bass voice that Kim found pleasant and fervently wished she didn't.

"It certainly seems like it, doesn't it." She reached into the cupboard to find a bowl into which to pour enough milk to satisfy Charity's sudden, very noisy, craving.

As the cat began lapping at her milk, the coffee maker was just winding down to its last few spits and sputters. With her hand on the handle of the carafe, Kim waited for it to finish before pouring coffee into two cups. Leaving hers black, she added a little sugar and milk to Vaughn's cup and carried the mugs to the table. She noticed that he seemed a little thoughtful and preoccupied, so she silently sat down across from him to sip at her coffee.

"Ah, Kim, I was wondering—"

"Wondering what?" she prompted.

His eyes suddenly came to rest on the cat. "How exactly did the cat come by the name Charity?"

Kim wasn't fooled. That hadn't been what he'd intended to ask. But she decided to play along. She could afford to be magnanimous. She'd be seeing the last of Sheriff Garrett within the hour. "That's easy. When she wasn't much more than a kitten, she showed up at the door one morning—asking for charity, Aunt Viv said. When she stayed, the name stuck." Vaughn nodded as though he was really interested, but Kim could see that his mind was elsewhere. "Now, do you want to tell me what it really was you wanted to say?"

"That obvious, huh?"

"That obvious," she agreed.

"I just realized that I don't even know what you do for a living. Where do you work?"

"A friend and I have a small gift shop. We sell books, crafts, that type of thing."

"I see. So you're your own boss. There's nobody to tell you when you have to work and when you can take a few days off?"

Why was he watching her so intently? "That's right, I guess. Although Kathy can be pretty demanding." She thought she noticed an expression of satisfaction flit across his features before he looked down at his cup.

Vaughn cleared his throat and toyed with his cup. "I don't quite know how to say this." He cleared his throat again, and Kim began to get a decidedly apprehensive feeling. Finally he set aside his cup, leaned forward and looked directly at her. And Kim knew that whatever it was he was going to say, she didn't want to hear it. "Kim, it's obvious that the guy we're after has now focused his attention on you. That puts you a unique position."

"No kidding!" Kim set her cup on the table and got up to pace the room. "Most people who die at my age aren't given enough warning to get their affairs in order. He's a very considerate guy, this murderer."

"That's not what I meant, Kim, and you know it. Hear me out."

"No!" Her voice rose as panic once again bubbled too near the surface. She forced it down, but not soon enough to avoid the adrenalin surge. "No," she repeated more calmly despite the renewed shaking of her hands. "If whatever you have to say puts me and that. . . that creature out there in the same breath, I don't want to hear it. I think I'd like you to go now, please. I'll be leaving shortly."

Vaughn rose and walked toward her. "Kim, you're in a position to help us catch him. If you stay here, when he comes after you, we can get him. If you insist on going home... well, he could still get to you, and there'll be nobody there to protect you."

"What do you mean? How can he get to me in Seattle?"

"He's already struck in Seattle once." Vaughn studied her tense face. "Do you remember Candace Smyth? She used to spend her summers here until her grandmother passed away." He paused when he saw the sudden recognition of the name flare in Kim's eyes. "Candace was killed a year ago in the same way Trent was killed. She was living in Seattle at the time."

"Oh, God." Kim closed her eyes tightly for a moment.

"Don't you see? You're the best chance we have."

The darkness she'd felt earlier suddenly crowded closer. "You don't know what you're asking." A scream from the past echoed in her mind. Fear clutched her heart in an iron fist as remembered terror began to seep through the chinks of the wall in her mind. Desperately seeking to fortify that wall, she focused her gaze on the sheriff's golden eyes. "I'm sorry. I just can't." The words seemed barely audible to her own ears. She wondered if he had heard them.

He had. "So you'll run away." His tone was suddenly merciless, accusing. "You've let this creature, as you call him, scare you so much that you'd rather let him get away with Trent's murder than stay and help us catch him."

He was close enough now that she had to tilt her head back to look into his face. His eyes were as cold as stone—topaz stone. She saw the shadow of the whiskers beneath the skin of his clean-shaven jaw. A jaw that, at the moment, was clenched tightly enough to provoke the rhythmic leap of a muscle beneath the tanned flesh. He placed his hands on her shoulders. The warmth of them burned through the thin fabric of her blouse.

Was that what would happen? Would another murderer escape because of her weakness? A chill shuddered through her. Oh, God. Could she live with another unsolved murder on her conscience?

"I'm asking you to reconsider, Kim. We need you."

She closed her eyes and swallowed the fear rising in her throat. He was right. She'd been planning to run away. And that was something she couldn't allow herself to do. "All right," she whispered. "I'll stay. As long as I can, I'll stay." This time the killer would pay for his crime. Opening her eyes, she met Sheriff Garrett's implacable gaze with one equally unwavering. "I'll stay," she repeated firmly.

CHAPTER 4

Vaughn had seen the intensity of the panic in Kim's eyes before she'd concealed it. It startled him. Knowing what he knew of her character, somehow it seemed too extreme for it all to be attributable to what had happened here tonight. If he'd been dealing with Deirdre, he might have expected it. He'd seen her go into hysterics when a mouse had run over her foot at one of the town dances. But Kim was made of sterner stuff. He decided it wouldn't hurt to ask around town and see if he'd missed some critical piece of gossip concerning Kimberley Clayton Tannas over the years.

As she continued to stare up into his face with her large smoke-blue eyes, realization struck him with the force of a blow. The barrier of a husband had been removed. And as he met Kim's eyes, he recognized two things he didn't want to see swimming in their depths: pain and courage. Damn, she was one hell of a woman. He fought the urge to pull her into his arms and cover her soft, sensual mouth with his. Instead, he gave her shoulders a quick squeeze. "Good girl," he said. "Don't worry. We won't let him get you."

She nodded in response, without comment, but the expression on her face didn't change.

"Well," he stepped away from her. "I'll make arrangements for Deputy Cheney to station himself here tonight. We'll have one deputy outside, watching the house at all times. Is there anybody you'd like to call to come and stay with you?"

Kim shook her head. "No. Even if there was, I'd be asking them to risk their life. I couldn't do that."

Vaughn studied her drawn face for a moment. She had a very highly developed sense of responsibility. Finally he nodded. "All right. But see if you can't get some sleep. It's extremely unlikely that he'll return tonight."

Kim nodded. "Right." Her droll tone said she wasn't banking on anything. But she seemed to be getting her emotions back under control. Turning away from him, she retrieved her mug from the table and poured herself a fresh cup of coffee.

Even though he now had what he wanted from her, he found himself peculiarly reluctant to leave. "I'll go make the arrangements then. I'll talk to you again tomorrow."

"Fine." She sat at the table looking drawn and tired as she sipped her coffee. He didn't think she would even try to sleep, but short of knocking her over the head, he didn't know what he could do about it. Then again, why should he care?

* * *

Vaughn tossed in his sleep. A pale face shimmered in the black rectangle of an upstairs window. He reached out. He needed to grasp it, to hold on to the faint picture. But the features began to recede. Shrinking. Disappearing. He was terrified. His heart felt like it would burst through the cage of his ribs. He cried out. The sound emerged as a hoarse shout, waking him. He bolted upright.

Slowly, the unreasoning terror began to fade and he recognized the familiar confines of his bedchamber. He breathed a sigh of relief. At least the tendency to sleepwalk hadn't returned with the nightmares. He remembered the added terror he'd suffered as a child when he'd awakened from a nightmare only to find himself in an unfamiliar place. As his pulse slowed, he swung his legs over the side of the bed, raked his hands through his tawny, sweat-damp hair and cursed in weary disgust.

He'd been free of the nightmares for more than ten years. Why the hell did they have to come back now? As if he didn't have enough to deal with. The dream that had awakened him this morning was one of the worst. Not for its visual content, but for the way it made him feel. Hollow, empty, and alone. Utterly alone. Yet he'd never been able to recall the cause of the intense fear and sense of loss. Once again, as he always had, he closed his eyes and concentrated on the visual remnants of the dream, trying to bring the whole of it into focus. It was no use.

He opened his eyes and concentrated on the sight of ancient firs and cedars bathed in the morning sunlight. When he had built his home he had installed garden doors in the living room, dining room and master bedroom in order to achieve a sense of space throughout the house. Now, by focusing on the world beyond the garden doors, he allowed the simple beauty of the mountain wilderness to soothe him. He loved it here. He always had—despite everything. Despite the pain and terror, the sense of being different and the ever present loneliness, Vaughn had always managed to feel at home in the mountains.

Perhaps that was why, of the four foster children raised in Anna Irving's home, he was the one to have returned to Lillooet Creek. He had lived the most formative years of his childhood in this town. It was home.

He'd left at 18, like most youngsters anxious to test their wings. But even then, he'd known what he wanted to do. It had just taken him a while to work up to it.

After completing his police training at the Criminal Justice Training Centre in Seattle, he'd worked in Seattle for a while. Yet he wasn't happy. Even though he'd liked his work, he hadn't liked the tumult of the city. He'd desperately sought a position with a smaller municipal law enforcement agency. Finally, just as he'd been about to quit police work and fall back on his carpentry and carving in order to earn a living in a smaller city, a position had come up. He had moved to Chelan without looking back. But finally, even life there had worn thin. It wasn't home; Lillooet Creek had drawn him like a magnet. He gave up a job he loved to return to his hometown. A year later the sheriff's position here had opened up. He'd run for it and won, and he hadn't looked back since.

He rose, stretched his lean, tanned body, and walked naked to open the doors. The sounds of the mountain morning greeted him. Errant breezes sighed in the tops of the tall evergreens; small birds sang and squirrels chattered; a nearby waterfall roared its mastery over mere soil and stone. He breathed deeply, absorbing the fresh scents, opening his senses to life. But despite the beauty of the morning, he could not long avoid his thoughts. Duty called.

Turning, he looked at his bedside clock. It was six a.m. He'd had five hours sleep. Enough to face the day when necessary. He wouldn't be able to fall asleep again in any case. There was too much invading his mind, demanding attention.

A few minutes later, fresh from the shower, Vaughn donned a pair of faded jeans and a blue chambray shirt. He just didn't feel like wearing a uniform today. After clipping on his badge and strapping on his 9mm Smith and Wesson semi-automatic, he was ready to leave.

This morning he intended to go to Erma's coffee shop for breakfast, and listen to the latest town gossip. It was something he did at least twice a week in order to keep abreast of things. Erma's was next to the

Fairview Hotel which Erma and her husband Tom Mills owned. Flanking the other side of the hotel was T.J.'s Bar also owned by Erma and Tom, but operated exclusively by Tom. The situation had been born out of necessity. Erma disliked alcohol and, in particular, drunks. When she had helped to operate the bar in its early days, she had refused to serve anyone who was becoming, in Erma's words, a bit tipsy, ordering them in her gruff smoker's voice to go get a cup of coffee. In the interests of preserving his business, Tom had built Erma a restaurant where she could sell the coffee she loved and keep her nose out of his bar. The agreement had worked well for more than 20 years now.

As Vaughn parked his Bronco on the street in front of the restaurant, he noticed the Barlow brothers leaning against the building. "Morning Bill, Phil," he nodded to them. "What are you boys doing up so bright and early?"

Phil barked a laugh. "Well, Sheriff it's bright," he squinted reddened eyes against the morning sun, "It's early," he continued with a grin. "But we ain't up yet."

Bill laughed and slapped his thigh. "Hell, no, we ain't up yet, cause we ain't been to bed yet." That was one thing about the Barlow boys. They were always in a good humor. Even hung over. It was absolutely remarkable. The scent of stale beer was almost strong enough to give Vaughn a hangover.

"I thought you boys only let loose on the weekends." The previous night had been a Thursday.

"Gettin' an early start this week. No work," Phil mumbled with a sheepish grin as he rubbed his temple.

The Barlow brothers worked for the town as maintenance men. Among other duties, in the summer they helped mend sidewalks, patch roads, and repair playgrounds; and in the winter they cleared snow and spread salt or sand on icy patches. They took their work seriously, were hard working, and they earned a good dollar. But they were weekend alcoholics. Vaughn could barely remember a time when they hadn't been. Now, he took in the sight of their rumpled clothing. The Barlows lived a good ten miles out of town. "You spend the night at the hotel?"

"Nah. Didn't want to waste good beer money. Just sat out back in the truck," Bill said with a jab of his thumb over his shoulder.

"You going to head home now and sleep off those hangovers?"

Phil shrugged and looked at the toes of his boots more like a sheepish five year old than a man somewhere in his mid-thirties. "Um, we'd kind of decided not to bother wastin' gas. The wife'll just tear a strip off me anyway. Thought we'd just wait for T.J. to open up and get a bit of the hair of the dog. You know?"

Vaughn shook his head in exasperation. "Do you guys ever put anything nonalcoholic that might contain a few vitamins down those gullets?"

Bill barked a laugh. "Hell, Sheriff, we get up every morning and beat the shit out of each other just to put some color in our faces."

"Hah, that's a good one Bill," Phil slapped his brother on the shoulder in appreciation.

Vaughn grinned. "Why don't you let me buy you breakfast at Erma's?" Maybe if he got them to eat something, he could send them home to get a few hours sleep before they started their weekly Friday celebration.

"Nah. Thanks anyway, Sheriff. We got money. We just don't want to spoil our appetites."

"Suit yourselves then," he said. "Just remember to tap it cool tonight. And I don't want to catch you driving under the influence."

Phil Barlow's eyes widened in one of the best imitations of innocence Vaughn had ever seen. "We learned our lesson last time, Sheriff. No more DUI. Honest."

"Right," Vaughn said, drawling the word in disbelief. "Catch you later boys." He winked in warning as he turned to continue into the restaurant.

Most of the regulars were already in place. John Winslow, the local plumber, sat on his usual stool at the counter flirting with wide-hipped, busty Florence Potter. Florence was one of the nicest, friendliest women in town. She liked variety, which accounted for the fact that she was still single at 40-something. Of course there were a good number of men in town that were more than a little appreciative of the fact that Florence had never married.

"Mornin', Sheriff."

Vaughn looked toward the caller. Erma was leaning through the opening in the partition separating the dining area from the kitchen.

"Morning, Erma. You cooking this morning?"

"You betcha," she answered with a smile. "You want the usual?"

Vaughn returned her smile. "Please."

"Give me five minutes." She turned away and began moving around in the kitchen.

Vaughn chose a booth near the back of the room where he could watch the goings on. Sliding across the red vinyl seat, he propped his back against the wall and stretched one leg out before him on the seat. He liked the relaxed atmosphere at Erma's. He felt at home here. But then everybody did. Erma was just that way— soft-hearted, motherly, caring, a bit bossy, and a damn good cook. Vaughn's mouth was already watering at the thought of her flapjacks covered in maple syrup, whipped cream, and peaches.

"Coffee, Sheriff?" Florence interrupted his thoughts.

"Yes, please." He smiled automatically in thanks when she'd filled his cup. He shifted in his seat to add milk and sugar to his cup.

"Mornin', Vaughn."

He glanced up. "Morning, Steve. Join me?"

"Don't mind if I do." The man slid onto the opposite bench.

Steve Riley was the local mayor, head of the local school board, and—following in his father's footsteps—a small-town lawyer. He'd been born and raised in Lillooet Creek. Because he was about four or five years older than Vaughn, they'd never been more than acquaintances in their school days. Ever since Vaughn had achieved the sheriff's office, though, they'd developed a good working friendship.

Florence automatically flipped over the coffee cup on his side of the table and began to fill it. "What can I get you this morning, Mayor?"

"The biscuits fresh?"

"Yes, sir," Florence grinned setting the coffee pot on the table as she readied her pad and plucked the pencil from over her ear.

"Okay then, biscuits with some of that fresh strawberry jam that Erma got from Sally Winslow and one egg over easy."

"Be two minutes," Florence said as she tucked her pad back into the pocket of her pink waitress uniform and picked up the carafe to refill coffee cups on her way back to the kitchen.

As she moved away, Steve looked back at Vaughn, his eyes suddenly grave. "Anything new?"

Vaughn didn't have to ask to what he was referring. "Yeah. But not good. He's already picked another target."

"Good, Lord. Who?"

"Kim Tannas." At Steve's baffled expression he added, "She used to be Kimberley Clayton."

"Oh, that poor kid. As if she hasn't had enough problems in her life."

Vaughn frowned. "What do you mean?"

Steve's blue eyes stared at him incredulously. "I can't believe that you don't know. I thought everybody did." He shrugged, and passed his hand over the bald spot in the center of his head. "Then again, I guess you were just a kid yourself when it happened. You probably had too many other things on your mind to pay attention to details."

"What details? What exactly are you talking about?"

"You knew that Kim's father passed away, didn't you?"

"Yeah," Vaughn nodded and sipped his coffee. "It was just a month or so later that they moved away."

"Do you remember how he died?"

Vaughn frowned. "I'm not likely to forget." He didn't bother mentioning the fact that he'd been reminded of it just two days earlier by Kimberley herself. "It was the first official murder this town had ever seen. But that was... what? Seventeen years ago. It's tough losing a loved one. I know that. But grief doesn't last forever."

"Unless there's something unresolved about it."

Vaughn stared at his coffee cup without seeing it as he tried to bring half-forgotten details from the past into focus. He saw Florence approaching with his flapjacks, the mayor's biscuits and a fresh carafe of coffee. Sitting back, he allowed her to serve them before picking up the thread of conversation. "What do you mean?"

Steve picked up a biscuit and began to slather it with jam. "Kim was with her father at the garage the night it happened. They figured she saw everything. But the poor kid was like a zombie for days afterward. She couldn't remember a thing." He took a bite of biscuit and talked around it. "I heard that, later on, she even underwent hypnosis."

"No luck?" Vaughn asked as he cut a piece of flapjack and used it to scoop up a dollop of whipped cream.

Steve shook his head and swallowed. "I guess we'll never know what really happened that night. But talk is that Kim blames herself for the fact that her father's murderer was never caught."

Vaughn froze as his conscience gave him a severe nip. And he'd used guilt to get her to stay in Lillooet Creek. Still, she'd had no compunction whatsoever about laying the blame at the door to the sheriff's department. Had Vaughn known about the guilt she suffered over her father's death, he might have exercised a little more sensitivity. Then again, if sensitivity hadn't worked, he would've done exactly as he had, so there was no sense worrying about it.

As Steve fell silent to dig into his biscuits with gusto, Vaughn concentrated on eating and observing the regulars at Erma's. Old man Harper and old man Aimes occupied the same table they had every morning ever since the restaurant had opened. And, as they had every morning for just as long, they complained about their wives. Vaughn had finally decided that the reason they'd both stayed married to women they supposedly hated—but with whom they'd both managed to father at least three children apiece—was because they needed to be able to complain.

Vaughn and Steve finished their meal with small talk, rehashing town gossip. Some of it Vaughn had heard before, most of it was inconsequential in any case, but there were a couple of rumors he would check out. It seemed that Tyler Dobbs was knocking around his young wife and kids again. Vaughn knew that Sarah would never press charges. She was terrified and, typically, blamed herself for riling Tyler. But Vaughn would keep an eye on the situation. Also, it seemed that Skeeter Barnes, the local Peeping Tom, was up to his peeping activities again despite countless warnings and a short stay in jail accompanied by a fine. Vaughn decided to have a talk with him real soon.

* * *

It was eight a.m. when Vaughn pulled up in front of the two-story brick building on Jackson Avenue that housed the County Court House and the sheriff's department. As he walked through the door he noted that Melissa was already there spooning coffee into a filter. Melissa was a brunette with large brown eyes and a warm, golden-tinted complexion. She was very attractive and very married, but even had that not been the case Vaughn doubted that they would ever have been more than friends. Melissa was one of those people who just took life too casually. Vaughn, by nature, was much more serious and introspective. He stopped now in surprise. "I wasn't expecting to see you here this morning. You were here late last night, weren't you?"

"No, I'd just finished getting groceries. I was dropping off some office supplies when Dee called. That's all."

Dee? "You're friends with Deirdre Ward?"

"Not Deirdre Ward. Deirdre Farris and I used to be quite close though. We kind of drifted apart when she married Kyle."

Vaughn leaned against the doorframe to his office. "You don't like Kyle?"

"Nope. And the feeling's mutual."

"Why?"

Melissa looked at him incredulously. "I can't believe you haven't noticed!"

Vaughn frowned. "Noticed what?"

"He's an asshole!"

Vaughn's expression cleared. "Oh, well, that explains everything. I'll try to be more observant the next time I meet him. Can I get you to bring me a cup of that coffee when it's finished?"

"Sure." Melissa took a seat at her desk and began sorting the mail she'd picked up on her way to work. Vaughn turned to enter his office. "Vaughn," Melissa's voice halted him.

He turned. "Yeah." He didn't like the grin on her face.

"I love it when you wear jeans, honey. When are you going to put those buns on a calendar so I can take them home with me without risking divorce?"

He frowned in mock severity, but somehow he kind of thought the expression was lost on her. "God, Mel. I swear the way you talk sometimes I just can't figure out what the hell keeps Curt married to you."

Her grin widened. "And the pity is, you'll never find out." Her brows lifted and she widened her eyes in innocence. "I'm a married woman."

"Right," Vaughn drawled. "If you weren't such a good office manager, I'd fire you for. . . for—"

"Sexual harassment?" Melissa supplied helpfully.

"I was going to say insubordination but, yeah, that would work."

"Well, then, I guess I'd better make sure my work quality stays up there."

"Now you got it." Vaughn turned and walked into his office. He grinned as soon as he turned away. A little lighthearted banter with Mel had been just what he needed. The woman was worth double her salary. Of course, he'd never tell her that. She'd ask for it.

* * *

At 11 a.m., Special Agent Stone arrived. Vaughn sized up the man as Melissa showed him into his office and they greeted each other. He liked what he saw. Stone looked fairly young, no more than mid-thirties. He had thick, wavy, almost-black hair and a high forehead. His dark brown eyes were clear, friendly, and forthright. He was average height and average build with a clean appearance.

"How do you do, Special Agent Stone?"

"Fine, thank you. Please, call me Stone. Everyone else does."

Vaughn nodded. "Have a seat. I guess the first thing we should discuss is exactly what you'll need from us."

Stone smiled. "Sure thing."

By the time Vaughn had Stone ensconced in an office, had finished his own paperwork, and found the time to drive over to Vivian Farris' place to speak with

Kim again, it was early afternoon. After pulling up in front of the house, he chatted briefly with Deputy Martin Lewis, more commonly known as Marty, who had relieved Ray Cheney on watch early this morning. Neither deputy had seen anything unusual.

Vaughn popped a cinnamon-flavored toothpick into his mouth to alleviate a sudden craving for a cigarette and walked up to the front door of the house. Charity came running up, her tail held high, as she yowled to be let in. When Vaughn merely rang the bell and waited, she looked at him with large gold eyes that seemed just a little puzzled. "I don't live here, cat. I have to wait for somebody to open the door for me just like you do."

"Meowww."

"Right." *Now I'm talking to a cat.* Impatiently he peered through the window on the door for signs of movement. Nothing. He rang the bell again, waited— and knocked, waited—knocked again louder.

When Kim finally opened the door, Vaughn just about choked on his toothpick. He barely noticed as Charity dashed through his legs and disappeared into the shadowy interior of the house. Somebody had kidnapped the ice queen he'd talked into staying in town and left a slightly rumpled incredibly warm-looking woman. Kimberley looked sexy enough to seduce on the spot. Her unbraided, honey-blonde hair framed her features in a tousled mop. Her large, smoky eyes were still dazed with sleep. And one shapely shoulder had escaped the neckline of the oversized, mid-thigh-length, red T-shirt she wore. The realization that that was probably all she wore left him momentarily incapable of speech.

"Sheriff. You woke me up." her tone, thick with sleep, was accusatory. "I didn't get to sleep until dawn." She stepped back, opening the door wider. "But, come in and make yourself at home." He opened his mouth to respond, but she forestalled him with a raised hand. "Not a word until I dress and have my coffee."

"Sure." Vaughn sat on the arm of the sofa and watched as she mounted the stairs. She had nice legs, pale and creamy. When the door to her room closed, he heaved a sigh, only then realizing how tense he'd been. Maybe he hadn't done such a smart thing by keeping her here for the investigation. His reasons for wanting her to stay had been simple and straight forward. But the only word that even came near describing the tangle of emotions he'd felt when he'd looked at her just now was *complicated*. Damn, the last thing he needed in his life right now was more complication—especially with a woman like her.

Barely two minutes passed before Kim emerged from the bedroom and walked back down the stairs. She'd merely donned her faded Levi's and tucked the hem of her T-shirt into the waistband. She kept hitching the neckline up onto her shoulders as she descended the stairs, but as soon as one shoulder was covered, the other insisted on provocative escape. She'd run a brush through her thick mane of hair, taming it somewhat, Vaughn noted. But she still looked damn desirable.

"Do you mind talking in the kitchen?" she asked.

"Not at all." He rose and followed her into the next room, purposely avoiding looking at the delicate sway of her feminine hips.

"Have a seat." She indicated a chair at the kitchen table. The same one he'd occupied the night before.

"Thanks." He watched her move about the kitchen.

Kim set the coffee production in motion, but found that her anticipation just wasn't what it should have been. She was really beginning to miss the cup of Starbuck's coffee that had become part of her morning routine Seattle. Turning her attention to the starving feline who had planted herself in front of the refrigerator, Kim put out some food. That done, she sat opposite Garrett.

Propping the heel of her right foot up on the chair,

she wrapped her arms around her bent knee as she faced him. Her eyes still felt a bit foggy. She rubbed her face for a second. "You'll have to forgive me if I seem a little vague. I didn't get to sleep until the sun came up."

He nodded. "You mentioned that. You're going to have to learn to trust us, Kim, or you'll make yourself sick."

Kim looked at him without comment. He was asking her to trust him with her life. She thought he was asking a bit much. There wasn't a man alive that she trusted that much. Not one.

Since she hadn't made a full carafe of coffee, the coffee-maker hissed its last and she rose to pour herself a cup. "Would you like a cup, Sheriff?"

"No, thanks. I've had my quota of coffee for a while. And I thought we agreed last night on less formality."

"Sorry. I'd forgotten. Can I get you something else?"

Vaughn hesitated. "Do you happen to have a soft drink, something cold?"

Kim opened the refrigerator door and bent over slightly to peer into its depths. "No pop," she announced. "There's orange juice."

"That would be great."

Kim poured him a glass and brought it to the table when she resumed her seat. "Now, Sheriff—"

"Hey," Vaughn interrupted.

Kim nodded her head in acknowledgement of his objection. "Vaughn," she amended, "what brings you here this morning?"

He hesitated. "I wanted to go over the FBI profile with you, if you're up to it? Just see if anything clicks. Maybe there's something that Trent, and Candace had in common with you—something that made him focus on you. What do you think?"

Kim swallowed and sipped thoughtfully at her hot coffee. "Okay." Her voice was a bit hoarse.

He cleared his throat. "Well, according to the profile done by the FBI, based on the information they have concerning Candace Smyth's and Trent's deaths, we're looking for a white male offender. Statistics indicate that he will probably be in his late twenties or early thirties." He paused to sip his orange juice. This was going to be harder than he'd thought.

"Special Agent Stone says that he would typify the guy as organized and fastidious. It's possible he is married or has a steady girlfriend, and it's probable that he is bisexual. He will be adept at boy-next-door conduct. Stone says this type of killer is the kind nobody believes capable of the crime." He studied Kim's pale features. "You with me so far?"

"Yes. But, I don't think I know anyone like that." Suddenly she pinned Vaughn with her gaze. "How can they know those things?"

"What things?"

She shrugged. "How old he is? That he's organized? That he's probably bisexual? Things like that."

Vaughn tensed slightly. "A lot of it comes from statistics and experience I guess."

"And the rest?" She was asking for details.

"From the individual case."

"So how did they characterize him as bisexual? How could they know such a thing?" Her eyes widened in sudden comprehension. "Oh, my God. Trent was—" She swallowed. "He was sexually assaulted, wasn't he? That's the only way they could make an assumption like that. Isn't it?"

Vaughn nodded and avoided her gaze. "Yeah. That's right."

"Jesus," she whispered as her hands clutched her cup with white-knuckled fingers. "That's sick."

"Yeah," Vaughn agreed. He poured the remainder of the orange juice down his throat. Somehow though, a bad taste remained.

An uncomfortable, tense silence reigned for a full minute. Suddenly Kim rose to stride across the kitchen. After pouring herself another coffee, she turned to face him. "I want to know everything you know about this guy. I want to know everything he did to Trent. Please?"

Vaughn studied her tense face. "I don't think that's a good idea, Kim."

"I don't give a damn what you think." Her voice rose, and she halted, holding up her hand as though to forestall any comment he might make. "I'm sorry. But you have to understand. I need to know his modus operandi. I need to know"—she paused, swallowing nervously—"I need to know what he has planned for me," she concluded on a whisper.

CHAPTER 5

Vaughn contemplated her. One delicately boned shoulder had again escaped the confines of her oversized T-shirt, but she seemed oblivious to it. Her head was canted slightly to one side as she awaited his response. The early afternoon sun had found its way in the kitchen window to highlight her blonde hair with molten gold. But it was her eyes that reached out to him. The banked terror in their depths tempered by an equal measure of determination that convinced him. A protective instinct surged within him. He suppressed it. She might require the physical protection he and his department could provide, but she sure as hell didn't need emotional protection. If she wanted to know all the gruesome details—particulars that had been indelibly engraved on his mind by his persistent examination and reexamination of the case file—then, by God, he'd tell her.

"Okay," he said. "But I must have your word that you won't pass on any of this information to anyone. No friends, no relatives, and no reporters. Barney McCarthy is the local reporter for *The Observer*. He's a good man and nine times out of ten won't bother anyone to excess, but"— Vaughn shrugged—"well, he can also be as determined as any pit bull once he gets his teeth into something he thinks is meaty. So if he does happen to come around, you'll have to be prepared. Agreed?"

"Agreed."

"Could I have another juice?" He was stalling. He hated talking about this.

"Sure."

He watched her as she bent slightly to get the juice from the fridge. She had a nice ass. *Real* nice.

"You'd better sit down," he said as she set the refilled glass down on the table before him.

Kim nodded and resumed her seat across from him. She took a deep breath and used the exhalation to blow an errant hair from her forehead. "All right. I'm ready."

Vaughn nodded and stared thoughtfully out the window at the beautiful mountain morning. How could a vicious murder have taken place in such a setting? It just didn't seem right. He sighed and looked back at Kim. The best place to start was probably at the beginning.

"According to the information I received, Candace Smyth was killed with a sharp-edged drawknife. Because the drawknife is a construction tool, Special Agent Stone believes that the perp may work in construction, probably carpentry. Based on the assumption that a high percentage of men who work in construction drive half-tons to convey their tools from job site to job site, Stone speculated that he probably drives a late-model, well-maintained truck."

He cleared his throat. "That brings us to the signature."

Kim's eyes narrowed thoughtfully. "I read about that in a novel not long ago. A repeat killer's signature is usually a product of fantasy, isn't it? Something that he rehearses in his mind?"

Vaughn nodded. "It's the ritual aspect of the crime. This killer has a rather unique signature, according to

Stone," Vaughn said. "Candace Smyth and Trent—" He stumbled briefly to a halt. It was so difficult to maintain professional distance, to speak dispassionately. "Both of the victims had their heads shaven. The killer then braided Candace's shorn hair. In Trent's case, because his hair was worn short, the perp glued strands of it to a thin nylon rope. Both victims had their wrists bound with their own shorn hair. Because Candace was also bound with ordinary rope, we know that this gesture is symbolic. But Stone had no theories as to what it might mean to the killer." He sipped his orange juice and stared out the window again as he tried to organize his thoughts.

Finally he sighed. "You sure you want to hear more?"

Kim nodded. "I have to."

"I thought you'd say that."

Kim watched as his long brown fingers slowly turned the glass of orange juice on the table.

"Both victims had a note printed in small block letters inserted into their mouths."

"What did it say?"

Vaughn shrugged. "Nothing terribly illuminating. Tick, tock. Tick tock. The clock strikes one! The deed is done! Tick tock. Tick tock.

Almost primary school level in its simplicity, Kim noted. But still poetic, like the note she had been left. A shiver traced its way up her spine. *Danger's kiss*. Jesus! She'd be lucky if she didn't go completely insane before this was over. If she was still alive to see it end, that was.

"What else do you know about him?" she asked a little too quickly.

"They don't think he had ever killed in this manner prior to killing Candace in Seattle," Vaughn responded. "She was his first victim, his first attempt at acting out his fantasy. The shaving of her head was much more sloppily accomplished, indicating that he hadn't yet refined his technique." Vaughn frowned. "And, despite the evidence of rape"—he paused and cleared his throat uncomfortably—"we don't believe that lust is in any way a motivation for this guy. He uses the sexual assault as a means of demonstrating his power over the victims, to degrade and humiliate. But every move he makes appears to be very well planned."

"What about physical traces?" Kim asked. "I've read about DNA fingerprinting. What about that sort of thing?"

Vaughn shook his head. "Both victims were clean. No physical evidence linked to the killer, other than a couple of cloth fibers, was found on either of them."

Kim frowned. "But how could that be? What about. . . you know. . . semen traces." Kim felt her face flush. She found it difficult to speak in such specific terms to anybody, let alone Garrett.

If Vaughn noticed her discomfort, he ignored it, merely shaking his head again. "No. Nothing. Even the rape is methodical and well planned—an exercise in subjugation. We believe he uses a condom. There weren't any prints either. He knows what we'll look for."

Kim drained her cup of coffee. She had heard about the condition of Trent's body when it had been found. She had thought it sick. She still thought it sick. But she needed to know if, perhaps, they'd discerned a reason for it. She cleared her throat. "Um, when they found Trent, his. . . his body wasn't just dumped, was it?"

"No." Vaughn sighed. There had been no way to keep some details from becoming public knowledge. Three adolescent boys had found Trent's body. After the initial shock had passed, they seemed to rather enjoy the attention and notoriety they received. "No, his body wasn't dumped. The killer posed the body."

"Why?" The single word emerged as a plea. She hadn't meant it to sound like that, but she needed to understand.

"You have to recognize the fact that what is important to this type of killer is the ritual. All the little details: shaven heads, braided hair around the wrists, the posing of the victims as though for a funeral with their hands folded on their chests, placing the weapon that killed them in their hands. It's almost as though he's saying they took their own lives. Stone believes it's probable that he even conducts a mock funeral after he's killed them.

"I don't believe his victims are in any way random. He chooses them carefully. They have something in common. You have something in common with Candace and Trent," Vaughn clenched his fist. "I just wish I could figure out what it is. There was never any evidence of poetic notes sent to Candace, but the ones sent to Trent contained undertones of vengeance, of retaliation for a wrong. Can you think of anyone who might hold something against you?"

Kim frowned in concentration. "No. I can't think of anything at all."

"Does one o'clock have any significance for you?"

"No. Why?"

"The time of death. The window is placed at late evening to early morning in both cases. The time may be another part of his ritual. *The clock strikes one*," he quoted. "Could be that one a.m. has some significance."

"This doesn't get any easier, does it?" Kim rose to stride nervously across the shiny white tile of the kitchen. Pivoting at the other end, she turned to face Vaughn. "Do you have any leads?" It was a repeat of one of the questions she'd asked two days earlier. She was hoping for a different answer.

Vaughn cleared his throat. "So far, just the profile and—"

"And what?" Kim prompted.

"And... you," he told her bluntly. His response, although different, offered her no comfort.

* * *

Sunlight struck the windshield with strobic glare as it lanced through the tops of the evergreens. Liz squinted against it as she gave the reluctant van a little more gas to keep it heading up the mountain road. She tried again to get the obstinate air conditioner to work, but it was no use. She wished she'd thought to recharge it before leaving Seattle. Damn, this July heat was enough to render fat. Well, maybe that wasn't so bad after all. She might actually melt off that last 15 pounds she'd been trying to diet away without any success. She opened the side window in an effort to alleviate the baking temperature, but even the breeze seemed hot. And she'd thought it would be cooler in the higher altitudes.

She'd worn a long-sleeved blouse with a loose flowing skirt to match. The material was a bright summery rayon, a multicolored turquoise, fuchsia, and jade mix that she loved, but it was too hot for the day. She should have worn short-sleeved cotton, she concluded as she drummed her long, glossy nails on the steering wheel. White cotton. The breeze provoked an errant strand of midnight-black hair into tickling her face and she brushed it away with a lightly tanned, thoroughly beringed, hand. She breathed deeply, taking in the smell of mountain air.

Her thoughts swung in the direction of the killer. Would he still be in Lillooet Creek? Or were her senses playing tricks on her? In the bright light of day, her certainty had wavered more than once. But each time she'd stopped with the intention of turning around, the compulsion, the need, returned to drive her on. What kind of person did it take to kill so viciously? A psychopath? Someone so twisted by hatred and malice that his own humanity had been lost beneath the weight of his malignancy? She hated to think about it.

How much further was it to Lillooet Creek? she wondered. The drive from Seattle seemed endless and she was anxious to get settled. A favorite song came on the radio and Liz reached to increase the volume. She sang along with it as she negotiated another curve in the road. Suddenly, she squealed and hit the brakes. An enormous bear stood before her. In the next instant, she realized that he held a sign welcoming her to Lillooet Creek.

"Jeez, they could give a person a little warning," she muttered as her heart slowly slid back down where it belonged. Then, she realized the she had reached her destination. "Finally." Giving the cedar grizzly a dirty look, she turned down the radio and inched the van forward.

"Okay, Liz. Where to now?" She coasted the vehicle forward as she looked for signs to orient herself. As the van rolled forward, crossing a small bridge spanning a creek—probably the source of the town's name, she mused—she noticed a poster stapled to a nearby pole advertising the Summer Finale Festival scheduled for August twenty-second, more than a month away. She hoped the small town would be able to celebrate. She passed an Amoco Station. Then a small sign proclaiming Main Street came into view. She turned the corner deciding to start there. She could tour the town and just see—

On the corner, a small brick building with the flag waving sporadically in the breeze called itself the Lillooet Creek Post Office. Beside it was the office of *The Lillooet Creek Observer*. A small local newspaper, Liz surmised without too much of a stretch of the imagination. On her right, directly across from the post office was a sign for a Chinese restaurant, the Chopstick Dining Lounge. Beside it was Reece's Sporting Goods store, Hilliard's Hardware, Vannah's Internet Café, Simpson's Pharmacy and the Danish Bakery. Liz liked the looks of the town.

Geraniums and petunias bloomed cheerfully in planter boxes along the streets, while colorful hanging flower baskets suspended from lamp posts. The town was well cared for and clean. A few cars lined the streets, parked diagonally. A number of pedestrians walked the sidewalks; several turned to study her van curiously as it passed.

Smiling at small-town inquisitiveness, Liz halted at a stop sign and looked back over her left shoulder to see what she'd missed on the other side of the street. A building larger than the others, nestled in beside *The Observer* to occupy most of the block—the Mountain View Supermarket. Beside it, a paved parking lot stretched right up to the cream-colored brick wall of the last building on the block, Kelsey's Photo and Frame.

Liz continued her tour of the town, locating the town hall, the county courthouse and the Office of the Waterford County Sheriff's office, the local medical clinic, a beauty salon, three clothing stores and the Village Cobbler Shoe Store. But nothing gave her a feeling of trepidation, a sense of impending doom. So, slightly reassured, she postponed any further exploration until she got settled.

She stopped at a small convenience store named Snodell's Grocery. After parking her van to one side of the small paved lot, she entered the shop. A profusion of small bells hanging on the door tinkled loudly as it opened. A peppermint-herbal smell permeated the atmosphere. Liz walked to the cooler and withdrew a bottle of Coke before stepping up to the counter. Seconds later, a friendly faced, rotund woman emerged from the back room still smacking her lips appreciatively over something she'd been in the process of eating.

"What can I do for you?" she asked as she patted the short curls of her slightly brassy hairdo.

Liz indicated the Coke. "I was wondering if you can tell me where I can rent a camping spot?"

"You won't find anything in town. About six miles out—you would have passed it on your way in—the

Cedar Ridge Campgrounds rents space."

Liz frowned. "I really didn't want to stay that far out of town."

"Then I suggest you go see Erma over at the hotel. She'll rent you a room without chargin' you an arm and a leg for it."

"All right. Thank you." Liz paid for the Coke.

"You betcha." She handed Liz her change. "I'm Kate Hobsin, by the way. And you are—"

"Liz, Liz Murphy." She offered her hand.

"You another one of those journalist types, Liz?"

"No, why?"

Kate shrugged. "Oh, no reason. I just wondered. We already have one young fellow staying over at the hotel. John Lambert, I think his name is. He's the only one that stayed on after the hullabaloo died down. I've been wondering why he's sticking around. Oh, well. You plannin' on being in town long, Liz?"

"I'm not sure yet. But it seems like a nice town."

"Oh, it is." She shrugged. "We've got a few undesirables like any place. But Sheriff Garrett's a good man. He keeps the place in better order than some."

* * *

Kim watched Vaughn Garrett walk down the steps and across the yard to his Bronco. Lord, he looked good in denim. Damn him! She placed her fingers over the tingling spot on her collarbone where his hand had lingered in a feather-light touch as he'd bid her goodbye. Why the hell was she reacting like this to a man now? Why a man like him? Why here? And why did it have to be another cop who could affect her this way? She wished she could ignore it, pretend there was no chemistry. She didn't even like the man for heaven's sakes. But even now the flesh he'd barely grazed with the pad of his thumb ached for a real caress.

It had been two years since Ken had died. There had been no one since. But since her sex life could never have been classified as anything more than satisfactory, even at its best, Kim didn't think it likely that her two years of celibacy had anything to do with her reaction to Sheriff Garrett.

Turning away from the door, Kim rubbed at the spot that persisted in tingling with the memory of his touch. Enough. She had to think about other things. She had decided last night, while passing the hours until dawn, that she was going to have to face the past if there was any hope of dealing with her present situation in a responsible and adult manner. She refused to allow herself to become a prisoner in her aunt's home. She'd go stir-crazy.

And thanks to the questionable methods of the local sheriff, she'd finally faced the fact that she'd been running away. She hadn't wanted to remember the times she'd walked happily down the streets of Lillooet Creek with her parents. Remembering those times would prompt the return of the pain that accompanied the acknowledgement of her father's death. To avoid remembering, she had hidden in her aunt's house whenever she'd visited. She could count on the fingers of one hand the number of times she'd been downtown in the last 17 years. It was time the running, and the hiding, stopped.

Fear could be controlled. You just had to be determined enough. If she faced it, dealt with it like she had her grief when Ken passed away and again when Trent died, she was convinced she could overcome it. So instead of phoning Dee and letting her know that she was still in town, Kim decided she'd drive up to her cousin's home. She was going to need to borrow some clothing anyway. She'd only brought enough of her own clothing with her to last a couple of days.

A few minutes later, Kim hooked the strap of her purse over her shoulder and stepped from the house. Immediately she saw the cruiser parked in her aunt's driveway. She'd forgotten about that. She'd better introduce herself and let the deputy know her plans.

Slowly, enjoying the early July warmth, she walked out to the green vehicle with the bold sheriff's department symbol on the door. The side window was down and a tanned elbow had been propped in the opening. Kim sensed that the deputy watched her progress, but the sun was in her eyes and his face was shadowed by the interior of the car.

She stepped up to the car and shaded her eyes. "Hi," she said extending her hand. "I'm Kimberley Tannas."

The man inside reached across his body to take her hand in a brief handshake. "We've already met," he returned solemnly as he studied her with dark, serious eyes. "I'm Deputy Lewis. Are you going out?"

Kim nodded. "Yes. That's what I came to tell you. I'll be going to my cousin's for a while. I'll probably be gone a couple of hours."

He looked at his watch. "Okay, I'll meet you back here at four-thirty. If you get back first, under no circumstances are you to go into the house before I have checked it out. Is that understood?"

"All right." Kim was a little taken aback by his vehemence. "Sure. If I get back and you're not here, I'll just wait in my car until you get here. Okay?"

"Fine."

Kim could feel him watching her as she walked to her small, red Ford Focus. He was an intense individual. Dark serious eyes. Somber expression. A little peculiar. But Vaughn had said Lewis was one of his best deputies precisely because he did take his job seriously. He never overlooked a thing.

Kim started her car and swung around in the wide drive to face the valley below. Lillooet Creek sprawled before her. How could a person have so many confusing feelings all linked to a single place not even worthy of a dot on many maps? "You can do this," she whispered to herself. She closed her eyes seeking the well of internal fortitude that had sustained her many times in her life. She would do this. She would not allow herself to be crippled by fear because . . . . She allowed the real dread within her to surface.

She was in another situation where her life or, possibly, the lives of others could be dependent upon her actions or her memory. Gritting her teeth, Kim headed for the town below. She had a number of places to stop before she went to Deirdre's.

Parking in front of the post office, Kim stared at it. For the first time, she actually sought out the associated memories. Her father on the steps gossiping with old man Hilliard. Her father inside, talking to the postmistress, Mrs. Johnson, about the price of postage, the weather, and the difficulty of raising children. Her father lifting her onto his shoulders as he descended the steps. She closed her eyes. She could remember the nervous excitement she had felt seated on his broad shoulders, looking down. She'd been sure Jack Clayton was the tallest man in the world. With a soft smile on her face, Kim searched her purse for a tissue. Finding one, she brushed self-consciously at the tears tracking down her cheeks. It was time to move on.

She pulled her car to the curb at the park. This was where she'd played softball. Getting out of the car, she strolled onto the rich green grass. Paths had been worn in many places. A young mother pushed her toddler on the swings. Kim didn't approach them closely enough to tempt conversation. Focusing her attention on the faded bleachers, she walked toward them. She could remember her parents sitting on the dulled and splintered wood, cheering on their only child as though she were champion material.

Kim had been terrible at baseball. She'd been terrible at most sports. But she'd always had heart, and the will to try. That had been what her parents had given her—especially her father. She climbed up on the seats and stared at the empty field, listening to the echo of her own girlish voice as she complained that she was never any good at anything. And her father's deep bass as he spouted another piece of wisdom learned during a life of hard work. *There isn't anything in this world you can't accomplish if you want it badly enough, girl. You remember that. You hear me?* God, she'd forgotten those words for a while. But she'd never forget again.

"Yes, Daddy," she whispered to the ghost in her memory. "I'll remember."

The pain in her chest was becoming almost unbearable. But she couldn't allow it to surface yet. Not here. Not in public. Tonight, when she was alone, she would exhume the memories of her father and face her grief and her overwhelming guilt for the first and the last time. It was what the psychiatrists had told her she had to do. But she hadn't been ready. Rising, Kim made her way back to her car. There was still another place she had to go.

The house where she'd spent the first 13 years of her life had fallen on hard times. It was occupied. It still echoed with the sound of life and joy and sorrow. But the creamy paint was scarred and peeling. The brown trim that her father had painted every second year looked as though it hadn't seen a paintbrush since his death. Four happy but extremely dirty children squatted in what had once been a graveled drive to make mud-pies which they decorated with dandelions. Kim smiled and allowed her eyes to roam.

She looked at the upstairs windows, seeing not the smeared glass that was there, but the gleaming windows of the past. There, beyond the sturdy branches of the big old tree that had been her private access, was her room. There'd been frilly white curtains at the window. Her mother had made them on the new sewing machine that her father had purchased as an anniversary present. The next window had belonged to her father's study. It had been a cluttered place, full of treasure that appealed to the sportsman. Jack Clayton had often sat up there on a winter's night, tying flies and dreaming about trout fishing in the spring.

Her parents had camped regularly. Kim had always enjoyed fishing despite that fact that she'd rarely caught anything and almost invariably ended up falling in and getting soaked. It had been the time spent with her parents away from civilization that had been special. Listening to the sounds of the wild creatures. Listening to her parents arguing over who had caught the biggest fish, making bets about who would have to cook the next evening. Listening to her parents singing together, harmonizing "You Are My Sunshine", as her mother cooked dinner over the old portable camp stove. Special times. Times she had almost allowed herself to lose forever by her simple unwillingness to remember. Sure there was pain. But the memories were worth that.

Her eyes drifted to the next room. Her parents' bedroom. The first thing you saw upon entering the room had always been the white and gold vanity that her father had made as a birthday present for her mother. It was so beautiful, so lovingly crafted. On its surface had been all the mysterious pots of cosmetics and perfumes that her mother had used to so magically transform herself from Mom into glamorous stranger on the nights that her parents had gone out together, leaving Kim with a sitter. She closed her eyes, remembering how handsome they had looked together.

And then it had all ended. Julia Clayton had not been a native of Lillooet Creek. When her husband had been murdered and her daughter had fallen into a deep and terrifying depression, her only thought had been to get away. To move back near her parents where she could receive the familial support she needed at such a time.

Kim opened her eyes and watched the children playing in the mud without really seeing them. There was still one more place she needed to visit. The service station. But she wasn't up to that yet. She thought she'd done well enough for one day. She'd shed a few tears, but she hadn't broken down. She hadn't allowed pleasant memories to unleash the terror in her mind. She hadn't lost control. Turning the key, she started the car. It was time to see Deirdre and Aunt Viv.

* * *

Liz Murphy sat in the sheriff's office, half wondering what she was doing there, but determined not to leave until she'd satisfied her instincts. As she'd left Snodell's Grocery, she'd had a sudden desire to meet Sheriff Garrett, whom Kate Hobsin had spoken of with such respect. Liz had decided to do so immediately. She sincerely believed that procrastination was one of the most deadly sins in existence, a usurper of the first order. It deprived people of their potential. It fooled them into thinking they had all the time in the world and then stole that time out from underneath them. And eventually, it leached away their chance at happiness. Liz knew. She had watched it happen.

So she had entered the sheriff's office and asked to speak to Sheriff Garrett. The pretty young woman behind the desk—Melissa Adams, her nameplate read—had informed her that the sheriff was out. When Liz had refused the help of one of the deputies, Melissa had directed her to a chair where she could wait. Liz sat sipping the Coke she'd purchased at Snodell's as she examined her surroundings.

She liked Melissa. She had a husky, slightly-scratchy voice, but it was friendly. It was obvious that she enjoyed her job and her life. That was something that was becoming a rarity. Everybody wanted more than they had. Which was fine—ambition was great—as long as you could enjoy yourself along the way. It was all in how you looked at life. The analogy Liz always made was that a good career choice was like a vacation. But if you didn't enjoy the route, why the dickens set your sights on the vacation in the first place?

"Hi, Ray. What are you doing here so early?"

Melissa's voice drew Liz's attention to the new arrival.

The deputy shrugged. "I woke up craving your coffee. What do you put in the stuff anyway? It sure isn't the best tastin' stuff I've ever had."

Melissa grinned. "That's my secret."

"Hmph." Ray poured himself a cup of black coffee and turned to survey the office. His eyes lit on Liz for the first time and, with the cup only halfway to his lips, he stared. Then, as though the aroma of the coffee had suddenly tickled his nostrils, he completed the gesture, taking a sip. But he still hadn't taken his eyes from her. Liz saw the masculine appreciation in his gaze. Lord it had been a long time since a man had looked at her like that.

He had wonderful eyes Liz noted. Clear and blue, like a spring sky. His hair was streaked with white, but it had once been a light brown. He had a slight pot belly, but he wasn't too overweight. He was simply a man who enjoyed good cooking, Liz thought. She couldn't fault him for that. She did, too. That's why she was constantly fighting that extra 15 pounds. And for some reason, the older she got the more determined those pounds were to stay on. Liz figured it was probably the same for a man as for a woman. They just put on the pounds in different areas of their anatomy.

"Hey, Ray. Could you come here a second?" The masculine voice emanated from an office door to Liz's left.

Ray looked toward it. "Yeah, sure. Coming." He smiled at Liz, a smile full of a promise that Liz was almost afraid to recognize.

"Marty, I thought you were up watching over Kim Tannas?" Ray said as he entered the office.

"I was, but she said she was going out for a couple of hours. I have to meet her up there again in an hour or so. I told her, if she got back first, not to go into the house until I get there to check it out."

"What d'ya need?"

"Well, I was wondering if maybe we shouldn't have someone staying in the house with her? You know, kind of double protection? I took a tour around the place today. Up on the hill like that, a quarter mile away from the nearest neighbor. It wouldn't be too difficult for a really determined guy to find a way to sneak into the house that wouldn't be visible from the driveway at all."

Liz, unashamed in her eavesdropping, cocked her head to cast a glance at Melissa across the room. Could she hear the conversation? It didn't look like it. She was busily pounding away on her computer keyboard. Liz went back to listening.

". . . thinking that way myself last night." It was Ray's voice again. "I just don't know. We don't have enough manpower to have two men up there. And by placing a deputy inside, you could be placing him in a dangerous situation. This bastard has already killed one man. And Trent Farris was no slouch. He kicked your ass last year in that boxing competition."

A tickle in her throat caught Liz unaware, and she coughed.

"Yeah, that's right. But he got caught by surprise. Knocked out." There was a pause. "Is somebody out there?"

"Oh, yeah, I forgot." The door to the office closed with a click.

Liz started thinking. This Kim Tannas was obviously in danger from someone. Was she the one Liz had been drawn to protect? She'd have to find a way to meet her.

A second later, the outer door opened and a young man wearing jeans and a blue chambray shirt entered. "Sheriff, I'm glad your back. There's someone waiting to see you."

Vaughn glanced at the waiting area. He saw a woman somewhere past middle age, but not by much, maybe late forties or early fifties. His first thought was that she was a stranger; his second was that she was a little strange—by Lillooet Creek standards anyway. Enormous multi-colored discs dangled from her pierced ears complimenting her bright, multi-hued attire almost perfectly. She appeared to have a ring or two on each of her ten fingers, and gold and silver bangles glittered on her arms. The nails on her hands and her sandaled feet were polished a bright shade of fuchsia that exactly matched the shade of the fuchsia splashes in her skirt. A number of black tendrils of hair escaped her loose chignon to snake around her neck or down her perfectly made-up cheeks. "Ma'am," Vaughn nodded as he strode toward her. "I'm Sheriff Garrett."

She rose, smiling, as she took his hand. "Liz Murphy, Sheriff." Vaughn noticed that she avoided his eyes. Her gaze fixed instead on the star attached to his shirt.

"How can I help you?"

Her smile faltered slightly. "Well, to be honest with you, I'm not exactly certain." Shc hesitated, glancing at Melissa. "Um, would it be possible to speak privately?"

He sighed inwardly as the tension and fatigue that had been building all day tightened its clutch on his shoulders. It must have shown briefly in his face because Liz Murphy hastened to reassure him. "It won't take long. Really. Please?"

"All right, Mrs. Murphy—"

"Ms. Murphy," she interrupted, "I'm widowed."

Vaughn nodded in acknowledgment. "Ms. Murphy. Just take a seat in my office," he led her to the door, "I'll be with you in just a moment." Closing the door, he turned to Melissa and raised a questioning eyebrow.

"Beats me," she responded quietly. "She didn't want to speak to anyone but you."

Vaughn nodded in frustrated acknowledgement. He'd been looking forward to a few solitary moments to organize his thoughts. He decided to pour himself a coffee. He'd noticed Ms. Murphy carrying a bottle of Coke so he assumed she wouldn't want one.

* * *

Liz was a little surprised by the sheriff's youth and attractiveness. The jeans, blue chambray shirt, and scuffed black boots he wore had only accentuated his youth in her mind. When the people in authority got younger every year, you knew you were getting old. While she waited for him to return, she studied his office.

The venetian blinds on the window behind the desk were closed, blocking out the view of what would probably be an alley. The walls were a light tan; the floor, tan linoleum with darker brown streaks in it. Two large, tan, four-drawer, lateral filing cabinets resided against one wall. On top of them sprawled a single, enormous, piggyback plant. One wall held a county map. Another, an enormous map of Washington state. Still, the office revealed next to nothing about the character of the sheriff himself. A green blotter occupied the exact center of the desk. To the right of it, a telephone sat on a perfect 45 degree angle. To the left and near the top, a desk organizer held three pencils and two pens along with tape and an assortment of colored paperclips. There were no pictures on the desk. Not even a single loose paper marred the immaculate order.

She heard the click of the door as it opened, and turned to watch the sheriff make his way past her and around his desk to take a seat. "Now, then, Ms. Murphy. What did you want to speak with me about?"

She had decided to be completely honest with him. But it wasn't going to be easy. She couldn't look him in the face. Not yet. She was afraid she'd lose her nerve. She stared at the closed blind instead. "What I'm about to tell you may sound farfetched," she said. "I'm asking you to keep an open mind."

"I'll do my best, ma'am."

"Please don't call me ma'am. It makes me feel old. Call me Liz."

The sheriff nodded without comment, and she

sensed his impatience. Just start, she thought. Open your mouth and say the words. What does it matter if he thinks you're crazy? A lot of other people do, too. He's just one more.

She cleared her throat. "I'm from Arizona," she said. "Flagstaff, Arizona. I'm a travel writer and an artist. I've only been in Washington a few days." She ran her fingers up and down her Coke bottle, collecting the moisture on her fingertips. "Last night before going to my hotel, I picked up a copy of *The Seattle Times*." She swallowed convulsively as memory of the visual flashes, vivid and frightening, interfered with her thoughts. "Um," she took a large swallow of Coke.

Slowly, haltingly, she forced herself to tell him what she had seen and felt as she read that article. She dared a look at him now and again. He didn't change position, merely sitting back in his chair, his chin propped thoughtfully on linked fingers as he observed her.

"You see, Sheriff," she said, finally daring to face him, "I've always been a bit psychic. It's something that's been passed down for generations in my family. I inherited it from my grandmother. But my impressions are usually closer to home, attached to family, friends and acquaintances. Sometimes to children. I don't know why I've been drawn here. I don't know what I can do to help. But I wanted you to know because. . . if there's anything I can do. . . I'd like you to ask."

Sheriff Garrett finally sighed and stirred. "I'll be honest with you Ms. Murphy; I've never put much stock in psychic phenomena—of any kind." Liz opened her mouth and he raised a hand to forestall her comment. "Neither am I completely ignorant of the fact that psychics have been successful in helping the police in a few isolated cases. I am not ruling out the possibility that you may provide us with assistance.

"However, I want to make myself perfectly clear. You are not to involve yourself in this investigation in any way without prior authorization from myself or one of my deputies. I will not have you placing yourself or others in jeopardy. Do we understand each other?" His tone had become condescending.

"Perfectly, Sheriff." Liz didn't know why she should be annoyed; she should have been used to it. He obviously thought he was talking to a kooky, old lady. And that was just fine. Their relationship had been defined. To start it off with a bang, she would have loved to kick his arrogant little butt.

She rose to leave. Reaching across his desk, she extended her hand. "Thank you for your time, Sheriff." For the first time, she looked directly into his eyes. A jolt like a bolt of lightning passed through her, paralyzing her. Oh God, it couldn't be! It wasn't possible! She was imagining things. But she'd seen those eyes before.

"Are you all right, Ms. Murphy?"

Stunned, Liz slowly backed toward the door. "I'm fine. Thanks." She wrenched open the door and fled.

CHAPTER 6

The woman closed the door so quickly as she exited that her long, full skirt caught in it. Vaughn stared at the bright swatch of fabric wondering if she'd torn the chunk right out of her skirt or if she was standing on the other side of the door playing tug-of-war with it. A second later the door opened enough for the piece of fabric to be quickly extricated. Vaughn grinned. There went one strange lady. What the hell had set her off like that? He stared speculatively at the closed door. Finally he shrugged in defeat. Damned if he knew, and he had more important things to think about.

After he'd left Kim's, he'd gone over to Carter's Lumber to check into buying a burglar alarm system. Bill Carter hadn't been there, so Vaughn had spoken with the yardman Mike Drayton. Even though Vaughn was a fairly regular customer at Carter's, it was the first time since Drayton had moved into town a year ago that Vaughn had actually spoken to the man. That struck him as peculiar. One would almost think that Drayton had been avoiding him or something. He tried to remember exactly when it was that Carter had pointed out his new employee for the first time.

Vaughn had been giving Jimmy Coontz a ride home

from school when he'd decided to stop off at the lumber-yard and pick up a couple of things. So school hadn't let out for the summer yet. He rubbed the bridge of his nose as he tried to bring the details of the day into focus. The grass had been green, and it had been warm because the Coontz boy had been wearing a short-sleeved T-shirt. That would have made it May or June. He didn't think it could have been as early as April, although there had been occasional balmy days in April too.

Okay, so Drayton had moved into town in May or June of last year. Candace Smyth had been killed in Seattle at the beginning of April. He wondered if Mike Drayton had been in Seattle at the time. He was probably grasping at straws. He was almost certain he'd been told that Drayton had come here from Tacoma. Still, people didn't necessarily tell the truth. It wouldn't hurt to make a few phone calls.

He wondered what it was about the man that rubbed him the wrong way. Drayton was average height, about five foot nine or so. He appeared to be about Vaughn's age, with green eyes, glasses and brown hair. Premature baldness had attacked with a vengeance—probably because of the caps Drayton constantly wore. And he was about ten pounds overweight, all of which appeared to have settled around his middle. But there was nothing in any of that that could explain why Vaughn had felt vaguely uneasy while speaking with him today. He shrugged, and picked up the phone. He'd make a couple of calls. Ease his mind. He'd have to place an order for an alarm system too. Carter's hadn't had one in stock.

* * *

Crystal Falls was a quaint little village. Much of it had been designed to imitate Swiss styling. Kim had had to look up the address in order to find Deirdre's raised bungalow home. Now, as she knocked on the door, she looked around the yard. Deirdre and Kyle had done a nice job of landscaping. Bright-colored perennial flowers added their rich sweet scent to the mountain air from numerous well-cared-for beds. The drive was paved with red, interlocking brick and bordered with colorful petunias. Climbing roses cloaked a trellis as it arched over the walk. Their home was attractive and friendly without being in the least ostentatious.

The door opened and Kim turned. The warm smile she'd been about to deliver cooled a degree, becoming merely polite, as she recognized Kyle. She couldn't help it. Kyle was an arrogant, big-city boy, born and bred, who'd always looked down on small-town hicks, and Kim was one of them. He and Deirdre had moved to Crystal Falls immediately following their marriage five years ago. Kim had often wondered why had he let Deirdre talk him into moving here since he so obviously disliked it. And why wasn't he at work right now? Kyle operated the only exclusive men's store in Lillooet Creek. Of course, he'd learned shortly after opening it that, in order to make a dollar, he had to stock just as many flannel work shirts as he did silk suits. She noticed that his own attire had changed considerably since the last time she'd seen him. He stood before her now clad in T-shirt and jeans.

"Hi, Kyle. Is Deirdre here?" What had Deirdre ever seen in the guy? Besides his devastatingly, handsome appearance that is. Fully clothed he exuded enough masculine sexuality to qualify as a *Playgirl* centerfold. Deirdre was just a sucker for tall, dark and handsome, Kim concluded. Thank God she'd always been immune to such impermanent trappings. Personally, she preferred personality.

"Yeah, sure. Come on in." He didn't bother to smile as he stepped back, allowing Kim to step into the house.

"Daddy. Who is it, Daddy?" Four year old Kaleigh came barreling out of a doorway to grasp her father's leg and stick her thumb in her mouth as she looked up at Kim with unabashed childish curiosity.

Kyle laughed and swooped the dark-haired child up into one arm. "It's Mommy's cousin, Kim. Do you remember seeing her at your birthday party last year at Grandma's?"

The child frowned and shook her head. "Well, that's okay," Kyle said. "You were a whole year younger then. You'll remember her next time. Won't you?"

Kaleigh nodded and smiled around the wet thumb in her mouth. "'im," she said, pointing with the pudgy index finger of her other hand.

Kim watched as Kyle gently removed the thumb from the little girl's mouth. "Kim," he enunciated clearly. "You can call her Auntie Kim. Okay?" He certainly seemed good with children. Perhaps the guy had some redeeming qualities after all.

When Kaleigh nodded and promptly stuck her thumb back in her mouth, Kyle put her down. "You run and tell Mommy she has company." He turned to Kim. "She's in the kitchen." He led her down a short hall. "I heard about the trouble you had last night," he said over his shoulder. "Figured you'd have lit out for home by now."

"Me, too. But I guess I'll be staying around for a while."

He stopped. "You're kidding!"

"No. Sheriff Garrett seems to think I should stay."

Kyle shook his head. "Well, you've got guts." His tone implied she might not have any brains.

Kim ignored him and turned into the doorway he indicated. Kyle disappeared. She assumed he went to watch television. She could hear an announcer giving a play-by-play on some sports game. Deirdre and Aunt Viv sat at the kitchen table sipping from mugs and talking while Deirdre monitored two-year old Tyler as he sat in his high chair eating a snack.

Aunt Viv looked up. She seemed haggard and spent.

"Kim! I was certain I'd misunderstood Kaleigh when she said Auntie Kim was here. I thought we'd be getting a call from you saying you were back in Seattle by now."

"Sorry, Aunt Viv. I'd have called sooner, but I didn't even wake up until early afternoon." She pulled out a chair and sat down. "And then I ended up talking to Sheriff Garrett for well over an hour."

"Why?" Deirdre asked as she set a cup of coffee in front of Kim.

Kim sighed. "It's a long story." Sipping coffee, she launched into her explanation. She saw Deirdre's spine stiffen in preparation for argument and forestalled her. "There's nothing you can say to change my mind, Dee. I know what I'm doing." She sipped again and ran her finger thoughtfully around the brim of the cup. "Dad's killer got away because I couldn't remember anything about that night. I can't let Trent's killer get away, too. Not when I might be able to do something about it. Do you understand?"

Dee opened her mouth to argue, thought better of it and let her spine sag slightly as she nodded. "Yeah, I do. But that doesn't make it any easier."

"I know that."

"Well, if you're determined to do this, I'll move back home tonight," Aunt Vivian said. "You can't stay in that big, old house all alone."

"Mom, no!" Dee's voice was almost frantic. "I couldn't stand the thought of both of you there. Please?"

"Calm down, Dee." Kim turned to her aunt. "I'd prefer that you let me stay there alone, Aunt Viv. It's your house, and I really don't have any say in the matter, but I'd feel better if my staying wasn't jeopardizing anyone else's safety. There's a deputy sitting outside the house whenever I'm there. When I return after going out, they're going to go in and search the house before letting me back in." She reached across the table to hold her aunt's hand. "I'm as protected as I can be. You're being there wouldn't make me any safer. And I don't mind staying alone. I've been alone for a while now. Remember."

Her Aunt Vivian's bright blue eyes searched hers, seeking sincerity. Finally she nodded. "All right, if that's the way you want it. But there's one thing I want you to know. A few years ago, after Jake left, I decided I didn't like being in that big old house all alone and I— well, I bought a handgun. I've kept it clean and well-cared-for so that if I ever needed it—" Her voice trailed off. "Anyway, it's in the drawer of my night table. For heaven's sake, if you need it, use it."

"I will. Thanks, Aunt Viv." She patted her aunt's hand reassuringly.

"I'm going to worry constantly." Aunt Viv shook her head in dismay. "Will you promise to call me every day to let me know how things are going?"

"I promise." Kim smiled reassuringly and then jumped as Tyler threw his cookie into her hair. "Young man, that was incredibly rude," she said with mock severity as she extracted the sticky mess. "You're going to pay for that." And waving her fingers in warning, she attacked his fat, baby ribs. His full-throated gurgling laugh was music to her ears.

A few minutes later, as she bounced the sticky toddler on her knee and realized that her jeans needed washing, she remembered that she'd meant to ask Deirdre to lend her some clothes.

"Sure. What do you need?" Deirdre asked.

"Everything. I'll stop and buy some lingerie in town on the way home, I guess. And I know I won't be able to wear any of your slacks or jeans because your legs must be at least four inches longer than mine. But if you could lend me some skirts, a pair of shorts, and some blouses and T-shirts, I'd appreciate it."

She nodded. "Let's go raid my closet." She took Tyler from Kim and, setting him on the floor with a pat on his chubby bottom, told him to go and play.

* * *

Liz carried her case down the upstairs hallway at the Fairview Hotel. She examined the numbers on the doors she passed, searching for number 212. There. Just to be sure, she compared it once more with the number on her key tag—no card locks yet for the small town—before putting the key in the lock. The door swung open to reveal a surprisingly spacious room for such a small-town hotel. After closing the door and setting her case down, she walked to the window.

Rooftops glinted with fire in the setting sun. Tall firs stood dark and sharply delineated against a distant mountain and the purpling sky. Four young men sat on the bridge dangling fishing lines into the creek. It really was an attractive little town. She noticed a square of light from a house high on a hill and remembered the conversation she'd overheard. Would that be where Kim Tannas lived? Probably not, but Liz intended to find out first thing tomorrow just exactly where she did live.

With a sigh she turned away from the window and walked the three steps to the bed. Lord, she was tired. Closing her eyes, she let herself collapse onto it. Not bad, she thought after a moment. A little hard maybe, but she'd slept in worse. Rolling over, she opened her eyes and stared at the ceiling. It was white stipple with little flecks of silver in it. Attractive, but impossible to wash. She supposed that, being a hotel, they would just paint it when it discolored.

Damn! It was no use. No matter where she focused her attention, she ran out of pertinent thoughts within seconds. Rising, she went to the mirror and stared at her reflection. His eyes were gold. But hundreds of people had very similar eyes. There was nothing unusual in that.

Had she really seen Sheriff Garrett's eyes before, or was it her imagination? No. Some instinct, some sixth sense had told her she'd seen those eyes—not just eyes like them, but *those* eyes. The knowledge had released a tempest of emotion that she hadn't understood, and still didn't. First, there'd been fear and rage—immeasurable rage. Then pain and grief, a hurt so strong that she'd thought her heart might burst. Then joy and wonder. And finally disbelief—the doubt in her own faculties. But she'd learned long ago to ignore the doubt and trust her instincts. Where had she seen Sheriff Garrett before this day? And why had seeing him again induced such an overwhelming emotional storm from her subconscious mind.

Turning away from the mirror, she opened her case and extracted her stretchy exercise outfit. It hadn't been getting worn nearly often enough lately. After quickly changing clothes, she went through an abbreviated form of her yoga routine before positioning herself for meditation. She hadn't mastered the technique yet, but it always relaxed her, and tonight she was willing to accept even that small measure of comfort. If she could just clear her mind. She did the breathing and focusing exercises, but it wasn't working. The remnants of the powerful emotions she'd felt continued to haunt her. Rising, she walked into the bathroom for a cold cloth.

She remembered feeling those emotions with such intensity only once before. A suspicion surfaced in her mind. She swallowed uncomfortably as she stared at her own aging reflection in the bathroom mirror. But, no. It wasn't possible after all these years. Was it? *Anything is possible, child*, her granny's voice emerged from the past to guide her. Okay. She wiped the cool cloth across her forehead and nodded to the reflection in the mirror. Tomorrow she'd see what small town gossip she could uncover. Within the week, she intended to know Sheriff Garrett as well as he knew himself. Maybe better. Now, it was time for dinner at Erma's and an early night.

* * *

He slept. The memories of the past, unfettered by conscious thought came to haunt his dreams. It was a hot July day. The sun shone down through the trees, warming his back as he sat on the boulevard watching her house—or, rather, her grandmother's house—a small one-story home surrounded by carefully tended trees and numerous beds of perennial flowers and herbs. The backyard had a large carefully tended garden. He knew because he'd circled the entire house before taking up his current position. He was almost certain that, should he gain entrance to her home, it would smell like cinnamon and sugar cookies. It looked like that kind of place.

Abruptly, his gaze sharpened. He could see a form through the sheer of the living room curtains; it was Candace. He would recognize her silhouette anywhere. For the hundredth time in the last hour, he tried to convince himself that he should get up, walk across the street, knock on the door and ask her to go to the movies with him. She had smiled at him today; she liked him. But the warmth of the sun on his back seduced him to linger. He'd just watch for a few more minutes. He liked to watch.

Unexpectedly the door opened and Candace emerged. "See you later, Grams," she called. Her high, clear voice engraved itself in his memory and he heard the words over and over again like an echo. Her grandmother must have spoken to her, given her some direction, because she said, "I will." And then, closing the door on the small cottage-like house, she walked down the narrow bricked walk toward the street.

She wore cut-off denim shorts that showed most of her long, golden-tanned legs. Shapely legs. Legs he wanted to touch. His gaze moved up. Her sleeveless black top left her delicate shoulders bare to the kiss of the sun. He could see her small breasts bounce slightly at each step and knew she wasn't wearing a bra. The knowledge tantalized him. He pictured her naked, smiling and reaching for him. A second later, she turned onto the sidewalk and began walking toward town. The realization that she was leaving wrenched him from his fantasy and filled him with a sense of urgency. There was no more time. He had to ask her now.

Without being fully conscious of his own actions, he rose and raced across the street to trail after her. The sunlight turned her hair to spun gold. In fact, she looked golden all over. A youthful goddess. Perfection. Too good for the likes of him. No! He shoved the unwelcome thought away. She had smiled at him.

Suddenly she turned. Her eyes shone like blue turquoise. She saw him and her lips curved in welcome. "Hi. Are you going to town too?"

He managed to nod.

"Want to walk with me?" she asked.

"Sure," he said. The word felt like a foreign object as he forced it past some constriction in his throat. He tucked his hands in his pockets and looked sideways at her. "Um, I've been meaning to ask you, if you—I mean—" He trailed off horrified by his ineptitude. But if he stopped now he would just look like more of an idiot. So, drawing a deep breath, he fixed what he wanted to say in his mind and blurted it out. "Would you like to go to the movies with me tonight?"

She halted in her tracks. He stopped, too, and slowly, hesitantly forced himself to meet her eyes. They held a combination of surprise and. . . pity. He ground his teeth, knowing the words that would come, hating them. Hating her.

"I'm sorry," she said. "I already have a date for tonight. Trent Farris asked me a week ago. I'm going to meet him and some of the others now."

"Forget it," he said, turning away from her. "I gotta go." Stretching out his legs he continued walking, moving ahead of her. He heard her call his name, but he ignored her. He ignored the ache in his chest and the burning behind his eyelids. He ignored the little voice in his head that said *I told you so*.

"Maybe next Saturday," she called after him. But he knew the offer came from pity. And next Saturday, she would have second thoughts. He didn't bother turning around.

A second later, he saw Trent coming toward him. Mr. Perfect with his movie-star smile and athletic build. Why was it that the people who had everything only seemed to get more while the ones who had nothing faded away? Hate stirred in him. He refused to fade away, to become a shadow.

"Hi," Trent said to him, nodding and smiling as they met and Trent passed him.

Controlling his anger, he returned the nod. "Hi." And then, a moment later, he heard Trent meet Candace. He heard them talk and laugh together. Laughing at him. About him. The hate curdled in his gut and he made himself a promise. Someday, in some way, he would pay them all back. And they wouldn't laugh anymore.

The street faded away and he watched them line up at the movie house. Popular Mr. Perfect. Smiling Trent Farris with his arm around the girl that should have been *his*. And Candace lapping up Farris's football-hero style like a pet dog. All the people around them laughing and joking on a warm July evening. An impromptu party. A party to which he'd never been invited. And never would be.

The dream ended and faded into the murk of long buried memories. He shifted in his sleep. Why was he so uncomfortable? Slowly he opened his eyes. Shit! He'd fallen asleep in his chair again. He stared around the darkened room and saw the even darker square of the window. He wouldn't be able to get to sleep again for hours. Might as well stay up. Turning on the lamp, he picked up his copy of the latest Patricia D. Cornwell novel and resumed reading. He loved to read, and his favorite novels were always those that taught him something.

* * *

Night's dark wings pressed at the windows like a living creature. Kim's imagination was getting the better of her as she walked through the house, turning on every light. But no amount of artificial brightness could dispel her agitation.

She had done what she promised herself. She'd taken out the memories of her father—and the guilt. She'd examined the grief and her own feeling of culpability from all angles. And she had cried. She'd cried as she had never cried before—for his death and the years they had both lost. She'd cried until she couldn't cry any more. Her eyes were swollen with it. And she felt better.

It was being in this enormous old house alone that was getting to her. It made her feel like a fly on the wall. The flyswatter was descending and she wasn't certain she'd be swift enough to escape it. Finally, realizing that pacing and ringing her hands wasn't doing any good, she decided to sit down and read one of Aunt Viv's copies of *Reader's Digest*. But no matter how many times she read an article, she didn't absorb a single word.

"Meow-ow."

"Charity." It was nice to just have someone to talk to. "Come here, kitty." The cat jumped up on her lap without waiting for a second invitation. "Lord, you weigh a ton. I think I'll have to talk to Aunt Viv about putting you on a diet."

Charity looked at her with accusing golden eyes as she began to knead Kim's thighs. As the cat lay purring on her knee, Kim focused her complete attention on her, mindlessly stroking Charity's long blue-gray fur until it became staticky. Then a stray cat hair worked its way up to tickle her nose, destroying her peaceful trance. Oh well, it was time to unpack anyway.

Setting the cat down, she rose to go up to her room. A suitcase and a shopping bag sat on the bed awaiting her attention. The case, from Deirdre, held all the clothes she'd lent Kim. Many more than Kim had asked for, and more than she could hope to use she was certain. But after one glance at Deirdre's extensive wardrobe, she'd decided not to argue. She supposed a wardrobe was one advantage to being married to a fashion-conscious male like Kyle.

She opened the shopping bag containing her purchases from Cleo's Ladies Wear first. Immediately the floral scent of sachet escaped into the room, making the chamber seem more like home. She'd been surprised and pleased to discover that Cleo's carried the sweet, gardenia-scented sachet that she always kept with her lingerie.

Lingerie was Kim's one personal indulgence. She'd been known to spend a small fortune on it. But then she didn't spend a lot on makeup, so she thought she was entitled.

Kim had always loved sexy clothing. Unfortunately her yearning hadn't come accessorized with guts. So when she'd found lingerie, she'd discovered the means to indulge that aspect of her feminine core without anyone the wiser. It was always concealed beneath more dignified apparel. Having the delicate fabrics next to her skin had allowed her to celebrate her womanhood while simultaneously camouflaging it from society's judgmental eyes.

She looked into the shopping bag full of delicately scented lingerie in a profusion of rich, vibrant colors. Slowly, savoring the moment, she began to remove the silk, satin, and lace undergarments, putting them lovingly away in the drawers: teddies and camisoles and tap pants and matching bra and panty sets, and stay-up stockings, and even some garters and stockings, although she wasn't certain when an occasion might arise to wear them. But no panty hose—

even when the sales clerk had attempted to tempt her with a lace topped pair. She'd always found them uncomfortable, and they were about as economical as caviar as far as she was concerned. When Kim got a run in a stocking, she threw away one stocking. Not a pair of stockings.

As she was about to place the last teddy in the drawer, she heard a noise to her left and looked quickly toward the window. For an instant, she saw nothing but the blackened rectangle of night. And then, she froze.

CHAPTER 7

On his way home from the office, Vaughn had stopped to speak with Jordan Hall, who was on duty outside the Farris home. Both men looked at the house with startled eyes as Kim's first scream split the air. When the second unintelligible shriek sounded, Vaughn was already on a run for the house. She shouted again and again, the frantic sound reverberating through the night air. And still he could not understand a word of what she was shouting. His heart was in his throat. He heard Jordan on his heels. Jordan was taller and leaner that Vaughn, and, despite his graying hair, age hadn't slowed him down a bit. But what had they missed?

Vaughn almost knocked the locked front door from its hinges in his anxiety. He didn't have a chance to take more than one run at it before it flew open and Kim ran into him, practically knocking him onto his backside. His arms closed around her as his gaze sought out the threat. "Whoa. What is it?"

"He's here." Her eyes were wild, barely focusing on him.

"Where?" He grasped her arms, shaking her a little. "Where, Kim?"

Although she didn't appear to be crying, a sound like a sob caught in her throat as she turned to point. "In the tree. Looking in my window."

Vaughn's heart slowed slightly as he guided her back into the house. That sounded more like Skeeter Barnes' style. But why the hell hadn't they seen him? He nodded to Jordan who moved off, gun drawn, to investigate. Tremors began to shudder their way through Kim's body.

"Okay, honey. Deputy Hall's gone to check it out. You're all right." He rubbed Kimberley's back for a moment, easing some of the tension from it. For an ice queen, she felt damn good in his arms. Too damn good!

Then, just as he thought she'd relaxed a bit, he felt her stiffen and lift her head from his shoulder. Questioningly, he looked down into her upturned face. He was startled by the depths of the anger he saw there.

She pushed away from him. "You, bastard!" she yelled suddenly. She began to pummel his chest with her fists, one of which still grasped some scrap of red material that she seemed oblivious to holding. "I hate you. I hate you. I hate you."

Vaughn caught her fists and held them, preventing her from doing him any actual hurt. "What the hell did I do?" Vaughn raised his voice slightly to be heard over her enraged harangue.

"What did you do?" she asked incredulously. "What did you do?"

"That's what I said."

"You talked me into staying here. You said you could protect me. It was bullshit. All bullshit." She struggled to release her fists from his grasp. "He walked right by you. Let *go* of me!" She emphasized the words with a kick to his shin.

"Ouch. Dammit! Will you calm down?" She continued to struggle in his hold. "Stop it!" But she ignored him. Her smoky eyes were wild with anger and fear. Strands of golden hair escaped her French braid to coil sensuously around her features. Her lush coral lips parted as she exerted herself. And suddenly Vaughn wasn't even thinking about placating her anger.

He used the grasp he had on her wrists to maneuver her fists behind her back, bringing her body hard against his. At the sudden change in their positions, she froze. Her eyes widened. Instantaneously, the atmosphere altered, thickened. The lush lips of her mouth drew his eyes like a magnet. God, he wanted to taste her. Had to.

"L–Let me go." The words were whispered, barely audible. He felt the soft exhalation of her breath against his face as she said them. But he ignored them as he lowered his mouth to hers.

Sweet. . . so sweet. He pulled her more tightly against him. She gasped slightly at the contact, and he took advantage of her parted lips to plunge his tongue into the warm, moist interior of her mouth. She moaned. The sound, low and animalistic, reverberated from deep within her throat. Desire, like a desert heat-wave swept through him. But the specters of reason and willpower surfaced.

What was he doing? Now was not the time for a tumble in the hay. He released her wrists and moved his hands to her waist. Slowly, he broke off the kiss, trailing his lips over her smooth soft cheek to her temple. She brought her hands to his shoulders as she leaned against him and he caught sight once more of the scrap of red material. What the hell was that?

As he massaged her back slowly and soothingly with one hand, he eased the clump of lacy, red fabric from her fingers with the other and examined it. His eyes widened. Holy . . .! Quickly, self-consciously, he dropped it onto the small mail desk that stood nearby. But not soon enough to forestall the picture his mind supplied of her clad in the skimpy little teddy. His blood pressure rose more than a few notches.

Just then the screen door squealed a protest as it

opened. Kim jumped away from him as Jordan returned. "Looks like there was definitely someone there all right. The grass is still flattened in spots where he walked. But there's no sign of him now."

Vaughn nodded, avoiding Jordy's knowing brown-eyed gaze. "Thanks, Jordan. I'll be out to talk to you in a few minutes." Jordan nodded, smiled, and closed the door.

Kim's face flamed with embarrassment as she moved to take a seat on the sofa.

"Kim—"

She held up a hand to stop him. "Don't say anything. I don't know why you kissed me, and I don't want to know. But I'm warning you not to do it again."

Vaughn stared at her. "It was just a kiss, for Pete's sake."

"I know what it was. But I don't like you in the least. And I can't get involved with another cop. Ever. Do I make myself clear?"

"I think you're presuming a bit much from a kiss. I don't believe I've mentioned anything about getting involved. Have I?"

The flame in Kim's cheeks flared brighter. "You ass. Why don't you—?"

It was Vaughn's turn to interrupt. "I'm sorry. I shouldn't have said that." The best thing for them both right now was to ignore what had just happened between them on a personal level.

"Let's talk business. Okay?" He sat on the arm of the chair facing her. "I don't think you had anything to fear this time. It was probably Skeeter Barnes."

Kim rubbed her palms on her denim clad thighs as she warily met Vaughn's eyes. "Who is Skeeter Barnes?"

"Skeeter is Lillooet Creek's resident Peeping Tom. He was fined and jailed for it a while back, but reports indicate that he's back at it. We just have to catch him in the act again."

"Oh." She frowned and shivered, crossing her arms over her stomach. "I think I remember him. Vaguely."

"Yeah, he hasn't changed much. He's still a little weasel." He watched her in silence for a second. "Look, I'm going to talk to Deputy Hall. We'll figure out how Skeeter slipped by us and make sure it doesn't happen again. All right?"

Kim nodded, refusing to meet his eyes. "Fine."

"I'll check back with you tomorrow."

"Sure."

She was still angry with him. Actually he couldn't say that he blamed her. Gritting his teeth, he left before he could say or do anything else that he might regret later.

* * *

Fifteen minutes later, Vaughn had just finished speaking with Jordan and had returned to his Bronco when his radio crackled. It was his part-time night dispatcher, Ethel Wright. Now what? He slumped forward to rest his aching head against the steering wheel. Maybe if he didn't answer she'd go away. Another call belied that hope. He picked up the handset. "Garrett here."

"Sheriff, there's a disturbance at T.J.'s." Ethel insisted on complete formality while she was working, even though she was old enough to be the mother of every man on the force with the possible exception of Ray Cheney.

"What happened?"

"One of the Hanson boys broke a pool cue over Phil Barlow's head."

Vaughn started the Bronco and began backing up. "Shit," he muttered to himself as his mind dealt with the implications. He knew for a fact that the Barlows had been drinking since T.J.'s had opened that morning. And the Barlow brothers weren't called cement heads for nothing. He'd never seen one of them knocked out in a fight, which meant that Phil Barlow was probably royally pissed off. It was rare indeed when a Barlow lost his sense of humor, but when he did it wasn't pretty. The local hospital might find itself doing some business tonight.

"Who'd you send?" he asked Ethel.

"Deputy Killian." Ethel's high voice reminded Vaughn of a parrot's squawk as it came over the radio. "But the whole place is in an uproar."

Vaughn sighed. "On my way."

Vaughn considered what he was in for. He'd known both the Hansons and the Barlows for more years than he cared to remember. Had he not been the sheriff, he would love nothing better than to allow the Barlows to give the Hansons the comeuppance they deserved. The Barlow boys at least had a code of ethics. He could respect them. But the Hansons—he hated to even consider himself a member of the same species. They'd damn near had to install a revolving door on the jail just for the Hanson brothers. Vaughn tried to remember if one of them was in prison at the moment or not. Sighing, he came to the conclusion that they were all home right now. Damn. That meant there'd be four of them to deal with.

The only place any of the Hanson boys ever went without the others was to jail—and maybe to the bathroom, although he wouldn't have bet on that assumption. After being raised with those creeps, it was no wonder his ex-girlfriend, Doreen, hadn't been able to retain a shred of sentiment for the male of the species. She'd refused to maintain any contact with her family since she'd left home. For once, Vaughn understood her reasoning.

When he arrived at the bar five minutes later, he found that a number of T.J.'s patrons had abandoned the premises for the comparative safety of the street. He opened the bar door to find a small skirmish in progress. Shouldering onlookers aside, he strode in. "Move it out," Vaughn said as he elbowed his way through the small throng. "Clear it on out of here."

Tom stood behind the bar surveying the fracas with concern. A couple of tables had been tipped over. One of the Hanson boys was laying in the rubble of a broken chair tipping back a beer as he watched the brawl continue around him. Bill Barlow landed a punch square in the middle of Kip Hanson's paunchy stomach. Young Deputy Killian stepped into their midst and, with a hand at each of their throats, held them apart and began talking to them. Killian was doing his best to prevent out and out war from breaking out. The tall, blonde deputy with his Nordic good looks might be young, but he was naturally brawny, and Vaughn had complete faith in his ability to prevent the fracas from resuming in that quarter.

Jason Hanson already looked a little the worse for wear. He was probably the idiot who'd taken it into his head to hit Phil Barlow with his cue. A trickle of blood wormed its way down Phil Barlow's forehead, but other than that he looked just plain mean.

"Evenin' boys," Vaughn said, as he walked up to them. "Having a little problem here, are we?"

"That fuckin' asshole owes me twenty bucks," Jason Hanson growled. He bounced on the balls of his feet, still spoiling for a fight. He reminded Vaughn of a bantam rooster. "He cheated."

"I don't fuckin' cheat, you lyin' sack of shit." Spittle sprayed from Phil's mouth as he swayed drunkenly toward his tormentor.

Vaughn nodded and stepped between them, counting on Deputy Killian to watch his back and warn him of any approaching trouble as he faced Jason Hanson. "How many times have you won a twenty from Phil here?"

Jason smirked. "Lots."

"And he usually pays up. No problem. Right?"

Jason avoided his eyes.

"Right?" Vaughn pressed him.

"Right." Jason was sullen now.

"You wanna be able to keep winning occasionally?"

"Yeah." Jason met his gaze belligerently. There was a challenge there. Vaughn only smiled.

"Then forget this twenty and go home." He eyed Jason's silent backup with dislike. "All of you. Unless you want to be registered guests in my jail for the night."

He heard Phil Barlow growl in his ear. Phil wasn't happy with the thought of his harasser leaving without more punishment. As Killian began to herd the Hansons out of the bar, Vaughn turned to face the Barlows. He nodded at Bill who was spitting on his scraped knuckles. "Well, Phil, I'll be damned if you didn't find someone else who could put a little color in your face."

Phil stared at him uncomprehendingly for a minute, as the alcohol fog slowed down his thought processes. Suddenly he blinked. Slowly, a grin shaped his lips. "How's it look, Sheriff?" he asked. Humor was restored. Vaughn hadn't been sure if it would work or not.

Vaughn considered him seriously for a moment. "Not bad, I guess. Considering. But I still think food might do a better job."

"But this is more fun. Gives us something to talk about for a whole week."

"Right," Vaughn drawled. "Well, I think you boys have gotten yourselves into enough trouble for one evening. Don't you? Maybe you'd better go next door and see Erma about a room for the night."

"Ah, Sheriff, there's still a lot of good drinkin' time left." Bill Barlow had moved up to complain over his brother's shoulder.

"Not for you boys there isn't. T.J.'s will be open again tomorrow. Go on. Move it out."

Muttering and grumbling and giving him dark looks over their shoulders, Bill and Phil began to move toward the door. Tom was already moving around straightening up his bar. Another Friday night crisis had been handled.

* * *

The next morning at ten o'clock the doorbell rang. Kim rolled over and stared blearily at the bedside clock. Dammit! It had been nearing five a.m. when she'd finally managed to get to sleep. The last thing she needed was to be aroused a mere five hours later. She was one of those people who found it nearly impossible to function without a minimum of eight hours sleep. Who could it be?

Remembering who it had been yesterday morning, and what had passed between them last night, she groaned. Not again, please. The bell continued to ring insistently. Finally, Kim rolled out of bed and sleepily tore a blanket from it to wrap around herself. No sense leading the man into temptation—if it was Vaughn. For the first time in her life, Kim felt the need to go out and buy one of those ankle-length fluffy housecoats that her mother had always owned. She'd never needed one in Seattle. There, no one had ever awakened her. Of course, she'd always been an early riser, too—until coming here.

Stumbling down the stairs, tripping over the blanket hem at every second step, Kim made it to the door just as whoever it was decided to abandon the bell and begin knocking on the door. She opened the door expecting to see Sheriff Garrett. Instead, a profusion of vibrant, sun-drenched color assaulted her sleep-drugged eyes. She raised a hand to shield them from some of the glare and staggered back a step as she attempted to focus.

"Good morning. You must be Kim Tannas." The voice was as bright and vibrant as its owner's taste in clothing.

"Yes." Kim stared at the woman. She was probably about Aunt Vivian's age, but she appeared younger. She wore gold hoops in her ears that seemed to refract every ray of sunlight they caught directly into Kim's eyes. Gold and silver bangles clinked together on her suntanned arms as she gestured. Gold rings, a couple of them sporting enormous stones, glinted in the morning light. Jeez, was the woman trying to rival the sun itself for brightness?

"I'm Liz Murphy. I'm a friend."

Kim waited for her to continue. Silence. "A friend of whom?" Kim finally asked.

"Why yours, dear. May I come in?"

Kim stared at the woman. She frowned. "Have we met?" She felt she had to ask although she was certain she'd never met Liz Murphy. She was, quite simply, not the type of woman anyone would forget upon having met her.

"No, dear."

Kim shook her head. She was beginning to get a headache. "Then how can you say we are friends?"

"Because we're going to be friends. Good friends. You need me and I'm here to help you."

Oh-oh. A nutcase. Here? Impossible! Kim stared at the woman incredulously. If this had been Seattle, she could simply have closed the door. But this was Lillooet Creek. If she closed the door in Liz Murphy's face, whoever she was, everybody and their dog would hear about it. Then she'd be inundated with callers who would run the gamut from indignant ladies come to admonish her for her rudeness to gossiping old biddies seeking another juicy tidbit for the coffee rounds. The mere thought was enough to cow her. She stepped back.

"Come in, Mrs. Murphy. I'm afraid I just woke up. Would you like to join me for a coffee in the kitchen?"

"I'd be delighted, dear." Liz followed Kim into the kitchen. "Oh, my, it's beautiful."

Kim looked over her shoulder at the woman. "What is?"

"The kitchen, dear. It's been over a month since I've been in a decent kitchen. I love cooking."

Kim waved Liz to a chair as she wrapped the blanket more securely around herself and began her morning coffee routine. "Do you?" she asked rhetorically. "I love eating, but I hate cooking. I usually find it just as easy to grab an apple or an orange or a chocolate bar when I'm hungry."

"Well, the apple or the orange is fine. But let me tell you, in another ten years or so those chocolate bars will start clinging to your hips and thighs like leeches."

Kim pivoted to stare at Liz. "God, what a horrible picture." She bent to break a package of cat food open in Charity's dish.

Liz smiled. "Think of it the next time you decide to reach for one of those chocolate bars."

"Yeah." Kim took a seat on a chair opposite Liz while she waited for the coffee. "Mrs. Murphy—"

"Oh, no. Please call me Liz."

"Liz. Would you please explain what you meant when you said that you were here to help me? Did somebody send you?"

"Well, no. Not exactly. Do you believe in psychic phenomena?"

Kim stared at her. "You're not from here, are you?"

"No, dear. I'm not."

Ah, hell. She could have closed the door on her and gone back to bed. Kim sighed and looked at the vibrantly clothed woman. Who was she kidding? She'd never closed a door in anyone's face in her life. You could take the girl out of the small town, but you couldn't take the small town out of the girl.

Kim rose to pour coffee into two cups and carry them back to the table. "Sugar or milk?"

"No, thank you. Do you believe in psychic phenomena?" Liz repeated her question.

"I read extensively," Kim allowed. "And I've always believed that I have an open mind about most things."

Liz nodded. "Well, that's better than I'd hoped." Liz had decided to be totally honest with Kim Tannas. Actually, Liz always decided to be totally honest with everyone. The thing was, she made that decision anew at each and every turn. Honesty was, after all, the best basis for the commencement of any relationship. And the moment she'd seen her, Liz had felt that she and the young woman truly would be friends.

Taking one more sip of coffee, Liz launched into her explanation, starting with the familial tendency to be a little clairvoyant or psychic and how it tended to work, through to the incident in Seattle that had prompted her to come here. She left out the graphic description of the vision. That would serve no purpose other than to further frighten an already anxious young woman. When Liz had finished, she waited silently, patiently for Kim's response.

Kim frowned and stared into the depths of her coffee. "So how do you know for certain that it's me you were. . . drawn here to protect?"

"I don't. But you are, at present, the only one being threatened. Aren't you?"

Kim shrugged. "As far as I know."

"Then it just makes sense."

"How did you discover my identity?"

Liz smiled. "No great test of my abilities there. I overheard a couple of deputies at the sheriff's department discussing the case. They mentioned your name. Armed with a name, all I had to do was ask Erma where to find you."

Kim nodded. "I see." She sipped her coffee thoughtfully and ignored the rumbling of her stomach. "I still don't understand exactly what you think you can do to protect me."

"I don't really know myself, dear. I have no special training or qualifications. My gift did not come with a user's manual. Neither I, nor it, are infallible. Perhaps my presence here with you will be enough. I do know that I am needed here in Lillooet Creek."

"Do you have some kind of a plan or something?"

Liz shrugged. "At the moment, my plan is merely to get to know you." She smiled. "To be a friend."

Kim studied the older woman. She didn't doubt Liz's honesty for a moment. What exactly was it about the woman that inspired that kind of confidence? "Well, I've heard it said that a person can never have too many friends." Kim smiled. "Would you like some toast for breakfast?"

"No, thank you. I ate at Erma's Restaurant before I came this morning. But if you don't mind, I'll help myself to some more coffee?"

Kim was scanning the shelves in the refrigerator for some jam. "I don't mind a bit," she said over her shoulder.

"Tell me, dear. What do you think of Sheriff Garrett?"

Kim looked over the fridge door and met Liz's eyes. "I think he's an ass." She resumed her search for jam and finally found a jar hidden behind a sealer of her aunt's homemade pickles.

"You don't think he's a good sheriff?" Liz asked.

"Oh, I think he's probably a fine sheriff. He seems to take his work very seriously." Kim's temper was already rising again as she remembered the previous night. *I don't believe I've mentioned anything about getting involved. Have I?* What a jerk!

"Then what's the problem?" Liz asked. There was a slight frown between her brows.

Kim flushed and shrugged depreciatingly. "He's just a supercilious, manipulative pain who looks real good in a snug pair of jeans, and he knows it. You know what I mean?"

"I know exactly what you mean." Liz smiled a so-that's-the-way-the-wind's-blowing smile that made Kim grit her teeth. "Unfortunately that is also the type of male to whom we women usually find ourselves irresistibly attracted, despite ourselves. My theory is that it has something to do with our primitive instincts. A male who's assertive is usually also a self-confident individual. Self-confidence implies a man capable of providing protection from—well, whatever it was primitive women needed protection from. Sabre-toothed tigers or something, I suppose. We modern women have to constantly struggle to overcome our instincts."

Kim turned away from the toaster to stare at Liz. "You know, it's scary how plausible that sounds on five hours sleep," she said. "How did you figure that out?"

"I've lived a long time, kid," Liz smiled. "And I've spent much of that time watching people. It's a personal hobby."

* * *

Vaughn glanced into Special Agent Stone's temporary office on his way by and stopped short. The enormous cork-board bulletin board Stone had asked for was already covered. Stone was standing in front of it examining photographs of the victims with a magnifying glass. Vaughn stepped into the office. "G'morning, Stone."

"Garrett." Stone didn't bother turning around to greet him.

"What are you looking for?"

Stone shrugged. "Maybe nothing. Maybe something. Won't know till I find it." He paused, sighed, and turned away from the bulletin board to put the magnifying glass on his desk. "Do you have a minute, Garrett?"

"Sure." Vaughn turned to close the office door. "What do you need?"

Stone sighed again and ran his hand over his chin as he sat down. Vaughn had noted that the FBI agent had a tendency to sigh whenever he was deep in thought. "I've gone over all your notes on the case. I just have a couple of questions."

Vaughn sat down. "Okay."

"What made you eliminate all the Hanson's as suspects? All but the oldest of them seem to come darn close to being categorized as dangerous offenders."

"I checked back. At the time that Candace Smyth was murdered in Seattle, they were all here in Lillooet Creek."

"There's no mistake about that?"

Vaughn shook his head. "None. They were in jail for causing a ruckus at a church social they'd decided to attend."

"And this Skeeter Barnes? He's a little further off base as far as the profile goes, but I'm interested as to why you ignored him as a suspect."

Vaughn met Stone's perceptive gaze. "Skeeter never went to school long enough to learn to read a poem, let alone write one. And he's not capable of torturing and killing animals. He's been rescuing and caring for hurt wild creatures for as long as anyone can remember. He gets along better with animals than he does with people."

"Yet it doesn't seem to bother him to terrorize helpless women by sneaking around their homes to watch them through their windows at night."

Vaughn frowned, considering the apparent inconsistency. "I don't think Skeeter realizes that he frightens them." He leaned forward in his chair propping his elbows on his knees. "You've got to understand that this is a grown man who never managed to get beyond adolescent awkwardness when it comes to dealing with women. They fascinate him at the same time that they terrify him. He's not normal. You could even say he's sick. But he's a different kind of sick than the killer is."

Stone nodded and steepled his fingers beneath his chin. "Just now, you said that Barnes was not capable of reading poetry, let alone writing it. Are you assuming that the killer is writing his own poetry? Or is this something you know for a fact?"

Vaughn frowned. "I guess it's an assumption. I never really thought about it. A couple of the poems we found sounded familiar to me. The others didn't. And since, as a kid, I read an awful lot of poetry, I guess I just assumed that he was writing them."

Stone stared at him. "You surprise me, Garrett. I didn't take you for the poetry reading sort."

"It was a long time ago, Stone."

"Hmm." Stone tilted back in his chair and stared thoughtfully out the office window for a moment. "Is there anybody else in town whom you might suspect? Somebody whom you think is perfectly capable of the perpetration but whom you have disallowed for one reason or another? Perhaps somebody who has a history of cruelty?"

"Yeah, sure. I questioned Tyler Dobbs closely. He likes to kick around dogs, cats, women, and children. Basically anyone smaller than he is. He has a history of throwing his weight around with his wife Sarah. But he was working here in Lillooet Creek when Smyth was killed in Seattle."

"Does he have an alibi for the time period when Trent Farris was killed?"

Vaughn grimaced and rose to walk to the window and stare out at the sunny day. "Not one I'd place a wager on, but it's good enough to stand up in court. He was with a bunch of his rabble-rousing buddies playing poker."

Stone rubbed the bridge of his nose thoughtfully. "Okay. Let's not discount him yet. It's a slim chance, but it is possible that the killing of Trent Farris was a copycat killing done by somebody who had read the account of the Smyth girl's death in the newspaper." Stone looked at Vaughn. "Is there anybody else you suspected and wrote off? Is there anybody whom your gut tells you isn't quite right? I need feedback. Since I'm a stranger here I have to get it from you."

Vaughn stared out the window uncomfortably. "Well, yeah, there is. But it's just a gut feeling. Nothing more."

"Go on."

"Well, there's a guy down at Carter's Lumber. Mike Drayton. He's been in town not quite a year, I guess. I have no idea where he was when Candace Smyth was killed, but I made a few calls to check. I hope to hear back in the next day or so."

"And what makes you suspect him?"

"Well, the first thing that made me consider him was that, in the whole time he's been in town, I've never encountered him anywhere. In a town this size, that's strange. I wondered if maybe he'd been avoiding me. But other than that, I don't know. He's done nothing wrong. I just don't like the guy." Vaughn frowned. "I don't trust him."

"Okay. I'll check him out, too. See what I think." Stone leaned back in his chair and stared at the ceiling. "In your investigation, did you encounter anyone from Lillooet Creek who was in Seattle at the time of the Smyth killing?"

"Yeah. Three people. Skeeter Barnes was there picking up some vehicles for his wrecking yard. Joe Frazer, from the Amoco station, was there dropping off his wife for a visit with her sister. And, I was there selling some of my wood carvings." Vaughn wondered again if he was being framed. If so, how had the killer known he was going to be in Seattle last April?

Stone considered him silently for a moment and Vaughn wished he could see his thoughts. Then Stone nodded. "Okay. Anybody else you know of that was out of town at the time."

Vaughn frowned. "My deputy, Martin Lewis, was on vacation at the time. I remember because I almost postponed my trip to Seattle." He shrugged. "A couple of fellows were out of town on vacation, but they were with family members, so I placed them at the bottom of the list Their names are in the file."

Stone nodded. "Okay. I guess that's all I need to ask you right now. It gives me a little more to work with. Thanks."

"No problem."

* * *

Liz pulled up in front of Snodell's Grocery and parked. She didn't really need anything, but she hoped to engage Kate Hobsin in an illuminating conversation concerning Sheriff Garrett. The bell over the door tinkled as she stepped into the store and began to look around. Coming across a magazine rack, she picked up a copy of *USA Today* just as Kate Hobsin emerged from the back to stand behind the counter.

"Hi, Liz. How are you today?"

"Fine, thanks. And you?"

"Couldn't be better. Anything I can help you with?"

Liz hesitated. She didn't want to start asking questions too quickly. "I think I'll just look around for a moment."

"You betcha." Kate began adding some cash register slips.

Liz picked up an enormous bag of Doritos and a large bottle of Coke, which her waistline certainly didn't need, and headed for the counter. "I think that's everything," she said as Kate looked up.

"Sure thing. You're staying over at the hotel, I hear?"

Liz smiled. "Yes. I met your Sheriff Garrett yesterday, too. He certainly seems like a nice young man. Has he lived here long?"

"Oh my, yes. That boy's been around since he was, oh, seven or eight years old, I'd say."

"So his family is here. They must be very proud of him."

"No." Kate shook her head with a frown. "Vaughn's an orphan. Hearsay is that his folks were killed in a car accident. He was one of the foster kids that Anna Irving took in. And Anna passed away a few years back." Kate paused and clucked her tongue. "It was a horrible death. Her house burned to the ground. The local kids won't go near the place to this day. They say her ghost is still there."

Liz nodded sympathetically. "So Garrett has no family here then?"

"Um-um," Kate shook her head in the negative as she popped a peppermint into her mouth. "No, the closest that boy has to family is old Aunt Willie. Anna was her sister."

"That's sad."

"Yeah," Kate agreed. "But he turned out okay. And handsome! Lord, if I was fifteen years younger and thirty pounds thinner I'd make a play for that boy myself."

Liz smiled. "He certainly is attractive." She took the bag that Kate handed her. "Well, it's been nice talking to you. See you."

"You betcha. Drop by anytime for a visit."

Liz put the bag on the seat beside her in the van, turned the key and considered her options as she listened to the purr of the motor. She didn't think she'd be able to learn any more concerning Garrett's life before Lillooet Creek from anyone other than Garrett himself. She frowned thoughtfully. The question was, how could she introduce the conversation?

* * *

It was early evening a couple of days later, Kim had just returned from shopping with Liz when Sheriff Vaughn Garrett knocked on the door. He wore his uniform and carried his dark green, Western-style hat in his hand. "Good evening, Sheriff." Her voice was as cold the mountain spring water that babbled through the town creek. She was still furious with him for the comment he'd made after kissing her.

"Kim." He nodded without smiling. "May I come in?"

Kim stared at him for a moment. Finally, she

stepped back and allowed him entry. She stayed near the door, however, and didn't ask him to sit down. "Do you have some news for me, Sheriff?"

He sighed and twisted the brim of his hat in his hands. "No, I don't have any news. I thought we'd gotten by that sheriff stuff."

"You thought wrong."

He nodded, opened his mouth as if to say something and took a step toward her. But that single step was a mistake. They were too close. Invisible electricity arced between them. Because she was already standing against the wall, she had nowhere to go but sideways. She refused to give him the satisfaction of intimidating her into such an obvious retreat. Stubbornly, she looked up into his face. But she wasn't prepared for the mesmerizing power of his golden gaze. Her eyes widened in recognition of what she saw in those molten depths. The air between them thickened to the consistency of butter. Kim's breathing faltered, then quickened.

"Kim, dear, who was at the door?" Liz's voice jerked her back to reality with a jolt.

Vaughn merely turned his head to see the owner of the voice. Hell, it was that damn psychic again. Maybe she was psychic. She certainly had a knack for turning up when he least wanted to see her. "Ms. Murphy, isn't it?"

"Sheriff," she smiled a wide welcome. "I'd hoped we'd meet again soon."

Vaughn stared at her. The last time he'd seen her she'd been in such a hurry to escape his office that she'd closed her skirt in his door. Now she was greeting him like a long-lost friend. "What are you doing here, Ms. Murphy? I thought I specifically told you not to become involved in this investigation without authorization."

She smiled. "Oh, you did, Sheriff. And I'm not. Kim and I are simply friends."

"I see." He looked at Kim questioningly, but she didn't seem inclined to elaborate on just how this friendship had come about so quickly.

"Could we offer you something to drink, Sheriff?"

"Liz!" Vaughn almost smiled at Kim's scandalized tone. It was obvious she wanted him gone. Maybe the psychic would have her uses after all.

"Well, I am off duty. Do you have anything stronger than orange juice?"

"Kim and I just put some beer in the fridge this afternoon. Sound more like what you had in mind?"

"Perfect." He followed Ms. Murphy, or Liz as Kim had called her, through the house into the kitchen. He could sense Kim following sullenly behind them. He found himself thoroughly enjoying her pique.

He declined Liz's offer of a mug for his beer and refused a chair, preferring to lean against the kitchen counter and sip his beer from the can. It was another exceptionally hot July day, and the beer tasted even better than he'd anticipated. Liz opened herself a beer and sat at the table. Kim busied herself putting some groceries away.

"You never did say exactly why you came by, Sheriff," Kim reminded him.

"Oh, yes. That's right. One of my deputies—Jordan Hall—you remember him?" Kim nodded and he continued. "Jordan and his wife Lillian are having a barbecue tomorrow night. It's something they do fairly regularly during the summer. Anyway, I was wondering if you'd like to go?"

Kim stared at him as if he was completely obtuse. He knew exactly what she was thinking. And he thought he knew exactly what to say to change her mind.

He held up a hand. "Don't say anything yet. Let me assure you this isn't a personal invitation. If you don't come to the barbecue, then either myself or one of my men has to miss it in order to watch this place. And that seems unfair when it's so easily avoided."

"I see." Kim frowned into the cupboard she'd opened. "Well, that's not really a problem, I guess. I'm sure Liz will stay with me for one evening. The two of us should be safe together."

"I hate to disappoint you, Kim, dear. But I'm afraid I can't stay with you tomorrow night."

Kim pivoted to stare at her. "What do you mean?"

Liz seemed to flush slightly. "Actually Deputy Cheney invited me to the barbecue. I didn't think it would present a problem."

If she didn't know better, Kim would have been certain she was being manipulated. "I see." So, short of staying home alone—which she was not foolhardy enough to do—or forcing some hapless deputy to miss the social event of the month—which she was not selfish enough to do—she had no choice. She looked at Vaughn. "Well, I guess I'll have to go then, won't I?"

* * *

It was dark now. A faint gibbous moon shone through the thin clouds overhead. He stood in the shadows watching the house. Bright yellow light spilled through the windows, creating rectangular squares of brilliance on the veranda. He could hear faint feminine laughter from within. His gut twisted with hate and his fingers curled with the intense desire to shut off the sound of their merriment. They were laughing at him again. Just as they had always laughed at him, made fun of him. Taking a deep breath, he forced the intense emotion deep down inside himself. He felt it flicker and then still.

Slowly he circled the property. A green cruiser partially concealed by the cascading branches of a weeping willow sat in the drive. They were doing a reasonably good job of protecting her. But then, he had expected they would. It was a minor irritation. The convenience of having her stay here rather than returning to Seattle was well worth the minor nuisance of decreased accessibility. He was certain that, when he was ready, he would have no difficulty getting into the house. He planned to test that assumption soon. But not yet.

Kimberley Clayton's presence had distracted him briefly from his original schedule. But her name was well toward the bottom of his list. He could afford to bide his time for a short while before delivering her punishment. There was another name on his list, more immediate. Another punishment to deliver. Another funeral to plan. His teeth flashed in the darkness. It would give the sheriff's department something else to do, too. He didn't want Vaughn becoming bored. Vaughn. He was disappointed in him. He had expected so much more stimulation from the match of wits that he had planned. Oh, well, it didn't really matter.

He stared at the house, so like another he had known. And his mind's eye saw the other. It crackled and creaked and groaned like a living thing as the flames of his hatred engulfed it. And beneath the thunderous roaring of the fire, another sound. A woman's scream. The scream echoed with the agony of slow death. Once again his teeth flashed briefly in the darkness. There were so many kinds of pain. As many as there were crimes. When imposing the death sentence, it was important that the level of pain correspond to the gravity of the crime. It was an art form that authorities would never understand. But the bitch had seen his face before she died. She had known the nature of her crime. He had seen the understanding flare in her eyes as he struck the match.

A woman's laugh floated to him on the still night air, hitting him like a dash of cold water and memory receded. He gritted his teeth as he watched Kimberley's silhouette walk by one of the brightly lit windows. Perhaps he would arrange a double funeral. It was an intriguing thought. Something new. A challenge. He would have to think about it.

CHAPTER 8

I t was 5:30 and Kim was a nervous wreck. Why had she accepted Garrett's invitation? Or rather, why had she allowed herself to be manipulated into accepting? She hated the man. She couldn't think of an evening more torturous than one spent in his company. She'd rather stay home alone. No, she wouldn't. She enjoyed life too much to risk losing it over her inability to tolerate men like Vaughn Garrett. But, Lord, she fervently wished the evening were over. She'd already changed her clothes three times in an attempt to find the perfect outfit. But they just didn't make cool and unapproachable outfits suitable for attending barbecues. On top of that dilemma, she was anxious about meeting a group of people whom she either didn't know at all or hadn't seen in years.

She checked the plastic wrap on the bowl of potato salad she and Liz had made earlier in the day. She checked the clock on the wall. 5:35. He was late. Maybe he wouldn't show up. Then Deputy Lewis would have to stay on duty, and it wouldn't be her fault.

The doorbell rang. Her hand flew to her throat. He was here! She was never going to make it through this night. Despite Vaughn's reason for asking her to the

151

barbecue, the outing was very reminiscent of a date. And that scared the hell out of her. Every bit of confidence she thought she possessed flew out the window. She sincerely hoped he didn't consider it a date. Because it wasn't. And she was going to make certain it was never repeated.

Butterflies ran rampant in her stomach as she walked into the front room to answer the door. Five feet in front of it, she stopped to take a deep calming breath and wipe her sweaty palms on her cream, linen walking-shorts.

The bell rang again. She opened the door. The butterflies twisted themselves into a knot in the pit of her stomach. She'd forgotten how devastatingly handsome he was. "Hi, I . . . ah, I'll just get the potato salad."

"Sure."

She walked a couple of steps toward the kitchen. Stopped. Turned around. "Come in for a moment if you like."

"Okay." He stepped into the house, quietly closing the door. "You look very nice." He called the words after her as she entered the kitchen.

"Thank you." Grabbing the potato salad, she slung her purse over one shoulder and returned to the living room. "Ready," she said.

He nodded without comment, but she thought she detected the ghost of a smile on his face. Damn him anyway! He was going to have her on the defensive all evening. Handing him the bowl of salad, she closed and locked the door behind them.

As soon as they began walking toward Vaughn's Bronco, Deputy Lewis pulled out of the driveway and drove off with a wave. "He's anxious to get home to change," Vaughn said as he opened the passenger side door for Kim.

* * *

In spite of herself, Kim had enjoyed the barbecue.

Avoiding Vaughn, she spent most of her time with the other women. Now, she sat silently looking out the passenger window of the Bronco as Vaughn drove her home. It was dark. One of those nights that was as black as the inside of Jonah's whale. Kim was nervous about returning to the house with Vaughn. He had taken the job of watching her house tonight. It should have been Ray Cheney on duty, but he'd requested that Vaughn take his shift.

Liz and Cheney were getting on very well. Kim smiled. They obviously found each other very attractive. Romance was the same at any age. Liz and Ray had stolen a number of private moments at the barbecue. Hands touched. Arms brushed. Ray had reached to smooth a hair from Liz's face. It was sweet. Kim hoped it worked for them. Growing old alone was frightening. Something that no one should have to do.

Observing Liz and Ray had reminded her of her own single state. And she'd been forced to admit that she missed having someone around to notice if she was late from work. She missed having someone with whom to share the ups and downs of the day. And hardest of all to face was the realization that she missed having someone to hold and to be held by. Dammit! She didn't want to need anyone. But she was beginning to realize that she did.

Was that why she'd found herself acting so strangely around Vaughn tonight? He was a man she didn't like. The embodiment of not one but two types of men that she had promised herself never again to become involved with: an excessively handsome, egocentric man, and a cop. Yet despite how she felt about him consciously, she could not deny the knowledge that her body responded to his proximity. Why? Was she simply vulnerable because she was lonely? She'd become a stranger to herself. She couldn't remember feeling this off balance and uncertain since high school.

All evening, no matter what she was doing, or

whom she'd been talking to, her eyes had continually— of their own volition—sought Vaughn out. She'd observed him as he'd laughed and joked with the other men as they monitored the progress of the burgers. She'd noted the way his dark gold hair caught the patio light, making him stand out among the others. She'd liked the way he'd looked in his tan chinos—casual but classy. He was about five foot eleven, a good three inches shorter than a couple of his deputies, and years younger than both Cheney and Hall. And yet his stance, his air of authority, left no doubt as to who was the superior officer. What was the matter with her? Why was it that, in a crowd of at least ten men, he had stood out above all others?

What irked her more than anything was the fact that he'd caught her looking at him more than once. And each time he had, he'd smiled at her in a way that set her heart racing in a manner completely uncharacteristic of her. She'd been so certain that she would never again be beguiled by masculine attractiveness. After all, she had been so thoroughly burned the first time that she had never recovered. She had sworn to never again allow herself to be bowled over by the dominant male type, as Liz referred to them. So what did her reaction signify?

For the first time in a long time, Kim realized that she was emotionally afraid of a man, and she didn't like it. She was afraid of Vaughn. Afraid of the feelings he aroused in her. And afraid of herself, of a vulnerability that she hadn't known existed.

Vaughn pulled into the driveway of her aunt's home, drawing Kim out of her preoccupation. "I'll have to check out the house," he said. "You want to come with me, or wait here?"

"I'll come."

As Vaughn got out of the vehicle to walk around and open her door, he wondered why she was suddenly so subdued. Just shortly before they'd left the barbecue, she'd become quiet and withdrawn. Until then, she had seemed to enjoy the evening. She'd gotten along well with the other women. She'd thoroughly spoiled Deputy Killian's toddling son. And she'd smiled as she watched the budding romance between Ray and Liz. That was something that Vaughn could only shake his head over. A cop and a psychic. What next?

He grasped Kim's elbow to steady her while she rooted around in her capacious shoulder bag for keys as they walked over the uneven ground toward the house. It was a warm night. Insects chirruped in the grass. Finally extracting her keys, she handed them to him. He opened the door and stepped cautiously into the house. Charity came running up to him, yowling her dissatisfaction about something. He sensed, rather than saw, Kim step into the house behind him and kneel to greet the cat. "I'll check the kitchen first."

He opened the kitchen door, turned on the light, and scanned the brilliant yellow counter top before stepping into the room. He checked the cupboards, the fridge, and the garbage. "Everything seems all right," he said to Kim as he emerged a minute later.

"Good." She rose and walked into the kitchen as he proceeded to check the living room, study and family room.

Kim poured herself a glass of Coke and sat down to sip it as she listened to Vaughn's footsteps checking out the bedrooms overhead. She didn't really want it. She'd drunk enough Pepsi, interspersed with coffee and beer, at the barbecue to last her into next week. But she needed something to do.

She jumped as Vaughn reentered the room. "Everything seems fine." His soft bass voice washed over her seductively.

Damn it! Why was everything about him attracting her tonight? She nodded her acknowledgement of his statement without comment. She'd hoped that, with his search completed, he would leave to sit outside and observe the house. But he didn't seem to be going anywhere. She glanced at him out of the corner of her eye. In fact, he was leaning against the cupboards in a relaxed fashion that indicated he might want to stay a while. She didn't know what to say to him.

Go away, she willed.

It didn't faze him. "So what did you think of the barbecue?" he asked.

"It was nice. I liked Lillian Hall." Kim avoided his eyes as she rose and rooted in the cupboard. What the hell was she looking for? She removed a package of cookies and set it on the counter. Then grimaced mentally. She didn't even want one.

"Okay, Kim. What's bothering you?"

She pivoted to face him. Was she that obvious? "Nothing. Why do you ask?" She noted that his eyes had a peculiar inner glow that she'd not seen in them earlier.

"You're as jumpy as a jackrabbit. Something's bugging you."

Kim sighed and rubbed her forehead. She needed to get away. To get out of this town and away from him. To get out of this limbo and resume her life. "I'm considering returning to Seattle." The idea had been nebulous, half formed until she put it into words. But the instant the words left her mouth, she realized that it was exactly what she wanted to do.

"You're what?" He took a step toward her. "Tell me I'm hearing things. I thought I heard you say that you were considering returning to Seattle." His tone was smooth. Intuition told her it was too smooth.

Kim turned to face him. Her instinctive gumption rising to do combat with the displeasure she sensed in him. "You heard right. This waiting for something to happen is ridiculous, not to mention nerve-wracking. And I have things to do at home. Maybe he's just decided he doesn't want me."

Vaughn's golden gaze narrowed as he took another

step toward her. The smooth stride of a predator. "It's only been a few days. You're certainly in a hurry." His voice was deceptively calm. His features misleadingly expressionless. "What scared you off this time? This is the second time since I've met you that you've decided to go home rather than face something. Is it Skeeter Barnes? He's a dirty-minded little creep, but he's harmless."

Kim stared at him in surprise; she wasn't good at dealing with censure. She *was* running, she admitted to herself. But it wasn't Skeeter Barnes she feared. It was Sheriff Vaughn Garrett and the strange combination of emotions he aroused in her. How could you dislike somebody and be attracted to them? It just didn't make sense.

"I've got better things to do than sit around in this godforsaken town waiting for something to happen. If the killer has given up on me, what difference does it make to you whether I stay or go?"

"None. None at all," he assured her. He was standing directly in front of her now, at the edge of her personal space, trying to intimidate her. She refused to let him succeed. Tilting her head back, she continued to meet his implacable, topaz gaze. "But you see, he hasn't given up. He's meticulous. He plans things carefully."

Vaughn took another step toward her, and despite herself Kim took a small, hasty step back. He was getting too close. The air between them crackled with tension—or was it electricity? "Okay," Kim said. The word emerged on a whisper and she repeated it more firmly. "Okay. I'll give it a while longer. Now, I think you'd better go."

"You didn't answer my question." He took another step toward her. Kim retreated a step to find herself up against the cupboard.

"What. . . what question?" Her chest felt constricted.

"What are you afraid of?"

"Nothing. I'm not afraid of anything." Had the

words emerged just a shade too quickly?

"Good. I'd hate to think I misjudged that tough-as-nails little bitch that came into my office that first day."

She almost slapped his face. Was that how he'd seen her? Was that how men saw her? If so, he was the first one to say it to her face. But she realized with sudden clarity that that was exactly the persona she'd subconsciously begun to cultivate a long time ago. At first, it had been an act, self-defense. But it had become second nature, a part of her. It was something Ken had complained about.

Can't you ever let your guard down? Be yourself? I'm your husband! How many times had she heard those words during the four years of their marriage? She had never really understood what he was talking about until this moment. Kim narrowed her eyes as she met Vaughn's uncompromising gaze. "You haven't," she assured him.

He smiled. Vaughn was in a dangerous mood and he knew it. But he seemed incapable of stopping it. He wanted Kim. Wanted her more than he'd wanted a woman in a long time. Maybe it had been the sight of all that sexy lingerie that he'd found in the drawer in her room when he'd hastily checked the bureau to ensure there were no dead creatures in it. He'd heard that a lot of women had started wearing that sexy stuff again, but Kim was only the second woman he'd encountered who actually did. The first had confided, during a brief stay in Vaughn's custody before being charged for prostitution, that she considered lingerie a uniform. Somehow it wasn't the same.

His imagination was running rampant. He saw Kim with her hair free of the ever-present French braid. As it had been that morning when he'd awakened her. He saw her laying in the center of that thick white duvet on her bed wearing nothing but the fiery red teddy she'd had in her hand the other night. He saw her in the delicate pink camisole and panties that had snagged on the callouses of his hands when he'd searched the drawer. And he saw her in the black garter belt and stockings that had been laying beneath the scented sachet.

And Vaughn came to a conclusion. No matter how much he disliked ball-breaking career-woman types, he wanted her. And no matter how much she might deny it, she wanted him too. The more he thought about it, the more certain he was that he knew the reason for her nervous behavior. He would have bet a week's pay that what Kimberley needed at the moment was a good lay. Of course, a team of Clydesdales couldn't have pulled that admission out of her. But she hadn't been able to keep her eyes off of him tonight. And he'd had the same problem, which explained how he'd managed to catch her looking at him so many times.

The question was: what did they do about it? As far as he was concerned, the solution to their problem was simple. A bout of good, wholesome sex. But it was obvious that Kim had never considered sex outside of a relationship. The first time he'd kissed her, she argued against getting involved with a cop. Involvement was the furthest thing from his mind. He took another step toward her and saw her tense. She had nowhere left to retreat. He noted the increasingly rapid rise and fall of her breasts with interest, and wondered what kind of lingerie she was wearing.

Her eyes darted to the side, and anticipating her attempt at escape, Vaughn planted his hands on the counter on either side of her. "I think we have a real problem here, honey."

She leaned away from him until her head almost reached the cupboard door. "Wh—what do you mean? What problem?"

"I want you," he murmured. He leaned forward until his face was mere inches from hers. "I think you want me, too."

Kim stared at him. "You're crazy." The words

emerged on a whisper. "I hate you," she said more firmly.

His lips twisted in a self-depreciating grin. "The feeling's mutual, honey. But somehow that doesn't seem to make any difference. Does it?"

"Don't call me honey." Oh, Lord! Was he telling her that his feelings for her were as confused as hers were for him? He was. And being male, he obviously thought they could just solve the problem with a one-night-stand. But she wasn't the one-night-stand type. Maybe if sex had ever lived up to the promise alluded to by the fire and excitement of arousal, she might have been more inclined in that direction on occasion. But she knew from experience that, for her, the promise was empty. Despite the pulse pounding in her throat, her next words emerged firmly. "I think you should g—"

But suddenly his mouth swooped down on hers, cutting off her words. Not hard. Almost tentatively, as though testing her, tasting her. But Kim couldn't have broken that speculative contact had her life depended on it. She didn't recognize the high panicked sound she heard as coming from her own throat, but she felt its emergence. Her lips parted slightly of their own accord, and he pressed closer. God help her, she had wanted this. . . and dreaded it.

Heat flooded through her, robbing her limbs of strength as his tongue invaded her mouth. And she knew how it felt to be a moth drawn to the seductive flicker of a flame. Fear raced through her in waves, but the hypnotic enticement of warmth and sensation tempered each surge of anxiety. His hand closed over her breast. A torrent of desire, stronger than anything she remembered feeling, poured through her. Her nipple tautened and tingled. Oh, God, she had been wrong. She had missed this. That was her downfall.

His mouth left hers as he trailed a path of kisses over her face. She felt the warmth of his breath as he traced the shell of her ear with his tongue. He made a sound deep in his throat, half growl, half purr, and everything that was feminine within her responded. Her heart fluttered wildly in her chest. Her breath came in small, labored gasps. Her limbs trembled.

"I can't believe what you do to me," he muttered as he distanced himself from her. "Let's get the hell out of this kitchen." Before his words had even penetrated the fog that enshrouded her mind, he picked her up and, cradling her in his arms, left the room.

As he walked across the living room with her in his arms, Vaughn knew the exact second when her arousal faded enough for her to become aware of the situation. He read the series of emotions that crossed her face as though he'd known her all her life. Surprise, fear, desperation, resignation. He saw them all. What he didn't understand was why he had seen them. Especially when her dilated pupils and rapid pulse still told a different story. As he began to climb the stairs, she found her voice.

"Please, put me down. I can walk." He loved her husky, breathless tone.

He saw her eyes widen nervously as he continued to climb, and she tightened her grasp on his neck. She was afraid he'd drop her! "Haven't you ever been carried before?"

She sighed as he reached the top of the stairs without mishap and entered her bedroom. "Just across a threshold," she answered. She eyed the bed with something akin to horror reflected in her eyes. "I really don't think this is a good—"

He covered her mouth with his briefly as he lowered her to the bed. Then he quickly slid the sandals from her feet. Sitting beside her, he bent to trace the delicate shape of her ear. He whispered calming words as he stroked the soft flesh of her upper arms soothingly. He heard the soft sound of surrender in her throat and began to work the buttons of her blouse. As the edges of the fabric parted and he drew back to look at her, he wasn't disappointed.

A bra of bright pink, transparent lace cupped the rich, creamy globes of her breasts. As he raised Kim slightly to work the blouse from her arms, he lowered his head to pay homage to the taut rose-pink nipples that peeked through the lace so temptingly. He was rewarded by a gasp as she threaded her fingers through his hair, holding him to her. Then, lowering her again, he undid the fastening of her shorts and began to slide them from her hips. Her panties matched the bra. The sheer lace did more to enhance her sexuality than it did to conceal it. A renewed rush of heat stabbed at his groin. He was rock hard.

Standing, he slipped the skirt-like shorts from her shapely legs. As he quickly undid his shirt and shrugged it off, she opened her eyes to watch him. His hand moved to the fastening on his pants, and paused. There was still something there, half hidden, in the passion-dark depths of her eyes that he hadn't seen before. It was that cognizance, more than anything else, that made him decide to wait a while longer before removing the rest of his clothing. Instead, he joined her on the bed.

Kim ran her hand over Vaughn's shoulder and arm as he joined her. His smooth, sun-bronzed skin stretched tightly over his muscular frame. The heat of his flesh surprised her. He was lean and muscular, wide shouldered and narrow hipped. She ran her hands over the crisp brown hair that dusted the center of his chest in a small V, tracing it as it formed a thin line that bisected his hard, flat belly. His stomach jumped at her tentative touch, startling her. Could he possibly be as sensitive to her touch as she was to his?

As he released the elastic on her braid and threaded his fingers into her hair, she rested her face against the warmth of his chest. He smelled good. It was a warm, male smell that was uniquely him. There was no doubt in Kim's mind that Vaughn was one of the handsomest men she'd ever seen without a shirt on. But then she'd always tended to avoid alpha males and jocks like the plague. Ken Tannas certainly hadn't been homely, but physically he couldn't have competed with a man like Vaughn Garrett. Ken had been a kind and loving man, a good man.

What was the matter with her? Here she was in bed with a man that nearly every heterosexual woman in the state would have considered a hunk, and she was thinking of her late husband. Raising her head slightly, she met Vaughn's golden gaze. Suddenly there was no more room for thought. No room for anything but sensation. Molten heat swam in his eyes, and something ignited within her in response. As her hands explored his body, enjoying the warmth and texture of him, she was only vaguely aware of him removing her bra. He lowered his head to suckle her breasts and sensation washed over her. Her eyelids drifted closed. His teeth grazed her nipple. A whimper of excitement escaped her. It had been so long. . . too long.

Basking in the pleasure of Kim's hungry response, Vaughn covered her full-lipped mouth with his own. His fingers worked beneath the elastic of her panties, exploring the springy, blond curls, seeking the moist core of her. Heat. Slick, wet heat. His jaw worked as he struggled for control before inserting a finger into the warm, moist sheath of her body. She gasped, the sound halfway between a moan and a sob. She was tight, soft as velvet, smooth as satin. Damn, she was beautiful.

He stood for a second to slide the panties from her limbs and quickly strip himself of his pants. Then, straddling her body, he trailed his mouth over her torso. Worshipping her, arousing her with lips and teeth and tongue. The silence was punctuated by the rhythm of her labored breathing, by her gasps and moans and sighs. And when finally he could prolong the agony of suspense no longer, Vaughn gently nudged her soft white thighs apart to settle his hips between them. Kissing her as hungrily as she had kissed him earlier, Vaughn pressed himself into the soft, moist depths of her body.

A moan of consternation escaped her, and her body tensed against his intrusion.

Oh, God. Please, don't stop now. "It's all right, honey," he murmured, attempting to soothe whatever anxiety plagued her.

"I. . . I'm sorry," she sounded close to tears and Vaughn winced inwardly at the thought that he might be hurting her. "It's been a long time for me."

Murmuring soothing sounds, and with more willpower than he thought he possessed, he reigned in his passions and relaxed against her. Not moving. Stroking the hair from her face with gentle fingers. "It's okay. Just relax. Relax," he whispered as he stroked and kissed her. And slowly the tension left her as inch by inch her body stretched to accommodate him. Sweet, sweet agony. He groaned as Kim once again began to move her hips in instinctive invitation. "God, you're tight. Where the hell have you been keeping yourself?"

Kim didn't answer. Her fingers clutched spasmodically at his back as he pressed his hips slowly forward, finally able to bury himself within her to the hilt. She moaned and lifted her hips to meet each of his thrusts and cupped his buttocks pulling him deeper.

A few minutes later, Vaughn abruptly sensed that something had changed. Kim still sighed and moaned, still stroked his body with a lover's hands, but he detected a difference. He couldn't say what it was. He wasn't even one hundred percent certain *that* it was. He tried to slow. To test this intuitive awareness. But he was too near the edge. He groaned as climax claimed him. Kim clutched him, pulling him tightly to her, moaning her own release.

Or was she?

As his heart slowed, he rolled to one side, cradling

her against him. Gently brushing the hair from her cheek, he studied her face. "Why did you fake your orgasm?"

Her head jerked as if she'd been stung. She stared at him with a stunned expression on her face. "How. . . how did you know?" she asked softly.

He sighed. "I didn't, for certain. But I suspected. Why?"

Kim shrugged and moved away from him, pulling a blanket from the bed to wrap herself in as she moved to raise the blinds and stare sightlessly from the window. "I always have," she whispered. She knew he would be staring at her in shock and disbelief. She couldn't meet his eyes. "I. . . I never wanted anyone to know that I'm frigid. That I'm incapable of. . . of. . . it. It's always just easier to pretend."

Vaughn remembered the passionate, hungry woman he'd held in his arms earlier. She wasn't frigid, of that he was certain. If she was incapable of having an orgasm, as she put it, there had to be a reason. He raised himself up on his elbow as he studied her tense form. "And you've never—?"

"No." She plucked at something on the blanket, avoiding his eyes.

Vaughn's eyes narrowed. There was something she wasn't saying. The inquisitive aspect in him that had prompted him to become a cop refused to let it lie. "Were you raped?"

She sighed. "No, I wasn't raped."

"But something happened. Didn't it?"

She swung her head to pin him with her smoky gaze. "You're a nosey son of a bitch, aren't you?"

He grinned. "Always." He fell silent. Waiting. Giving her time. Although she still looked toward him, her eyes had grown so distant he wondered if she remembered his presence.

Finally she blinked. "I've never told another soul. No one. Not even a girlfriend. But maybe it's time I told someone," she said the words almost musingly. "It could be the catharsis I need." Smiling a small humorless smile, she returned her gaze to his face. "And since you're the first man I've encountered who was perceptive enough to even suspect that there was a problem, then perhaps it should be you."

Kim wondered what she was doing. It was stupid to tell him. Knowledge was power. She would be giving him the power to hurt her as deeply as she had been hurt before. But something drove her. Some instinct that she could only pray to God was not wrong.

"I was sixteen," she said quietly, avoiding his eyes as she looked out the window. But she didn't see the yard bathed in moonlight. She saw herself as she had been back then—trusting, confused, still missing her father. "His name was Gage. He was eighteen. A high school football player." She smiled sadly, a little cynically. "A real jock. You know the sort. Mr. Macho." She waved one arm in a rough imitation of a male flexing his biceps and looked back at Vaughn. "The first time I saw you, I was irrepressibly reminded of him.

At his expressive grimace, she shrugged a bit sheepishly. "Sorry."

"Don't worry about it. Please go on."

"We'd been dating for a few months," Kim said. "Gage had a wandering eye and, because I was young and stupid and desperate to hang onto the only male in my life, I gave him my virginity. At the time, I really didn't see what all the fuss was about. Sex, after that first time, was pleasant enough. But there sure as hell weren't any fireworks." She shrugged and looked in the direction of the dresser across which Vaughn had thrown his.

Vaughn watched her, wondering what was coming. Knowing that whatever it was, the mere remembrance still caused her pain.

Still wrapped in the blanket, Kim moved across the

room to gently touch an old picture among the memorabilia crowding the shelves there. Then, sighing, she retraced her steps. Shoving some things aside on the dresser, she sat on it to stare thoughtfully in his direction. Vaughn didn't think she saw him.

Abruptly, she blinked and focused. "Anyway, like I said, I didn't think sex was anything special. But Gage did. And if sex was what it took to hold on to him, then I was willing to use it. I was too immature to realize that you couldn't build a relationship on sex."

She paused and used one hand to lift her hair away from the nape of her neck. "I've tried a thousand times since then to figure out why I was so desperate to hang onto somebody like Gage. When I look back, I realize he wasn't even worth the time of day. But, somehow, he made me feel whole, complete." She shrugged. "I guess I needed that.

"But Gage's friends didn't like me. I wasn't the wild, partying type. I refused to have anything to do with any of them, no matter how many times they hit on me." She closed her eyes briefly. "And because I provided a ready supply of sex to Gage, virtually on demand as long as we were in private, he was spending less and less time with his friends." She threw back her head with a groan. "God, I'm so ashamed of who I was back then."

Vaughn watched her as she wrapped her arms around herself. "I don't think you have anything to be ashamed of. We all do things we're not proud of. That's life."

"Don't spout platitudes. Nothing anybody says can change the way you feel in here." She tapped her chest. "Anyway, one day, Gage met me in the hall after school and took me to the gym. It was quiet there, empty. He took me to one of the small side rooms where they stacked the gym mats. And. . . and he began to make love to me." She looked at Vaughn. "Just foreplay, you know." She sighed. "God, this is even harder than I thought it would be."

Kim slid off the dresser and walked to the window again. Her guts were churning with self-loathing and a hatred for Gage almost as strong as it had been back then. How could she have been so naive? She detested even thinking about this. Talking about it was pure torment. But she had started. It was too late to back out now.

She allowed memory to carry her back. "With Gage, foreplay had always been rather perfunctory," she continued. "Of course, I didn't know that at the time. I thought that was the way it was supposed to be. But on this day, the foreplay just went on and on. I didn't understand what he was doing. I began to feel things I had never felt before. And for the first time I actually wanted him to make love to me." She stopped and turned to look at Vaughn. He had surprised her by being a good listener. "You have to understand, that I was still quite inexperienced. I was still rather shy about the whole process. I attempted to show Gage that I was ready by kissing him and trying to maneuver his body on top of mine. But he ignored me."

"It was then that he started talking to me, saying, "Tell me what you want, baby. Show me how much you want it." Finally, I was so aroused that all sense of shyness and reticence faded away. All I could think of was how badly I wanted him to make love to me. And I gave him what he wanted. I said the words. I asked him to make love to me. Begged him to make love to me."

Remembered pain and hate rose in her throat, choking her. "And that was when he got up and stood looking down at me." Unconsciously, she clenched her fists. "My jeans were down around my knees. My blouse was undone. My hair was a mess. And he just said, "See you later, baby."

Kim shrugged. The words had been uttered in a way that was as matter-of-fact as the way she had probably heard them. But Vaughn had heard and felt the pain hidden behind the words, and a protective instinct rose within him.

"I was in shock," Kim's voice was low now. "I don't think I truly realized what he had done until I saw him reach down to pick up his books. That was when I saw the recorder. He clicked it off and left me sitting there.

"I found out later that night, when he came to apologize, that he'd done it on a dare from his friends. They had told him that they thought I controlled him with sex. He had told them that he could walk away from sex anytime, anywhere, even if the woman was begging for it. And the bet was on. Gage won. He seemed to think that I should have understood his need to reaffirm his macho image with his buddies. He couldn't understand why his apology wasn't enough for me."

Vaughn stared at Kim as she started pacing the length of the bedroom. The words he'd heard couldn't begin to describe the depths of hurt and shame she'd suffered. The teen years were bad enough without something like that.

"Anyway," she said as she walked. "Ever since then, whenever I reach the point where I'm so desperate for sexual release that I know that my orgasm is only seconds away, something shuts down inside me. Like somebody flicking a switch. All the feelings die. There's nothing left." She closed her eyes briefly, inhaled deeply, and then walked to the window. "I never again begged a man for anything." She said the words so quietly that Vaughn almost missed them. He wondered if she was aware that she had said them aloud.

He couldn't begin to feel the total humiliation that 16-year-old girl had felt all those years ago, but he could understand what she'd felt. And he wanted nothing more in that moment than to get his hands on the man who had wounded her so badly. Since that was impossible, he vowed the next best thing. The next time he made love to Kimberley, she would experience an orgasm. Somehow, he'd figure out a way to undo what had been done.

He was unaware that the single bout of good wholesome sex he had envisioned had just been transformed into something else.

* * *

She'd said good-bye to Vaughn almost an hour ago. God, what had prompted her to tell him everything? She felt her face flame with embarrassment. How could she have been so stupid? He probably thought she was a real nut case. An emotional cripple. How was she ever going to face him again? Of course, he probably wouldn't want to see her again except in the capacity of his job. Which, when she thought about it, was exactly what she wanted. Wasn't it?

Kim jumped as her Aunt Vivian's big grandfather clock chimed one a.m. The clock's fading reverberations immediately brought to mind Vaughn's suggestion that that particular time might be important to the killer. Shivering, she wrapped herself more tightly in the blanket that she'd torn off her bed to bring downstairs. Despite the brilliantly lit house and Vaughn sitting outside in his cruiser, Kim knew she wouldn't be able to sleep for hours yet, not until the sun began to rise.

"Might as well settle in for the night," she said to herself as she rose and moved into the kitchen to pour herself a glass of 7-Up. She'd specifically chosen it because it was caffeine free, and she'd begun to wonder if her sleeplessness might be due, in part, to a burgeoning sensitivity to the effects of caffeine.

Awkwardly clutching the blanket to her while she carried the soda in one hand and a bag of air-popped popcorn in the other, Kim settled herself on the sofa in front of the television. She'd decided to watch a late-night movie in the hopes that it would be boring enough to lull her to sleep. She'd just keep the volume low so that the commercials—which always seemed to be at least three decibels louder than the movies—wouldn't awaken her.

The first movie she found was an old one featuring Lindsey Wagner as she persistently dodged the attempts of recently dead corpses to have her join their ranks. It didn't take Kim long to determine that the movie was definitely not meant for someone who hoped to be soothed to sleep. She switched the channel and consulted newspaper for the latest television listings. Finally, she decided to watch another old movie, *K-9*. She'd seen it before, but it seemed to be the least threatening of the late-night movies offered.

Kim had just gotten involved in the movie and had picked up her glass when the discordant ring of the phone exploded into the near silence. It startled her so badly that she spilled the drink down the front of her nightshirt.

Who the hell would be calling her at this time of the night?

Brushing in annoyance at the wet spot on the front of her over-sized T-shirt, Kim stretched across the sofa to answer the phone on the opposite end table. "Hello."

There was no immediate response.

"Hello," she said again.

"Hello, Kimberley." It was an odd voice, low and scratchy. She didn't recognize it.

"Who is this?"

Once again there was only silence on the other end. Kim was about to hang up the receiver in disgust when he spoke again. "Vengeance is mind sayeth the Lord of Death. That's who I am, Kimberley. The Lord of Death."

Kim froze. She gripped the receiver so tightly that her hand hurt. Her throat closed. There was silence on the other end. And then a strange, sibilant laughter. Finally, Kim found her voice. "Why are you doing this?" There was too much fear in her tone. She knew it even as the words emerged.

"You feel it, don't you, Kimberley? You feel her cold, cold kiss. She's Death's companion, you know? Her name is Danger."

Kim shivered as the grotesque whispering hiss of his voice washed over her. She ignored the strange poetic threat, using her anger to steel herself against fear. She had to get a clue to his identity.

"Tell me why you are doing this," she demanded. There'd been no fear in her voice that time.

"I didn't want you to think I'd forgotten you. I'll never forget you, Kimberley." There was a click, and then nothing but silence. Ominous silence.

CHAPTER 9

Vaughn discovered that his attention had wandered from the fax in his hand. A week had passed since the night he'd spent with Kim. The morning after their encounter, she had reported receiving a threatening call. She'd been unemotional and abrupt as she related the words of the caller. She had spoken to him only a handful of times since then, and only long enough to demand updates on her cousin's murder investigation. Why had their association, uncertain though it was, regressed? Why had she had reverted to the cold-as-ice, hard-as-steel little bitch that constantly rubbed him the wrong way?

Vaughn shook his head. He had to really force himself to concentrate on his work. Kim was always on his mind. Whenever he relaxed, he found himself thinking about her. The slight glimpse he'd had of her without her persona, without the tough-as-nails act, had well and truly hooked him. But her persistent animosity was beginning to frustrate the hell out of him.

Forcing his attention back to the paper in his hand, he reread it and frowned. The communication concerned Mike Drayton. Mike's sin, in this case, was not one of lying, but one of omission. He had omitted telling anyone that, although he had lived a number of years in Tacoma, the last year and a half, prior to moving to Lillooet Creek, he had lived in Seattle. Vaughn added one more name to the small list of people who had been in both Seattle and Lillooet Creek at the times the killings took place. He would definitely keep an eye on Mike Drayton. It might even be worth his while to go over to the lumberyard and ask Drayton a few questions.

There was a knock on his office door and Melissa poked her head in. "Doreen Hanson's on the phone, Vaughn. She wants to talk to you, and she sounds really pissed."

Although his mind was still a million miles away, he automatically picked up the phone. "Garrett."

"How long is it going to take you to catch this son of a bitch? He killed my bird. Left me a real cute poem about a fucking corpse."

She had his complete attention. Doreen worked hard at achieving a veneer of class. She studiously avoided using coarse language. If she was using it now, something had to really have frightened her. He was one of the few people in town who knew her well enough to recognize that.

"Whoa, Doreen. Calm down. What are you saying?" He recalled the one and only time she had spoken to him of her upbringing. Her mother had died when she was a small child, and she had been raised by her father and four brothers. She had likened the experience to being raised by a pack of hyenas. At the time, he had wondered what she meant by the comparison. Then he'd happened to catch a nature show about hyenas. When he'd seen a wounded hyena ripped to shreds by the members of its pack, he thought he understood her meaning.

"Are you dense? I'm saying that the goddamn killer's been here. He left his calling card."

"Don't touch anything. We'll be right there." Replacing the receiver, Vaughn rose and strode into the outer office. He paused briefly outside Stone's door to see if he'd returned from his latest round of questioning. He had. "You might want to come with me on this one, Stone. It looks like he's chosen another target."

Stone rose without comment, grabbed his suit jacket and flung it over his shoulder letting it hang from the hook of one crooked finger as he picked up his evidence collection case with the other hand. As they got into the Bronco parked out front he asked, "Man or woman?"

"Woman."

"Targeting two women at the same time is new. Interesting. Who?"

"Doreen Hanson. She's one of our local elementary school teachers."

Stone nodded and looked out the passenger-side window without further comment. Five minutes later, they turned onto McCurdy Road and pulled up in front of the large two story house that Doreen rented at a reduced rate from the school board. An elderly teacher had willed the house to the board when she'd passed away a few years back.

Doreen, wearing beige slacks and a bright yellow blouse, sat on the front step waiting for them. She held Landon on her lap. Vaughn allowed himself a brief moment to drink in the sight of his son.

The boy had Vaughn's eyes, but his hair instead of being blond was as black as coal. Vaughn wondered where that came from. Doreen's hair, like that of the other Hansons, was light ash brown. Landon smiled and waved his chubby hands as Vaughn and Stone drew nearer the house. He was a beautiful child.

"Go on in," Doreen said. She seemed to have calmed down somewhat. "I'd rather not go back in there until you're through, if it's all right?" Vaughn nodded and she looked beyond him to Stone.

"Doreen, this is Special Agent Stone of the FBI." Vaughn introduced them. "Stone, Doreen Hanson."

"I'm pleased to meet you, Ms. Hanson."

Doreen managed a slight smile and a nod. "Special Agent Stone." She briefly shook the hand that Stone bent to extend to her. "You're going to catch this guy before he catches me. Right?"

"That's the plan, Ms. Hanson," Stone assured her.

"Good." Doreen turned her face away to stare out at the road.

Vaughn opened the front door, and he and Stone entered the house. As he led Stone through to the kitchen, he noted how the FBI agent's eyes seemed to miss nothing. His gaze swept everything, from ceiling to floor. Suddenly he stopped and stared up the staircase toward the second floor. Vaughn followed his gaze. "Do you see something?"

Stone shook his head. "Baby powder," Stone said enigmatically before moving past Vaughn and continuing into the kitchen. The statement left Vaughn baffled. What did baby powder have to do with anything?

When he entered the kitchen, he almost ran into Stone. The guy had a habit of just stopping short. "What are you doing now?"

"Looking."

"For what?"

"Everything. When you try to catch a killer, you have to try to think and to see things the same way he does. The first thing I saw when I entered this room was that bird cage." Vaughn saw the bright yellow canary hanging from a string in the center of its cage. Limp, obviously dead. "A pet," Stone continued. "He appears to like killing animals. So we have to figure out why."

Stone moved closer to the cage and stood looking up at it. "A lot of psychotic personalities enjoy killing animals. It makes them feel all-powerful. Maybe our perp sees another purpose in it. If you take the theme of vengeance that he used in the Farris killing one step further, what do you get?"

Vaughn stared at Stone in silence for a moment as he tried to follow the line of thinking. "Well, I'd already assumed that, when he killed Farris's dog, it was part of his campaign of vengeance. A warning. A terror tactic. What you're saying is that when he kills the animals, it might not be a warning. It might be an element of the revenge."

"Exactly. He may like to kill something that his target is attached to."

Vaughn frowned. "But that doesn't fit in with the squirrel he left for Kimberley Tannas."

"True," Stone admitted. "But then, Ms. Tannas is not a resident of Lillooet Creek. Her pet, if she has one, is not here. And he might have thought that, because she is a woman, she would react strongly to the killing of any creature."

Stone set his evidence case on the table and opened it. After donning a pair of gloves, he removed a stick which he lengthened and used to remove the bird cage from its ceiling hook. "So, does all of this have anything to do with the smell of baby powder?" Vaughn asked as he watched him.

"Animals are innocent creatures. When they're our pets, we consider it our duty to care for them, to protect them." Stone set the bird cage carefully on the table and turned to look at Vaughn. "What does the smell of baby powder suggest to you?"

Vaughn's eyes widened in sudden comprehension. "Innocence," he breathed as his mind raced. "You don't think he'll go after Landon, do you?"

Stone shrugged. "Only he knows that for certain. But we have to remember that this guy doesn't see things the same way we do. His thought processes are. . . distorted. But if his reason for killing pets is the one we just hypothesized, then it doesn't take too much of a stretch of the imagination to see him going after a young child."

"Jesus." Vaughn felt as though he'd been hit in the stomach. It was his child, his son, Stone was talking about so matter-of-factly.

"Yeah," Stone agreed, shortening his stick. As Stone continued working with the dead bird, Vaughn walked over to check the exterior kitchen door for signs of forced entry. There were none. He made a mental note to ask Doreen about it. Then, using the supplies in Stone's case, he began dusting for prints.

"Hey, Garrett, come here, would you?"

Vaughn stepped up beside Stone.

"See here," said Stone, pointing with his stick. "The string is tied into a perfect hangman's noose. It looks to me like he killed the bird, probably broke its neck, and then hanged it. The hangman's noose is symbolic of punishment for a crime. I think what we have here is a fellow who considers himself judge, jury and executioner. He knows his victims. Maybe not well. For all we know their crime could be something as simple as bumping into him on the street and forgetting to say excuse me. But I think it's a pretty reasonable assumption that he's had some contact with them."

Vaughn nodded and looked at the slip of paper taped to the birdcage. Using a pair of tweezers from Stone's evidence case, he removed it. He frowned as he read the typewritten words.

Then come to me. I will give you a cold, cold kiss.
My roses are dead, they, too. My lips are gray. My
    eyes
Have neither irises nor pupil. They died, and now all is
    white;
White in a face of stone. Sister, cold lover, come.

When Vaughn looked up, there was an expression in Stone's eyes that he couldn't quite interpret. "You recognize that poem?" Stone asked. No doubt, in Stone's eyes, everyone was a suspect. Even the local sheriff who'd called him in. But there was nothing Vaughn could do about that except catch the killer. Preferably before he managed to implicate Vaughn anymore.

There was no sense denying it. "Yeah, I think I do. I've just got to remember from where." Vaughn carefully placed the paper in an evidence bag.

Stone nodded as he carefully placed the dead bird in a paper pouch. "I can finish up in here if you want to go ahead and get Ms. Hanson's statement," he said.

"Sure. I want to check around the yard, too." Vaughn went back outside to sit beside Doreen on the steps. He took the opportunity to extend one of his fingers for Landon to grasp with his chubby baby hand. "I've got to ask you a couple of questions, Doreen."

She looked at him. "Shoot."

If she had said that to him just a few months ago, he would have been almost tempted to take her at her word. Now, however, he found that his anger had begun to fade. She was a young woman who had been raised in an environment not only devoid of love, but rife with abuse. He knew what it was like to grow up in that kind of an atmosphere.

Reluctantly, Vaughn released his finger from Landon's grasp and removed his note pad and pen from his pocket. "What time was it when you found the bird?"

"What time was it when I called you?"

"About eight-fifteen."

She nodded. "That's what time it was when I found it. I had just come down to start breakfast. I noticed that Mimi wasn't singing. I looked and saw her hanging there. I—" She frowned and rubbed her arm as though to ward off a sudden chill. "I saw the note and walked over to read it. Then I called you."

Vaughn nodded. "Did you touch anything?"

"No. I don't think so."

"Did you hear anything unusual last night."

She shook her head. "Nothing."

"Were your doors locked?"

"Of course." She frowned. "At least I think they were. I make a point of locking my doors when I hear that—" she paused and swallowed as though struggling with an admission. "When I hear that my brothers are in town drinking. But it is possible I forgot last night."

"Well you're going to have to start checking them. All the time. Okay?"

"Sure." Doreen lowered her head to nuzzle the baby's ear as she tightened her hold on the child.

She was a good mother. Vaughn hated to frighten her more than she was already, but she had to be warned. "Stone seems to think that Landon could be in danger."

Doreen's head jerked up. "Why?" she demanded.

Vaughn swallowed uncomfortably. "This guy seems to like to punish by hurting what we care about, what we're attached to."

"Oh, no," Doreen whispered as she closed her eyes and clutched Landon to her so tightly that the little boy squirmed in protest.

Vaughn closed his note pad and returned it to his pocket. "We're going to have a deputy sitting outside the house whenever you're home. I'll need you to inform him when you plan to be out and arrange to meet him here again on your return. Agreed?" He knew first hand just how stubbornly independent Doreen could be, but he didn't expect an argument this time.

She nodded. "All right." She looked toward the street with a grimace. "How long are you going to baby-sit me?"

"As long as it takes to get him." He'd already brought Killian down from his post in Crystal Falls to help out. Now, he'd either have to call in more deputies from outlying villages, hire additional manpower, or justify a lot of overtime pay to the town council. But he intended to do whatever it took.

She nodded without comment. Vaughn studied her. She was a beautiful woman. Hazel green eyes. Light ash brown hair. Heart-shaped mouth. But she didn't stir the same feelings in him that she once had. She was the mother of his son—thanks to her machinations—and she was a friend. Although, at the moment, his feelings of friendship were still tempered by resentment. But there was nothing more. Not anymore. When had his feelings changed?

"I dusted the kitchen for prints. Stone is dusting some of the other more prominent areas. It'll leave a bit of a mess, but it can't be helped."

Doreen nodded. "That's all right."

"We'll need to get a sample of your prints. Do you think you can come inside now?"

She rose without comment and moved into the house. She was scared to death and trying to hide it.

A short time later, Landon sat contentedly in his high chair munching cereal pieces from the tray while Doreen wiped the residual ink from her fingers. Stone and Vaughn had just begun packing up their supplies when there was a knock at the front door. Frowning slightly, Doreen walked into the living room to answer it.

"Hello, Barney."

"Oh, hell," Vaughn groaned when he heard the greeting. "Reporter from *The Observer*," he said to Stone. "Nice guy. But I swear he's half bloodhound." Before Barney McCarthy could begin trying to worm details out of Doreen, Vaughn strode into the other room.

"Barney," Vaughn nodded in greeting as he came up behind Doreen. "What brings you by?"

"Got a tip that Doreen had a spot of trouble this morning. Hinted that she might have had a bit of a scare. That true?"

Vaughn saw the curtain twitch in Mrs. Babchuk's window across the street. It wasn't too hard to figure out where Barney's tip had come from. Now Vaughn arched an eyebrow as he looked at Doreen. "I didn't think you ever got scared."

"I don't." She looked at Barney with a frown. "Somebody gave you bad information, Barney."

"Cut the crap, you guys. Quit treating me like one of them big city reporters. I deserve better than that."

Vaughn studied Barney's round face. The guy was right. He did deserve better. He'd always worked with the sheriff's department rather than against it. And he'd always obliged when Vaughn had asked him to hold off on a story. Of course, few people in Lillooet Creek needed *The Observer* to give them news of the sensational. That usually travelled by word of mouth in a manner that was much faster and grew much more sensationalistic with each telling than anything Barney could have printed.

No, what the people of Lillooet Creek needed from *The Observer* was information about the next church social or community bazaar. They wanted to know who was having garage sales, what the score had been in the local basketball game, and whose daughter had married whose son. The most popular sections of *The Observer* were its weekly recipe section, and its gardening tips. When Barney did print something sensational— something that the big city newspapers would have latched onto like moss to the north side of a tree—he was often taken to task by citizens of the town for not getting the details right. Because, of course, they'd already heard the story, and that wasn't the way Uncle Waldo had told it. It took a special kind of person to be a reporter in a small town.

Doreen stepped back. "All right, Barney. Come in."

Just as Barney stepped into the living room, Stone emerged from the kitchen carrying his evidence case and the birdcage. "Agent Stone," Doreen said. "I'd like to introduce you to our local reporter, Barney McCarthy, affectionately known as Blarney Barney. Barney, Special Agent Stone."

Barney, slightly red-faced due to Doreen's needling introduction, stepped forward to take the FBI agent's hand. "Pleased to meet you, Agent Stone."

Stone set the evidence case down for a moment. "McCarthy." Stone nodded and then turned to Vaughn. "I'll be outside." Picking up the case, he exited the house.

"Unfriendly sort?" Barney asked of Vaughn.

"No. Preoccupied sort," Vaughn clarified.

"Ah, I see." Through the screen door, Barney watched Stone walk out to the Bronco. Then, with a quick sigh, he turned to face Doreen. "So what happened?"

Doreen looked at Vaughn questioningly. Barney followed her gaze. Vaughn sighed. "I suppose Doreen can tell you as much or as little as she wants to tell you, Barney. But I'm going to have to ask you not to print anything yet. We still have that reporter out of Spokane staying at the hotel. You print anything that catches his interest, and he'll have his cronies coming down on this place like a flock of vultures again."

"He's no ordinary reporter, you know," Barney said. "He's a free-lance investigative journalist."

"There's a difference?"

"Of course, there's a difference." Barney seemed a bit perturbed. "He—"

Vaughn held up a hand to forestall a detailed explanation. "I'll take your word for it. Right now, I have work to do. And remember, no story without my go-ahead."

"Yeah, okay. You know, someday I'm going to move somewhere where I can do my job the way it's supposed to be done."

Vaughn grinned. "Later, Barney." He looked at Doreen. "Take care. I'll have a deputy stationed outside before I leave. Okay?"

She nodded. "Sure."

Vaughn found Stone checking the ground near the house. "Find anything?"

"No. The soil's too hard."

"You should look out back, across the clearing." Both Vaughn and Stone whipped around at the sound of the voice. It was Liz Murphy.

At sight of her, Vaughn came to the resigned conclusion that it just was not going to be his day. He sighed as he watched her walk toward them. "Stone, I don't believe you've had the honor of meeting Liz Murphy yet, have you?"

"No, I don't believe I have." He stepped forward to offer his hand in greeting. "Ms. Murphy."

"Liz, this is Special Agent Stone."

"How do you do, Special Agent Stone?" she said. Vaughn noted that her expression was unusually solemn. She didn't smile.

"Fine thank you. What was it you said earlier?"

"I said that you should check out back. Not in the yard, but across the clearing behind it. Near that junk yard."

Stone looked at Vaughn questioningly. "She means Barnes Auto Wrecking."

Stone nodded and turned back to Liz. "Why do you say that, Ms. Murphy?"

Liz frowned. "I'm not really sure." She closed her eyes. "But I think you'll find a piece of cloth. Dark blue, or maybe black. He tore his jacket." She opened her eyes and looked at Stone. "I'm sorry. That's all I can tell you."

Once again Stone cast Vaughn a look of inquiry. "Ms. Murphy is psychic," Vaughn explained. "She arrived in town a little over a week ago."

"I see." Stone turned back to face her. "We'll certainly check out the lead you've given us. Thank you."

"I wish I could do more." Liz looked beyond Stone

and Vaughn to the house. Her eyes travelled slowly over its surface, rising to the second-story window. She shivered. "I wish I could do more," she repeated in a whisper. Then, without further comment, she turned and walked out to the road, got into her van, and drove away.

"Strange lady," Vaughn commented as he shook his head.

Stone turned to face him, studying him for a moment with his penetrating gaze. "She's a little strange," he said. "But don't discount anything she has to say because you don't understand it. Granted, sometimes these psychic types are way off the mark. Then again, sometimes they're right on the money."

"You've worked with a psychic before?"

"A good one... once." Stone looked after Liz Murphy's van. "The experience taught me a lot."

"Well, I'll arrange to get a deputy over here, and then we can check out that clearing."

"Sure." Stone was standing back, looking at the upstairs window that Liz Murphy had looked at only moments before. "Wonder why she looked so chilled when she looked at that window?"

Vaughn followed his gaze. "Beats me." He really didn't want to know. What with the tangible fears that plagued his days, and the intangible fears that haunted his dreams at night, Vaughn just didn't have the capacity to deal with psychic fears, too. Leaving Stone staring at the window, Vaughn walked out to the Bronco where he could speak without risk of being overheard, and contacted the office.

* * *

The knee-high grass rustled dryly as they walked through the vacant lot that separated the rear yards of the houses on McCurdy Road from the wrecking yard.

"There's a trail here," Stone said.

"Kids use this empty lot as a shortcut all the time."

They continued scanning the property. They were

nearer the auto wrecking yard now, and Vaughn began to look more carefully for the scrap of dark blue or black cloth that Liz had mentioned. Since they hadn't been able to find anything within the tamed confines of Doreen's yard, he really didn't hold out much hope of finding anything out here. But he didn't say that.

When they reached the fence that enclosed the wrecking yard, they both began to walk along it in opposite directions. Vaughn noted a couple of depressions in the grass that looked like they might have been made by man-size feet, but there was nothing definite enough about them to provide any kind of a lead.

Suddenly Stone shouted. "Here." Vaughn turned and, at Stone's beckoning wave, walked toward him.

"Whatcha got?"

Stone held up a jagged square of material with a pair of tweezers. It was dark blue denim. "Looks like he snagged his jacket while coming over the fence." He indicated a fiber still snagged on a barb of the fence. "There's a small stain on the fabric. Could be blood. We'll have to send it out for testing."

"I'll be damned. She was right."

CHAPTER 10

When Kim opened the door in answer to the persistent ringing of the bell, she didn't know who she expected to see, but it certainly wasn't Aunt Willie. "Stopped by for some coffee," Willie said without preamble.

Recovering from her surprise, Kim smiled. "It's good to see you, Aunt Willie. Come in." She noticed a dish in Wilma's hands. "What's that?"

"Macaroni and low-fat cheese casserole. I know you young women. Can't be bothered cooking to feed yourselves properly; and won't eat anything with too much fat in it. But I never met anybody who wasn't tempted by macaroni and cheese."

There was enough food left in the house from the gathering after Trent's funeral to feed Kim for months, but she didn't say that. "You're right. I love it," Kim said with a smile. "We'll share it for lunch."

"Oh, no." Willie waved a hand dismissingly. "I ate before I came. It's for you. Should last you a couple of days anyway." Aunt Willie's voice was as abrasive as it always was as she followed Kim into the kitchen. "So when's Vivian going to quit hiding out up at Deirdre's and come home?"

They visited for a while, until Aunt Willie got around to the real reason for her surprise visit. "What's all this nonsense about a psychic? You know this Murphy woman everyone is talking about?"

Kim smiled. "Just what she told me about herself. But she seems like a nice person. I like her."

"Is it true that she's psychic?"

"Who knows? She certainly thinks she is. But she says the ability isn't completely reliable. All she knows is that she was drawn to Lillooet Creek to protect someone. She thinks that someone may be me."

"Hmph," Willie snorted. "Is she one of those martial arts people or something?"

Kim couldn't help but smile. "Not that I'm aware of."

"Then how's she think she's going to protect anyone from a killer. More'n likely she'll just end up getting herself killed. I never put much stock in that psychic stuff."

Kim wasn't quite certain how to respond to Aunt Willie's almost antagonistic attitude. She was saved by the ringing of the doorbell. "Excuse me," she said as she went to answer it.

As Kim opened the door to see Liz standing on the veranda, she knew instantly that something was wrong. Despite Liz's usual bright clothing and flashy jewelry, a shadow seemed to hover over her.

With only a fleeting hesitation due to her incomplete conversation with Willie, Kim grasped Liz's arm and led her into the house. Aunt Willie would just have to accept Liz as one of Kim's friends. "What's the matter, Liz?"

"I wish I knew for certain."

"Come into the kitchen. You can join Aunt Willie and I for a visit."

"Oh, no." Liz halted in her tracks. "If you've got company, maybe I should come back later."

"Don't be silly."

Liz allowed herself to be coaxed into the kitchen and Kim introduced her two visitors as she pulled out a chair for her. "Aunt Willie, this is Liz Murphy." She gave Aunt Willie a speaking look that she hoped the older woman would be able to interpret. "Liz, meet Wilma Nielsen, affectionately known as Aunt Willie."

"I'm pleased to meet you." Liz extended her hand in greeting, but her smile was tight and forced.

"Likewise," Aunt Willie said as her enormous, calloused palm swallowed Liz's hand. "Been hearing a lot about you." As Kim placed a cup of hot coffee in front of Liz, she noticed Aunt Willie's penetrating dark, green eyes sweeping the psychic from head to toe.

Liz sighed and leaned forward, resting her braceleted arms on the table with a clink while she worked at shredding a tissue she had wadded in one hand. "I guess that can be expected in a town this size."

Kim placed a calming hand over Liz's agitated ones. "Tell us what's bothering you." Liz shot an uncertain glance at Aunt Willie. Kim hastened to reassure her. "Don't worry about Aunt Willie. She'll keep whatever you say to herself. Won't you, Aunt Willie?"

"Hmph," Aunt Willie snorted. "I've never repeated a private conversation in a gossip session yet, don't know why the hell I'd start now. Mind you, I've got to admit, I like listening to gossip as much as the next gal. I'll even go so far as to make my rounds to find out what's goin' on. But you don't have to worry about me. The only stories I tell are the ones that are mine to tell."

Liz considered Aunt Willie briefly. Then she nodded. "I like you."

To her surprise, Kim saw a slight flush deepening the dusky tone of Aunt Willie's weathered complexion. "You don't know me," Aunt Willie responded in a tone slightly more crusty than usual.

"I know enough," said Liz. She sipped thoughtfully at the coffee Kim had placed before her. Then she looked at Kim. "Something's going to happen," she said. "Soon. And because I don't know exactly what it is, I don't know what to do to stop it."

Kim frowned as a shiver travelled down her spine. "What makes you so certain that something will happen, Liz?"

Liz shrugged and shivered. "I woke up this morning feeling really down, depressed. That's unusual for me. I knew I had to speak to Sheriff Garrett as soon as possible, so I called his office. Melissa said he wasn't in. When I asked her if she knew where he was, she didn't want to say. But I managed to get her to tell me that he'd gone over to talk to Doreen Hanson. As soon as she said the woman's name, it was like somebody had pulled back the curtains in a darkened theatre. Scenes started flashing in my mind. I was so disoriented I had to sit down. Suddenly, I could see—" Liz sipped hastily at her coffee. "And I wished I couldn't," she whispered.

"Why? What did you see, Liz?" Kim asked.

"At first, all I saw was a two-story house, a little like this one but a bit smaller with red trim. There was a woman sitting on the front steps, holding a baby in her lap."

"What'd she look like?" Willie demanded curtly.

Liz shivered. "Slim, attractive. Shoulder-length, light brown hair. But—"

"That's Doreen, all right," Willie acknowledged. "But what?" she prompted.

Liz rubbed her arms. "Her lips were gray. Her eyes"—she hesitated, swallowing convulsively—"Her eyes were completely white and her features looked gray white like those of a statue."

"A corpse. Are you sayin' you saw Doreen as a corpse?" Willie demanded.

"I don't know. I think so." Liz frowned and rubbed her forehead between her brows. "Suddenly the scene shifted and I was seeing the house from the rear, moving toward it. For some reason, I looked down at my arm—only it wasn't my arm—and I noticed that I'd ripped the sleeve of my jacket. It was a dark jacket, blue or black. I moved on. It was night, but the moonlight was bright. A dog barked.

"Then I was in front of the two-story house looking up at the second-story windows. Suddenly, as though I was fifteen feet tall, I was looking directly into one of those upper windows. And inside—" She stumbled. "Inside were coffins. Lots of coffins." Shivering, Liz rubbed her arms before picking up her cup of coffee with both hands.

Both Kim and Aunt Willie were momentarily speechless. "The next person who tells me that my psychic ability is a gift is going to land flat on their behind in the middle of next week," Liz said through gritted teeth. She raised her gaze to the ceiling. "You hear that granny? You never had to deal with one like this."

Aunt Willie found her voice first. "So what you're saying is that you think my girl's in danger?"

Liz looked at her questioningly. "Your girl?"

"Doreen." Willie nodded. "She lived with me for the last few years of her schooling, you know. Had to if she wanted to finish school. That father and those useless brothers of hers were just working the poor kid to death, caring for them. Not a one of them would lift a finger. When I saw what was happening, and realized that the kid just couldn't take much more, I told her to pack her stuff and move in with me. I never once regretted it. She's a good girl. Went on to get her own teaching certificate.

"'Course I see a lot of the stuff that goes on in the schools, what with being a maintenance trustee, and all. That's just the fancy term they use here for a janitor, in case you were wondering." She paused, apparently realizing that she'd been sidetracked. "You think Doreen's in danger?" she asked again.

Liz nodded hesitantly. "I don't know what else that horrible vision could mean. And the feeling it gave me was chilling, sinister."

Kim stared at Liz, her mind still reeling with the implications. Would she now be free of him? Despite the week of renewed and intensified fear that she'd suffered due to his phone call, Kim found hope swelling within her. Did this mean the killer had switched the focus of his attention? Found someone new to terrorize? Perhaps she really could go home soon. Immediately upon the heels of those thoughts came guilt. Here she was wondering if she could go home, and not once had she spared a thought for the woman who was now in danger. She hadn't realized she could be so callous.

"I'm going to talk to Vaughn," Aunt Willie's voice cut into Kim's thoughts. "Find out exactly what he has to say about being at Doreen's this morning. Then I'm going to talk to that girl. Tell her that she and the baby can stay with me for a while. It'll be safer." Willie suddenly pinned Liz with her gaze. "I'm not saying I believe everything you say, mind you. Just figure there's no harm in being prepared." She eyed Liz over the brim of her coffee cup for a second. "And why aren't you staying here with the girl you're supposed to be protectin'? You can't be much help in a hotel room across town, can you?"

"Willie!" Kim was shocked by her audacity. She thought she'd remembered Aunt Willie pretty well, but it was obvious that either her memory was faulty or Aunt Willie had grown even more brusque with age.

"That's all right, Kim," Liz assured her with a smile. "Actually, Willie, I had hoped that Kim would invite me to stay with her after she got to know me well enough. And if she doesn't get around to it soon, I've been planning on asking her about just parking my van in the driveway and camping in the yard to stay nearby."

Kim stared at Liz incredulously. "You see, girl," Willie said. "Now aren't you glad I brought it up?" Kim switched her gaze to Willie. She didn't know what to say to either woman.

* * *

As Vaughn drove into Carter's Lumber, he looked for Mike Drayton and finally caught sight of him near the rear of the yard. He was unloading logs. Armed with the knowledge that Drayton was here, Vaughn walked into the store in search of Bill Carter. He stood behind the counter tallying a bill.

"Hi, Bill," Vaughn said.

Carter looked up and smiled. "Vaughn. What can I do for you today?"

"I was just wondering if I might have a word with one of your employees?"

Carter's smile faded. "Trouble?"

"Not that I know of," Vaughn assured him.

Carter nodded. "Okay. Who'd you want to see?"

"Mike Drayton."

"He's out back. Just go on through. You can't miss him."

"Thanks." Vaughn exited the store through the rear door.

It was a hot day. As he crossed the yard toward him, Drayton stopped working, removed his cap to wipe the sweat from his forehead with his shirtsleeve and then stood watching him. When he was within speaking distance, he nodded a greeting. "Drayton," he said.

"Sheriff," Mike Drayton nodded coolly in return. "Something I can help you with?"

"I'd like to have a word with you, if you don't mind?"

"Sure thing." He strolled to the side a few steps to a shady spot provided by a large stack of lumber.

Vaughn followed. "I understand you lived in Seattle for a while before coming here?"

"That's right."

"You wouldn't happen to remember where you were fifteen months ago, on the evening of April eighteenth?"

Drayton stared at him for a moment with his cold,

pale green eyes. Then he smirked and shook his head. "You got to be kidding! I don't even remember where I was last month on the eighteenth. Do you?"

Vaughn returned his smile. "Okay. I agree that question might have been a bit tough. Let's try this month. Do you remember where you were the night of July tenth?"

Drayton considered him with a narrowed gaze. "What are you tryin' to pin on me, Sheriff? What happened on July tenth?"

Vaughn shrugged. "You tell me."

Abruptly, Drayton's eyes widened. "That's the night that Farris guy got himself offed, isn't it? And you think that I—" Drayton's face split into a wide smile and his shoulders shook with silent laughter. "Sorry, Sheriff. The night that guy bought it, I was over at Tyler Dobbs' losing a whole fuckin' week's pay at five-card stud. I ain't your man."

Vaughn nodded. "I hadn't realized you had become part of Dobbs' crowd."

For the first time, Drayton frowned. "I'm not part of Dobbs' crowd. I just hang around with those boys every now and then."

"Okay," Vaughn nodded. "Thanks for your time."

As Vaughn walked back across the yard, he decided to skirt the store and just walk directly around to his Bronco. He had little doubt that Dobbs would verify Drayton's alibi. Dobbs would do anything to thumb his nose at the law—even commit perjury.

* * *

It was late-afternoon by the time Kim drove Willie home. Aunt Willie never drove. She either walked everywhere she went or took a taxi. Kim had refused to allow her to take a cab when she could just as easily drive her home.

Liz had returned to the hotel to check-out and pick up her luggage. She would be camping in the yard until Kim managed to reach her Aunt Vivian to get permission for another person to stay in the house with her. She had called earlier, but her aunt had been out. It was just a formality, Kim knew. She was certain her aunt wouldn't refuse. Still, she felt obliged to ask. After all, it wasn't her home. So the request would just have to wait until she made her regular evening call, that was all.

She pulled up in front of Aunt Willie's small bungalow on McCurdy street, two doors down from Doreen Hanson's place. Kim noticed a deputy sitting in his car, watching the house. It looked like it might be Deputy Killian, but she wasn't certain from this distance. However, the deputy's presence certainly made it *seem* as though the killer had chosen another target.

Across the street, a man was helping an elderly lady carry her groceries into her town house. Kim didn't recognize either of them. There were a lot of townspeople whom she hadn't recognized after all the years of being away. Still, she was curious. "Who are they?" she asked Willie.

Willie followed the tilt of her chin. "Oh, that's old Mrs. Crenley. She must be pushing eighty-five now. Her husband passed away about ten years ago. All their kids were already long gone—living out of state the last I heard—so she's pretty much alone now. I stop over to check on her about once a week. The man with her is Mike Drayton. He just moved into town about a year ago. He works down at the lumberyard." Willie shrugged. "He seems like a nice enough fellow. He's certainly helpful. Always doing things for the old people in the neighborhood." Willie opened the door and got out of the car.

"But. . ." Kim prompted as she followed Willie up the walk.

"But what?"

Kim shrugged. "The tone of your voice suggested you weren't quite sure about him. Why?"

Willie hesitated and turned to glance at him as he

emerged from Mrs. Crenley's apartment and walked to his metallic-green truck. Kim followed her gaze. The truck he got into seemed to be adorned with more accessories in polished chrome and black then Kim had known existed. The box had a topper on it painted the same shade as the truck.

"Damned if I know," Willie finally answered, drawing Kim's gaze back to her. "It's probably just an old lady's imagination."

Kim turned to glance at the man again only to meet his gaze head-on. A shock ran through her as she recognized him. His elbow was propped on the open window of his truck door, and he was looking at her. His round face was solemn as he stared at her with unnaturally bright, pale green eyes. This was the man she'd almost run into that day when she'd first arrived in town. Abruptly he smiled. The gesture reminded Kim of a dog baring its teeth. There was no warmth in it. Pulling the brim of his ball cap further down, shielding his eyes, he started his truck and drove off down the street. Kim shuddered. The coldness in his gaze had been pure fancy, she was certain. Still, Kim felt unaccountably relieved when he left.

* * *

Heading back home, Kim decided to stop and talk with Sheriff Garrett. She really didn't want to see him again. She was still terribly embarrassed by what had passed between them and what she had told him. She wished desperately that she had ignored the impulse that had prompted her to reveal the most humiliating moment of her life to a man she hardly knew and wasn't even certain she liked. It had taken all her willpower just to face him the next day when he'd come to see her. And it didn't get any easier. Perhaps that was why the enticement of returning to Seattle had grown more appealing with each passing day. And if the killer had switched targets, perhaps she could leave Lillooet Creek without jeopardizing the investigation.

The only way to find out was to talk to Garrett.

As Kim parked her car in front of the sheriff's office, she noted that Garrett's Bronco wasn't there. He probably wasn't in then. She hesitated. Should she go in and check? Or, should she return home? She'd told Deputy Lewis that she'd be gone less than an hour. Deciding that it wouldn't hurt to check, she got out of the car and strode quickly up the walk. A small bell tinkled on the outer door as she opened it and Melissa looked up from behind her desk.

"Hi, Kim," she smiled. "What can I do for you today?"

Kim returned her smile. "Is Sheriff Garrett in?"

"Not at the moment. He said he had a couple of things to look into at home. You can probably catch him there if you want. You have to drive right by his place anyway."

"I might just do that. Thanks, Melissa."

"No problem. See you later." Melissa was already bowing her head back to her paperwork as Kim left.

As Kim followed her usual route out of town, she was abruptly halted by a crew doing repair work on a storm drain. Dammit! There was no way around them. The detour sign pointed toward Ponderosa Street. Kim swallowed. She was going to have to drive by her father's service station; the place where he had lost his life. She wasn't certain she was ready for that.

Kim felt sweat begin to bead her forehead as she turned the corner. Her hands clenched on the steering wheel. She knew what she would find. She could picture it clearly, like a scene from a movie.

The old signs hanging by their rusting chains would creak in the summer breeze. The grass, tall and wild, would be growing up through the cracks in the scarred and ancient tarmac. And the station—its walls peeling and its windows broken by the passage of time, a relic of the past—would stand as a painful reminder of happier days. It would be a place of ghosts. She was terrified that it would trigger memories. Memories that she would be incapable of dealing with. Memories that she might never be strong enough to face.

Kim took a deep breath. Fear could be controlled. And she really didn't believe in ghosts. The only ghosts she had to face were the ones in her mind. She rounded a curve in the road and tried to prepare herself for the sight that was mere seconds away. Suddenly, she slammed on the brakes and stared in open-mouthed astonishment.

The station—an Esso now—was nothing like she'd imagined it at all. Two young boys busily pumped up bicycle tires. A young woman in a pink dress conversed with a man at the pumps as he filled her car. A middle-aged man emerged from the office, stuffing a package of cigarettes into his skirt pocket as he walked to his truck. Kim shook her head. There were no ghosts here, nothing to haunt her. This was a place for the living. The place had changed completely.

Why had she thought that, because her father had passed away, the station would die? The mind played strange tricks on us at times. She felt almost disappointed. She had feared this moment for so long it was rather anti-climactic.

A few minutes later, as Kim followed the winding road back up to her Aunt's house, she tried to decide whether she should stop and see Garrett or not. She really wasn't sure if it was a good idea to meet him on his own territory, so to speak. He'd be comfortable and she'd be at a disadvantage. Still, she'd been wanting to see the house he'd built for himself ever since she'd heard about it, and she did need to speak with him. The stand of tall trees that bordered the narrow driveway entering his property was coming up on the right. Kim slowed, still undecided. Ah, what the hell? She swung the wheel to take the turn. Her business partner, Kathy, was always telling her she needed to live a little, and take some risks.

When Kim emerged from the shadow of the trees flanking the driveway, she stopped rather abruptly. The place was beautiful! More than beautiful—it was breathtaking! Like a small oasis of natural wilderness into which the house had been set. The one-and-a-half story house, constructed from vertical cedar planks, harmonized with the grounds. A red shale driveway formed an oblong circle in front of it, drawing the eye to the enormous weeping willow in its center. From the drive, a wide stone walk led up to front steps which were also constructed of stone and flanked by enormous stone planters full of blooming flowers. She had never imagined Vaughn Garrett in a place like this. The idea that he was capable of creating it was completely inconceivable. And yet she had the proof before her eyes.

Coming out of her shock slightly, she eased the car slowly forward, taking the right-hand drive until she was in front of the house. She parked beside Garrett's Bronco and walked up to the house. Little things about the landscaping that had initially escaped her attention drew her eye now. A number of fluted concrete birdbaths enhanced the naturalistic setting. And carvings. There were wood carvings everywhere. An eagle, its wings stretched skyward, looked as though it had just landed at the edge of a bed of shrubs. A doe, its graceful neck elongated as though it sniffed the air, stood in the shadow of the willow. There was a bear cub and a ram, a family of squirrels, and a fox. All seemed exquisitely detailed.

Kim rang the doorbell and continued to scrutinize the yard as she waited for an answer. There wasn't one. That was strange. She looked at the Bronco. As far as she knew, he didn't have another vehicle. Maybe he'd been doing something that had prevented him hearing the bell. She rang it again. Waited. No response.

Backing up, she looked at the upper windows. Where could he be? She'd have to go home without speaking to him after all. Well, as long as she was here, she wanted to see as much of the house as possible. She might not have another chance. She descended the stairs and started walking around the house to the right. The heels of her sandals sank into the soft earth beneath the lawn and she wished absently that she'd worn her jeans and sneakers today. But she couldn't wear them all the time. Today she was wearing a summery skirt outfit she'd borrowed from Deirdre.

As she rounded the corner of the house, she forgot all about her inappropriate attire. Her mouth dropped. She had almost chosen architecture or interior design as a career. Every time she saw a place like this, she wished she had that choice to make all over again. An enormous multi-level cedar deck stretched the entire length of the house. In its center, a latticed gazebo was almost completely concealed by clinging vines of ivy. Kim stepped onto the cedar planking.

A pair of garden doors faced onto the deck. Feeling a little guilty, she used her hands to shield her eyes from the exterior light and peered into the house. The room she looked into was a bedroom. She drew back rather quickly at that realization. Somehow, it just seemed a little too personal. Still, in the brief minute that she'd seen the room, she had noted a number of things. A shirt hung over the back of a chair. A pair of shoes rested in the middle of the floor. And a pair of jeans had been left in a heap at the foot of the bed. But despite those few indications of untidiness, the room had not given her an impression of disorder. Quite the opposite in fact. It had seemed almost spotless. The bed had been made. The furniture gleamed. And potted plants thrived. But then she'd never really been much of a clean fanatic. And she could kill a plant faster than a rain shower could spring up on a sunny day in Seattle.

As she moved along the deck toward the rear of the house, she tried to peer into a couple of smaller windows but they were too high. On the rear corner of the house, a greenhouse style window had been installed at an angle. She stood on tiptoe to peer into it. To her surprise, she recognized herbs growing in small pots: parsley, chives, and thyme. Jeez, Garrett could cook, too? Was there anything the guy wasn't into?

Craning her neck, she looked beyond the plants, trying to see the kitchen. She couldn't see the lower cupboards, but the upper ones were of light-colored wood that had been lavishly varnished. An elaborate carved design embellished each cupboard door. She could just barely make out a counter top of rich, dark granite. Almost beyond her range of vision to the left was the corner of something she thought must be an island. To her right, she saw a kitchen table and four chairs sitting in a brightly lit alcove.

"What the hell do you think you're doing?" a deep male voice growled in her ear. Kim shrieked and jumped three feet.

With her heart still in her throat, she recognized Vaughn. "You scared me half to death."

"People who are doing something they shouldn't are easily frightened." His gold eyes appeared unusually cool. "Do you make a habit of going around invading people's privacy by staring in their windows? I thought Skeeter was the only Peeping Tom we had in town."

Kim felt a flush creeping up her neck. Damn the man, he seemed to have a knack for making her feel like an idiot. "I am not a Peeping Tom." Her voice was reserved and even. "I came by to see you. When you didn't answer the doorbell, I decided to try to see as much of your house as possible. It's beautiful."

"Thank you." His tone remained cool.

Kim's back stiffened. "I'm sorry to have bothered you. I'll let you get back to whatever you were doing."

It was only as Kim backed up a couple of steps that she noticed he was carrying a large wicked-looking knife in his right hand. Her eyes widened. He must have interpreted the shock in her expression because he explained in a brusque and irritated tone.

"I was carving," he said. "I do that when I want to be alone to think."

"There's blood on your hand." She'd just noticed it. His thumb and forefinger were stained with it. A small amount smeared the blade near the hilt. Despite his explanation, the knife made her nervous. What did she really know about this man? Suddenly he seemed much more sinister, much more of an unknown quantity than he had before.

"I cut myself," he responded curtly to her observation. "Now, do you want to tell me why you came by?"

Kim decided she really didn't want to broach the subject of returning to Seattle while he held an evil-looking weapon in hand. But for the life of her, she couldn't think of an alternative explanation for her presence. She stared up at his handsome face, into those hard, topaz eyes and froze. "Um, I, ah—"

He raised a mocking brow, and waited.

Kim's eyes narrowed. What an ass! She always thought better when she was angry. And she'd just received inspiration. "Actually, I came by to ask you if you'd like to come to dinner. But since you can't even bring yourself to be civil, you can forget it." Turning, she stalked away, her heels clicking on the cedar deck.

"I'll be there at eight."

Kim whirled. "I told you to forget it. The invitation is withdrawn."

He grinned. "Since we both know you never really intended to make it, the withdrawal doesn't count."

Her heart skipped a beat. How did he *do* that? "You can't just make up rules to suit yourself."

"Sure I can. I'll be there at eight," he repeated.

Kim didn't trust her voice to respond. What the hell had she gotten herself into now?

CHAPTER 11

Furious with herself for being outmaneuvered, Kim drove home, staying only long enough to inform the waiting deputy that she would be returning to town for a few minutes. Now she had to buy something to cook for Garrett. She supposed she could have pulled one of the frozen dishes that had been left by the townspeople after the funeral from the freezer, but somehow that wouldn't seem right. So she had to cook. She wondered if she could buy arsenic at the local grocery store. Of course, the way her luck was running when it came to Vaughn Garrett, she'd probably just end up poisoning herself.

Damn! She didn't even know what to make. She wasn't a hopeless cook, but she certainly wasn't capable of turning out cordon bleu quality. She'd simply walk down the aisles in the store and see if inspiration struck.

Kim emerged from the Mountain View Supermarket a few minutes later with all the ingredients for lasagna. It was the one thing she'd always been able to make with consistent results. Unlocking the passenger door, she set the bag of groceries on the seat. When it came to lasagna, she had a never-fail recipe.

Oh, no! The recipe was in her apartment in Seattle! The sudden realization startled her into trying to stand upright before she'd withdrawn her head from the car.

"Ow! Dammit!" Kim rubbed the back of her head and scowled at the roof of the car. Now what was she going to do? She didn't trust herself to try to make the meal from memory. Her Aunt Vivian probably had a ton of recipes somewhere, but it was already late afternoon. She didn't have the time to search for them and then try to wrest one exceptional recipe from years of accumulation.

Kim frowned and tapped her nails on the shiny, red paint of the Focus as she looked down the street. Aunt Willie! Willie loved to cook. She must have a good recipe for lasagna. And since Willie only lived about three blocks from here, she could walk over. She hadn't been getting enough exercise lately.

She'd only gone about half a block when a large woman wearing a lime green pant suit coming along the sidewalk from the other direction suddenly stepped into her path. "Hi! You're Kim Clayton, aren't you?" The woman, only a few inches taller than Kim, had an exuberant voice and an enormous smile.

Kim returned the smile hesitantly. "It's Kim Tannas now actually."

"Oh, yeah. I'd heard. I was real sorry to hear about your husband."

"Thank you." Who was this woman?

"You don't remember me do you?"

Kim felt awful. She shook her head. "No. I'm sorry. I don't."

The woman waved her hand. "Don't worry about it. It's not your fault. Since the last time you saw me, I've had three kids and put on a hundred pounds. I'm Susan Granger, only it's Susan Barcley now."

Kim's mouth dropped. This was Susan? Little Susie Granger who, always bored, had managed to instigate more mischief than five other girls. "Susan!" Kim smiled. "It's good to see you again." They spoke for a few minutes about kids and husbands and life in general. Then Kim checked her watch and realized the afternoon was slipping away from her. "Listen, Susan, I have to go. It was really nice seeing you again. If you get a chance, give me a call sometime. I'm staying up at my Aunt Vivian's."

Susan grinned. "I'll do that. We have a lot of years of girl talk to catch up on." With a wave, she moved on.

Breathing in the scent of the mountain air and the flowers blooming in their planters, Kim walked on. A block away from Aunt Willie's, she found herself walking along a piece of property protected by a chain-link fence. The compound appeared to contain nothing but the skeletal remains of myriads of vehicles, from the steeply sloped hill at the rear of the compound to the more level tract of land along the fence. Each and every cranny of the property held a vehicle. Kim frowned. She remembered this place.

Years ago, it had belonged to a man named Milo Barnes. He'd been a coarse, hostile man whom her father hadn't liked. But Milo Barnes had been an old man. It couldn't possibly still belong to him. Who ran it now? And why hadn't the town taken the opportunity afforded by a change in ownership to have the unsightly business moved?

As she walked along the fence, a shiver traced its way up her spine. She was being watched. She could feel it. She quickened her step, but her eyes were continually drawn back to the vehicular graveyard. It was a perfect place for someone to hide. She hugged the edge of the sidewalk, walking as far away from the fence as possible. Not too far ahead was the corner of the compound where the chain-link fence disappeared to be replaced by the normal plank fencing of someone's backyard. Kim tried to quicken her steps even more. Perhaps it was ridiculous to be so nervous in the bright light of day in a town the size of Lillooet

Creek. But there was a murderer on the loose. A murderer who had singled her out. And at the moment, she was more inclined to listen to her instincts than she was to the voice of reason. She wanted to leave this eerily silent compound behind her.

Suddenly, out of the corner of her eye, she saw a shadow move. She gasped and her hand flew to her throat as her head whipped around to identify the source of the movement. A man stepped forward from between two cars just inside the fence. He was thin. His filthy clothing hung on his bony frame as though it had been made for a much larger man. His sparse, greasy brown hair had been combed straight back, exposing a pronounced widow's peak. Twining long, grimy fingers in the links of the fence, he smiled at her. Small, pointed, widely-spaced teeth made him seem vampirish.

"H. . . hello," Kim stammered and resumed walking.

To her horror, he began to move along the fence with her. She glanced to the side. "Is there something I can help you with?" she asked, hoping he would get the hint. He didn't even answer. His gleaming blue eyes appeared to be riveted to her breasts. With sudden intuition, Kim knew that it was Skeeter Barnes whom she faced through the fence. He had obviously taken over the junkyard from his grandfather, old Milo. This was the man who had watched her through her bedroom window the other night, scaring the wits out of her. His eyes skimmed her body lasciviously as he strode along the fence, keeping pace with her. Kim wished desperately that she'd worn a loose fitting blouse rather than a T-shirt. The thought made her angry. She hated feeling like a victim. She hated feeling exposed when she was decently clothed. And most of all, she hated lecherous men. The kind of man who could make a woman feel half-clothed no matter what she wore.

With her hands clenched into fists, she stopped and

swung to face him. "Either you stop bothering me, or I'm going to report you to the sheriff. Do you understand?"

"Sorry," he said. His voice sounded rusty and unused. He hung his head sheepishly for a moment, sticking his hands in his pockets as he backpedaled a couple of steps. Kim resumed walking, but an instant later realized that he continued to follow her. Within seconds, his eyes established contact with her again, flicking over her face briefly before travelling down over her hips and legs. As his gaze moved up to cling to her breasts again, spittle drooled from one corner of his mouth. He wiped it on the dirty sleeve of his shirt. Disgust curdled in Kim's stomach.

It was at that point that she came to the conclusion that Skeeter Barnes had been shortchanged in the brains department. When he unself-consciously reached down to rub his crotch, Kim fled. Racing to the corner of the street, she turned and kept going until she'd managed to place the security of a house between herself and Skeeter's view.

Feeling more secure, she slowed and made an effort to breath more evenly. She tried to find a shred of pity within herself for the mentally handicapped man who—although capable of living independently—would never lead a normal life. It just wasn't there. She felt sickened, disgusted and frightened. As she turned up the walk to Aunt Willie's house, it took her a moment to remember why she'd come. When she did, she took a deep breath to calm herself before knocking on the door.

* * *

It was after five o'clock. He'd just settled into the old car up on the hill—*his* car—to watch the town. He liked sitting up here. He always had. You learned a lot about people by watching them. And he could see so much from here. It was the highest point in the wrecking yard.

The wrecking yard bordered Jackson Avenue, Cascade Crescent, and the rear property of the people living on the west side of McCurdy Street. From this vantage point, he could see people in their yards and, when he brought his binoculars, he could even watch them in their houses. It was almost as good as television.

Suddenly he sat up. Kimberley was walking by on Jackson Avenue. She'd crossed the street to walk on the far side, but he had no doubt that it was her. She looked almost as fresh and buoyant as she had all those years ago in school.

It had been a day much like this one except that it would have been late May or early June. He had seen Kimberley standing alone, leaning against the bricks at the corner of the school. Her blonde hair had been pulled into pigtails and secured with blue ribbons. She'd worn blue overall-style, knee-length shorts and a cute white blouse with scallops around the neck. She'd been so pretty, so pure. He'd decided then that he would be her friend.

With his heart hammering in his throat, he'd walked up to stand beside her. She hadn't noticed him right away because she was looking the other way. But finally, she'd looked his way. "Hi," he'd said, smiling at her.

"Hi," she'd said back, but she didn't smile.

He remembered how his throat had closed with anxiety, but he pressed on goaded by the desire to have someone pretty in his life. "Could I walk you home?" he'd asked.

And Kimberley had looked at him as though he were some type of creature she'd never seen before. "No, thank you," she'd said. "I'm meeting a friend." Then she'd turned her back on him and walked away. He remembered the pain of that rejection as though it was yesterday. That was when he'd realized that someone who was pretty on the outside was not always pretty on the inside. Still, he had often forgotten that lesson. It had been taught to him a number of times. Enough times now that he knew he would never forget it again. Just as he would never forget those that had forced him to learn it.

* * *

Vaughn's mind wasn't on what he was doing as he prepared to go to Kim's. It was on Kim. He knew she hadn't planned to invite him for dinner. He would have had to have been a complete fool to believe that, after days of avoiding him, she had suddenly had a change of heart. No, there had been something else on her mind. But it didn't matter.

She had managed to take his mind off his problems for a while, and he needed that. He needed to forget, if only for an evening, that the killer that occupied his town and his mind had chosen another victim. He needed to forget that his infant son was in danger. And he needed to forget that he had no right to separate Landon from his mother for the boy's protection. He'd made no claim to the child. God, if he had it to do over again. . . To hell with propriety, he'd sue for joint custody.

Later in the afternoon, he'd gone back to speak with Doreen, without Stone present, and had tried to convince her to place the boy with a sitter for a few days. She could say that she was so upset that she needed some time alone. There wasn't a woman in town who would have faulted her for that. No one, but Doreen herself. She had been taught at an early age never to admit to weakness. She wouldn't do it now. Damn, the woman!

Vaughn had been so angry, so frustrated by his inability to get her to listen to reason, that he'd left the office to seek the solitude of the woods at the rear of his property. He'd always found that working with wood relaxed him. He'd begun working on a carving of a mountain lion that he'd begun almost a month ago. But even that had failed to clear his mind, and as his attention wandered, he'd cut himself on the carving knife. Irritated with himself, he'd been returning to the house to find a bandage when he'd discovered Kim peering in his kitchen window. The sight reminded him of the killer who seemed to gain access to his home at will, invading his privacy. At any other time he might have regarded Kim's snooping with humor, but today it only served to exacerbate an already unpleasant day.

Then, in the next instant, he really had wanted to throttle her. How could she have reacted with fear to the sight of the knife and the small amount of blood on his hand? In the last couple of weeks it seemed that his every waking moment had been concerned with her safety. He couldn't believe that she would think him capable of harming her. Of course, her fear hadn't lasted long. He was fast learning that, with Kim, all you had to do was piss her off a bit and she was a pretty spunky little thing.

He grinned as he looked at his reflection in the mirror. That had been the point at which she'd issued, and withdrawn, the dinner invitation that she'd never intended to make in the first place. And because his mind had spent almost as much time dwelling on Kim—and her confession—within the last week as it had spent thinking about the killer, he, of course, had been quick to ignore the withdrawal and accept. He was almost certain that he had figured out exactly what had to be done to overcome her difficulty. And be damned if he wasn't looking forward to trying out his theory.

* * *

The lasagna was in the oven. Kim was just in the process of preparing her mom's special salad when the doorbell rang. She looked at the clock. It was already 7:15. Had she locked the door? No, she was certain she hadn't bothered because Deputy Lewis had returned within moments of her arrival at home, and with the deputy sitting out front in full daylight she felt safe.

"Come in," she yelled, hoping that whoever it was would hear. She wanted to finish the salad. A second later, she heard the door open.

"Hello?" It was Liz's voice.

"Hi, Liz. I'm in the kitchen."

"Hi, Kim, dear. I've parked my van in the drive over near the garage. Okay?"

Kim nodded. "Sounds fine. I managed to get hold of Aunt Vivian a little while ago. She says if you want to stay here, it's fine with her. You're welcome to use whichever guest room you prefer. Deirdre's old room is upstairs next to the room I'm using. And there's one just behind the living room. It was my Grandmother's room until she passed away."

"I think I'd prefer the one down here," Liz said, as she eyed the salad Kim was creating. "I hate climbing stairs if I don't have to, especially at night." She reached to pluck a small piece of tomato from the cutting board. "That salad looks delicious. What's in it?"

"Romaine lettuce, black olives, tomatoes, Spanish onion, green onion, cucumber, radish, purple cabbage and grated carrot."

"Mmmm. I'm going to have to remember that. What kind of dressing do you use?"

"Whatever you like. It's versatile."

"And what have you got cooking in the oven that smells so delectable?"

"Lasagna."

"Sounds scrumptious," Liz said using two long fuchsia-colored fingernails to pluck a slice of cucumber from the salad bowl. "Something special happening this evening?" The question sounded as though it was loaded with buckshot.

"Don't be ridiculous." Kim frowned. "Somehow, Sheriff Garrett managed to con me into inviting him for dinner. That's all." Suddenly Kim was struck by inspiration. "Would you like to stay?" She waited for

Liz's reply with bated breath, hoping that she would no longer have reason to be nervous about the upcoming evening.

"I'd love to, dear. But I can't. I've already agreed to have dinner with Ray." Kim's disappointment must have been evident on her face because Liz apologized. "I'm sorry. I tried telling Ray that I should be spending my time here with you, but—well, to be honest, my dear, that man is a real sweet-talking devil. Do you know what he said to me?"

Kim grinned. "No. What?"

"He said that women are like fine wine. They only get better with age." Liz shrugged. "It kind of loses some of its charm in translation, so I don't expect you to understand. And I know he didn't come up with it himself. He probably heard it the same place I did. . . on television. But still, the way he says it kind of strums the heartstrings. I just couldn't refuse the man. Do you know what I mean?"

"I understand, Liz. I think it's wonderful."

Liz smiled. "Me, too. I did tell him that I had to be home by eleven. I don't want to be leaving you alone at night. Your date should be over by then, shouldn't it?"

"It isn't a date." Kim's eyes shot sparks at Liz.

Liz shrugged nonchalantly. "Whatever you say, dear."

"And, yes it will certainly be over by eleven," Kim said as though Liz hadn't spoken. She put the salad in the refrigerator and rinsed her hands.

"I'll give you a key for the door in case I've gone to bed by then." She reached into the pantry where her aunt had hung a number of hooks that held various labeled keys. "It doesn't look like she has another one for the front door, so I'll give you one for the back." She pointed at the door that opened into the kitchen from the veranda.

"That's fine," Liz said. "Thanks. Well, I guess I'd better get going. Ray's supposed to be here any minute."

Kim followed her gaze to the clock on the wall. It read 7:28.

"Bye, dear. See you later. Have fun."

Damn! She still had to shower, change, and put on fresh makeup. "Bye, Liz," she called absently as she checked the lasagna and turned the heat down a bit. She was going to have to move at lightning speed.

* * *

It was precisely eight o'clock when the doorbell rang. Kim groaned. Although she'd managed to shower, blow dry her hair and put her makeup on, she was still in the process of dressing. She hastily finished pulling on her black stay-up stockings, smoothed her yellow skirt down over her hips, and grabbed a pair of black pumps before racing down the stairs. She made it to the bottom of the stairs before the doorbell rang again. Halting long enough to slip on her shoes, she took a deep breath and called, "Just a moment," as calmly as she could.

She stepped forward, felt something beneath the ball of her foot and damn near jumped through the ceiling when the object let out an ungodly yowl. With her heart in her throat, Kim watched Charity tear off down the hallway still loudly protesting the insult to her tail. "If you're going to lay at the bottom of the stairs you can expect to get stepped on," she called after the fleeing feline.

She hated being rushed like this. She was off balance already, and she hadn't even begun to deal with the good sheriff of Lillooet Creek yet.

Taking another deep breath, she walked to the door and paused in front of the mirror over her aunt's mail desk to check her appearance. Damn! She'd forgotten to put her earrings on. Oh, well. Too late now.

She opened the door. Vaughn Garrett stood before her in black pants and a pin-striped turquoise silk shirt looking cool and calm and more attractive than any man had a right to look. "Hi," he said, flashing that engaging smile that set her heart racing like a schoolgirl's. His eyes travelled down her body and back up again. "You look beautiful. I like your hair like that."

Self-consciously Kim raised a hand to her unruly mass of blonde hair. She hadn't had time to braid it. "Thanks. Come in," she said as she stepped back. Her heart was pounding so forcefully—from her race down the stairs and her encounter with Charity, she told herself—that she wasn't certain whether she smiled or not.

He stepped into the house and Kim closed the door. When she turned to face him, he held up two bottles of wine. "I didn't know what to bring. Red or white?" He held a bottle of white Bordeaux and one of red Italian Chianti.

Kim stared. She hadn't expected him to bring wine. She hadn't even thought of it because she'd never been much of a wine drinker. And she didn't have a clue what kind of wine you were supposed to drink with what. Wait. Lasagna was an Italian dish. She'd choose the Italian wine and hope. "The red, I think," Kim said.

She led the way down a short hallway from the living room to the dining room, just right of the kitchen. Her aunt's dining room was full of antique furniture. An old sideboard cluttered with ancient pieces of unmatched china, each with its own history, rested against one wall. The enormous old table with its eight ladder-back chairs occupied most of the room. Kim had set two places, complete with placemats and napkins, at right-angles to each other. At the time, she had wondered why she was doing it. Now she was glad she had. Somehow the formality seemed more suitable for the consumption of a meal complete with wine.

But she hoped Vaughn wasn't getting the wrong idea. Kim by no means intended this to become a romantic evening. There were no candles or flowers on the table. There was no romantic mood music waiting to be played. And there were definitely no amorous notions in her head. He should understand that very clearly. As the memory of what had already passed between them came back to haunt her, Kim flushed. Muttering something about a corkscrew and wineglasses, she exited through the dining room door that led to the kitchen.

Vaughn startled her by following. While he opened the wine, Kim set about completing the salad preparations. When next she turned, she found Vaughn using her aunt's pot-holders to remove the lasagna from the oven. "Mmmm. Smells delicious," he said as he turned the oven off.

Within mere minutes he had demonstrated that not only was he quite at home in a kitchen, he enjoyed being there. The man was forever surprising her. But no matter how much she learned about him, she still wasn't prepared to like or trust him. The phrase 'too good to be true' popped into her mind and stuck. That was exactly how she was beginning to feel about him.

He was a bachelor with a gorgeous house and beautifully landscaped yard, all of which he had done himself, according to the local grapevine. Her peek at the interior of his house had revealed that he cooked and cleaned and that he was organized. One would assume from his status as the local sheriff that he was also an honest man. In addition to his obvious artistic talent, the man was handsome enough to turn any woman's head. And, although she'd found him a bit rude at times, he had yet to exhibit the callous disregard for the feelings of others that Kim had expected to find in a man so attractive. So what was the matter with him? He had a bit of a temper. And Kim had the distinct impression that he'd resort to almost anything to get his own way. But there had to be something more. She eyed him suspiciously as he carried the lasagna into the dining room.

After her initial constraint passed, Kim discovered that Vaughn was actually an entertaining conversationalist and their time together was quite pleasant. They spoke of their lives during the last 16 years and how things had changed. Discussion of Kim's happy but short marriage led to questions concerning her childless state, which led to an explanation.

Vaughn watched her closely. "Are you saying that you definitely *can't* have children, or that it's merely unlikely?"

Kim sipped her wine and replaced the glass. "I don't see that there's much of a difference. The doctors say that women with endometriosis are unlikely to conceive. I suppose that means it's not impossible, but I've pretty much decided on adoption as a course of action."

Vaughn nodded and stared thoughtfully at his wineglass for a moment. "If you can keep a secret, I would like to share a confidence with you."

Kim hesitated only a second before raising her right hand. "Word of honor," she said. Curiosity would not allow her to do otherwise.

Vaughn looked at her. His golden eyes suddenly intense and brimming with an emotion she didn't recognize. "I have a son," he said.

Kim was stunned. A dozen questions raced through her mind. Where? Who is his mother? How old is he? But none of them seemed appropriate. Neither was the one that popped out. "How did that happen?"

He stared at her blankly for a second. "I was under the impression, from the tone of our conversation, that you understood the reproductive process," he said dryly.

Kim smiled and waved her hand dismissingly. "You know what I mean." She waited for Vaughn to elaborate. He did. And, for the first time, Kim began to see Vaughn Garrett as a person who could be hurt. Up until this moment, she had seen him only as someone from whom she must guard her own feelings, her own emotions.

"And how do you feel about Doreen now?" She wondered if he would tell her why he'd been called to Doreen's today. That would give her the opening she'd been waiting for to broach the subject of her going home.

Vaughn shrugged. The gesture was an effort at a nonchalant attitude that didn't quite work. "We're friendly, but it was touch and go there for a while. Even though I understood her reasons, I came real close to hating her for what she did." He sighed and raked his fingers through his hair. "Enough about me. What about you?"

Kim sighed. Oh, well, she could wait to discuss Seattle. "What about me? I've already told you my deepest, darkest secret." Now why the hell had she said that? She felt her face begin to burn with the heat of her embarrassment.

"Do you want some help with the dishes?" Bless him for changing the subject, she thought.

"Actually I still have dessert to serve, if you're interested?"

He closed the short distance between their hands on the table. As he covered her hand with his, he gently stroked her wrist with his fingertips. "What's on the menu?" His suggestive expression made her flush deepen in hue.

"Fresh fruit with a cream cheese dip," she answered with decorum. She couldn't help but smile at his exaggerated expression of disappointment.

"Tell you what," he said. "The lasagna was delicious and I'm stuffed, so why don't we save the fruit for later."

"Sounds fine," Kim said as she self-consciously removed her hand from beneath his and began gathering up dishes. "Liz might even be back by then to share it with us."

"Liz?"

"Liz Murphy," Kim said over her shoulder as she

walked into the kitchen. "You know, the psychic. I've invited her to stay here while she's in town."

She had just set the dirty dishes on the counter when Vaughn grasped her arm and turned her to face him. "What did you say?" he asked. His too-smooth voice communicated disapproval. Now what had she done?

CHAPTER 12

"I said, I've invited Liz to stay with me while she's in town," Kim repeated as she frowned up at him.

"And she's supposed to be here soon?"

"She said she'd be here by eleven or so. Why?"

Vaughn stared at her. For an instant, he was annoyed that she had so thoroughly subverted his designs for her seduction. But then Kim couldn't have known of his plans. And he suspected from her behavior over the past week that, had she known, she would have done nothing differently. As he studied her upturned face, he wanted her more than ever. His mind whirled, seeking new possibilities. With sudden clarity, he realized that Liz's presence in the house could actually fit in with his plan quite neatly, and might indeed work to his advantage.

He smiled and looked at the clock. It was 9:40. "Well, we'd better get these dishes done." Kim looked at him suspiciously as though she didn't quite trust his sudden shift in temperament. He turned up the wattage on his smile before going to retrieve the last load of dishes from the dining room. As he set them on the counter, he scanned the kitchen. "Your aunt doesn't have a dishwasher?"

"No," said Kim as she squirted some dish soap into the stream of water pouring into the sink from the tap. "Uncle Jake bought her one once, as an anniversary present. It was one of those portable ones that you roll up to the sink and attach to the taps. But when their marriage broke up, she sold it. She said she'd never had much use for it anyway."

Vaughn found a dish towel hanging from a hook and took the opportunity to study Kim as he waited for her to begin washing the dishes. She removed her rings and set them on the windowsill next to a small prayer plant. Her hands were small with long, elegant fingers. God, she was beautiful. He liked everything about her, from her wild mane of blonde hair to her slim, elegant feet. Suddenly he realized that he'd begun to think in terms of keeping her in his life for a while. When had that happened? That was the last thing he needed!

"What's the matter?" Kim's voice drew him from his reverie.

He met her smoky-eyed gaze and felt his heart trip a beat. Dammit! He didn't want another relationship. Not yet. He was still licking his wounds after the last one. There was no reason they couldn't just be friends. A lover and a friend—that was all he wanted.

"Well?" she said.

"Well, what?" He picked up a plate and began drying it.

"I asked you what was the matter."

"Nothing. Why?"

"You were scowling darkly enough to win a thundercloud competition."

He smiled. "Sorry. Don't worry about it. I was just thinking."

Her eyes searched his face for a moment, and then she nodded. They worked in companionable silence on the dishes. "There. That's about got it, I think," she said as she pulled the plug in the sink and dried her hands. "Thanks for the help."

"Don't mention it. Just a token of my appreciation for a delicious meal."

Kim waved a hand depreciatingly. "I'm just glad it turned out. My cooking doesn't always yield consistent results. Would you like a coffee?"

"No thanks. I think I'd rather wait a while."

"Oh. Well—" Her eyes began scanning the room as though seeking inspiration. She was suddenly stuck for a course of action.

He wasn't. "Kim."

"Yes?" She turned to face him.

"Come here."

She read his expression. "Oh, no." She took a step away from him. "Look! I'm not willing to have that kind of a relationship with you. Or any man for that matter. I thought you would have understood that after the last time."

Vaughn couldn't believe his ears. He hadn't realized that she intended to completely shut off the sexual side of her life. "What are you planning to do? Enter a convent?" he asked incredulously.

"Don't be ridiculous. I lead a full and happy life." She was lying. "I've just decided that it isn't necessary to share that life with a man. I mean, it's not as if I have a lot of luck in that area. I've only loved three men in my entire life: my father, Ken and Trent. And each of them was killed. I'm beginning to think I'm cursed or something. When you add the fact that . . . . that sex is—" She swallowed and flushed as she met his gaze. "Well, let's just say I don't see much reason for pursuing a relationship."

He folded his arms and leaned against the counter. "You don't honestly expect that course of action to work, do you?"

She raised her chin. "I certainly don't see why not?"

"You're a very sensual woman, honey."

She stared at him as though he'd lost his marbles. "Either you have a very short memory, or you're thinking of someone else. And don't call me honey."

"My memory is just fine." He straightened and took a step forward. "Come here, and I'll prove it."

"No!" She fairly yelped the word as she took a series of small steps away from him. Her body would betray her with Vaughn; she had no doubt of that. Because—if things in the sex department were better—she would want nothing more than to be in his arms.

He took another step forward. "What are you afraid of, Kim?"

"Nothing."

"Prove it. Come here."

"No."

"You know I'm right, don't you?" Another step.

"No. I know you're wrong." Her eyes betrayed her unease as she began looking for an avenue of escape. She scrambled another couple of steps out of his reach.

"Chicken," he taunted as he moved forward.

Her lips compressed. She was getting angry. Good! Her back would get ramrod stiff, she'd raise her chin in defiance, and she'd refuse to retreat another step. Which was just what he wanted her to do.

"I think you'd better go." Her tone was as icy as a midwinter day.

"If you're honest with yourself, honey, is that really what you want?" She tensed at the endearment and took root only an arms-reach away, not answering his question. That was telling in itself. He smiled and stood looking down at her. Her delicate shoulders were creamy white against the black spaghetti straps of the top she wore. He placed his hands on them, felt their warmth and softness. A subtle trace of perfume rose to tempt his nostrils. "We have an argument to settle. And I intend to prove you wrong."

Her mouth opened, no doubt to make another flimsy protestation, but before a word could emerge, he swooped. Pulling her into his embrace and covering her lips with his, he plunged his tongue into the soft, warm cavity. She tasted of wine. Her soft throaty sound of objection died almost instantly while the exhalation of her small, quick breaths against his cheek betrayed her burgeoning desire.

And she thought she was frigid!

Kim's sense of equilibrium deserted her. She felt consumed by Vaughn's kiss. The blood pounded in her ears. Her lungs constricted. And the room suddenly seemed much too warm. Instinctively she clutched his broad shoulders, seeking stability. She felt the warmth of his flesh through the thin fabric of his shirt. Felt the muscles in his arms flex as he tightened his embrace. Felt the erotic caress of his hands on her back.

Oh, God. It felt so good to be held this way.

He gently nudged her thighs apart and pressed his own hard masculine thigh against the heated core of her. She moaned as fire ignited deep within her. Maybe it was worth it. Even if she never experienced the satisfying conclusion, at least she could lose herself in this carnal madness for a while. His mouth left hers to trace kisses over her face and neck. She closed her eyes, caught up in the heated vortex of a tropical cyclone.

No! What was she thinking? She'd only be hurt again.

"Vaughn, this isn't a good idea." Even her traitorous body ignored her assertion, spreading languorous heat through her, robbing her limbs of strength. She just hoped Vaughn wouldn't sense it.

But he, too, ignored her words. His hands moved down her back, kneading, massaging. She gasped as he found the soft rounded flesh of her behind and lifted her more firmly onto his muscular thigh. Sparks exploded in her abdomen.

"Vaughn!" She clutched at his muscular shoulders.

"Lift your leg, honey." She heard his words through a fog of sensation, but they didn't make any sense.

"Why?" The word emerged hoarsely through numbed lips.

But even as she waited for an answer, he gripped her left thigh and tugged it forward.

"Vaughn—" He covered her mouth with his as he propped her knee on his hipbone. For a moment the consuming heat of his kiss blocked out everything. Kim felt as though she'd been submerged in a pool of warm, dark water, insulated from the world. And then his fingers pushed aside the leg of her panties and with sudden, stark clarity Kim understood why he had raised her leg. Panic gripped her as his fingers found the soft, warm folds of flesh between her thighs. Alarmed, she jerked her mouth away from the seductive pressure of his. "Vaughn, I don't want this!"

He pressed a finger into the slick moisture of her body, and Kim's eyelids fluttered closed as she tried to hold back the groan that rose in her throat. It was no use.

"Liar," he said softly. "Tell me again that you don't want this?" Vaughn's voice was husky. Kim opened her eyes to look into his and saw raw hunger burning in the golden depths. Everything that was feminine within her responded to that masculine call.

"I hate you," she murmured without heat as his caressing fingers coaxed a renewed onslaught of molten heat from her deceitful body.

He grinned. "I can deal with that."

Suddenly in one last desperate attempt to save herself, Kim pinned him with her gaze and asked, "Why?"

Vaughn discerned the anguish in her eyes and understood her meaning instantly. "Because this time will be different."

"No it won't."

"Trust me."

"I don't think I can."

Instead of responding, he lowered his head to kiss her and lifted her in his arms to carry her from the room. When he reached her bedroom, he stood her next to the bed and lifted the thin camisole-style top over her head. His breath caught in his throat. A strapless, lacy, black bra supported the twin globes of her soft white breasts. Coral-tinted nipples peeked through the thin fabric tantalizingly. With a sigh, he lowered his head to tug at the enticing little buds with his lips and teeth through the bra fabric. Kim made a small squeaking sound deep within her throat.

Her hands began to tug his shirttail out of his waistband, and Vaughn allowed himself to hope that she was beginning to trust him, to trust her own response. He released the button on her skirt, and slid the soft fabric down her hips. He trailed his lips up her neck until he recaptured her mouth and plunged his tongue into the warm recess. As his shirt joined Kim's clothing—except the sexy black stockings—in an undignified heap on the floor, Vaughn lifted her once again in his arms to place her on the bed. Then he hastily peeled the last of his clothing away.

He took Kim in his arms, cuddling her against him, just holding her as he trailed his lips gently over her face. Her hands began to explore his body, to caress him, and he reached to halt their progress.

"No," he said simply. "Tonight is for you, honey. Just you. I want you to relax and enjoy it. Okay?"

Vaughn allowed his hands to tenderly explore her body as he considered her, awaiting her answer. Kim was so accustomed to faking her sexual response as soon as she reached a certain plateau in lovemaking that Vaughn wasn't certain she'd be able to control that instinct. He would only observe the indicators that she couldn't fake: dilated pupils, flushed skin and rapid pulse.

She met his gaze, and he read uncertainly there although he wasn't sure of its cause. "Okay?" he prompted again as he softly nibbled her lips with his own.

Finally, she nodded. As though her nod of acquiescence had somehow changed something between them, Kim felt some transformation in Vaughn's manner. He began to trail his lips and fingertips over her body in feather-light caresses, the like of which she'd never before experienced. Almost immediately her flesh began to tingle and ache as it goose-pimpled in reaction to the gentle, almost non-existent stroking that went on and on. He seemed determined to explore every inch of her body with just his fingertips. What was he doing? Her body arched in involuntarily supplication. Oh God, she wanted to caress him. She wanted him to caress her. Real touching. Not this soft brush of his fingers designed to drive her insane.

He trailed his lips gently up her torso and over her breasts. He memorized the shape of her collarbone with his fingertips. He laved her nipple with his tongue and then gently blew on the taut bud. Her breath caught in her throat as pleasure sparked through her like a million fireflies. A soft moan escaped her as the pressure within escalated.

Then, abruptly he grasped her hips in his strong hands to shift her position on the bed and she suddenly felt very small and feminine. Her insides melted at the leashed strength she felt in those fingers. *Finally*, she thought, certain that he would take her then. But he didn't. Once again his fingers stroked her so lightly that, had the fine hair on her body not risen in response to his touch, she wondered if she would have felt it at all. Tension and frustration mingled in equal measure within her.

He continued caressing her like that. Kim barely recognized the animalistic sounds emerging from her throat. Her whole body tingled with need. She had to clench her teeth to keep from begging him to release her from this delicate torture. But that was one thing she could never do. God, would he never stop? The urgency within her was building, and building. And then, she felt it coming.

"No, Kim. Don't tense up, honey. Relax." Kim heard Vaughn's words from a distance as he massaged the muscles in her thighs. "That's a girl. Relax. Picture yourself floating on a soft, white cloud."

Vaughn felt the tension slowly seep from her thigh muscles as she gradually relaxed again. But he noted that, even as she had tensed, she had continued to softly sigh and moan as though nothing was wrong. His suspicions were confirmed. Faking had become so habitual for her that it had become automatic. She mechanically offered what she felt was the expected response. Vaughn didn't want that. He wanted to know that the sounds that came from her were involuntary— a result of the intense feelings she experienced, not a practiced response designed to camouflage something she perceived as a personal inadequacy.

"Shh, honey," he said. "I think I may have just heard Liz come in." In actuality, he hadn't heard a thing. He felt almost guilty for using the ruse. Almost.

"Oh, no." Kim tensed. "I'd forgotten about her." The simple admission did wonders for Vaughn's ego.

"Relax, Kim. As long as we're quiet, she'll never suspect a thing." He gently stroked the tension from her muscles as he looked into her eyes, darker now due to the dilation of her pupils.

And Kim managed, once again, to relax. For a few minutes. Until Vaughn began to trail feather-light kisses over her stomach and hipbones and she realized exactly where his mouth was heading. Although she was 28 years old, she had ceased being sexually adventurous at the age of 16. Now, shock and fear of the unknown battled with her the awareness of her agreement to relax and enjoy. Fear won. "No!" she exclaimed as quietly as possible.

He raised his head to look at her. "What's the matter?"

"Don't do that."

He frowned. "Do what?"

Kim flushed. "Kiss me. . . there." She let her eyes indicate just where *there* was.

To her surprise, he seemed genuinely puzzled. "Why?"

"I don't like it."

"Have you ever been kissed there before?"

Kim hesitated. Damn him! Why did he always pursue a subject to an unconditional conclusion? She decided against a direct answer. "I don't like it."

"But I do." He began to kiss her stomach again.

"Vaughn!"

"Forget about me, Kim," he ordered in a low voice against her abdomen. "Think about the cloud."

She tried. She really did. But when the heat of his mouth touched her, when she felt him begin to kiss her as deeply *there* as he had kissed her mouth, her thigh muscles tensed and she experienced the beginning of the withdrawal that haunted her.

"The cloud, Kim," Vaughn's husky voice reminded her. "Feel the sun warming your skin. Relax." And once again, with infinite patience, he began to massage the tension from her thigh muscles. But this time he didn't stop what he was doing with his mouth. And that other pressure continued to build within her until she thought she would explode. It kept trying to draw her back from the imaginary cloud. Her breath came in small gasps. Tiny involuntary animalistic noises escaped her throat despite her best efforts to suppress them. As Vaughn inserted a finger into her body to supplement the tender torture he was performing with his mouth, the tremendous pressure within her suddenly reached its zenith.

Wave after wave of incredible, indescribable pleasure rocked her. Now, Vaughn slid his body up hers in one long, intimate caress. She reached for him, hugged him to her, the only stability in a world suddenly reeling in a tropical storm. Heat exploded over her. Sound, like an ocean tide, roared and pulsed in her ears.

Slowly, she opened her eyes to stare at him uncomprehendingly. He was smiling at her. "Well, honey. How did it feel?"

"Jesus!" Kim breathed as she managed to find her voice.

He laughed and hugged her to him. "I'll take that to mean that you've finally discovered what all the fuss is about."

She nodded against his chest as lethargy gripped her. And then she realized that he was still huge and hard against her thigh. He hadn't even entered her. And she was so replete with pleasure, so satiated, that all she wanted to do was sleep.

But gradually, as his knowledgeable hands stroked her body, all thoughts of sleep faded into oblivion. Once again he drew her inexorably toward the heights of passion. And this time as he slid his body over hers she was eager for his possession. She wrapped her arms around his neck as he reared up over her, entering her in one long, powerful thrust. There was a brief flash of discomfort as the newly contracted muscles stretched to accommodate him, and then there was only pleasure. A pleasure so unique, so beautiful, that Kim knew she never wanted it to escape her again. She stroked Vaughn's body with her hands, seeking to know him as only a lover can.

Vaughn closed his eyes as enjoyment so exquisite it was almost painful shook him to his core. Kim's body held him within its soft sheath as though she had been made exclusively for him. Need burned in his chest, unfamiliar and barely recognized. The primal need to brand her with his body, to wipe out the memory of every man who had ever touched her, to make her his and his alone. And then, as he began to move within her, everything ceased to exist but the woman beneath him, and the pleasure.

* * *

Kim stirred and opened her eyes to a room still

black with night. She frowned into the pitch-darkness, wondering what had awakened her. And then, as sleep retreated even further, she remembered that, on this night, she had not been sleeping alone. Slowly, she reached across the bed to establish contact with Vaughn. He wasn't there. Perhaps it was his rising that had awakened her.

Where had he gone? She knew he would not have left because, after their lovemaking, he had dressed and gone out to inform the deputy that he would be spending the night. Kim flushed at the memory. She had asked him not to so blatantly announce their affair to his men, but he had seen no way around it. The sheriff's office was drastically understaffed at the moment and he didn't want to leave a man sitting outside watching the house unnecessarily.

Suddenly Kim heard a sound. Half moan, half mutter, it seemed to come from the corner of her room. Perplexed, she slid across the bed until she could reach the lamp. As the faint illumination of the 15 watt night light dispelled the darkness, she saw Vaughn huddled on the floor near the door. He wore only his shorts. His knees were drawn up to his chest, his arms wrapped around them. Fear or panic shone from his unfocused eyes.

Kim realized that, still in the grip of a nightmare, he was, in fact, sleepwalking. But she didn't know what to do about it. Having never encountered anyone who suffered from the affliction, she knew little about it. She remembered hearing that it was extremely dangerous to wake somebody too suddenly because they could go into shock. Whether that had even a shred of truth to it, she didn't know. She gnawed her bottom lip indecisively. What should she do?

"Vaughn. Wake up." She called the words softly, not wanting to startle him, but the reaction was instantaneous and fierce.

"Stay away from me, you bitch!" He roared the

words so loudly that Kim felt certain that, had there been any close neighbors, the entire block would have been roused from their sleep.

Although not really frightened, Kim was neverthe-less unnerved and cautious. Slowly, she rose from the bed and slipped her nightshirt on. His head didn't even turn toward her. His gaze remained fixed at some point higher and to her right.

"Kim?" It was Liz's voice calling to her from the other side of her bedroom door. "Kim, is something wrong?"

Vaughn didn't seem to hear her.

Slowly, Kim moved toward the door and opened it enough to allow Liz to enter. Too concerned to be in the least embarrassed, she indicated Vaughn's position behind the door. "He's sleepwalking, I think."

Liz frowned as she looked at him. "Vaughn?"

The response to her calling his name was once again instantaneous. "Keep your fucking hands off me," he shouted. His eyes were wild and his arms swung violently as though warding off unwanted handling. "Don't you *ever* touch me. I'll kill you. I swear I'll kill you."

"Kim, do you have an alarm clock?"

"Yes." She walked to the dresser and picked up an old Big Ben wind-up clock. "Right here."

"Good." Liz took it from her and began turning the hands.

"What are you going to do?"

"What I used to do with my son when he had a nightmare that didn't seem to want to let him go. Set the alarm off and call him for school. It always worked like a charm."

Even as she finished speaking, the alarm began to blare discordantly in the small bedroom. She waited a moment until the fear began to fade from Vaughn's eyes as the piercing sound began to loosen the grip of the nightmare, and then shut it off. "Vaughn, it's time to wake up, dear." Kim marveled that she could call to him so calmly in exactly the same tone that her mother had always used to call her for school. Did all mothers sound the same? she wondered.

Vaughn blinked.

"I think I'll leave him to you now, dear," Liz whispered as she backed from the room. "I don't want to embarrass him unnecessarily. I'll go downstairs and make some hot cocoa for us all."

Kim nodded, her attention already focused on Vaughn. "Sure. Thanks." She knelt on the floor in front of him, her hand on his shoulder. "Vaughn? Are you all right?"

He blinked, focused on her face, and then slowly looked about the room. His eyes revealed the instant that cognizance returned. Even in the dim light Kim saw his features darken with embarrassment. He ignored her hand on his shoulder as he pushed himself up off the floor and stepped away from her.

"Are you all right?" she asked again.

"Yeah." His tone was gruff. "I'm fine." He looked around the room once more and laughed, but the sound was harsh; it held no mirth. "One hell of a protector I turned out to be, huh?"

Kim shrugged. "Well, as it turned out, I didn't need a protector. Liz is making us some hot chocolate. Do you want a cup?"

Vaughn grimaced as he began pulling his pants on. "Shit! I woke her up, too?"

Kim nodded without comment.

He straightened and looked solemnly at her. "I'm sorry you had to see. . . that." He waved in the general direction of the corner where he had huddled. "I hope I didn't frighten you."

Kim shook her head, waving off his apology. "Forget it. You didn't frighten me. And you don't have to apologize for something that you had no conscious control over." She opened the bedroom door. "C'mon."

The grandfather clock in the hall chimed the half hour as she stepped into the corridor. It was 1:30.

* * *

When they arrived at the kitchen, Liz was just dropping some miniature marshmallows onto the tops of three steaming mugs of hot chocolate. She wore a pink chenille bathrobe and fluffy slippers to match. Her face was devoid of make-up and her thick black hair was tousled. Without her cosmetics and flamboyant clothing, she looked motherly. And yet, for the first time, Vaughn could almost acknowledge her *psychic*ness, if there was such a thing. It was in the way she looked at him. Her golden hazel eyes seemed to look both at him and through him as he entered the room. Her eye color was in fact quite similar to his own, perhaps a trifle more greenish gold. Funny that he'd never noticed that before. Perhaps her eye shadow had somehow camouflaged it.

"Sit down," she said softly. Although the words seemed to be directed at both Kim and Vaughn, her gaze continued to cling intently to Vaughn. What the hell was the matter with her?

Trying to ignore the strangely intense expression in her eyes, he tore his gaze away from hers and pulled out a chair for Kim at the table. When he'd seated himself, Liz placed a mug before each of them and then took a seat on the opposite side of the table.

"Vaughn—" she said. Her tone, her expression, even her manner was hesitant. Yet her eyes continued to cling to his face. She took a sip from her mug and suddenly avoided his eyes.

"Yes," he prompted.

She swallowed. "The people who died in the car accident, orphaning you, were not your biological parents."

Vaughn jumped as though he'd been stung. The statement, coming out of the blue like that, left him momentarily unable to complete a coherent response.

Kim looked at him with a puzzled expression. Conflicting emotions ricocheted through him. Anger was the one that took root. The thought of people prying into his background, digging out the details of his existence as though they had to right to dissect his life, infuriated him. "How the hell did you know that? Nobody knows that."

Liz ran the polished nails of her fingers up and down the surface of her mug. "I know. . . because you are my son."

CHAPTER 13

"Bullshit!"

His eyes were hard as he looked at her, but Liz knew that she had to get him to listen to her tonight or he would fade out of her life forever. She wondered if that mightn't be kinder in the long run. But she couldn't do it.

"No! It's the truth. Will you hear me out? Please?" Liz heard the pleading tone in her voice and didn't care. She had been robbed of so much already, what was a little pride. "Please?" she repeated.

Vaughn's eyes were still hard, his expression unyielding. His gaze flicked briefly to Kim before he responded. "I'll listen," he said. "I've got nothing better to do anyway. But I'm not making any other promises."

"Fair enough." Even though she felt like she was on the verge of tears, Liz looked at Kim and smiled. "You don't mind listening, do you, dear?"

Kim shook her head. "Of course not." Truth be told, she probably would have fought tooth and nail had anyone asked her to leave the room.

Liz switched her gaze back to Vaughn. "It's a long story, and it begins years ago, when I was fifteen.

She focused her eyes on the black night beyond the

kitchen window. "I lived with my parents and my maternal grandmother on a small farm in Montana. My father was a deeply religious man, fanatical by today's standards. My mother was a quiet woman who bowed to his wishes in almost all aspects of their lives. Yet they seemed to truly love each other. He was never cruel to her. And, on the rare occasions when she asked for something, he almost always granted her wishes.

"My grandmother was a spritely, incorrigible, old woman who was the life of the family. She was the one who refused to allow us to take ourselves too seriously." Liz smiled at the memory. "My father was always castigating her for her blasphemous tongue. She invariably responded in the same way. 'The good Lord gave me a mind and a mouth for a purpose, Cyrus. And I'll keep speaking my mind until he tells me different.' " Liz shook her head. "Sometimes she'd so enrage my father that I thought he'd drop dead of apoplexy.

"Anyway, my entire world revolved around my family. We saw very few outsiders except at Sunday services, and we always returned home immediately afterwards. I was allowed to attend school, of course, but never to socialize.

"I was fifteen the summer that Richard Worth entered our lives. He came by the farm asking if he could do some work in exchange for a meal. My father, ever one to respect the value of a hard day's work, hired him. Richard ended up staying with us for most of the summer." Liz swallowed and looked briefly at Kim before switching her gaze to Vaughn. "Lord, this is going to be more difficult than I had imagined after all these years."

Kim smiled and got up to refill the electric kettle and plug it in. "Take your time. There's plenty of chocolate, and I'm getting downright accustomed to going to bed at sunrise."

As Kim resumed her seat, Liz continued. "Richard was the first young man I'd ever had any real, prolonged contact with. He was kind and attentive. And very handsome, with a head of thick tawny hair and hazel eyes. Within days, I began to imagine myself in love with him. When he first noticed my infatuation, I think it merely amused him. But as time passed, his attitude began to change. Before three weeks had gone by, he had seduced me. In his defense, I have to say that he probably didn't find the task too difficult. Despite my religious upbringing and fear of my father's wrath, I was completely and totally enamored." She paused to sip from her mug. "By the end of the summer, when he was supposed to leave, it had become obvious to both of us that I was pregnant."

Kim rose to unplug the whistling kettle and Liz paused to finish off her hot chocolate. After handing her empty cup to Kim, she resumed. "I was absolutely terrified, of course. My father had an extremely volatile temperament when something displeased him.

"But Richard said everything would be all right. He would leave the farm, but he would get a job in town. As soon as he had a job, he'd get a place for us to live, and I could join him. I seemed like the only solution, so I agreed."

Liz looked at Vaughn, but could not yet perceive any softening in his expression. "Richard was true to his word. Within six weeks, just as my pregnancy was beginning to show a little, he came for me." Liz closed her eyes as the pain of that time came back to haunt her. Her mother's tears. The hurt in her father's eyes when she told him the truth. And his horrible, hateful words. *'You are Satan's child now. I have no daughter. You are no longer welcome here.'*

Then, opening her eyes, she squared her shoulders and continued. "Richard and I moved into a small apartment in town. I felt as though I'd entered another world. I'd never been away from home before. I wasn't even certain what to do. But within a couple of weeks, I managed to stop feeling so unanchored. Richard and I settled into life together. We talked of marriage often, but somehow we just never got around to it. And because we lived in sin, as our good, God-fearing neighbors called it, there weren't that many people who would socialize with us—although I believe that the ladies of the town were more cruel to me than the men were to Richard. Anyway, we spent most of our time together, and basically we were happy.

"Six months later, Danny was born." Liz felt tears sting her eyes as she remembered the birth of her first child. She smiled. "He was a big boy, almost eight pounds, and healthy with a lusty squall that could be heard in the next apartment. He had his father's dark, gold hair." She blinked back the tears that threatened to spill and took the fresh cup of hot cocoa that Kim handed her. "But he had my eyes," she said with a smile. "We lived reasonably happily as a family for two years.

"Then, one day Richard came home early. He'd lost his job. Every day for a week, he got up in the morning and went out looking for work. On the last day, he never came home." Liz fell silent for a moment, assailed by memories of her youth and naiveté, and the sense of helplessness that had followed Richard's abandonment. At first, she'd tried to convince herself that he had simply ranged too far afield in his hunt for work to make it back. Then, the next day, when she discovered that he'd taken most of his clothing and half of their small hoard of cash, she'd faced the truth.

"Even though I knew he'd abandoned us, I continued to hope that he'd come back. For the next week, all that I bought with the little bit of money I had was milk for Danny. We lived on oatmeal porridge. Finally, when both the money and the food were almost gone, I realized I was going to have to do something.

"I knew I couldn't go home, so I had to find work. But first I had to find someone willing to care for Danny." She sighed. "I was soon to discover that it would not be an easy task in that isolated and close-knit religious community. Danny was a bastard. Although times had changed and a sexual revolution had swept most of the world, none of it had touched the devout citizens of Rock Springs. In those days, people there still didn't want much to do with illegitimate children. They certainly didn't want their own children playing with one. So in the end, the only woman I could find to care for Danny was another woman who herself lived on the fringes of the town." Liz frowned thoughtfully. "I never did find out why the ladies disliked her so." She shook her head. "Anyway, old Mrs. Ramsey was a brusque woman who spoke her mind even more plainly than my grandmother." Liz looked at Kim. "Your Aunt Willie reminds me of her a great deal.

"Mrs. Ramsey agreed to care for Danny while I looked for work. Unfortunately that, too, proved more difficult than I had imagined. An entire week passed, and still I hadn't found anyone willing to hire me. I was out of money. If Mrs. Ramsey hadn't been feeding Danny, I don't know what I might have done. Perhaps I would have swallowed my pride and begged for help from somewhere. But my pride was all I had, and as long as Danny was being cared for, I refused to abase myself to people I was beginning to despise."

Liz stared at the darkness beyond the kitchen window without seeing anything. Mrs. Ramsey had known the straits she was in and, unbeknownst to Liz, had taken it upon herself to walk out to the farm and castigate Liz's parents for their attitude. Liz had later learned from Granny that Mrs. Ramsey had repeatedly quoted the scriptures at them. "Nehemiah 9:17," she had said. "Thou art a God ready to pardon, gracious and merciful, slow to anger, and of great kindness." Liz remembered Granny's laughter as she recounted the story to Liz. "The Bible teaches forgiveness and tolerance, Cyrus, not self-righteousness," old Mrs. Ramsey had said. Somehow, the old woman's words must have gotten through to Liz's father, because the next day, he and her mother had come to town.

"My parents surprised me by coming to town to take me and Danny home with them," Liz said in a soft voice. "I wasn't fool enough to believe that all had been forgiven, but I thought that perhaps we would be able to come to some sort of understanding. Danny was their grandchild.

"Unfortunately, I was a fool," Liz heard the bitterness in her voice, even after all these years, but there was nothing she could do about it. "It was a mistake that I was destined to pay for dearly.

"Although Granny fell in love with Danny immediately, my parents would have nothing to do with him. I was home a month and a half before my mother agreed to watch Danny. At the time, I took it as a sign that she was finally beginning to accept him." Liz swallowed and closed her eyes. She had been so wrong!

"Danny was a little more than two years old. I had gone upstairs to do some cleaning while my mother watched him. I heard the screen door slam like it did a hundred times a day, but for some reason it sounded different—ominous. I remember feeling my arms chill. I knew I had to get downstairs. I went to the door and turned the handle." Liz swallowed. "The door wouldn't open. I had been locked in my room."

Liz felt again the icy fear that had charged through her like an electrical current. Moving quickly to the bedroom window, she had narrowed her eyes against the brilliant summer sunshine and looked down in the weed-grown driveway. She had seen her father with Danny in his arms, standing in the center of the drive with foot-high dandelions dancing gaily in the breeze. And yet, the day had turned suddenly dark, shadowed by a young mother's instinctive terror.

"I saw father carrying Danny to his truck." She could still see the battered, old, red pickup. She remembered how, with sudden gripping certainty, she had known what he was doing.

"My chubby little baby boy was screaming his lungs out. He had spotted me in the upstairs window, and his little arms were outstretched toward me. He called Mama in one long endless litany." Liz was unaware that the tears she had been fighting since she'd began the story now tracked freely down her cheeks.

She remembered how she had fumbled desperately with the latch so that she could raise the window. Her father had already placed Danny on the seat of the truck and was just getting in himself, when it finally slid up. She had barely been able to see through the tears that fogged her vision as she begged her father to reconsider. "Papa, please. Please don't do this. He's my son—your grandson. I'll take him away. Please, Papa." She had said that and more—much of which she couldn't remember now—in an attempt to sway her father. She remembered the hope that had flared briefly in her heart as her father paused and looked up at her. But his only response had been, "The child is the work of the devil."

"That was the last time I ever heard my son's voice. I never did discover what my father did with him. He refused to tell me. And although I begged my mother to tell me, I finally came to believe that she was telling the truth when she said she didn't know. Six weeks later, Granny and I left. I never saw my parents again. I was never able to forgive my father for what he did, nor my mother for allowing him to do it.

"Granny and I moved to the city where I could get work, and we began looking for Danny. As weeks turned into months and then into years, I never gave up hope that someday I'd find him. But no matter how much heartache we feel, life goes on. Eventually I married and had two more children, David and Caroline. From the beginning, I raised them with the awareness that somewhere out there, they had a brother. Still, after all these years, I had almost given up hope."

Liz looked at Vaughn. "I *know* you are my son. I

know because every time I see you I see another aspect of you that reminds me of your father. I know because you have my eyes. And I know in here." She tapped her chest. "Whether you can accept that or not is up to you. I have no way to prove it to you, although I suppose there are medical tests that could do that. I'd be willing to take a test if you like."

Vaughn swallowed and rose to walk across the room and stare blindly through the window of the back door. His anger was gone. In its place was a distinctly uncomfortable awareness. Liz had described in perfect detail one of his own recurring nightmares. He had only to close his eyes to see it again as he had dreamed it so many times over the years. The white-faced woman in the upper window of the old house. His own hands reaching for her, knowing he had to hang on to her. The face fading into oblivion. And his own sense of unparalleled fear, desperation and isolation.

That awareness left him with only one of two possible conclusions. Either she really was psychic and had somehow plucked the dream from his mind. Or she was his mother. He wasn't comfortable with either deduction. He was extremely uneasy about acknowledging the existence of the mystical. All in all, he was a hell of a lot more comfortable with the idea that Liz Murphy was his biological mother. Though what the hell he was going to do with her now that he had her, he didn't know. Getting to know her a little better would be the first thing. Then. . . what? Visit her on Sundays? That seemed to be what most men his age did with their mothers.

"Vaughn?" It was Kim's voice.

"Yeah?" He didn't turn around. Not yet. He needed a cigarette more right now than he had at any other time since he'd begun trying to quit smoking. But he wasn't wearing his shirt and his tinder-dry, week-old cigarettes didn't hold enough allure to make him go upstairs to get them.

There was a brief silence. "Would you like another cup of chocolate?"

"I think I'd prefer something a little stronger if you have it?" Why tonight? he wondered suddenly. What had happened tonight that had prompted Liz's sudden revelation? Slowly he turned. Kim was looking through her aunt's liquor cabinet. Vaughn studied Liz curiously.

"You've got a choice of beer, Scotch, or dark rum." Kim's voice distracted him briefly.

"Scotch, please." He spoke almost absently as his mind continued to seek possible reasons for Liz's sudden certainty. He couldn't find any.

"On the rocks, with water, or with a soda?"

He glanced at Kim. "With water, if you don't mind." He heard her begin mixing drinks as he shifted his eyes back to Liz. "Why tonight, Liz? What suddenly made you so certain that I was your son?"

Liz met his gaze. She'd wiped the tears from her cheeks, but her eyes were still rimmed with red. "Your nightmare," she answered simply.

Vaughn frowned. "I don't understand."

She hesitated. "It's nothing really. And it doesn't mean much until you add it to all the other little things I've already mentioned." She didn't seem to want to elaborate, but Vaughn simply waited and watched her expectantly. He'd learned long ago that people often said more than they planned if you didn't jump into every stretch of silence. Finally, Liz sighed. "You won't like the explanation."

"Try me."

Liz took a deep breath. "Nightmares run in my family. Particularly among the men who seem to have a harder time learning to accept the hunches they receive from their subconscious mind. The nightmares appear to be a result of the subconscious mind trying to force communication. My son, David, suffered the same affliction until he learned to accept and use his intuition, or sixth sense, if you will."

She had spoken so quickly that it took Vaughn a second to interpret her meaning. When he did, he thought he must have heard incorrectly. "Pardon me?" he asked incredulously.

"Look," Liz said. "You're a cop. As a cop you must have had occasion to do things based on hunches. Am I right?"

"Yeah," Vaughn allowed, wondering if he'd just stepped into something he shouldn't have.

"Well, all I'm saying is that your hunches or cop sense or sixth sense, or whatever you want to call it can be a lot more reliable if you accept it and learn to use it. I can help you do that."

"You're trying to tell me that I'm psychic!" Vaughn concluded incredulously. "Oh, that's funny." He took the glass of Scotch that Kim handed him, saw the censure in her eyes and avoided meeting her gaze again. What the hell did she want him to do? Accept everything and anything Liz wanted to tell him at face value?

"No. It's not funny." Liz's voice was calm, but for the first time since meeting her, Vaughn sensed anger in her. "And I'm not saying you're psychic." She met his gaze unflinchingly. "For the last six generations when psychics were born among my Irish ancestors they were always women. But many of the men of my family have had a heightened sense of awareness, of intuition.

"Have you ever been faced with a decision and felt a tightness in your chest, or a little tickle in your mind that made you feel uncomfortable? Have you ever ignored that warning and gone ahead with something and then wished you hadn't?"

Vaughn stared at her. He wished he could laugh off her statement again, but he couldn't. "Yes," he finally said, then frowned. "But I'm sure that's common for a lot of people. And what does that have to do with nightmares?"

"When you either can't or don't acknowledge

repeated warnings from your subconscious mind, it begins to seek other avenues of communication. At least that's the explanation that David and I came up with, and it seems to fit."

"So you're saying that my subconscious mind is trying to tell me something, and because I haven't been listening, it's trying to communicate through my dreams?"

"Basically, yes." Liz nodded.

Vaughn shook his head. "It doesn't wash."

"Why?"

"Because the dream I had tonight was a recurring nightmare that I've had since I was a kid."

"Can you tell me about it?"

Vaughn stared at her for a moment. The woman didn't know what she was asking. He shook his head. "It's not something I talk about."

"Well, perhaps it's not necessary. You see, Vaughn, it is possible for a person to always have a particular dream or nightmare when they feel a certain way. One woman I knew always dreamed of taking a trip in a hot-air balloon when she felt the pressures of life closing in on her. She didn't understand the dream's significance, however, and ignored it. Within two years, she suffered a heart attack. Fortunately, she survived. Eventually, she realized that her dream was a message delivered by her subconscious mind to warn her to slow down.

"So," Liz continued, "a dream can be representative of a certain feeling. It might be warning you of something that induces the same feeling. Do you follow me?"

Vaughn nodded. What she said made sense—a lot of sense actually. As a child, this particular dream he'd had tonight had always warned him of impending danger, and the sleepwalking that had accompanied it had removed him from that danger. The dream had recurred a number of times in the last few weeks—since finding the clipping concerning Candace's murder on his table. Still, the fact that nightmares in one form or another warned him of danger every goddamn night didn't do a whole hell of a lot of good when he didn't know from where the peril would come.

* * *

Only a week earlier, Vaughn would have barely acknowledged the little tickle in his mind, ignoring it—as he had many times in the past—because he would not have understood its significance. He felt it the instant that Doreen told him she was leaving town for a while. She planned on leaving Landon with Aunt Willie while she went on a week-long shopping trip in Chelan.

On the surface, Vaughn didn't see anything wrong with her plan. It would put her out of harm's way, wouldn't it? Landon would be safe with Aunt Willie. And there would be less strain on the sheriff's office. But something told him differently.

The late-morning sun haloed her hair as they stood on her front porch facing each other. Vaughn was just about to attempt another argument when Deputy Lewis interrupted them. "Excuse me, ma'am," he said to Doreen. "I was just wondering if I might use your washroom before I leave."

"Of course," she said with a smile.

As Vaughn waited for the door to close behind Lewis, he looked around and tried to figure out just what to do about his unease. Landon, already strapped into his safety seat in the car, watched with wide, curious eyes as he waited for his mother. A flatbed truck stacked with lumber sat in the driveway next door. Mike Drayton and Ron Obrich were unloading it and carrying it toward the rear of the Obrich property. Vaughn heard the loud clap of lumber against lumber as they stacked it somewhere out of sight. It seemed Ron was planning to take advantage of the nice weather to do some building.

"Look," Vaughn said finally. "I don't think that your leaving town right now is such a good idea. Why don't both you and Landon stay with Aunt Willie for a while?"

"What good would that do?" Doreen wanted to know. "The danger is in town. Anywhere in town." She paused and looked up into his face. "Besides I really need to get away from this place for a while, see some of my friends in Chelan who think I've forgotten them. It will probably be the only holiday I get before the school season starts again." Picking up the case that contained Landon's things, she descended the stairs.

Vaughn moved to block her path. "You're sure there's nothing I can say to make you change your mind?" He took the baby's heavy case from her.

"Nothing. Look, I really don't understand what you think you have to worry about. Landon and I will be spending the morning with Aunt Willie. I'll be making the trip to Chelan in broad daylight this afternoon. Once there, I'll be staying with friends. What could possibly happen?"

"I don't know," Vaughn was forced to admit. "Maybe nothing." As Doreen stepped around him and began walking to the car, he walked with her. He deposited the case in the back seat. "Where's your luggage?" he asked, suddenly realizing he'd seen no evidence of it.

"In the trunk," Doreen responded. "Actually I, uh, packed during the night." There was a wealth of meaning behind the hesitant admission. She had been afraid. She hadn't slept. The admission, even so indirectly made, would not have come easily. It was her way of explaining her determination to leave.

She walked around the car to the driver's side. Vaughn extended his hand through the open passenger-side window to stroke Landon's cheek. "How you doin', big fellow?"

The baby bounced excitedly in his seat and responded with a phrase that sounded like, "Doe An Wiwwie fo nicnic."

Vaughn looked at Doreen inquiringly.

"He means we're going to Aunt Willie's for a picnic."

"Oh." Vaughn looked again at his son. God, he wished he could spend more time with him. He smiled tenderly. "You have a good time then." He ruffled the little boy's thick black hair. Hair that Vaughn now realized he'd inherited from his grandmother.

"Doe! Doe! Doe!" Landon bounced determinedly, as though by will alone he could get the car moving.

Vaughn smiled. "I think you'd better get this demanding little cuss over to Willie's."

Doreen nodded. "Lock up for me, will you?" she tossed him a house key.

Vaughn nodded. "Sure."

Doreen settled herself behind the wheel. She must have seen the concern still reflected in his eyes as he bent to observe her through the side window. "Don't worry." She started the engine. "I'll be back within a week. Catch him before then, okay?"

"Sure thing." The tickle in his mind grew stronger as he watched Doreen's small black Corolla turn the corner. He clenched his fists at his sides. Damn Liz for making him more aware of it. It wasn't specific enough to do him any good. All he could do was hope that it was wrong.

* * *

He smiled to himself as he fit the key in the door. It was time to adjust his schedule again. Providence had decreed that he overhear Doreen's conversation with Vaughn, and now he must act. He stepped into the cool, shadowy interior. Drapes pulled closed over the windows kept it that way. Just the way he liked it. Without turning a light on, he walked unerringly into the kitchen and opened the pantry door. Slowly he moved things around until he accessed the large canister at the rear. Pulling it out, he opened the lid and removed a black leather bag. Taking it to the table, he opened it and checked its contents.

Methodically he removed each of the items and laid them out in order. Rubber gloves, surgical gloves and condoms to the right. Hair net, scissors, battery-operated barber's shears to the left. He removed the quarter inch nylon rope and unraveled it consideringly. Fifteen feet or so. Sufficient.

He went into his bedroom and removed a pair of white disposable coveralls and shoe protectors from his closet. He'd initially seen them worn by auto body mechanics in Seattle over a year ago and had realized instantly how perfect they were for his task. He didn't bother to count the stack remaining. He knew there were exactly seven pairs. Taking the coveralls back to the table, he set them beside the rope and considered his preparations.

Although he hadn't planned on delivering Doreen's punishment for another few days, the only harm done was that he hadn't had time to write an original piece of work to accompany her. He frowned in annoyance. He hated borrowing so heavily from the past masters. But, after consulting his watch, he realized there was no help for it. He couldn't take a chance on missing her.

Going to the computer he had set up in one corner of the living room, he turned it on. Wincing at the bright illumination from the monitor, he adjusted the screen and hastily accessed his word processing program. What to write? His mind traversed through the years, back to the time when he had first realized that Doreen was like all the others.

There had been a school dance. He had gone, even though he had known full well that he would not dance. Standing in the shadow of an enormous old tree, he had smoked cigarettes and watched the comings and goings of the other students. Some escaped the vigil of the chaperons, sneaking into the back seats of cars to neck.

It was a warm night. After the dance had been in

progress for a couple of hours, they opened the gymnasium doors and some of the dancing students spilled out onto the grounds. Adolescent excitement permeated the air like a perfume as young men and young women trifled with the seductive danger of flirtation. He stood on the fringes, watching, learning, too self-conscious to join in.

Suddenly he saw Doreen Hanson break away from the crowd and wander in his direction. He knew that she couldn't see him huddled in the shadow of the tree in the darkness. He watched her. Even in the shabby dress that she wore, she was a pretty girl. He knew the Hanson's were poor—just like he was. And although she'd never been friendly, Doreen had never looked down her nose at him like the other students had.

He watched her take a seat in the grass just a few feet in front of him. She swore and began to tear the grass near her, throwing it away with abrupt, vicious motions. Her anger didn't bother him. It was one of the few emotions he understood. He wondered what it would be like to kiss her. A small, fragile blossom of hope flared in his chest. Had he finally found a girl who could relate to him? Understand him? He continued to watch her for a while until her anger began to fade and she calmed. Then, slowly, he moved forward to join her.

"Mind if I sit with you?"

She jumped and looked up at him. Her hazel eyes glowed like a cat's in the moonlight. "Suit yourself." She shrugged.

He sat down. "Not enjoying the dance?"

She snorted. "Hardly."

He sat with her in silence for a time, not knowing what to say. He just liked looking at her, being with her. He noticed her casting sidelong glances at him occasionally and wondered what she was thinking. Suddenly she grabbed his hand and pulled him to his feet.

"Come on," she said, drawing him back into the darkness beneath the big, old tree. Propping her back against the truck of the tree, she grasped both his hands and looked up into his face. He could see moisture glistening in her eyes. "Kiss me," she ordered.

He couldn't believe his luck. Slowly, hesitantly, afraid to break the spell, he stepped closer and pulled her into his embrace. She felt so good, so soft. He touched his lips irresolutely to hers. But Doreen was not in the mood for uncertainty. Threading her fingers into his hair, she had pressed her lips firmly to his and urged him with her tongue to part his lips. The sensation that had rocketed through him as she'd pressed her soft, curvaceous body to his left him trembling and rock hard. He crushed her to him, letting her feel his need. And then—

"Doreen, where the hell are you?" a drunken voice shouted from the half-circle drive in front of the school. It was one of Doreen's brothers.

Doreen broke away from him guiltily and looked off in the direction of the school and the light. "Oh, Lord, I'm going to catch hell. I have to go. They told me to be waiting."

"Doreen," her brother bellowed again.

He followed her gaze to the rickety old farm truck parked not far away. He wanted to scream in frustration. "Don't go. Stay with me."

She looked at him incredulously and snorted a laugh. "Stay with you? How can I? They'll kill me."

"Why did you kiss me if you knew you were leaving soon?" he demanded, letting anger push frustrated desire to the back of his mind.

She shrugged as she backed away a couple of steps. "I don't know. I just wanted to see what it was like, I guess." She turned away. "See you," she said over her shoulder.

Grabbing her arm, he stopped her. "Can I see you again?" he asked.

She laughed without mirth and jabbed a thumb over her shoulder at the waiting truck. "You've got to be kidding."

Struck by the coldness of her response, he had allowed his hands to drop to his sides. His fingers curled into fists as he watched her walk away and get into the truck with her drunken brother.

Now, shaking his head, he emerged from the past. Hastily, from memory, he typed a few words from a poem by Sir Robert Ayton that he thought relatively well suited to Doreen.

I loved thee once; I'll love no more ----
Thine be the grief as is the blame;
Thou art not what thou wast before,

Then, for good measure he added a Shakespearean line:
Most friendship is feigning, most loving mere folly

And an original verse:
And more folly yet is thine
For daring to malign
The Lord of Death; he cometh
And to his hand thine will succumbeth

He considered what he had written with critical eyes. It was no masterpiece, nothing to be remembered in the annals of timeless literature, but it would have to do. With a quick click of the mouse, he sent it to the printer. He must hurry.

CHAPTER 14

A couple of days later, Vaughn was just leaving the mayor's office after a brief meeting with Steve Riley when Melissa called his cell phone. "Sheriff, Tyler McCurdy and Vincent Welsh just stopped by the office to report an abandoned vehicle a mile or so out of town." Her tone was strangely solemn.

Vaughn felt a strange tightening sensation in his chest. Tyler and Vincent were the same boys who had discovered Trent's body. "You got a make on the vehicle?" he asked.

There was a pause. "According to the boys, it's a black Corolla."

Vaughn closed his eyes and let his head fall back. For a few precious seconds his mind went blank. He couldn't think, didn't have to consider what the communication meant. Then reason intruded. "Where did they find it, Mel?"

"They say they found it in almost exactly the same location where they found Trent's body a few weeks ago."

Vaughn winced. Jesus!

"Cheney and Special Agent Stone are on their way out there now," Melissa added.

"Okay, Mel. I'm on my way."

When Vaughn arrived at the scene, Cheney had already strung out yellow tape to keep people out of the immediate area until they'd completed their investigation. He obviously expected the worst. Vaughn's eyes sought out the vehicle partially concealed by brush in a small depression at the edge of the road. Was it Doreen's? He noticed Stone taking pictures, making notations in a notepad and studying the ground around the vehicle with meticulous concentration. Vaughn wanted nothing more than to go and bury his head in the sand. Instead, he forced himself to get out of the Bronco. Ray met him within a few steps.

"The car is Doreen Hanson's, Vaughn. No mistake. It looks like she never made it to Chelan."

Vaughn swallowed and nodded. Why the hell hadn't she listened to him? "Doreen?"

"No sign of her."

Moving carefully through the roped-off area, Vaughn moved to join Stone just as he squatted near the driver's door. "How does it look?" he asked.

"It looks like we might be able to get a fairly good print from this handle," he muttered. Then, looking up, he met Vaughn's gaze and emerged from his cognitive trance enough to realize that Vaughn was speaking in more general terms. "There's a small amount of blood—" he pointed at it with his pen— "here on the steering wheel, so I'd say there was a bit of a struggle. I'll get a type on it and compare it to the type we got from that piece of fabric, but my guess is that they'll be different. I think this blood came from the victim. The keys are still in the ignition." He frowned. "One curious thing though. The stereo has been removed."

"What the hell would he want with the stereo?"

Stone shrugged. "Your guess is as good as mine."

"Have you seen anything to give us a clue as to what direction they went from here?"

Stone shook his head. "Sorry. I haven't been here that long."

Vaughn nodded. "I'll leave you to the car then while I look around."

"Garrett?"

"Yeah," he turned back to face Stone.

"Just for the record, I agree with you about Mike Drayton. I went over to have a talk with him. Something about the guy doesn't feel right. Whether he's our man or not, I don't know. But my instincts tell me to watch him. The problem is, we have nothing on him. Not even circumstantial. I'm making some inquiries."

Vaughn nodded. "Thanks." Then he returned to the task at hand. Standing back, he considered the density of the forest. It was thick here. Enormous ferns and leafy brush could hide a lot. But he didn't want to drag too many people into this. Not yet. Not until it proved necessary. He beckoned to Ray and moved to the perimeter. "Have Mel call Jordan and Marty in. Tell her to have Marty escort Kim over to stay with a friend. Killian has just gone home. There's no sense calling him to come back from Crystal Falls. Not yet at any rate. When Jordan and Marty get here, we'll set up a line search, double back every five hundred yards, or so."

"You got it." Ray moved off to use the radio in his cruiser.

Thoughtfully, Vaughn stepped outside the yellow tape and began to study the ground around the area, concentrating primarily on the north perimeter. Pulling a lighter and his package of cigarettes from his pocket, he lit a one and coughed. For an instant he looked at the source of his lung irritation in confusion. He didn't remember lighting it. It was his first cigarette in 3 days. Somehow, he didn't think it would be his last.

He'd have to remember not to put the butt out on the ground. One of the first things he'd learned all those years ago in training was that you never, but never, add anything to a crime scene.

He winced inwardly. Doreen was dead. He knew it; felt it with a certitude that was frightening.

A few minutes later, he heard a vehicle and turned toward the road expecting to see his deputies arriving. He did. But he also saw Barney McCarthy pulling up behind them in his classic 1964 Ford Galaxie. Sitting beside Barney, was the freelance investigative journalist that had been staying at the hotel. For an instant Vaughn felt an acute and irrational sense of betrayal, as though Barney had gone over to the enemy. Then, realizing how silly the emotion was, he shook it off. Barney was a reporter—had always been a reporter—and it was obvious that today he would not let himself be put off.

"Sheriff." Barney beckoned to him from the border of the crime-scene tape.

With a resigned sigh, Vaughn crushed his cigarette out on the sole of his boot, pocketed the butt, and went to speak with Barney. "Morning."

"Morning, Sheriff. I'd like you to meet John Lambert."

Vaughn extended his hand. "Lambert," he nodded, then switched his gaze back to Barney expectantly.

"John here is writing a book on killers who choose multiple victims."

Vaughn nodded, flicking a glance at the investigative journalist. "That's interesting. Well, if you don't mind—" he trailed off as he took a step away from them. He didn't have time to stand around exchanging chitchat.

"Actually, Sheriff," Barney said, stopping him, "I was wondering if you're prepared to make a preliminary statement about what happened here."

"Sure," Vaughn nodded. "Two local boys discovered a black 1987 Corolla abandoned in the brush over there." He gestured to the car which was still being minutely examined by Stone. "The vehicle is registered to Doreen Hanson."

"Doreen was supposed to have left for Chelan a couple of days ago. Wasn't she, Sheriff?"

"That's correct."

"Did she ever leave town?"

"That's something I can't comment on without further investigation."

"Sheriff, do you suspect foul play?" John Lambert asked.

Vaughn swung his gaze toward the man, considering him. He was about 30 with clear, intelligent, blue eyes and straight, slightly stringy, brown hair tied into a ponytail at the nape of his neck. He wore jeans, a Western-style shirt, and high-top Reeboks. Vaughn wasn't sure what he thought of him, and he didn't have the time to form a more detailed impression. "Yes," he said finally, succinctly. "Now if you gentlemen don't mind, I have work to do."

"One more question, Sheriff. Is your suspicion of foul play based solely on the note that was left for Ms. Hanson a few days ago? Or have you received additional information?"

Vaughn cast Barney an accusatory look. He'd thought they'd agreed to keep that quiet. Oh, well, he supposed it hardly made any difference now. Before long, Lillooet Creek would be once again inundated with reporters. He turned back to Lambert. "There has been no additional information received at this time. Excuse me."

Vaughn took his camera from the Bronco and hung it around his neck before removing his evidence collection kit and slinging it over one shoulder. Within minutes Vaughn, Ray, Jordan and Marty had organized themselves into a small but knowledgeable search party. Vaughn believed it would be the only search party necessary. He was fairly certain that the killer wanted the bodies of his victims found and would not have concealed the body very thoroughly. He hoped he was right because he'd hate to have to expand the search to include civilians who might stumble on the body ill-prepared for the sight of death.

They were just about to head out when another vehicle pulled up. This one, too, was familiar. It was Liz in her van. Vaughn hastily strode toward it, meeting her before she could even open her door. "What are you doing here, Liz?"

"I had to come." He saw a shadow hovering in her eyes.

He sighed. "What now?"

"I know who I've been brought here to protect."

"Who?" Vaughn frowned impatiently. He didn't have time for Liz's mumbo jumbo right now.

Liz swallowed. "You," she said quietly. "He wants to hurt you, destroy you." She closed her eyes. "He calls himself the Lord of Death. He wants to take your life."

He reached into the open window of her van and placed a comforting hand over hers. "Look, Liz," he said, "what you say may be true. I'm not disputing that right now. But he isn't coming after me yet. And I have work to do. So will you go home. Please?"

*   *   *

It was the stench that warned them. Even in the relative coolness of the forest, it hovered in the motionless July air like an invisible haze. Marty had been the first to smell it. Halting, staying back from the site, he'd called the others. Faintly through the brush, they could see a portion of the body.

Vaughn swallowed. "Marty—" he beckoned to his youngest deputy—"I'll need you to go back to the road and inform Stone. Then I want you to call Dr. Harcourt to tell him what's up. He'll need to bring the ambulance to transport the body. After that, take up a position at the road to keep everybody back. You okay with all that?"

Deputy Martin Lewis nodded solemnly. "Sure, Vaughn."

Vaughn watched Marty walk away. Since legally, a

body could not be moved until a preliminary examination had been completed by a medical examiner or a coroner, Vaughn wanted Doc Harcourt out here as soon as possible. Harcourt was the elected coroner for Waterford County. Although he wasn't a qualified forensic pathologist, that didn't concern Vaughn. He knew that Harcourt would call in a qualified M.E. as soon as he heard.

Vaughn caught another whiff of the sickening odor and felt his stomach roil. There was nothing quite so horrible as the reek of a human corpse. Turning away from the smell, he took a few deep breaths of clear mountain air through his mouth. Then, taking a small container of Vick's from his shirt pocket, he smeared a liberal quantity beneath his nose and passed the container on. It wouldn't block the scent, but it would numb the olfactory senses enough to make it bearable.

While he waited for his deputies to prepare themselves, he faced the realization that, despite his conscious certainty that Doreen was dead, subconsciously he had harbored a small and persistent hope that he was wrong. Now that hope died.

He closed his eyes. He didn't want to do this. He didn't know how he was going to do this. He didn't love Doreen any more, if he ever really had. But she was the mother of his son. And she was a friend. How could he possibly do his job objectively? But he had to do it precisely because it was his job. Squaring his shoulders, he turned and, shoulder to shoulder with his two remaining deputies, moved on.

Her body lay in a small clearing. She was naked, stretched out on her back as though for sleep, her legs crossed demurely at the ankles. A huge and hideous slash spanned her throat. Blackened by clotted blood, the edges of the wound had curled back, a savage and macabre caricature of a smile that seethed with flies and maggots. Her shaven head lay on a pillow of crushed and wilted fern fronds. Her hands, bound by nylon rope and what Vaughn knew would prove to be her own braided hair, lay between her breasts. Clutched tightly within her fingers was a small bouquet of wilted flowers. The hilt of the knife that had taken her life had been positioned beneath her arched palms. The blade, centered and pointing down, anchored a piece of paper on her body.

Closing his eyes for a second, Vaughn sought and found the emotional detachment he needed. Then, turning on the small voice-activated digital recorder in his shirt pocket, he removed the lens cap from the camera hanging around his neck and prepared to take pictures. Before they moved any closer, touched anything, the scene had to be photographed from all angles. As he took each picture, he recorded pertinent information concerning the camera setting, lighting, and the direction he was facing for each exposure. He'd transcribe the recording to hard copy later.

Being careful not to step on anything that might prove to be evidence, Vaughn and Ray moved closer. Vaughn continued to take pictures. "No blood or anything anywhere around," Ray commented. His tone revealed the fact that he was trying not to breath too deeply. "Looks like she was killed somewhere else."

Vaughn nodded and replaced the lens cap on his camera for the time being. "That follows the pattern." Squatting, he tried to avoid looking at her face—it no longer bore any resemblance to Doreen—as he gauged the temperature of the body. The skin was cold and clammy. The head, neck and chest had taken on a grotesque greenish-red hue. "I'd say she's been dead at least twenty-four hours, probably closer to thirty. You were right, Ray. She never left town."

* * *

As soon as she'd managed to drag the reason for the temporary withdrawal of her deputy protection out of Deputy Lewis, Kim had decided to have him escort her over to Aunt Willie's. Just a few days ago, Willie had called Doreen her girl. Sentiment ran deeply there, and Kim thought that for once Aunt Willie might be the one in need of a strong shoulder rather than the other way around. Her instincts had been right.

The news that Doreen's abandoned car had been found just out of town had spread like wildfire through pine tar along Lillooet Creek's grapevine. Although Willie was desperately trying to hide her worry as she cared for Doreen's young son, it was obvious that she was a nervous wreck.

As soon as Kim had arrived, Willie had turned over Landon's care to her while she had begun pulling bowls and pans from the cupboards. "I'm way behind on my baking," she'd muttered. But Kim had seen the sheen of tears in her eyes and knew that Willie was simply trying to keep busy.

Now, an hour later, with the oven full of cake pans and trays of squares sitting on the counter cooling, Aunt Willie paused long enough to take a breath. "Sit down for a bit," Kim urged as she jounced Doreen's toddler son on her lap.

Aunt Willie sank into the chair across from her with a sigh. She seemed to exhale whatever bolstering influence she'd been drawing on with that sigh. In an instant, she aged ten years. Propping Landon on her hip, Kim jumped up and hastily filled a glass with water. "Here. Drink this," she said as she pressed the glass into Willie's hand.

Willie sipped and then looked up at her. "That poor child never had a chance at life." Taking another sip of the water, Willie looked out the window and spoke almost musingly. "Her mother died when she was still a little girl and Doreen took on the care of an entire household. She washed clothes and cleaned house and cooked meals until her little hands were raw, and never once did her father or her brothers show any appreciation." Willie shook her head. "They just abused her more. Whipped her when things weren't done to their satisfaction. She never had a childhood."

Willie sipped silently at the glass of water, her gaze unfocused as she remembered the past. She grimaced. "When Doreen reached puberty, it only got worse. I know for a fact that she was sexually abused by at least two of her brothers. When I discovered that, I stepped in and brought her to live with me. Told her family if they tried to interfere I'd alert the authorities. I wanted to avoid that though. Didn't want Doreen subjected to a string of foster homes. Unfortunately for Doreen, I don't think it was soon enough. She mostly avoided talking about men, but when she did it was obvious that she regarded them as some type of alien creature—beasts without feelings."

Willie focused her gaze on Kim. "I used to hope that she and Vaughn would get together. They both suffered so much as kids that I thought they'd understand each other. But it just never seemed to work out. I don't think Doreen ever really understood that men, good men, can have feelings, too."

Willie looked briefly at Landon as he sucked contentedly on a pacifier and played with a shape-sorter toy on the table. "She never did tell me how she ended up getting herself pregnant. Never saw her date anyone." Willie shrugged. "I was glad when she had a boy though. I hoped that having a son would teach her about male feelings while she was still young enough to find herself a good man." Aunt Willie sniffed and looked out the window. "Nothing ever worked out for that poor kid," she whispered. "Not a damn thing. Why do you think that is?"

Kim shrugged. "I don't know, Aunt Willie. Life just doesn't play fair." They fell silent, each occupied with their own thoughts. Suddenly, Landon banged his toy on the table in frustration, making them both jump.

"Mama!" The pacifier fell from his mouth as he pointed at the door. "Mama," he demanded again, this time looking at Kim. "Doe 'ome."

"Soon, darling." She hugged his chubby little body. "Soon," she prayed.

The timer went off on the stove and Willie rose to remove her cakes. Kim watched her, but her mind was on the words she'd heard earlier. *They both suffered so much as kids*, Aunt Willie had said. How had Vaughn suffered? Was his childhood the source of the nightmares he wouldn't talk about?

"Aunt Willie?" She waited until Willie turned to look at her. "Can you tell me about Vaughn's childhood?"

Willie considered her silently for a moment. "It's not something he likes to talk about, child. I don't think he'd want me to tell you."

"I like him, Aunt Willie. I'm beginning to like him a lot." Too much for her own peace of mind. "But he's suffering from a recurring nightmare that he won't talk about." Willie continued to meet her gaze impassively. She didn't seem to be wavering in the slightest. "I want to understand him, to help him."

Willie turned back to her stove without comment and Kim sagged dejectedly in her chair.

"Vaughn and three other foster children, all boys, were raised by my sister, Anna. There were two older boys, Johnny Qualchin—he was Indian—and Freddy Sumner. Let's see"—she gazed sightlessly at the ceiling—"they both left within a couple of years of Vaughn's and Coyd's arrival, I think. Vaughn and Coyd arrived within the same year, but Coyd was two years younger than Vaughn as I recall.

"I don't know if you remember Anna." She glanced at Kim questioningly. Kim shook her head. "Well, she looked a lot like me. She was over six feet tall, as strong as an ox, and as independent as the day is long. She built her own house, did her own wiring and plumbing. There was nothing that woman couldn't do. The good Lord only knows how she managed to learn it all. She was illiterate." Willie shook her head in remembrance.

"She'd always made sure I went to school, but she never went herself. I still don't understand why. But as a result, she could barely print her own name. I used to read to her a lot before we grew up and left home. She loved stories, especially poetry."

"Anyway, Anna wanted kids. Somebody to teach all her self-taught skills to. So she found herself a husband and got married. *Hitched*, she called it. Within a year though, Anna discovered she couldn't have kids." Willie grimaced. "Anna never liked being denied something she wanted. The only person I ever met that could be more stubborn than Anna was me. So despite what the doctor said, she blamed Herman for her barren state.

"Herman Irving was a small man, certainly no match for Anna in a temper, and he was a travelling salesman. Before long it became obvious to everyone in town that Herman had pretty much left Anna. Oh, he still came back every now and then. But he never stayed long." Willie shook her head. "I never did figure that relationship out."

Pouring herself a cup of coffee, Willie brought the mug to the table and sat down. "A short time later Anna decided to adopt. But again she ran into a brick wall. Because of Herman's frequent absences from the home, it was not considered a particularly stable environment and Anna was not considered an ideal candidate for adoption. Actually, I think the adoption lady took a dislike to her, too. Anna could be more than a little coarse at times. Anyway, that was when she decided to take in foster kids." Willie gaze grew distant as she sipped her coffee. Suddenly she shook her head. "Where was I?"

"Anna decided to take in foster children," Kim said.

"Umm," Willie nodded. "Foster homes are always desperately needed, and somehow Anna managed to qualify. She taught those boys everything: cooking, cleaning, woodcarving, carpentry. It wouldn't have been a bad home if Anna hadn't been such a stern taskmaster. And if she hadn't—" Willie seemed to choke on her words. "She managed to keep it hidden from me for years. But she changed; the older she got, the worse she got. And just before Johnny and Freddy left, they found the courage to confide in me."

Willie fell silent, her face clouded by past pain. Kim stayed silent, waiting, knowing that, whatever Willie revealed, she would do it in her own way at her own speed. Landon seemed to be getting sleepy, so Kim rose and placed him in the playpen in the corner of the room. Without a protest, he rolled over on his side, pulled his blanket up to his face and stuck his thumb in his mouth. Kim poured herself a coffee and resumed her seat. Willie jumped slightly as though she'd forgotten Kim's presence.

"Somehow, without my realizing, it had gotten to the point where the boys did everything around there. They'd come home from school and cook the meals. They'd do all the maintenance, all the repairs. Everything. And Anna, I didn't even know her any more. Freddy complained that night after night, she forced the boys to take turns reading to her. Poetry mostly because that was what she liked best. Her favorite book was always *The Oxford Book of English Verse.*"

Using her thumbnail, Willie began to scrape at some dough that had somehow gotten stuck to the table during the afternoon's baking spree. "Johnny said that when they disobeyed her or balked in any way, she would tie them up in the woodshed, hanging them by their wrists to an overhead beam." Willie closed her eyes and brushed impatiently at a single tear that escaped the corner of her eye to track down her nose. "Then, she'd shave their heads until there was nothing left but a stubble that could pass as a brush cut and beat their bare bums with a wooden paddle."

"My God," Kim breathed. "How could anyone treat a child that way?"

"I don't know." Willie shrugged. "I wish I did. Perhaps I could have done more to stop it. But that wasn't the worst of it." She stared out the window at the sunny July day, but Kim didn't think she saw it. "Freddy told me that Anna had begun to sexually abuse the boys. She would wait until after midnight, when she thought they were asleep and then sneak into bed with one of them. Freddy was sixteen and almost suicidal when he came to me. Anna had managed to catch him in the midst of an erotic, adolescent dream. He had done the things she'd encouraged him to do before he was even awake enough to realize what was happening."

Willie fell silent and Kim's mind reeled with shock. She felt sick to her stomach. She didn't understand how these kinds of things could go on with no one aware of them. She had gone to school with Vaughn and Coyd. Although she barely remembered them, she did know that no one had suspected that they were anything other than two sullen adolescent boys who couldn't fit in. No wonder they hadn't been able to fit in. Like Doreen, they'd had their childhood stolen from them.

Willie sipped her coffee and cleared her throat, drawing Kim's eyes to her face. "Many people argue that it is physically impossible for a woman to rape a man or, in this case, a boy, but I don't know what else to call what Anna did to those boys. Anyway, after Freddy and Johnny told me what was going on, I took it upon myself to confront Anna. I told her that I was going to the authorities, that I was going to have the boys removed from her care."

"What did she say?"

Willie sighed and closed her eyes. "She threatened me."

Kim frowned. "How?" she asked.

Willie's mind's eye fixed on the past. She saw her husband's face twisted with rage as he raised his hand to strike her one more time. And she replayed, as she had countless times over the years, her own reaction. Whatever had possessed her to grab the whisky bottle from him and break it on the banister of the stairs? What demon had made her stab that jagged glass into his throat? She didn't know. She had just been so tired. Tired of the endless work of caring for a household full of drunks—Cecil had often brought his cronies home with him. Tired of the endless string of long, lonely nights and pitying glances from the townspeople because her husband had once again been seen openly consorting with some woman. Tired of the endless physical and emotional abuse.

She hadn't thought; she had only reacted. And, as her husband's body tumbled down the stairs, Anna had been there to see it fall. Anna had been there to help her make sure it looked like an accident.

Now, Willie looked across the table at Kim's young face. Kim would never understand. And because there was no statute of limitations on murder, Willie knew that her guilt was one secret that she would carry with her to her grave. "I can't tell you that. I've never told anyone. Anna was the only person who ever knew, and that was because—well, never mind. I will tell you that Anna had the ability to ruin my life. I couldn't face that. In exchange for her continued silence, I had to keep mine. So, I simply intervened constantly on a personal basis. Nearly drove Anna crazy." For the first time Willie's lips quirked slightly.

"I managed to stop most of the abuse, both physical and sexual, by my constant presence and interference. I took over the running of Anna's household. Short of physically throwing me out, there wasn't a whole heck of a lot she could do about it. Since I was the one giving the boys their instructions, it was up to me to deliver any punishments.

"I installed those sliding barrel-bolt locks on the boy's bedroom doors. Anna removed them the next morning. I went back and reinstalled them that evening. That little war of wills continued for well over a week until Anna finally gave up. The locks stayed.

"I don't think Anna and I spoke more than ten words to each other in the years that followed. Except in public of course. We did our best to keep up the loving-sister act. But any love that had been between us was dead."

Kim shook her head. "And were the boys all right? Where are they now?"

Willie shrugged. "I thought I'd managed to stop the abuse soon enough to prevent Vaughn and Coyd from being permanently scarred by it. They were both still young. But Freddy and Johnny—" Again she shrugged. "Although they kept in touch a bit over the years, it was obvious that they both had problems. Freddy was married and divorced three or four times before he finally ended up drinking himself to death. Johnny took risks, constantly. He had a death wish or something. He finally killed himself during some kind of a horse race on the reservation." Willie's voice cracked slightly and she cleared her throat. "It's strange, you know. I had such a short time with them. But both those boys had me down as next of kin on a card in their wallet. I think that's the best compliment I'd ever received."

Kim smiled slightly. "I agree. What about Coyd? How did he take it?"

Willie got up and refilled her coffee cup. "I was never sure about him. I never could get that boy to open up. It was like there was a wall between him and the rest of the world. But he was a good boy. Real smart, too. Neat. Quiet. Always did what he was told. Soaked up praise like a sponge, but you really had to watch to see the signs. He never showed his feelings."

"Where is he now?"

"Dead."

"Him, too?" Kim asked incredulously. "How did it happen?"

"He was fourteen. Went hiking near the gorge. All they ever found was his backpack lodged on a stone. There wasn't much in it, so it didn't look like he was running away or anything. Still, I never could figure out what happened. Coyd had a healthy respect for that gorge, and he wasn't the careless type."

"His body was never found?"

"Nope," Willie sat down. "But that gorge has to be a couple of hundred feet deep. The water in it moves fast. His body would have been washed downstream before the search even began."

"I wonder—" Kim began.

"Enough," Aunt Willie interrupted her. "The past is past. A closed chapter. I've talked about it all I'm going to for one day." Rising, she checked on the baby sleeping in the playpen.

* * *

He watched as they carried her body from the woods. A suitably solemn procession of professionals, they silently placed the body bag on a gurney and slid it into the waiting ambulance.

He smiled inwardly. Doreen's punishment had been the most rewarding so far. She had been so strong, so determined not to show her fear. She had tried everything. Everything from calling him a coward for tying her and challenging him to an equal fight, to feminine wiles and the promise of the best fuck of his life. But her words had rolled over him, meaningless, unfelt. In the end, she had accepted her punishment.

The door closed on the ambulance, startling him from his reverie. He looked around. Quite a crowd had gathered now. He observed and catalogued the expressions of the bystanders. He saw everything from pity and grief, to rage and fear, to fascination and curiosity in their eyes. Even Vaughn's eyes had a sheen of moisture in them. The display of weakness turned his stomach. Vaughn never had had any backbone. Oh, well, in the end Vaughn, too, would die. But he would be last. . . dead last. He smiled at the cliché. It was so interesting to watch Vaughn torment himself over his own stupidity.

For now, it was time to return his mind to business. He had another funeral to plan. He wondered if he could scare Kimberley into leaving town and then stop her on the outskirts as he had done with Doreen. No. It wasn't certain enough. He'd have to come up with something else. Something more challenging.

* * *

It was late afternoon by the time Vaughn stopped by Aunt Willie's. He came in his official capacity as sheriff. Wilma Nielsen was the only next of kin that had really mattered to Doreen. But the guise of sheriff faded rapidly in the face of Willie's obvious grief. And it was the boy she had all but raised, not the sheriff, who pulled her into his arms to comfort her.

Kim stood self-consciously to one side. As her gaze met Vaughn's over Willie's shoulder, she saw the raw pain in his eyes. She couldn't share their grief. Having been a couple of years younger than Doreen in school, she'd never known her well. But she understood their pain, and she didn't want to be a spectator to something so private. Quietly, she went into the living room, leaving them alone until Willie got herself back under control.

A few minutes later, Vaughn came into the living room to speak with Kim. "Deputy Killian will be on duty by seven o'clock," he said. "You can call the office to have him escort you home, then."

"Sure. Thanks."

He looked as though the load he carried at that moment would all but crush him beneath its weight. She wanted nothing more than to throw her arms around him and hold him close. But she didn't think he was ready to accept her support. Not yet. This thing between them was still too new. So, aching for him, she watched him open the door and walk to his Bronco.

It was dusk, around eight o'clock, by the time that Kim headed home with the sheriff's department cruiser tailing her. It had taken her considerable time to get Landon settled for the night and assure herself that Aunt Willie was capable of caring for the child. Despite her own nervousness, she'd offered to take Landon home with her, but Willie had point-blank refused.

Now as Kim negotiated the curving road home, all the feelings she'd had just after Trent's death once again came to the forefront. Doreen's death brought it all back. How was it possible that Trent's funeral had only been three weeks ago? So much had changed since then. She'd changed.

She remembered that morning that Vaughn had come over to discuss the profile of the killer with her. If she could have buried her head in the sand and avoided all mention of anything unpleasant, she would have. But she couldn't; the killer had seen to that.

Frowning, she wondered what condition Doreen's body had been found in. Had the killer left his signature? Had he shaved her head and bound her wrists with her own hair as he had with Trent?

Suddenly, Kim felt her throat close. No! It couldn't be. She was imagining things. But no matter how she tried to deny its existence, the sudden awareness would not go away.

Anna's foster children had had their heads shaven repeatedly as children. The victim's heads were shaven. The kids' hands had been bound while they were beaten for disobedience. The victim's hands were bound. The killer appeared to have an affinity for poetry. Anna's foster kids had been forced to read poetry to her on a regular basis. Coincidence? How much room was there for coincidence when you were talking about the personalized signature of a killer?

Kim swallowed against the enormous lump that had developed out of nowhere in her throat. Of the four foster children raised in Anna Irving's home, only one was still alive. Vaughn Garrett, Sheriff of Waterford County. Kim shook her head as her mind groped frantically for other possibilities. She couldn't find any. Oh, Lord! What should she do?

Kim parked her car and barely noticed Deputy Killian take up position in his cruiser. She noticed Liz's van sitting in the drive though. Her first thought was that she didn't want to see Liz right now. How could she face the mother when she was entertaining the possibility that the son might be a murderer?

Turning, Kim began walking toward the house. "Ms. Tannas." Kim turned at the sound of her name and waited while the deputy strode up to her. "I'd like to go through the house with you before you settle in for the night, if you don't mind? The place was sitting unguarded for much of the day."

Kim frowned. "I thought somebody would have done that already. Isn't Liz home?"

"Not that I know of."

"Oh. Well, all right. Sure." Kim answered distractedly as her mind once again began its insistent contemplation of the coincidences that pointed to Vaughn's identity as a killer.

She waited in the entrance as Deputy Killian checked out the kitchen. "It's fine," he said a couple of minutes later as he emerged. "I'll just check the rest of the place and be out of your hair in no time."

Kim nodded without comment. Moving into the kitchen, she methodically went about preparing the ingredients for a salad. She heard Deputy Killian's steps ascend the stairs and then forgot about him. How could Vaughn possibly be the killer? He was a gentle man. A caring man who, despite the abuse he'd suffered as a child, had managed to see the beauty in the world around him. Just one look at the carvings scattered so freely about his yard revealed that. But memory of the carvings brought to mind another memory. Less pleasant. Almost frightening.

Kim stared at the knife in her hand and remembered the day she'd gone, uninvited, to see Vaughn. She remembered how coldly angry he'd appeared. A stranger. And she remembered the blood smeared knife in his hand. "Stop it!" she told herself, slamming the knife down on the cutting board. "Just stop it." She raked her fingers through her hair. "It's not possible."

A thump overhead distracted her and she looked at the ceiling with a frown. Was Deputy Killian still up there? He should have been on his way down by now. Moving out into the hall, she went to the base of the stairs. "Deputy Killian?"

A muffled response drifted down the stairs. What was he doing?

"Is everything all right?"

"Fine. I'm almost through." Again the voice was muted. Where the hell was he? In her closet or something? She stood at the base of the stairs and waited for him. She heard a couple more steps, then nothing. Well, she didn't want him snooping around up there all night.

She'd just placed her foot on the bottom step when Charity suddenly howled loudly from the veranda. Kim looked over in time to see the enormous cat jump at the screen and hang there by her claws, peering into the house with demanding golden eyes. "Charity, get off of there before you tear the screen." The cat didn't budge. Sighing in frustration, Kim went to the door and opened it. The cat jumped down and streaked by her, racing into the kitchen where she commenced a caterwauling meant to convince Kim that starvation was imminent.

"All right," Kim muttered casting one more dark glance at the stairs. She'd feed the cat and then check on Deputy Killian.

Kim emerged from the kitchen a few minutes later and noticed immediately that the foyer and living room seemed darker. Frowning she looked at the front door.

The inner door had been closed, blocking out the sunlight that had filtered through the screen door from the veranda. Had Deputy Killian gone back out in the couple of minutes she'd been in the kitchen? Opening the door, she stepped out onto the veranda and looked toward the cruiser. Yes, he was definitely sitting in his car. He appeared to be watching the second story of the house. Kim frowned. Why hadn't he said anything when he'd gone back out? Rubbing her arms against the chill evening air, she turned and reentered the house.

Although she wasn't hungry, Kim forced herself to eat a healthy portion of salad. Then, still plagued by doubts concerning Vaughn, becoming more depressed by the minute, she decided to take a hot shower. Maybe it would relax her.

Pulling the blind in her room, she stood before the bedroom mirror to brush her hair before beginning to undress. Suddenly, something stopped her. Something didn't feel right. She looked at the closet. The door was ajar. She always closed her doors, and the deputies invariably left things exactly as they had found them. She shuddered.

Was somebody there? Watching her? Don't be an idiot, she told herself. Deputy Killian just forgot to close it. But the sense of something not right grew stronger. She looked around for something to protect herself with. Trent's old baseball bat was propped in the corner beside the closet. No. Too far away. She wanted something in her hand before she walked over there. Unplugging the lamp, she picked it up and warily moved toward the closet door. Grasping the handle firmly in one hand, she yanked the door open. Nothing. There was no one there.

She sighed in relief. Then, feeling a little foolish, she began once again to remove her clothes. A shiver ran up her spine. *Danger's kiss.* Suddenly she didn't care how foolish she was being. Grabbing her bathrobe, she went into the bathroom, checked the shower stall and then firmly locked the door. That done, she managed to finish disrobing without further discomfort.

Emerging from the hot shower a few minutes later, she felt much better. The knotted muscles in her shoulders had eased, and the massage of the water had loosened the tension in her scalp. Tying her robe securely about her waist, she wrapped her hair in a towel and opened the door. Picking up her discarded clothing, she placed it in the hamper and then, abandoning the steamy bathroom mirror, she moved into the bedroom to comb her hair out.

As she removed the towel from her head and turned to face the mirror, the blood froze in her veins. She tried to scream, but fear paralyzed her vocal cords and all that emerged was a small, helpless squawk. There, high on the right-hand side of the mirror was a blotch of bright, red lipstick—a shade she never wore. Someone wearing lipstick had pressed their lips to the mirror in a kiss.

CHAPTER 15

The strength faded from Kim's legs and she sank to the floor. Her mind seethed with a morass of half-formed thoughts and fears until she thought she'd go mad. And then one thought rose above all the others: *He was in the house.* He had done this during the brief moments when she was in the shower. If Vaughn was the killer, there was no way he could have returned home already. And, irrationally, what was uppermost in Kim's mind in that instant was not fear for her own safety, but a desperate need to reestablish her faith in Vaughn.

Galvanized into action she grabbed the bat from the corner and raced into her Aunt's room to use the phone on the nightstand. She dialed Vaughn's home number. The phone rang four times before being answered—by voicemail. Kim's spine sagged slightly. Oh, God! He wasn't home. If she called his cell phone, would she hear its ring... somewhere in the house? Was she brave enough to try? She chewed her lip in indecision. Then, before she could change her mind, she called his cell. She listened intently, but heard nothing in the house. Neither, though, did Vaughn answer. Once again her call went to voicemail. Where was he? She hung up.

Where was Deputy Killian? Why hadn't he stopped the intruder? Kim needed him, needed his help right now, but she was afraid. Too afraid to go outside in the dark. Too afraid to go downstairs alone. Too afraid to . . .

"Stop it!" she whispered fiercely to herself. She had to stop thinking that way before she became nothing more than a shivering mess too afraid to move.

She'd call the sheriff's office and report the intruder. They could get hold of Deputy Killian by radio. After dialing the number, she waited anxiously on the line while the dispatcher—not Melissa—tried to raise Deputy Killian on the radio.

"He's not answering Ms. Tannas," the old woman's voice squawked. "I'll get somebody else over there right away. You sit tight. You hear?"

"Yes, thank you." Her voice was barely audible to her own ears. She closed her eyes. Jesus! A killer was in the house and there was no one to help her. So much for Vaughn's plan to protect her and catch the killer. Vaughn's plan? No, she refused to think that way. Dammit, she didn't want to die. A tear snaked down her cheek, startling her. She dashed it away angrily. *Think! Dammit, think!*

If the killer, whoever he was, really wanted to kill her, he obviously could have done so already. That meant that he simply wanted to frighten her again. He'd succeeded. But if she kept her wits about her, then maybe—just maybe—she could catch him. Suddenly she remembered the conversation she'd had with her Aunt Vivian when she'd first decided to stay.

Slowly, she opened the drawer on the nightstand. It was there. Right where Aunt Viv had said it would be. A shiny pistol. Kim didn't know what kind it was. It wasn't loaded, but a full clip lay beside it in the drawer. With shaking hands, Kim withdrew the weapon and, with fumbling fingers, snapped the clip into place.

* * *

Vaughn stepped from the shower. He'd stood in there forever, trying to wash away the stench of death, trying to wash away his own failure. He'd known there was a murderer in town. He'd known that Doreen was a target. He'd known, or rather sensed, that her idea to go to Chelan was not a good one. Yet despite all that, he had failed to protect her. He'd let Doreen down. Somehow he had to learn to live with that awareness or the guilt would drive him crazy.

He toweled himself dry and strode into the bedroom to dress. Catching sight of the alarm clock, he hesitated. It was after ten. Where the hell had the time gone? He looked at the jeans in his hands. Should he get dressed, or simply go to bed?

He shrugged. He wouldn't be able to sleep anyway. He pulled on his jeans before walking barefoot out to the kitchen to get himself a drink. Scotch on the rocks was what this night called for.

Carrying the drink into the living room, he noticed the voicemail light blinking on his phone. Someone must have called while he was in the shower. Reaching over, he depressed the button to play back the message.

He frowned. Whoever it was hadn't said anything. There was the faint sound of breathing, a sound that might have been a sob, and then nothing. He felt a strange tightening in his scalp. What the hell was going on? *Kim.* He had to check on Kim.

He didn't hesitate. Even as the compulsion gripped him, he was striding toward his bedroom. He had to dress and get over there. Entering the room, he stopped short. Had that been the click of the screen on the garden door he'd just heard? He held his breath, listening. Hesitating only long enough to extract his gun from the holster that he'd hung over the back of a chair, he silently crossed the room. Flattening himself against the wall, he peered out onto the deck. A footfall. There was someone out there.

Slowly, he reached out to release the catch on the

sliding screen door. Then, with a sudden move that became one continuous, fluid motion, he slid the door aside and leapt out onto the deck. As he pivoted, seeking the intruder, his starving lungs suddenly demanded oxygen and he realized that he'd been holding his breath. There! Movement. A shadow slightly darker than the night.

"Stop right there!" he shouted. But even as he moved toward it, gun extended in readiness, the shadow faded into the night. He did a quick, thorough search of the shrubs in the area, but found nothing. His imagination? He didn't think so. But his nerves were so on edge, he couldn't have sworn to it.

Breathing deeply in an attempt to combat the aftermath of an overdose of adrenalin, Vaughn stuck his gun into the waistband of his jeans, returned to the house and reentered his bedroom via the open screen door. The compulsion to check on Kim had not lessened. If anything it had intensified.

His dirty shirt lay on the carpet. He frowned; he could have sworn he'd thrown it in the hamper. Plucking it from the floor, he'd just taken a step toward the closet to get a fresh shirt and put this one where it belonged when the phone rang. He contemplated ignoring it. It rang again. Muttering a curse, he strode over to the night stand to answer it.

"Yeah."

"Sheriff, you're there!" Vaughn frowned at the obvious relief in Ethel Wright's voice. Of course he was here. Where the hell else would he be? He ran the dirty shirt through his hands as he listened to her. What the hell was that red smear on the collar? "I tried reaching you a couple of times but I only got the machine. And you didn't answer your cell or the radio."

Vaughn forgot about the smear. She wouldn't have been trying so desperately to reach him unless there was something seriously wrong. He felt tension take root in his body. "What's up?" His throat felt tight.

"Ms. Tannas called. She said she had an intruder in the house. When I tried to raise Deputy Killian, he didn't answer either."

"How long ago was this?" Vaughn demanded.

"Twenty, maybe twenty-five minutes. I called Deputy Cheney and sent him over when I couldn't get you. He radioed me a couple of minutes ago to let me know that he'd gotten there, but I haven't heard from him since."

"On my way." Vaughn hung up the phone, grabbed a fresh shirt from the closet and his gun holster from the back of the chair in one motion. Shoving his bare feet into his boots, he was out the door and into the Bronco within seconds.

* * *

The house was brilliantly lit when Vaughn pulled into the drive and parked behind the two cruisers already there, but there was no sign of movement. Getting out of the Bronco, he began walking toward the house. It was quiet. Too quiet. He glanced into Ray Cheney's cruiser as he passed. Ray must be in the house. Peering at Killian's cruiser as he moved up to it from behind, he saw a form behind the wheel. Cautiously, he moved up beside the vehicle and glanced inside. It was his deputy.

"Killian," he called in a low voice. No response.

Frowning, he took his eyes off the house and looked into the car. He wished he'd remembered his flashlight.

"Killian," he called again, a little more forcefully. Still no response. His heart was in his throat as he reached into the cruiser and checked for a pulse on the deputy's neck. He sighed in relief. It was there. A bit thready maybe, but definitely there. "Hold on, Killian," he said. Where the hell was Ray?

He continued on toward the house, moving more swiftly now. His fear for Kimberley—like a raw, painful wound—made it difficult to think. He had just reached the front steps when he saw a shadow move at the corner of the house. Instinctively, silently, he slipped to the side to investigate. As he drew nearer the shadow, the moon came out briefly from behind a cloud and he saw a halo of blonde hair, silvered by the moonlight. Kimberley!

He also caught the glint of a gun. His concern over having an untrained civilian skulking around with a gun tempered his relief at finding her. Shit! Where had she gotten a gun? Did she even know how to use one? There was nothing more dangerous than a gun in the hand of an amateur. Not wanting to alarm her for fear of getting shot, Vaughn moved quietly toward her.

As he drew nearer, he peered in the direction where her gaze was fixed so intently. Had she seen something in the shrubbery? Then, the shrubs moved and for a brief instant Skeeter Barnes's face shone in the light spilling from one of the windows before he disappeared. Just as Vaughn's attention was diverted, Kim raised the weapon.

"No, Kim!" Vaughn shouted. He was above to dive for her legs and knock her to the ground when she spun to face him. It only took a fraction of a second for her gaze to find him crouching near her. "Kim, it's me." She kept the weapon trained on him. "It's Vaughn," he said, rising to face her.

He knew the instant that recognition entered her eyes, yet her expression was racked with indecision. For one horrible moment, Vaughn faced the possibility that Kim might shoot him anyway. Why? "Give me the gun, Kim. Please?" He carefully extended his hand toward her. "Please?" he repeated.

Slowly, with shaking hands, she lowered the gun and put it into his outstretched hand. Then, as though the weapon had somehow been the source of her strength, she crumbled. Catching her, Vaughn tucked the gun into his waistband and lifted her to carry her into the house. He wished he knew what the hell was going on!

As he walked around the side of the house carrying Kim, he met Cheney coming from the direction of the driveway. Ray, too, carried someone in his arms. A quick glance told Vaughn it was Liz.

"What the hell is going on here, Ray?" Vaughn had finally found someone to whom he could voice the tormenting question.

Cheney shrugged, but his eyes were laden with worry. He fell into step beside Vaughn. "I wish to hell I knew. When I got here, I found Killian unconscious in his car and the house lit up like a Christmas tree, but empty. I figured Kim and Liz might be in the van, so I checked it. I found Liz and couldn't wake her up. Found a lump the size of a plum on the back of her head. Thought I'd get her into the house and call the doc to see to her and Killian then take another look around."

* * *

Kim frowned. The rhythmic tapping on her cheek had begun to sting slightly. She brushed at it in annoyance. "Kim, honey, wake up."

Slowly, she pried her lids open and looked into Vaughn's concerned golden gaze. Lord, she loved his eyes. Then, she looked past his shoulder and saw Ray Cheney kneeling in front of the other sofa. "What happened?"

"You fainted," Vaughn explained in a gentle voice.

Kim stared at him incredulously. "Don't be ridiculous. I've never fainted in my life." She struggled to sit up but Vaughn pushed her back.

Vaughn's lips twisted in a small lopsided grin. "Okay, then I guess you got really tired and decided to take a nap in the flowerbed for a nap. How do you feel?"

The minute she'd lifted her head, a pair of invisible vise grips clutched her temples and begun to squeeze. "I have a headache the size of the Grand Canyon."

"Do you have any Tylenol?"

Kim tried to nod and winced at the stab of pain. "I

think there should be some in the medicine cabinet in the bathroom."

"Okay, just lie there for a moment while I get it."

Kim closed her eyes without argument. Before Vaughn made it back, she heard a knock on the door.

"Come on in, Doc." It was Ray's voice.

Why had he called the doctor? Kim wondered. She struggled again to sit up. This time she made it, although the effort made her feel decidedly nauseous.

"Liz Murphy's in the spare room through there," Ray was telling the doctor. "Killian's right here. He's in pretty bad shape. Liz just has a big goose egg."

Kim focused her fuzzy vision on the sofa across from her and gasped. Good Lord! Deputy Killian's dark blonde hair was matted with dried blood. "What happened?" she croaked.

Vaughn returned with the Tylenol and a glass of water just as Ray turned to answer her. "We were kind of hoping you might be able to tell us."

"Thank you," Kim murmured as she took the pills from Vaughn. She was vaguely aware of him turning and walking into the kitchen, but her attention was focused on Ray. Why did he think she could tell him anything? Frowning, Kim swallowed the pills and set the glass on the table. The relentless pain in her head made it difficult to think. She watched as Dr. Harcourt knelt to look at Killian and tried to force coherent thought to penetrate the wall of pain.

The last thing she remembered was sitting and talking to Aunt Willie. Aunt Willie had told her . . . . She frowned. It was there, just on the edge of her consciousness. She rubbed at her temples. Dammit! She would not allow a piece of her memory to be stolen from her again. *Think!* she commanded herself. *Remember!* And then suddenly, with chilling clarity, it all came back.

Oh, God! She had almost shot Vaughn. Had he made the slightest threatening gesture, she knew she would have pulled the trigger. She'd been so frightened. Her emotions had been so tied up in knots. And he had calmly carried her into the house and tenderly taken care of her. How could she have entertained the notion that he might be a killer, even for a second? It simply wasn't possible, was it?

He emerged from the kitchen and returned to her side. "Here," he said, smiling gently. "This might help." He'd wrapped a couple of ice cubes into a cool, wet cloth. Kim felt tears sting her eyes at this further display of his kindness. She blinked them back and pressed the cloth to her forehead.

"I don't mean to rush you, honey, but do you feel up to talking a bit now?" Vaughn asked her a moment later.

Kim looked at him. And although it was tempered by concern, she saw the impatience and determination in his eyes. She decided in that moment, to tell him everything—including her own briefly held suspicion. But she didn't want to do that in front of anyone else. "Can we go into the kitchen?" she asked.

Vaughn frowned slightly, obviously confused by her request. "Sure," he said. Extending a hand, he helped her to her feet and wrapped an arm around her waist as they walked to the kitchen together.

* * *

They were alone in the house. Killian, and possibly Liz as well, had suffered a mild concussion, and Doc Harcourt had had them both transferred to the hospital. Ray had gone with them.

Vaughn stared at Kimberley unable to believe his ears. He was hurt and angry that for the first time in his life, Aunt Willie had actually stooped to gossiping about his upbringing. It wasn't her place to tell Kimberley anything about his past. "What are you saying, Kim?" His tone was dangerously soft.

"I'm saying that, the way I see it, there are only three possible explanations for the similarity between your upbringing and the killer's signature. That's what you called it, right?"

He nodded without comment, watching as Kim paced the kitchen floor with the damp face cloth dangling, forgotten, from her fingers. Her headache seemed to be gone.

"Okay," she said, halting to face him. "One." She held up a finger for emphasis. "Somebody who has intimate knowledge of your upbringing is trying to frame you. Two." She held up a second finger. "Coyd didn't die in that gorge and he's come back." She held up a third finger. "Or"—she paused uncertainly—"three. You have a split personality and your alter ego is the killer," she concluded in a rush.

Vaughn eyed her incredulously. Even in the grip of another personality, how could she think him capable of murder? The idea was preposterous. But he couldn't deny the existence of the incredible parallels between the abuse he had suffered, and the signature of the killer. Damn! It had been right in front of his nose all along.

A chill swept through him. Why hadn't he seen it? But he knew the answer to the question even as he asked it. Because he hadn't wanted to see it. Because he'd struggled every minute of every hour of every day for years to block out those memories and live a normal life. Because facing that realization meant opening the tomb of the past, unearthing the worm-ridden, rotting memories from their grave and facing all the fear, the self-disgust, and impotent rage again. His guts churned.

He met Kim's gaze. Why was she just standing there watching him as though she expected some strange metamorphosis to follow the expounding of her brilliant deductions? He tried to smile, but his emotions felt as though they'd been caught in the violent grip of a tornado. The expression that twisted his lips felt cold and unnatural.

"Well," he said quietly. "*I* know I don't have a split personality, but I suppose that's no comfort to you. I guess we'll just have to go through your theories one at a time until we find the one that fits. With any luck, maybe Killian or Liz can shed some light on the situation tomorrow. For now, let's go see that kiss on the mirror you told me about."

He was angry. Angry with Kim for seeing what he hadn't. Angry with himself for his blindness, his cowardice. And angry with whoever was doing this to him. No, he was more than angry at that person. A rage so black and furious that it all but clouded his vision gripped him, and if he could have gotten his hands on the individual at that moment, he might actually become the kind of person that Kim had thought him to be. A killer.

As Vaughn stood in front of the mirror in Kimberley's room and saw the bright crimson stain there, he remembered a smear of the same shade on his shirt collar. He remembered the sound of the patio door latch clicking quietly into place. And he remembered the faint sound of a stealthy footstep on the deck. The rage that had gripped him earlier was nothing compared to the cold, deadly hatred that now took its place.

The killer wasn't trying to frame him. He was toying with him. Tormenting him, like a cat torments a mouse. He had come here tonight, not to hurt Kimberley, but to prove that nothing could stand in his way. To prove that Vaughn's effort to protect Kim was futile. To prove that he was unstoppable. Was he? All the bolstering anger and hatred fled him in a rush leaving him simply tired. So tired.

Raking his fingers through his hair, Vaughn sat on the edge of the bed and stared at the floor. What the hell was his next move?

"Vaughn?" He looked up at Kim's questioning call. "What's the matter?"

"Nothing," he said quietly. He tried to smile reassuringly. "Don't worry."

But Kim had seen the weariness in his eyes. She could imagine what this day must have been like for him. Impulsively, she went to him. Wrapping her arms around him, she cradled his head against her breast and pressed her cheek to his soft tawny hair. His arms came up to embrace her waist. "It's okay," she said, as she ran one hand over his shoulders and felt the tension there. Slowly, she began to massage the knotted muscles.

A couple of minutes later, he lifted his head and looked up at her. She didn't know what he sought there but he must have found it because he suddenly clasped her to him in a fierce embrace. With an abrupt move, he pulled her down beside him on the bed and then, with gentle fingers, traced the outline of her face.

"Kim, I"—but whatever words he'd been about to say were lost as his mouth suddenly slanted across hers in the hungriest, most devouring kiss she'd ever experienced. Her body responded instantly to that primal call, melting into his embrace, clutching him to her. Her intuition told her that his need, at that time, was for a gentle touch, for understanding and compassion, for a few brief moments of blissful oblivion. For love.

Her heart contracted with a brief stabbing pain. She wasn't certain she could give him that last. She cared for him deeply. She'd lusted after him shamelessly ever since he had forced her to recognize her own innate femininity. But gentle man and considerate lover that he was, he was still a cop. He would always be a cop. One of the highest risk professions there was. And Kim had already lost one husband to a bullet.

No, she would give Vaughn anything but her love. She couldn't risk her heart again. And as guilt stabbed at her for her cowardice, she clutched him to her as fervently as he clutched her.

They made love like they never had before, like two savage strangers intent on self-gratification. It was primal and hungry. It was wild and desperate. It was a laugh in the face of danger and a tempestuous promise for the future. It was oblivion and sweet, sweet release.

As Vaughn lay sleeping in her arms, his head pillowed against her breasts, Kim stared into the darkness, her mind once more plagued by her suspicions. If Coyd had come back to Lillooet Creek, where was he staying? How was it that no one had recognized him? Of course, it had been 14, maybe 15 years since he'd disappeared. He could have changed a lot in that time. Look how much some of the other people she'd run into had changed. Still, you'd think that someone in town would have recognized him if he'd come back. How many ways were there for someone to change their appearance? The changes incurred by natural aging could be quite considerable, but not enough to account for no one recognizing him. A weight gain might account for it though. The pounds that Susan Granger had put on had made her virtually unrecognizable. Kim gnawed thoughtfully at her lip.

She jumped at the abrupt sound of a distant crash. It sounded like glass shattering. Her pulse leapt in her throat. One of her Aunt Viv's porcelain lamps? But they'd locked all the doors. Had he come back? Broken in?

"Vaughn." He groaned slightly, but didn't wake up. Some protector! She watched him sleep for a moment, noting the absence of tension in his face and felt her heart swell with something she refused to name. After the day he'd had, maybe he deserved a slice of oblivion.

She listened to the house again. Silence. Maybe it had been her imagination. Had she heard something or not? Of course she had; she wouldn't have been startled otherwise. Still, she wasn't helpless. She didn't have to awaken Vaughn to check on a little noise. She'd lived perfectly independently for a couple of years now.

Reaching out, she turned on the small night-light and carefully slipped out of bed. Vaughn stirred slightly at her movement, but slept on. Taking her Aunt Vivian's pistol from the nightstand—she'd refused to allow Vaughn to confiscate it—she slipped from the room.

CHAPTER 16

She left the bedroom and headed downstairs, flicking on every light switch she encountered. She'd always felt, that if she kept herself surrounded by enough light, the nightmares and things that haunted the darkness couldn't touch her. It was a simplistic and juvenile rationale, she knew, but it helped her face the nights.

She hugged the wall as she moved slowly, silently down the stairs. She was terrified of what she might find. Frightened by the thought that she might actually be forced to use the gun in her hand if she encountered *him*. One more step and she'd be able to see the entire living room. She closed her eyes and swallowed, taking a deep breath to calm her racing heart.

She took the step and peered into the living room. It was dim, but enough light spilled into the room from the stairway for her to see that there was nothing amiss. Her aunt's lamps were in place. She looked across the foyer at the kitchen door with a sense of apprehension. Then, before she could race back to her bed and hide her head under the blankets like a coward, she descended the remainder of the stairs and flicked on the light switch.

Another glance into the living room confirmed her first assessment. Everything was fine. She took a deep breath and pushed open the kitchen door. Impenetrable darkness cloaked the room beyond. The switch for the overhead light was a good four steps to her left. Kim blinked, trying to adjust her eyes to the gloom before venturing into it.

A pair of eyes glowed in the darkness across the room. Her heart stuttered. Owlish, yellow eyes observed her unblinkingly. "Charity?"

"Me-ow-ow."

Kim shook her head in disgust. "Dammit, cat, you scared me half to death." Sidling sideways, she slid her hand along the wall searching for the switch. Light flooded the room. Charity blinked at her sleepily. "What are you doing up on the cupboard?" she demanded of the feline. "You know better than that."

"Meow." Charity didn't move so much as a muscle.

Kim donned a threatening expression and, gun hanging forgotten from her fingers, began to walk toward the cupboard. "You get down from there this instant," she said.

Saucer-like golden eyes stared up into hers with an expression of supreme innocence. The cat flicked a glance into the sink. "Meow," she said. Her tail twitched.

Kim followed her gaze. A shattered drinking glass and a broken ceramic pot—which, until a short time ago, had been sitting on the windowsill with a Prayer Plant growing in it—lay in a mess of loose soil and tangled vines at the bottom of the sink. Kim looked back at the cat and met her innocent gaze.

"I suppose you're going to try to tell me you don't know anything about that?" she said.

"Meow-ow."

"I don't believe you."

"Meow," Charity said one final time as she jumped down. With her fluffy tail raised indignantly over her back, she raced toward the double-hinged kitchen door, pushed it open with practiced ease and disappeared.

Kim sighed and looked at the mess in the sink. Well, at least the gun hadn't been necessary.

* * *

It was ten a.m. when Vaughn pulled up outside Skeeter Barnes's wrecking yard. He still couldn't believe that the thumb print Stone had lifted from the handle of Doreen's car had been Skeeter's. In fact, he'd been certain that it would belong to Drayton. Vaughn stepped out of the Bronco and began negotiating his way through piles of discarded tires and rims and other vehicular parts which had been roughly sorted into stacks until he reached the old construction trailer that served as Skeeter's office.

Opening up the door, he peered inside. Unpleasant odors assailed him. A pile of unwashed rags or clothing lay on the floor next to the door. The smell of stale coffee grounds and rotting food drifted to him from the overflowing garbage across the room. Combined with that was the odor of motor oil and grease.

"Skeeter?" he called. No answer. Hesitantly he stepped up into the trailer and looked past the counter to the room beyond, which served as Skeeter's sleeping quarters. Dingy gray bedding trailed half on and half off the mattress. There was no sign of Skeeter. Feeling somewhat relieved, he was about to step back outside into the fresh air and sunshine when he caught sight of something sitting on the counter. A CD stereo. He frowned thoughtfully.

He stepped outside, took a deep breath, and looked around the yard. No sign of Skeeter, but then Vaughn knew he could be just about anywhere. Inside a vehicle catching a nap, underneath a vehicle removing parts, on top of a vehicle soaking up the sun.

"Skeeter," he yelled. No sign of movement.

He turned the other way and cupped his hands around his mouth. "Skeeter," he called again. He waited. A minute later a red ball cap bobbed up at the edge of the property. Skeeter waved an arm in acknowledgement and began heading toward the office. His scrawny legs seemed dangerously inclined to become entangled in his filthy, loose-fitting jeans—the crotch of which hung halfway to his knees—but at each stumbling step, some miracle of balance prevailed and he continued to approach. His t-shirt, which might once have been white, was so full of holes that it barely clung to existence. It appeared to be about two sizes too small as it hugged Skeeter's gaunt frame. Over it he wore a flannel work shirt, its buttons undone and its tails flapping in the breeze.

"Skeeter," Vaughn said, with a nod, by way of greeting when the little man reached him. "How are you?" He managed to ignore the ripe scent of body odor.

"Fine. Fine," Skeeter drawled with a smile that revealed his stained and pointed vampirish teeth. "Can I do sumpthin' for ya, Sheriff? Lookin' for a spare tire, are ya?"

"Not today, Skeeter. I have a couple of questions to ask you, okay?"

Skeeter bobbed his head and fingered the dirty navy and white bandanna he wore at his neck. "Sure. Sure."

"Do you remember Doreen Hanson, Skeeter?"

He narrowed his murky blue eyes thoughtfully. "Pretty lady with brown hair. Yeah, I remember."

"Do you remember what kind of car she drove?"

"Oh yeah," Skeeter acknowledged without hesitation. He puffed up slightly with self-importance. "It was a black Toyota Corolla. Two-door," he added as an afterthought.

Vaughn nodded. "Did you know that Doreen died recently."

Some of the buoyancy faded from Skeeter's expression and he shoved his hands into his pockets, hunching his shoulders forward. He nodded and looked at the toes of his scuffed work boots.

"Skeeter, look at me, please." Vaughn waited until Skeeter lifted his eyes to his face once more. "Can you tell me why we found one of your fingerprints on the door handle of Doreen's car."

With the suddenness of a bolt of lightning, fear sparked in Skeeter's eyes. "I didn' do nothin', Sheriff. You gotta believe me. I wouldn' hurt nobody." He transferred his weight from foot to foot quickly, nervously.

Vaughn laid a calming hand on the little man's shoulder and felt the starkly raised collarbone beneath the shirt. Lord, didn't the guy eat? "I'm not accusing you of anything, Skeeter. I just need to know how your prints got onto the car. That's all."

Skeeter calmed somewhat. "I didn' do nothin'," he said the words almost defiantly. "There was this little bird, see. It had a broken wing an' I fixed it an' then it was time to let it go. When I was lettin' it go, I saw the car. It was just sittin' there, so I looked in it. The keys was in it, so I figured Doreen meant to come back. An' then I saw the CD player. I been gettin' a lot of call for those lately, so I figured—" His eyes widened as he suddenly realized that he had just confessed to theft.

"You took the stereo?" Vaughn pressed.

Skeeter nodded miserably. "I figured she'd get another one. Insurance or sumpthin'."

"I see," Vaughn said. "Do you remember when it was that you came upon the car?"

Skeeter pursed his lips thoughtfully. "Woulda been Tuesday mornin'."

That would have made it the day after she was supposed to have left for Chelan. "Did you see anything else that attracted your attention?" Vaughn asked.

"Like what?" Skeeter asked with a puzzled expression.

Vaughn shrugged slightly. "Something that you thought was strange? Anything that didn't belong?"

Skeeter frowned and stuck out his bottom lip in an expression of exaggerated thoughtfulness. Finally he shook his head. "Nope. Can't remember nothin' strange."

Vaughn nodded. "Okay. Now can you tell me why you were up at the Farris's place last night?"

Skeeter avoided his eyes and licked his lips nervously. "Who says I was up there?"

"I do, Skeeter. I saw you. Do you realize that you could have been shot?"

"Shot!" the little man echoed incredulously. "For lookin' in a window?" And then, suddenly realizing he'd admitted his guilt, he pinched his lips together.

"You could have been shot by Ms. Tannis," Vaughn said. "The people in town are all scared right now, Skeeter. If they catch you trespassing, they may shoot and ask questions later." Skeeter was once again avoiding his gaze. "Look at me, Skeeter," he said. When he complied, Vaughn continued. "The next time I see you or hear about you peeping, I'm going to put you in jail for your own safety. Do you understand?"

Skeeter nodded sullenly. "Yeah."

"Good," Vaughn said. "Okay, Skeeter. I guess that's all for now. But I'll need you to hand over that CD stereo."

Once again, Skeeter's expression turned decidedly glum. "Okay," he muttered petulantly, like a child accepting a punishment he feels is unjust.

Vaughn decided his next stop would be Mike Drayton's place. Where was Mike on Monday night? he wondered. For that matter, where had Drayton been last night? He intended to find out.

* * *

As soon as Vaughn had given her into the hands of Deputy Hall that morning, Kim had asked the deputy Hall to escort her up to the hospital to see Liz. But the intended visit proved impossible. A large, forbidding nurse, who reminded Kim of a prison matron, denied her admittance to her friend's room. "You'll have to wait for visiting hours," she was told firmly. "The doctor hasn't even seen her yet this morning."

So, putting that frustration behind her, Kim decided to go over to the library to see if she could find the book of poetry that had been Anna's favorite. *The Oxford Book of English Verse* Aunt Willie had called it. It felt exceedingly strange to have a deputy following her everywhere. It actually made her feel guilty. As though she were somehow at fault for wasting his time. But, there seemed to be little she could do about it, so she tried to forget his presence.

A few minutes later, Kim was elated to discover that the small Lillooet Creek Library actually had the book she sought. She had been more than half prepared for failure. However, her elation at finding the volume was tempered rather quickly by the sheer enormity of the task facing her. The book had over a thousand pages in it, and Kim had never been much of a poetry fan. How was she going to plod her way through all these poems in time for it to do any good? Determined to find a way, Kim signed out the volume, tucked it under her arm and walked down to Erma's restaurant to have a snack while she waited for the hospital's visiting hours to begin at eleven.

While she waited for the clock to tick its way through another hour, Kim indulged herself in Erma's famous apple pie and a cup of coffee that was almost as good as the Starbuck's coffee she could get back home. Although she had opened the book of poetry with good intentions, she found herself thinking of Vaughn.

Despite Vaughn's initial protestations that he didn't want to get involved, a relationship had developed between them. And in recent days it had begun to move rather quickly. It was obvious that Vaughn was beginning to develop feelings for her. How deep those feelings were, she wasn't certain. Occasionally, though he'd not yet voiced the words, she got the impression that they were strong indeed. That frightened her.

Vaughn had managed to eradicate her conviction that all handsome men were completely self-centered and manipulative. He had proven himself a kind and gentle man, a caring man. But Kim couldn't allow herself to care too much—about any man. How could she yield to the lure of a man's love when she feared in her heart that she would only lose him to death? She was afraid of the pain and of what it would do to her.

Perhaps if he'd been in another profession, something safer, she would have been able to let her guard down enough to involve her heart. But he was a cop, a man who placed his life on the line for others as part of his job. The risk of loving such a man was just too great. She should know. No, when this was all over, it would be better if she just said good-bye and returned to her life in Seattle.

The pain that knifed through her startled her with its intensity. Tears started in her eyes and she blinked them back. Was her heart already involved? Had Vaughn with all his contradictory guises—his toughness and sensitivity, his kindness and brutal frankness—somehow slipped past the walls of her heart? Oh, God, please no, she prayed.

Suddenly more frightened than ever, Kim wished she hadn't accepted Vaughn's invitation to have dinner at his place that evening. She sipped her coffee and stared out the restaurant window at the streets of Lillooet Creek and remembered.

She remembered the incredible intensity of their lovemaking last night. Was it just great sex? Or was it sex made great by the element of love? She had no way of knowing. Her sexual problem had prevented her from ever experiencing lovemaking the way it was meant to be experienced with any other man. She had thought that her increased attraction to Vaughn, the growing satisfaction that she drew from each of their sexual encounters, was just a result of her newly awakened passion. But what if she was wrong? She forced herself to consider the possibility that she was already in love with Vaughn Garrett.

She remembered the way he'd automatically pulled her to him when she'd returned to bed last night after cleaning up Charity's mess. The way he'd curled around her, spoon fashion, sheltering her within his muscular embrace. She had felt so safe, so loved. Kim closed her eyes in despair. It couldn't be. She didn't want it to be. She wouldn't let it be. What they had was simply a mutually rewarding sexual affair between two consenting adults.

She remembered the expression in his eyes when he'd prepared to leave that morning. With Killian in the hospital and another deputy off collecting evidence with Stone, he was short of deputies. Kim had tried to tell him that it was no problem. Telling him she was planning on leaving right away anyway, she had tried to push him out the door to the work she knew awaited him. But he'd refused to go. There had been something in his eyes besides concern for her safety when he'd told her he wouldn't leave until he'd seen her safely drive down the road to the town below. The soft, glowing emotion had made her knees weak as he'd kissed her good-bye and told her he'd see her that evening.

In sudden agitation, Kim raised her coffee cup to her lips and realized it was empty. Damn! She glanced at the clock. Oh, well, it was almost eleven anyway. She'd head on over to the hospital to see Liz.

* * *

Deputy Paul Killian lay in the hospital bed, his blonde hair hidden by swathes of white bandages. Vaughn had come to the hospital as soon as the doctor had informed him that Killian was awake.

"Hi, Paul," he said as he took a seat near the bed. "How are you feeling?"

Killian grimaced, his blue eyes reflecting pain. "You

mean aside from the fact that it feels like somebody is slowly hammering nails into my skull?"

Vaughn smiled slightly. "Yeah, aside from that."

Killian shrugged. "A bit stupid. I didn't provide much protection for Ms. Tannas, did I?"

Vaughn frowned. "You did just fine. Kimberley is all right, so don't worry about it. That's one tricky bastard out there, and I think that part of his game is to prove he can outmaneuver us." He studied Killian's face. "Can you tell me what happened, Paul?"

"Not enough to do any good," he said. "Ms. Tannas had just come home, and I was checking out the house. I'd already checked the main floor and was upstairs. When I entered Ms. Tannas' room, I checked behind the door and then went to check the drawers and things. Suddenly, I heard a noise behind me." He paused, frowning thoughtfully. "Not much of a noise really. It was more like I sensed movement. Anyway, I started to turn around, but before I saw anything I felt something hit my head and that was it. Lights out. I didn't see anything more until I woke up here this morning."

Vaughn tightened his lips as his mind raced. "Where do you think he came from?"

"Had to be the closet," Killian said. "That was the only place I hadn't checked yet. Unless he managed to hide in the hall somehow, but I don't see how he could have." He hit the bed with a clenched fist. "Why the hell didn't I check that closet before I checked the rest of the room?"

"You didn't see anything at all? Did you see what struck you?"

Killian frowned slightly. "It felt like a cannonball." He closed his eyes for a moment and then opened them abruptly. "Wait! Yeah, I think I did see it. It was a baseball bat."

Vaughn nodded. That made sense. He'd seen the bat in Kim's room himself a few days ago. Had it been there last night when he'd examined the room? He didn't remember seeing it? He'd find it and have it checked for prints. With any luck they might belong to Drayton.

He hadn't liked the alibis the Drayton had come up with either for Monday night, when Doreen was killed, or for last night. Monday night, Drayton had apparently been in T.J.'s Bar playing pool until 12:30. Vaughn had already confirmed that with T.J.. But, since the M.E. had placed Doreen's death at sometime between midnight and four a.m., Drayton's alibi didn't mean much. And last night, he had apparently been home alone watching television. Vaughn had confirmed the programs he said he'd watched, but hell, Drayton was the best lead he had. If you subtracted about 60 pounds; if you darkened the eyes from that strange pale green to the hazel green he remembered; if you thickened the hair and lightened it a bit, the guy could be Coyd.

"Okay, Killian, you get some rest. I'll stop by to see you again later."

"Sure. 'Bye, Vaughn."

Vaughn frowned as he left the hospital. The killer was getting bolder. Vaughn had a bad feeling about that. A real bad feeling.

* * *

Vaughn flashed Kim a beaming smile as he opened the door. "God, it's good to see you," he said, grasping her arm and pulling her into the house. He waved good-bye to Ray, who, following orders, had tailed her right into Vaughn's yard, not letting her out of his sight until she was safely in the custody of another officer. Then he shut the door behind her and turned to draw her into his embrace. "It's been so long." He kissed the side of her neck sending little shivers dancing along her nerve-endings.

"Mmm, it must be at least twelve hours," she responded dryly. Guilt ravaged her. She had come here tonight with the intention of telling Vaughn she wanted to end their relationship before they got in too deep. She wondered if she'd be able to do it.

"An eternity." He released her and stepped back. "Let me take your jacket." Shrugging out of it, she handed it to him and waited while he opened the closet. He reached into it to extract a hanger and suddenly stopped in mid-motion.

Vaughn lifted the sleeve of a denim jacket hanging there and stared at it. The tear was there. The jacket had gone missing prior to Doreen's becoming a target, and now that she was dead, it had been returned. Another article belonging to Vaughn that could be linked to the killings. Another element in the psychological war the killer waged with him. He fought the urge to tear it from the hangar and burn it. He would need to have it examined for trace evidence.

"Is something the matter?"

He started slightly and turned to look at her. It took another instant for his eyes to *see* her. Finally, he smiled tightly. "No, of course not. I thought I'd lost that jacket, that's all. I was trying to remember the last time I'd looked in this closet." He grasped her elbow. "Come into the kitchen. I have to check on dinner, and then I'll give you a tour of the house."

"Dinner smells delicious." Kim stood in the center of the kitchen and watched as Vaughn lifted the lids from a pot here or an pan there. Taking a deep breath, she tried to identify the aroma that permeated the air. She failed. "What is it?" she finally asked.

Vaughn shrugged. "A combination of my favorite oriental meals." He pointed to one container. "Deep-fried ocean perch fillets with orange sauce." He removed one pan from the heat source and set it aside. "Thai noodles with prawns." He indicated a stir-fry pan. "Beef chop-suey, and"—he pointed to a basket— "deep-fried chicken wings."

Kim stomach rumbled its appreciation. "I can hardly wait," she said.

"Well, you'll have to, my dear. Didn't your mother teach you that anticipation is the secret ingredient of all great cooks."

"No."

"Tut-tut. Your education is sadly lacking."

"Is that so?"

He walked up to her and, lifting her chin, planted a soft almost non-existent kiss on her lips. "That's so," he breathed. "Now come on and I'll show you my home so that you won't have to peek in the windows any more. We'll start upstairs, I think." Grasping her arm, he led her toward the wide, curving staircase that wound its way up from the near end of the living room.

"This is classified as a one and a half story home," he said as they climbed. "I didn't want a full second story because I like the cathedral ceiling affect over the kitchen and living room. There are two bedrooms, a full bathroom, and a loft. . . playroom up here." He sobered slightly as he mentioned the playroom.

Kim saw the pain reflected briefly in his eyes. "Are you going to bring Landon here to live with you soon?" she asked.

He considered her silently for a moment before nodding. "Yeah, I think so. As his godparent I'm now his legal guardian. But right now Aunt Willie seems to need his presence, and until this investigation is cleared up, I just wouldn't feel right about bringing him home."

Kim nodded. They had reached the top of the stairs. "I understand." She looked out the window at the end of the upstairs hall. She could just make out the roof of something half hidden in the trees out back. "What building is that?" she pointed.

Vaughn followed her gaze. "That's my work shed. It's where I go when I want to escape everything and do some carpentry or some carving. I wanted it quite a distance from the house so that I wouldn't be tempted by distractions." He placed his hand on the small of her back to propel her forward and to their left. "This," he said, opening a door, "is one of the bedrooms."

Surprise robbed Kim of her voice. The room was completely decorated for a little girl. The carpet was a pale petal pink. A pink gingham spread and matching curtains complimented the white Colonial furniture perfectly. And a doll in a pink dress sat in a child's rocking chair.

Vaughn cleared his throat, and Kim switched her attention to him. He seemed embarrassed. "I know I went a bit overboard, but after I chose the carpet the rest just seemed to follow." He drew her to the next room and flicked on the light. "This is the bathroom," he said. "Nothing special here. Tub. Shower. The usual." He grasped her elbow to lead her to the next room. "And this is Landon's room."

Kim smiled. The room was perfectly suited to a little boy. The walls were pale blue. A black-and-red freight train in the guise of a wallpaper border wound its way around the room at ceiling height. A number of plastic toys littered the deep, sapphire-blue carpet in orderly disarray. And a twin size bed with partial rails on its sides sat against one wall. This room, too, had a matching bedspread and curtains, but the design was in shades of light and dark blue with a bit of red accenting.

Vaughn guided her on. "And the last room up here is the playroom." He opened a door. "Nothing in it but space for little ones to run and make noise."

Kim looked into a long, narrow room with open beams and a skylight overhead. He was right. There was nothing in it but space. But knowing children, it certainly wouldn't stay that way once it became Landon's private domain. Kim's stomach rumbled with embarrassing intensity.

Vaughn grinned. "And now, I think we'd better eat before I show you the rest of the house. What do you think?"

Kim sighed. "I thought you'd never ask."

Vaughn laughed and invited her to precede him down the stairs. Within moments, they were ensconced in the dining alcove, feasting on some of the most delicious cuisine that Kim had ever tasted. She tried not to wax too effusive in her praise—she didn't want to magnify Vaughn's already sizable ego—but it was difficult to maintain a suitably decorous demeanor. She even found herself enjoying the wine, which surprised her because she'd never had much of a taste for wine. All in all, the meal was a smashing success. Which made it even more difficult for Kimberley to find a means of broaching the topic she knew she had to discuss.

They were enjoying a cup of coffee after having cleared the table, when Kim finally managed to force herself to bring up the subject. "Vaughn, I've been doing a lot of thinking lately."

"About what?"

"Us."

There was a tense pause. "I see. And what conclusions have you come to about us?" His tone was completely bland.

Kim studied his features, but they revealed absolutely nothing. "Well"—she paused, then forced herself to forge ahead. "I know you haven't said anything, but I get the feeling that our relationship is on the verge of getting serious. And I think that maybe we should cool it for a while."

Vaughn nodded thoughtfully. "This idea of getting serious really bothers you, does it?"

"You know it does. I explained that to you before."

"Oh, yes, I remember. Something about every man you ever loved being killed." He rose and walked over to the cupboard where he began scraping leftovers into storage containers for the fridge. "So what you're telling me is that you'd rather have a cold, lonely existence— starting right now—than risk falling in love with me and perhaps end up having a cold, lonely existence after something happens to me. If something ever does."

Kimberley stared at him stonily. "You make it sound stupid."

He placed the palms of his hands down on the counter top and stood there with his back to her, his posture radiating tension. "I don't need to make it sound stupid, Kimberley. It is stupid." His tone was still low, still evenly modulated, and somehow communicated more than if he would have shouted at her. "Dammit, Kim! You're running away again. Running away from something that might never happen."

Tears threatened and she blinked them back. She would not cry. "Can I help it if I'm an emotional coward? Do you have any idea what it's like to lose someone you love?"

"Yeah, I think I do." His voice rose slightly for the first time as he skirted the cupboard and walked toward her. He stood over her, looking down at her with a curiously intense expression that she couldn't read. "I've been getting a crash course lately in what it feels like to lose my friends. It doesn't take much of a stretch of the imagination to magnify that pain."

"I'm sorry." But Kim had time to say nothing more before Vaughn jerked her to her feet. Before she had time to do more than gasp in surprise, his mouth descended on hers with bruising intensity. Her breasts were crushed against his hard male chest. His hands began to roam her body with knowledgeable expertise. There was nothing warm or tender in his embrace, no sensitivity. It was ruthless and punishing. And yet, despite that, Kim felt her traitorous body begin to respond to the calculated caresses.

Suddenly he broke off the kiss. Continuing to hold her, he looked down into her face. "So, you want sex without any emotional involvement, do you, Kim?" he asked quietly. "Sex without friendship or love. Did you like it, Kim?"

As the meaning of his words sunk in, Kim stiffened in his arms. She was too angry to formulate a suitable response to such a cold, calculated assault. "Let me go." She forced the words through her clenched teeth.

He ignored her. When he spoke again his tone was more controlled. "No matter how much it might hurt to lose it someday, Kim, I would never deny myself the opportunity to love. It's love that makes us human, Kim. We may not love each other forever. Hell, we may not even fall in love at all. But we should have the chance to fall in love. Don't you understand that?"

Kim tested the limits of his embrace and found that he allowed her to step away. "Understanding it, intellectually, and feeling it, here"—she tapped her chest—"are two different things."

"Maybe, but you're an intelligent and a sensitive woman. Don't you believe, in there"—he tapped her chest—"that having love, even for a short time, is better than never having it at all?" He paused and studied her face. "Think about that. Think about what you may be throwing away for the sake of a fear that in all likelihood will prove to be totally groundless."

Kim studied his solemn face and compassionate gaze. He had done a lot for her. "I'll think about it," she said. She owed him that much.

"Good," he smiled at her so tenderly that she felt tears sting her eyes again. She looked out the window and blinked rapidly. What the hell was the matter with her lately?

Suddenly uncomfortable in the silence, Kim cleared her throat and bent over to pick her napkin up off the floor. It must have fallen when Vaughn had pulled her to her feet. "Well, I should be going soon. It's after ten and I don't want to leave Liz alone in the house for too long. She's supposed to rest."

Vaughn nodded and moved back to the cupboard where he began loading dirty dishes into the dishwasher. "I understand."

And he did understand. He understood that she needed time to think and space to do it in. He understood that she was terrified of the feelings that she was beginning to develop for him. And, he understood that he was terrified by the realization that he already loved her. This time, he knew what he felt was love. It was more intense than anything he'd ever felt. Thoughts of Kim invaded his mind at every unguarded moment. He felt an incredible sense of happiness, of completeness, whenever she was near. And sex had become the most incredible phenomenon he had ever experienced. The thought of losing all of that scared him to death.

Instinct had warned him that she wasn't ready for a declaration of love, and he had heeded it. Now he was infinitely glad that he had. When Kim had introduced the topic of *us*, the sudden tension in his chest had been so nearly unbearable that he had thought briefly that his heart might stop. Then he had simply reacted to her words intuitively. Avoiding any assertions of love, he had tried to argue his cause as diplomatically as possible. He had to convince Kimberley to give them a chance. He hoped he had done that. But he knew, too, that the next time they slept together, the initiative would have to be Kim's. He needed to be sure of her.

"Do you want some help with the pots and pans before I go?" Kim's voice startled him back from thoughts.

"No. No, that's fine. Let me just call Ray to escort you home. I'll see you tomorrow." Vaughn removed his cell phone from his belt clip and called, speaking briefly with Ray.

She stood indecisively watching him move around the kitchen for a moment while they waited for her escort. Finally, she heard a horn blast. "See me to the door?" she asked.

"Oh, sure." He walked her to the door and helped

her with her coat. "Thanks for coming," he said as he opened the door.

Kim nodded and stepped out. Abruptly, she turned back to face him. Her eyes searched his face hesitantly. And then, slowly, she moved forward until she stood so close to him that he could feel her breasts against his chest. As she wrapped her arms about his waist and hugged him, his arms went about her automatically. "Thanks for dinner," she said. Then, quickly, she raised herself on her toes and planted a soft kiss on his mouth. "Bye."

"Bye," he murmured as he let her go and watched her walk to her car. As she drove down the drive, with Ray tailing her in his cruiser, Vaughn turned away and closed the door. A faint smile curved his lips.

* * *

Kim sat in the living room reading poetry. She was quickly coming to the conclusion that it wasn't going to do her a heck of a lot of good to read it when she didn't have access to all the poetry the killer had written. She should have taken the volume over for Vaughn to read. Sighing her boredom, she set the volume aside. It was almost midnight. She'd get ready for bed, make herself a cup of hot chocolate, and then see if she couldn't plod through a little more. It certainly couldn't hurt and she just might come across something.

A half hour later, her hair still damp from the shower, Kim wrapped herself in a blanket—she still hadn't invested in a housecoat—and descended the stairs. Her mind on the words Vaughn had said earlier, she wandered into the kitchen to plug in the kettle. A sudden noise at the kitchen door startled her. She checked it to make certain it was securely locked and then listened for a repeat of the strange sound. It never came. It had sounded like a tree branch scratching the house, but she was certain there were no trees growing that close. Maybe it had only been some dry leaves rustling their way along the veranda. A chill undulated its way up her spine and she shrugged it off. Imagination could, at times, be an enemy. Look at what had happened the other night. She could have shot the damn cat, for Pete's sake.

Hot chocolate in hand, struggling with her makeshift housecoat, Kim returned to the living room. Resuming her position at one end of the sofa, she reached to retrieve the volume of poetry from the end table where she'd left it. Her hand froze in mid-air.

The book was no longer the way she'd left it. She distinctly remembered closing it in disgust before going upstairs for her shower. Now it lay open. Slowly, she leaned forward to read the title of the poems on the open page. *The Dream*, the first was called. Her eyes moved to the right page. *The Funeral.*

There was something teasing at the edges of her mind. Something important. But her eyes glued to the page of their own accord, and Kim picked up the book and read. Two lines, each from a separate verse, jumped out at her.

That subtle wreath of hair about mine arm;
As prisoners then are manacled, when they're condemn'd to die.

And then, with the force of a blow, the realization struck her. He was here. In the house. Again. Panic gripped her. Dropping her blanket, she raced toward the door to Liz's bedroom and stopped halfway there. What if he was in there? She needed to alert the deputy outside.

Her breath caught in her throat as she ran toward the front door. But what if he had incapacitated Cheney already, like he had Deputy Killian the other night? Kim yanked open the front door and froze in indecision. Was he out here waiting for her? She'd forgotten the gun. Her eyes scanned the darkness seeking the green cruiser. There! At the edge of the drive, camouflaged by the darkness and the foliage of her aunt's enormous weeping willow, the sheriff's department vehicle blended into the night.

Kim waved, hoping to attract the deputy's attention, wishing she could see him in the blackness. There was no response. Slowly, she descended the stairs, peering into the darkness as she walked onto the lawn toward the drive. She waved again. Again there was no response. A sob rose in her throat. She choked it back.

* * *

He stood in the shadows. She was so close he could smell the perfume rising from the heat of her skin. So close. His hand tensed on the knife in his hand. He had only to reach out and she would be his. She had not even sensed his presence. That disappointed him. He wanted her to feel Danger's kiss. He would wait. Soon, she would feel the chill and turn to look into his eyes. Soon.

But she did not. For endless seconds that stretched into moments, she stood in front of him her slender back rigid with tension as she stared silently at the empty sheriff's department cruiser. Finally, she turned to her right and walked back into the house. He frowned. If only she'd turned left instead of right, she would have seen him. Oh, well, it was not quite time yet anyway.

He wished he could stay to see her reaction to the message he'd left her. He was quite proud of it. But unfortunately, another matter demanded his attention. He looked off in the direction taken by the scuttling form that had descended the tree just prior to Kim coming out of the house.

* * *

Kim walked slowly back into the house and closed and locked the door. She had felt his presence, like a cancer in the night. It had stopped her cold. She had considered going on to the cruiser, but the fact that the deputy had not responded to her wave did not bode well. Instinct prompted her to feign ignorance, to hide her fear.

Now she leaned against the door and wiped the icy perspiration from her face. She had to get help. Vaughn. Galvanized into action, she headed for the phone. She had almost reached it when she stopped and looked toward the front of the house and him. Although she couldn't see him, he could see her easily through the living room windows. She couldn't stand that. She felt like an insect in a jar. She'd use the phone on the kitchen wall. He'd have to move around the side of the house to look into the kitchen window.

She pushed open the door to the kitchen and froze. The back door stood wide open. How could that be? It had been securely latched only a few minutes earlier. And then she looked beyond the door. Into the darkness. Into cold, dead eyes.

"No." The denial emerged as a faint whisper. "God damn you," she screamed as she ran forward and clutched desperately at Charity's swaying body. The enormous Persian had been hanged. It was only as she managed to release the noose from the cat's neck and lay her on the veranda floor that Kimberley realized that Charity also had been cruelly disemboweled.

Kim stared in horror at the blood and entrails staining her nightgown. Fighting back the bile that rose in her throat, she staggered back. Phone. She had to get help.

Shock blinded her to everything. She moved like an automaton as she raced back into the kitchen and picked up the receiver. Automatically, she dialed Vaughn's number. And then she saw it. Another note. Another poem. Attached to the wall with one of her aunt's steak knives.

Danger's kiss, with a serpent's stealth,
Crawls up your spine to warn
Of the impending storm.

Beware! The kiss of Death.

"Hello. I'm unable to come to the phone right now. If—" But Kim didn't hear the faint voice coming through the receiver. Fear and rage blinded her.

Seeking relief in an act of mindless violence, she used the only weapon at hand, the receiver of the telephone, to strike out at her tormentor.

"Bastard," she screamed as she knocked the knife from the wall. "I'll kill you. I'll kill you. I'll kill you."

And then, just as suddenly as it had gripped her, the rage left her and she crumpled to the floor, her mind numbed by shock. "Why are you doing this?" She directed her eyes and her question to the open kitchen door. "Why?"

CHAPTER 17

No one answered. She saw nothing but a rope, swaying in the night breeze and the soft stirring of Charity's gray fur. Tears streaming unheeded down her face, Kim half crawled, half stumbled back out onto the veranda where she slumped down next to the dead cat.

She could picture in her mind Charity's terror when faced with the unexpected cruelty of a human being. The cat would have fought for her life, Kimberley knew. But she was just a small animal. A domestic animal that had relied on people to provide her with her needs in exchange for her love and companionship. Guilt gnawed at Kim.

"I'm sorry, Charity," she said as she stroked the cat's soft fur. "I'm sorry I didn't protect you. I'm sorry."

Those were the words Liz heard as she pushed open the kitchen door. She stared in disbelief at the scene before her. The painkiller she had taken earlier continued to fog her thoughts, and for an instant, Liz thought herself caught in the grip of a nightmare. Noise, the sound of shouting— something, had pulled her doggedly from her drug-induced sleep to face this horror.

She was caught in a nightmare. But it was real. And suddenly Liz was very afraid.

Swallowing back the urge to panic, to scream in horror, Liz focused on her need to get help. She went to the phone and, catching the dangling receiver, replaced it briefly in its cradle before lifting it again and dialing the number of the sheriff's department. Time slowed to a crawl. She closed her eyes to the sight of the blood as she waited for the phone to ring, for someone to answer it. She had to stay calm or she'd be no help at all to Kim. But there was so much blood everywhere. It streaked the wall and the floor. She felt it's stickiness where it smeared the handle of the receiver. Was Kim hurt?

Someone answered the phone on the first ring.

"Hello. This is Liz Murphy. Could you please send some—"

"I'm sorry, but you'll have to slow down. I can't understand you. Calm down, Ms. Murphy."

Liz stared at the phone in frustration. What the dickens was the matter with the dispatcher? She had purposely made an effort to speak slowly and clearly. Was the woman deaf? She began again. "This is Liz Murphy. Could you please send someone up to Vivian Farris's? Something has happened."

"Can you tell me what happened?"

"No." Liz grit her teeth against the urge to scream hysterically at the woman on the other end.

"Hold on a moment while I try to reach Deputy Cheney. He should be up there."

Liz's heart suddenly stuttered. Ray was up here. Where was he? Why hadn't he stopped all this? She held her breath as she waited for the dispatcher to come back on the line. What was taking her so long?

"Ms. Murphy?"

"I'm here."

"Sheriff Garrett is on his way over now."

"Sheriff Garrett?"

"That's right, Ms. Murphy."

"But where's Deputy Cheney?"

"I'm afraid he's not answering his radio at the moment. He could be temporarily away from his cruiser."

Liz swallowed. "No. Something's wrong. What about his cell phone?"

"Please, Ms. Murphy, you must stay calm. The sheriff will be there any minute. Can you give me any idea what happened there?"

"I was asleep."

"Is Ms. Tannas all right?"

Liz looked at Kim, still sitting on the veranda in her bloodstained nightgown. "I think so. But the cat is dead."

* * *

Vaughn was cruising the streets, trying to put off the seductive lure of sleep and the inevitable nightmares that accompanied it, when the call came over the radio from Mrs. Wright. His heart leapt into his throat when he realized there were more problems at Kim's. Shit! He already had one deputy hospitalized. Where the hell was Cheney? And if Cheney was incapable of answering his radio or cell what had happened? Was Kim all right? Why hadn't Liz known Kim's condition? The questions burned in his mind as corrosive as acid.

He pulled up behind the cruiser already parked in the driveway and stopped so abruptly that the Bronco was still rocking when he leapt from it. He barely paused long enough to direct a beam of light from his flashlight into Ray's cruiser and ascertain that it was, in actuality, empty before racing to the house. Barely slowing his momentum, he turned the handle of the front door and leaned his shoulder into it with enough force to throw it back on its hinges—if it had been unlocked. Damn! He hammered at it in frustration. And then, not bothering to wait for someone to open it, he ran along the veranda to the side of the house.

His brain registered the components of what he saw without drawing any conclusions: a dangling hangman's noose. A small, dark lump lying in front of the door. Blood. His heart stopped and his breath froze in his lungs as he opened the kitchen door. Kimberley sat numbly on a kitchen chair while Liz stood next to her wringing a cloth out into a bowl of water already red with blood. "Kimberley?" His voice sounded choked and barely audible even to his own ears.

Liz looked up as he entered the kitchen. "Kim's all right, Vaughn," she hastened to assure him after a single glance at his face. "She's all right."

His heart began to beat again. "What happened?" he asked.

"I'm not certain. I haven't pressed Kim for details yet. I thought it would be best to clean her up first."

Vaughn nodded and looked at the blood-streaked kitchen. "I'm going to call, Stone. I think he'll want to see this." Pulling his cell phone from his belt clip, Vaughn went into the living room. The room appeared untouched. It was as he was hanging up that he glanced down and saw the open volume of poetry.

The words of *The Funeral* stared up at him. "Coyd," he whispered. Kim was right. Coyd was alive. He had always had a fascination with that poem. Vaughn had grown to hate it. Now, for the first time in almost 20 years, he forced himself to read it. A chunk of ice settled in his stomach. Suddenly he knew the motive behind the killings, understood the interpretation Coyd would glean from the last line: *since you would have none of me, I bury some of you.* The motive was revenge. But it was revenge for rejection—childhood rejection.

Coyd had always been friendless. There had just been something about him that seemed to keep people at arm's length. They had both been loners, but solitude was something that Vaughn had usually wanted. Lack of acceptance had always forced Coyd into isolation.

Vaughn closed his eyes as memory, painful and caustic, assailed him. He remembered the last words they had spoken.

"You just don't want me," Coyd had shouted at him.

"It's not that I don't want you. It's just that I can't take you," Vaughn had said. He had been 16, Coyd 14. Vaughn had decided that he was old enough to leave Anna's. Aunt Willie had helped him to find a job after school and on weekends that would pay enough to supply him with room and board and a little spending money. How could he have taken Coyd? He couldn't have made enough money to support them both, and there wasn't any work for Coyd. Besides, Coyd was young enough that Anna could have started trouble if they'd both tried to leave at the same time.

Still, in the end, Coyd had left even before Vaughn. When Coyd had disappeared, there had still been a week to go before Vaughn could pay his first month's board and move out of Anna's. Vaughn had always wondered with a sense of guilt if Coyd had committed suicide. Now, he wondered how Coyd had managed to fake his death. Where had he spent the last 15 years?

Thoughtfully, he walked back into the kitchen. Despite the lack of proof, he agreed with Kim. His instincts told him Coyd was alive. But now was not the time to think of that. Where was Ray?

Liz looked up as he entered the room. "I'm just going to take Kim upstairs and help her change."

Vaughn nodded. "I'll be outside for a while. Stone will be here shortly."

Liz stared at him solemnly for a moment. "Find him, Vaughn."

He wasn't quite certain if she meant Ray or the perp, but either way the answer was the same. "Yeah." He stepped out the door, carefully avoiding the cat's body, and began to search the grounds by flashlight.

It took him almost 20 minutes to find Ray.

Trussed up and stuffed beneath Liz's van with a gag in his mouth, he appeared to be just regaining consciousness. Upon a cursory examination, Vaughn discovered a goose egg on his head the size of Mount Olympus. Kneeling, he untied Ray, removed the gag and did a more thorough examination for injuries. Other than the lump on his head, he seemed unharmed.

After Ray had coughed and sputtered for a moment, his tongue worked extremely well. The mildest comment was, "If I get my hands on that son-of-a-bitch, he's gonna wish he'd killed himself."

Vaughn ignored him as he gently examined the wound on his head again to see if the skin had been broken.

"Ouch," Ray said, jerking his head away and giving Vaughn an accusing stare. "You tryin' to finish the job or what?"

Vaughn just shook his head. "Can you make it to the house?"

"Of course I can make it to the house. What the hell kind of question is that? He hit me on the head. He didn't chop off my friggin' legs."

Without further delay, Vaughn helped Ray to his feet. Despite his assertion, Vaughn noticed that Ray swayed unsteadily for a moment and leaned on him rather heavily. At least with Ray concentrating on putting one foot in front of the other, his mouth wasn't working. Vaughn had always known Ray had a temper, but he'd rarely seen it in action.

Five minutes later, Vaughn had Ray seated at the kitchen table. Ignoring all of Cheney's threats and admonitions, he'd called Dr. Harcourt. The doctor had instructed him to bring Ray down to the hospital for an examination. They were just launching into that argument when Liz returned to the room.

"She's resting," Liz responded to Vaughn's unspoken question. "I gave her a couple of sleeping pill to help her relax." Seeing Ray, Liz moved swiftly to his side. "Are you all right?"

"Except for the knot on my head, I'm fine."

Vaughn noted that his tone lost a considerable amount of surliness when he responded to Liz.

Liz explored his head with gentle fingers. "This guy has a nasty tendency of just conking anybody who gets in his way, doesn't he?"

"It could be worse," Vaughn observed.

Liz looked up sharply. "Yes. It could, couldn't it?"

"What happened, Ray?" Vaughn asked.

"I heard a cat howling like somebody was stepping on its tail or something. But the sound was muffled, as if she was inside something she couldn't get out of. It was the damndest sound I ever heard. Made my hair stand up.

"Anyway, I figured it might be that big gray one that I've seen goin' in and out of here, so I went lookin' to see if I could figure out what she'd got herself caught in. I'd just passed the rear corner of the house—I was heading toward that old garage—when, out of the corner of my eye, I saw something coming at me. I tried to duck, but I wasn't fast enough. Next thing I knew, I was lookin' up at you."

Vaughn looked at Liz. "Neither you or Kim heard anything?"

Liz shook her head. "The pills that Dr. Harcourt gave me knocked me out. I wouldn't have heard an earthquake."

"And Kim?" he asked.

Liz frowned. "I'm not certain. Her hair was still damp when I found her, so she was probably in the shower."

Vaughn nodded and slapped his palm against the wall in frustration. "This guy has taken two of my deputies out of commission and we still don't even know what he looks like." Although he was certain he knew who they were looking for, Vaughn desperately needed to know what Coyd looked like *now*. What name did he go by? Where did he live?

There was a knock at the door. Special Agent Stone had arrived.

Almost three hours later, Stone had taken enough pictures to fill an album. He'd carefully bagged and tagged the mutilated feline, the note and the steak knife. After Vaughn had shown him the book of poetry, indicating the particular poem to which it had been left open, he had also confiscated the library book. Now, Stone and Vaughn stood together on the veranda at the front of the house.

"So, what you're telling me is that you think you know the killer's identity. But because fifteen years have passed since you last saw him, you have no idea who he is or who he's pretending to be."

Vaughn swallowed and nodded. "Basically that's it. Any Caucasian man in his late twenties or early thirties who arrived in Lillooet Creek"—he paused thoughtfully—"say within the last five years, could be Coyd. The only other criterion is that he would have had to have gone to Seattle in April a year ago. And for the most part, the people I have listed as being there told me voluntarily. That kind of information is easy to hide."

Stone nodded. "We're getting closer to him," he said. "But we need to move faster. We managed to get his blood type from that small amount we found on the piece of denim. DNA test will take longer though, so we can't count on that helping us. There was some blood embedded beneath the cat's nails that might be human. I'm going to have that checked too, see if it matches."

Vaughn nodded. "I'm going to search the grounds as soon as it's daylight. Maybe—" With a tense shrug that revealed his frustration, he let his voice trail off.

"Vaughn?" Liz called to him from the front door. He walked over to her. "There's no way that Ray is going to stay in the hospital for observation. I barely managed to convince him to see the doctor at all. So if you're going to be staying with Kim, I thought I'd stay with Ray. Just for tonight, you understand. I'd like to make certain he's all right. So, are you? Planning on staying, I mean?"

Vaughn held up a hand to forestall her flow of words. "It's all right, Liz. I understand. And yes, I'm planning to stay the night in Ray's stead."

Concern shadowed Liz's eyes. "If you're sure. I mean if you need me, I'll stay."

"I'm sure, Liz. Go with Ray."

She sighed and smiled slightly. "Okay, then. I'll see you tomorrow."

He rejoined Stone and they watched as Liz and Ray left together. "Has she come up with anything else that could help us?" Stone asked.

The question startled Vaughn. Despite Stone's earlier counsel concerning psychics, the thought of actively involving Liz in the investigation had not even occurred to him. He admitted as much to Stone.

Stone nodded. "I'm not surprised. Employing psychic techniques in an investigation is a direct departure from everything we are taught concerning the gathering of concrete evidence. Still, I think I'd like to get Ms. Murphy to look at some of the evidence and see if she can give us anything that might help."

Vaughn nodded. "I'll ask her to come in tomorrow morning."

Stone nodded and without further comment began walking toward his rental car. Just before he got in, he turned. "Good night, Garrett," he said. The words were mechanical, an afterthought, because Stone's gaze was still turned inward to the thoughts that occupied his mind.

"Good night, Stone." Vaughn didn't think the other man heard the words.

Vaughn went into the house and carefully closed and locked the doors. He then proceeded to check every window and latch in the house. When he'd finished that, he went up to check on Kimberley. Her face was drawn, and as white as the lacy spread on her bed. Yet as soon as he stepped into the room, her eyes opened.

"Vaughn?"

"I'm here, honey." He sat down on the edge of the bed and picked up her small, fragile hand in his. It was cold and he rubbed the flesh absently as he studied her face. It was strange how, within the matter of a few short weeks, her face had grown to be so dear to him.

"Will you stay the night?" she asked. Despite her fear, her voice was still as low and as rich as always. But he knew the question was prompted by fear, and that knowledge hurt.

"Tonight and every night until he's caught. You're not spending any more nights in this house without me. Okay?"

She studied his face briefly. Finally, she smiled slightly. "Okay," she agreed.

* * *

It was dawn. Vaughn had spent the night alternately pacing the house and sitting on the sofa. Liz had called once to let him know that, except for a definite bruise, the doctor had given Ray a clean bill of health. Now, as he watched the sun paint the horizon, he decided that there was probably enough light for him to do a thorough search of the yard. Just as he rose, he caught sight of Kim coming down the stairs. She was completely dressed and carried her purse over her shoulder.

He frowned up at her. "You didn't get much rest, did you?"

She shrugged. "Neither did you. Besides, I want to go up and visit Aunt Viv and Dee today. I can't just tell them about Charity over the phone. Aunt Viv had that cat for more than five years." She came to a stop at the bottom of the stairs.

Vaughn stared at her. He couldn't decide whether the matter-of-fact tone of voice was an act or whether she really had recovered that thoroughly from the evening before. The problem with Kim was that she never wanted to allow herself to reveal any emotion that might be construed as a weakness. And because she had completely lost her composure last night, she would attempt to maintain an absolutely rigid control today. He decided that it was an act.

"I don't think it's a good idea for you to go up to your cousin's today." Coyd had struck during the day when he'd accosted Doreen. And if he stuck true to the pattern that Stone perceived, he would strike at Kimberley within the next 48 hours. "Even with an escort, it may not be safe."

Kim smiled humorlessly. "It's not safe anywhere. Besides, I'll only be gone for the morning. I promised Aunt Willie I'd watch Landon this afternoon while she went to the funeral." She studied his face intently for a moment. "You are going, aren't you?"

"Yes, of course."

She nodded. "When are you planning to tell Aunt Willie that Landon is your son?"

Vaughn shrugged. "It will come out when they read Doreen's will this afternoon that I have been named as Landon's godparent. A lot of people will probably put two and two together then. But I still don't plan to take Landon home until this is over." He walked over to look out the window. "Everything is too uncertain." He didn't tell her that part of the uncertainty he faced concerned Kimberley herself. If he managed to convince her that she should spend her life with him, would she be ready to take on the responsibility of a child as well? She had said once that she planned to adopt. Had the statement been a serious intention or merely something she was considering? There were a lot of things for them to work out, and none of it could be done until Coyd was caught.

"I think that's a good idea," Kim said.

Vaughn turned at her words, a frown of confusion

on his face. "Pardon me? I was thinking."

"I said, I think it's a good idea that you're planning on leaving Landon with Aunt Willie until everything is more settled. It'll allow him a little time to begin adjusting to the loss of his mother. You are seeing him regularly, aren't you?"

Vaughn nodded. "Every day, for at least a few minutes."

"Good. You don't want to be a stranger to him."

"Yeah. I know." Vaughn put his hands in his pockets as he looked at her.

"Well, I'd better get moving. I want a quick cup of coffee and then I'm off."

"Listen, Kim. If you insist on driving up there, I want you to do something for me."

"Sure. What is it?"

"Phone Deirdre and let her know you're coming. Tell her if you're not there by"— he paused to look at his watch—"by eight o'clock she is to call me immediately."

Kim hesitated. Finally, she nodded. "All right. If you really think it's necessary."

* * *

Vaughn watched Kim back out of the driveway and Deputy Jordan Hall pull out of the drive to follow her. Then, taking a deep breath of the fresh morning air, he set about searching the property for any evidence that might lead them to the perp. There were a number of partial prints that could have belonged to anybody, but nothing obvious. Nothing conclusive. There was a cigarette butt that on examination proved to be fairly old. Certainly not from the previous night. He collected it, but he didn't think it would tell them anything.

He checked the area near the rear corner of the house carefully since that was where Ray seemed to think the perp had come from. Finding nothing, he moved on to the lilac bushes. He frowned thoughtfully as he studied them. There were a number of broken branches. But the bushes formed a dense growth. Vaughn couldn't understand why anyone would force their way through such an impenetrable hedge. Even a child would have found the task uncomfortable, to say the least. Unless, ...

Standing back, he considered the area. Unless, that person was frightened, very frightened. His pulse began to race. Had they finally gotten a break? Had there been two people here last night? The perp and a witness? His hopes soared. He crouched down near the lilacs and carefully studied the ground around them. Damn! Nothing. He walked along the hedge until he came to the garage. There, a small path alongside the garage went further back onto the property. He followed it back for a brief distance and then turned to walk along the lilac hedge from the other side. Once again, broken branches revealed the spot where the person had forced his way through the barrier. Vaughn squatted to study the ground and peer into the dense shrubbery.

Nothing. His high hopes began to plummet. Who could it have been? He stared thoughtfully at the base of the hedge.

Any number of kids, he supposed. There was a young gang that made a regular habit of raiding gardens and that kind of thing. Harmless pranks mostly. Still, he didn't think any of those kids had the confidence to act alone. And if there'd been any more than one person, he was certain they would have left more evidence of their passing. So where did that leave him?

He didn't know of any prankster adults who could have been up here last night. Or did he? "Skeeter," he said to himself. With sudden certainty, he rose. He would have bet gold that Skeeter had been up to his peeping activities last night and had had the bejeesus scared out of him by something he'd seen.

Vaughn had a visit to make. Walking purposefully

back along the hedge, his mind occupied, he almost missed it. In fact he would have missed it entirely if an errant breeze had not plucked at it causing it to wave in his face. He stopped and stared at the small scrap of navy and white fabric. A bandanna. A bandanna, filthy with grease and grime. Quickly donning a glove, he reached out and disentangled the material from the lilac branch. He had last seen it tied around Skeeter's neck. It confirmed his suspicion. Skeeter had been here last night. Skeeter was a witness. He placed the scrap of fabric in a plastic bag.

Vaughn was just getting into his Bronco to head over to Skeeter's when Ray and Liz pulled into the drive. He walked over to them. "Morning, Ray, Liz." He suddenly remembered his conversation with Stone last evening. "Listen, Liz, Special Agent Stone asked me to let you know that he'd really like to speak with you this morning, if you don't mind."

Liz stared at him speechlessly for a second. "Oh, um, no, I don't mind. When?"

Vaughn shrugged. "Whenever it's convenient for you, I guess, but as soon as possible."

Liz nodded. "Is Kim home?"

Vaughn shook his head. "No, she went up to Deirdre's for the morning. She'll be home this afternoon."

"Well, I'll just change and be on my way then." She looked at Ray. "I'll see you later?"

"Sure thing. I'll call you this afternoon."

Both men watched Liz walk toward the house. Then Vaughn turned to Ray. "I think we may have gotten our first break in this case."

"That's great. What is it?"

Vaughn proceeded to tell him about his suspicions and suppositions. "I'm just heading over to the wrecking yard now."

"All right if I meet you there? I just want to follow Liz to the office, and then I'm free."

"Sure. See you there." Vaughn got into his Bronco

and, taking advantage of the extra wide driveway, maneuvered around Ray's cruiser to head down into the town ahead of him.

* * *

As Vaughn parked his Bronco and headed up to the wrecking yard office, a sense of something not right assailed him. He paused. The early morning sun warmed his back through his shirt. Flies buzzed. A breeze rattled some bicycle chains hanging from a hook on a light pole. Yet it seemed too quiet somehow. He felt like he was being watched. Slowly, he made a full turn. He couldn't see anybody. "Skeeter," he called. There was no answer. Not even a hint of movement.

Squaring his shoulders, he shook off the illogical feeling. It wasn't even nine a.m. yet. Skeeter was probably still sound asleep in his bed. So who's watching you then? a distant part of his mind demanded. He ignored it. Stepping up to the door of the office, he knocked.

No answer. He knocked again. "Skeeter, it's Sheriff Garrett," he called. "You awake?"

Again, there was no reply. He frowned. That was odd. Grasping the handle of the door, he turned it. The minute the door opened, the unpleasant odors he remembered—although somehow more potent—struck him like a solid wall. How could anybody live like this? As he stepped up into the trailer, he realized that another smell had been added to the blend already present: the strong scent of human excrement.

It took only a second more for him to discover why. As he looked past the counter into the area used as living quarters, he saw Skeeter sprawled on the bed. One of his arms trailed off onto the floor. Three narrow streams of blood wound their way down the arm culminating in a black sticky pool. Skeeter was dead. In death, his sphincter muscles had relaxed, releasing bladder and bowel contents. Vaughn clenched his jaw. No matter how many times he saw it, he'd never get used to the fact that there was no dignity in death.

Why hadn't he gotten here sooner? As he listened to the silence, he remembered again the sense of being watched. He was 75 percent certain that his instincts were right. And it obviously hadn't been Skeeter watching him. Was the killer still here? Hiding in one of the hundreds of vehicles scattered about the property? Coyd, in whatever persona he used now, watching them, enjoying the game he'd devised?

CHAPTER 18

Vaughn had no doubt that—despite the obvious difference in the M.O.—Skeeter had been killed by the same man as the other victims. As Vaughn had surmised, Skeeter had been a witness last night. And his presence had been noted by the killer. Skeeter had died for being in the wrong place at the wrong time. *That* was why the M.O. was different.

Vaughn heard the door open behind him. Reacting on pure instinct, he whirled, grabbing his gun as he prepared to confront the man who, in his thoughts had the face of a boy, Coyd. Only it wasn't Coyd standing there, or anyone who could be mistaken for him. It was Ray.

With a sigh, Vaughn relaxed and returned his gun to its holster.

"Jesus, Vaughn. What the hell's the matter with you?" Ray stepped up into the trailer.

Vaughn gestured over his shoulder to Skeeter's body. "I think you'd better call Doc Harcourt. We're going to need the ambulance again. I'll call Stone. He'll probably want to have that M.E. he brought in stick around to do another autopsy."

"Ah, damn." Ray shook his head.

331

"Yeah," Vaughn agreed. "It looks like you were lucky you didn't see him last night, Ray. In all probability, Skeeter did."

* * *

Liz stepped hesitantly into the office indicated by Melissa. Unobserved for the moment, she regarded Stone at work. He was a young man, perhaps a little older than Vaughn, with a high forehead and intelligent eyes. But then, she'd noticed all that about him before. There was something different about him today. What was it? Abruptly, he looked up, and in that instant Liz knew what it was. Intensity. She had seen it before while observing chess masters in competition: a single-minded concentration capable of blocking out the world.

"Ms. Murphy, please have a seat." He indicated the chair sitting in front of his desk. "I appreciate you coming in."

Liz stepped into the office. "You're welcome. I'm just not quite certain what it is you expect of me." She took a seat in the chair he'd indicated.

Stone nodded. "Then let me explain. Vaughn told me some time ago that you had offered to help us by utilizing certain extrasensory abilities you possess. I believe the time has now come to attempt to use that capability in a more direct manner. Can you tell me what form your talent usually takes?"

Liz studied Stone's face seeking duplicity or mockery. She found none. Finally, she nodded. "Visions, usually. Sometimes they're very accurate in detail, and other times they seem to be almost completely symbolic. And feelings, emotions. I almost always feel an emotion as part of the vision. A couple of times I have heard a voice, but that occurs extremely rarely."

Stone nodded knowledgeably. "Clairvoyance with a touch of clairaudience. Have you ever attempted to help with this type of investigation before?"

"No."

"I see. Have you ever purposely sought the visions in order to try to clarify something or help somebody?"

Liz nodded. "Yes, a few times. But I wasn't always successful."

Stone leaned back in his chair to consider her. "Ms. Murphy, I'm going to be honest with you. I believe it is imperative that we learn all we can about this man as soon as possible. With that in mind, if you are willing, I would like to show you some of the evidence collected at the scenes. Then I would simply ask that you tell me of any impressions you might receive. What do you say?"

Liz plucked nervously at the material of her skirt. She wouldn't refuse, couldn't refuse. But the thought of what she was about to attempt made her dearly wish she could. "Yes, of course," she said to Stone. "I'll do my best."

"Good." Stone opened one of the drawers in his desk and began placing clear plastic bags before Liz. He smiled slightly. "I had anticipated your answer, Ms. Murphy. I hope you don't mind."

"Not at all," she assured him. "And please call me Liz. Ms. Murphy sounds stuffy."

His smile widened and she realized suddenly what an attractive young man he was when the tenseness in his expression eased. "Liz it is," he said. "And you can call me Stone. Everyone does."

Liz frowned. "It doesn't feel right for me to call you by your last name. Don't you have a given name?"

"Not one I'd want anyone to hear."

"Why ever not?"

He gave her a hard look.

"I'm sorry," she said hastily "I didn't mean to pry."

He waved away her apology. "It's all right, Liz. And, if you promise not to reveal it to another soul, I'll tell you."

"Well, of course, I promise. But you really don't need to tell me."

Stone smiled. "My given name is Huxley, full name: Huxley Elijah Stone."

Liz opened her mouth to respond, didn't quite know what to say and closed it again. Finally, she sighed. "Oh, my. I hate to say it, but I see what you mean. Stone, it is," she said.

Stone finished placing items on his desk. "Well, that's about it."

Liz sat forward in her chair to observe the articles. There were a number of notes, each in its own plastic bag, two large and deadly looking knives, and a number of snap shots. She extended her hand to pick up one of the pictures. Oh, Lord. It was the young woman she'd seen in her vision. Doreen. Her hand began to shake so badly that she returned it to her lap without picking up the photo. Her visions hadn't helped anyone so far. Certainly not Doreen. What was she doing here? Her mouth was suddenly very dry.

She looked at Stone. "May I have a glass of water, please?"

"Certainly," he said. "I'll get it."

While she waited for Stone to return, Liz studiously avoided looking at any of the pictures, focusing her attention instead on the poetic notes. They were. . . cold. She shuddered as she read them.

"Here you go." Stone set a glass of water before her.

"Thank you." She sipped at the water before once again focusing her attention on the pictures. She was silent for a long while as she looked at them, reread the poems, and looked at the pictures again. "This one. . . and this one," she picked up two of the poems and moved them to one side, "I associate with this. . . victim." She placed the picture of Doreen with the two poetic notes.

Once again, she read the poetry.

Vengeance, like a fine red wine
Aged, is potent. I savor its power;

I glory in the deed. Death is thine.
It awaits thee now, thy funeral bower.

"This one and this"—she indicated another—"and possibly this one as well, I associate with this victim." She positioned the three notes and the photographs of Trent Farris together. "These two were received by Kim." Liz indicated the last two notes. "She told me about them."

"These observations you're making, Liz—are they just feelings, or are you seeing something?" Stone asked.

"Just feelings, so far."

"That's fine. Continue whenever you're ready."

Taking a deep breath, Liz turned her attention to the murder weapons. With shaking hands, she closed her eyes and reached out to lay her hands over the first one. She gasped at the suddenness of the connection. Disjointed scenes and emotions assailed her with all the violence and force of a hurricane.

"Liz, are you all right? What is it?"

Liz sat gasping shakily for a moment. Realizing that her throat once again felt as dry as sandpaper, she reached for the glass of water and took another swallow. Finally, she raised her eyes to meet Stone's gaze. "That is the weapon used to kill Doreen Hanson. She was on her knees. Her—" Liz swallowed and reached for the glass of water again. "Her head was shaven and her hands had been bound behind her back when he—he cut her throat."

"Where did this happen, Liz?"

"In the cathedral," she replied. Then she frowned as she realized she didn't understand the connotation of the words.

"The cathedral?"

"Yes." She shrugged. "I'm sorry I don't know where that came from."

Stone nodded. "That's fine. Can you tell me what the place looked like?"

Liz closed her eyes and placed her hands back over the weapon. "There are lights, lots of little lights."

"Like Christmas lights?" Stone asked.

"No. . . no. Candles. There are candles everywhere. They are all around the altar."

"Describe the altar to me please. What color are the candles?"

She frowned. "The altar is just a slab of stone placed over two smaller ones, like a low table. The candles. . . are all colors: white, red, black, green." She opened her eyes and tucked her hands into her lap. "I'm sorry. I can't see anything else."

"Do you know anything about Satanism, Liz."

"Not really. Just what I've happened to read in magazines."

"I see." Stone frowned. "Do you think you'd be able to recognize the trappings of Satanism if you saw them?"

Liz stared thoughtfully at the knife before her. "You're wondering if the killer is a Satanist," she said.

"Precisely."

"I didn't get that feeling. It felt more as though—" she sighed in frustration as she tried to put the feeling into words. "As though he'd tried to create the atmosphere of an actual church. It wasn't a deliberate parody, but an attempt at authenticity. Do you understand what I mean?"

"Yes, I believe I do. Is there anything else you can tell me?"

Liz rose and walked to the window. She rubbed her arms as though to ward off a sudden chill. "He's insane," she said. "But he thinks he's very, very smart."

"What makes you say that?"

She sighed. "It's very difficult to explain the feelings that surround a vision. How do you explain to somebody what it feels like to experience an emotion?"

Stone propped his chin on steepled index fingers as he swiveled to face her. "All I'm asking is that you try, Liz."

She considered his intent features for a moment, then nodded. "I felt anger." Unconsciously, she clenched her fists and shook her head. "No, it was more than anger. Rage. He was consumed by rage. And there was confusion and hurt and grief. And then triumph and. . . strength. No, that's not right." She pounded her fist lightly against her thigh as she tried to grasp the essence of the emotion she'd felt. Finally she turned to face Stone. "I'm sorry I can't describe it."

"Power?" Stone asked.

Liz froze. "Yes, that's it. He felt powerful. He calls himself the Lord of Death, you know. He told Kim that."

"Yes, I'm aware of that." He gestured to the other knife on his desk. "Do you feel up to doing any more today? Or would you rather come back another time?"

"I might as well try it while I'm here," she said. She was just placing her hands over the weapon when the phone on Stone's desk rang. She waited, knowing that she wouldn't be able to concentrate until he was through.

He raised the receiver to his ear. "Yes," he said. He listened intently for a few moments. "I'll be there shortly." He hung up. Glancing at Liz, he held up a finger. "I'll just be one moment." He picked up the receiver again. "Melissa could you please ring the hotel and see if David Strilman is still there. If he is, tell him to drop by a.s.a.p." He paused. "Thank you." He looked back at Liz. "All right, Liz. Let's continue."

Liz closed her eyes and resumed the exercise. Then, after a moment, she frowned and withdrew her hands. "Nothing," she said. "I'm sorry. I seem to have lost my concentration."

Stone smiled slightly and began reorganizing the evidence bags. "Well, you've certainly been a help in any case. If necessary, we can always try again later." He rose and extended his hand to her. "Thank you very much for coming in, Liz."

"I'm glad I was able to help a little."

* * *

When Vaughn had discovered that Aunt Willie had planned on taking a taxi to the funeral, he had squelched the plan instantly. What on earth had she been thinking? Why hadn't she asked him to escort her? She'd known he was going. But there was no understanding Willie or her fierce independence. Now, as they turned into the driveway at Kim's and parked behind Jordan Hall's cruiser, preparatory to dropping off Landon before heading to the church, Vaughn studied Willie's manner with his son.

It was obvious that she was very fond of the child. But Willie had always loved kids. Thank God for that. Vaughn didn't know what he would have done without her. Even when he'd been at that awkward adolescent know-it-all age, Willie had always found a way to communicate. And she'd always been fair. His thoughts made him reconsider his position. It wouldn't be very considerate of him to let Willie find out about his relationship to Landon at the reading of the will. She deserved better from him.

Now, as she reached to open the door of the Bronco, he laid a hand on her arm to forestall her. "Willie, there's something I have to tell you."

She settled back in her seat and looked at him questioningly. Vaughn cleared his throat and looked out at the willow tree. Willie leaned forward a bit to peer into his face. "Is it more bad news?" she asked.

"Oh, no. Nothing like that. Well, at least, I hope you won't think so."

Willie frowned in irritation. "Well, come on, boy. Spit it out."

Vaughn forced himself to meet her clear-eyed gaze, wishing he knew what her reaction would be. Would she be hurt at the thought of losing Landon? There was only one way to find out. "Landon is my son."

Willie just stared at him.

"Doreen had papers drawn up that named me as his godparent. I think there are probably some papers that state that I'm his natural father as well. I didn't want you to find out that way." Willie continued to stare at him in silence. "Will you say something. Are you upset?"

"Upset?" Willie shook her head and looked out the window. "That's the first piece of good news I've had in days. I've been worried sick about what was going to happen to this little gaffer." She gave Landon a hug. "I'm way too old to raise him." She looked back at Vaughn with a hard look that Vaughn remembered well. "Lord above, boy, I could box your ears for waiting this long to tell me."

"So you're okay with it then?" Vaughn asked.

"Okay?" Willie shook her head in exasperation. "Look, if this wasn't the kind of day it is, I'd be happy enough to spit bubbles like one of them circus clowns. Is that clear enough for you?"

"Yes, ma'am," Vaughn smiled. He looked at the chubby little boy in Aunt Willie's arms. And suddenly it sank in. The pretense was over. "Can I hold my son?" he asked.

Willie looked down at Landon. "How's about you let your Daddy carry you into the house?" she asked, pointing at Vaughn.

Without hesitation, Landon reached out to Vaughn and in his demanding little voice said, "Doe 'ouse."

Vaughn's throat was suddenly too clogged with emotion to make a response. He got out of the car and, when Willie had joined him, began walking toward the house.

"Willie?" he said just as they reached the veranda.

"Hmm?"

"Will you keep him until all of this is over? I need time to—"

"You know I will," Willie interrupted him. "As long as you need me to."

Landon bounced demandingly in his arms. "Doe! Doe!" He pointed at the door to the house.

Vaughn smiled and stepped up onto the veranda just as Kim opened the door. "I saw you coming," she said to Vaughn as he stepped into the house. She looked at Landon and reached out to gently poke his rounded little belly. "I've been waiting for you, little man. You and I are going to have lots of fun. Do you know what we're going to do?"

Landon grinned and shook his head.

"We're going to finger-paint!" She held out her arms to him and Landon went willingly.

Then, before she could do more than take a single step, Landon turned in her arms, looked imperiously at Vaughn and Willie and ordered, "Tay."

"No, son," Vaughn said. "We have to go. But we'll only be gone a little while. Okay?"

Landon's lower lip began to tremble. "Tay," he repeated, but this time the word had a pleading quality. "Don' doe 'way."

Once again Vaughn felt his throat close. The poor kid. How could he leave with Landon looking at him like that? He shot a glance at Willie. There were tears in her eyes. She had turned away from Landon to hide them.

Suddenly Liz appeared behind Kim. "Well, now. What do we have here?" She walked around Kim to face the little boy in her arms. "Well, if it isn't the handsomest young man I've ever seen. Look at all that thick black hair. And those eyes—" her voice trailed off and she looked at Vaughn in sudden surprise.

Vaughn nodded in answer to her silent question. "I'll explain later," he said. Landon still refused to take his eyes off of Vaughn or Willie for more than a second.

Liz gently grasped the little boy by the chin. "Sweetheart, Aunt Willie just has to go shopping. She'll be back in just a little while. I promise."

"Soppin'?" Landon repeated hesitantly.

"That's right," Kim assured him. "Okay?"

He shot another look at Vaughn and Willie. Thoroughly examined Kim and Liz, and then said, "'kay."

* * *

It was said that funerals were for the living, not the dead. Vaughn supposed that was true. A funeral somehow imparted that sense of finality, that sense of saying good-bye that allowed the living to endure the loss of the loved one and get on with their lives. But rather than acceptance, Vaughn found himself becoming more and more angry as the funeral progressed. Doreen's death had been so pointless. Just like Trent's.

Remembering Trent's funeral brought to mind the daffodil and his awareness that the killer had been to Trent's grave. Had he come to Doreen's funeral too?

Vaughn's eyes scanned the assembly, settling on the Hanson family seated together ahead and to his left. All but the old man were dry eyed, stony faced, and, quite obviously, extremely uncomfortable in their Sunday clothes. Old man Hanson actually dabbed at his eyes with a dingy, gray handkerchief. Crocodile tears? Vaughn wondered. Or, unlike his sons, did the old buzzard really harbor some vestige of human emotion within him?

Vaughn grimaced inwardly. Doreen wouldn't have wanted them here. He wished he could have found a way to avoid informing them of her death. But they were her only blood relatives.

Vaughn swallowed. As a friend, and one of the few people who really knew her, it seemed that he had failed Doreen in a number of ways. He would not fail to catch her killer. He returned to scrutinizing the congregation.

Was Coyd here sitting in one of the pews, listening to the sermon? Vaughn searched the faces of the mourners, seeking a resemblance to the boy he remembered. And he wondered why Coyd had become a killer.

CHAPTER 19

$\mathcal{V}$aughn had just returned from driving Willie and Landon home. He and Kim were in the kitchen, working together to prepare a light dinner for themselves when Liz opened the door from the living room. "Liz. Hi." He looked from her to Kim and back again. "Did Kim tell you anything about Landon?"

Liz walked into the room and began emptying a small bag of groceries. "No. But that child looks enough like me to be my grandchild." She turned suddenly, pinning Vaughn with her gaze. "Is he?" she asked.

Vaughn shoved his hands into his pockets and rocked forward onto the balls of his feet for a second. "Yeah." He nodded. "Yeah, as a matter of fact, I guess he is. And well, I'd like to talk to you about that." He glanced at Kim. "Would you excuse us for a few moments?"

"Certainly." She gestured to the pile of vegetables they'd been cutting for a stir-fry. "I can finish this."

Vaughn flashed her a smile. "Thanks. We won't be long." Taking Liz's arm, Vaughn led her into the living room. As she took a seat on the sofa, he paced the room for a moment. "I don't quite know how to start," he said.

"How about at the beginning?" Liz asked. "Tell me how you managed to keep your connection to your son a secret, in a town this size, and why you would want to."

And so, for the second time in as many weeks, Vaughn told the story of his relationship to Doreen Hanson. When he was through, he sat down opposite Liz. "So that's why no one knew that I'm Landon's father. And that brings me to the point where I ask a very big favor of you."

Liz stared at him silently for a moment. "What is it?"

Vaughn raked his fingers through his hair in agitation and rose to pace the room again. "I've been thinking about this a lot," he said. He turned to face Liz. "If anything happens to me now, Landon will be an orphan. With no one legally appointed to care for him, he'd probably be put up for adoption. I"—he sighed—"I don't want that to happen."

Shoving his hands deep into his pockets once again, he hunched his shoulders forward a bit. "Go on," Liz said.

Vaughn cleared his throat. "I know Aunt Willie is attached to him, but she's almost seventy. She's just not able to raise another child. So—since I'm as certain as I can be without DNA testing that you are my mother after the way you described my recurring nightmare of being taken from you as a child—I'd like you to agree to act as Landon's guardian should anything happen to me."

Liz smiled. "Of course, I agree. He's a darling little boy, and he's my grandchild."

Vaughn sighed in relief. "Good. I had the papers drawn up this afternoon. There's really not that much to them. We just have to sign them and have Kim witness them." During his discourse, Liz's expression altered drastically. "Is something the matter?" he asked.

"Why?"

Vaughn frowned in confusion. "Why what?"

"Why the hurry? Why did you have those papers drawn up today? You sense something, don't you?" He watched her grow increasingly pale as the blood drained from her face. "What is it?"

He hastily sat down beside her and took her hands in his. "Liz, calm down. You're jumping to conclusions." He saw the uncertainty in her eyes. "Really," he insisted. "In case you haven't noticed, life, in general, has become quite hazardous for a lot of people lately. And I have a son to think of now. I can't allow myself to ignore the possibility that the danger you warned me of does exist, and that it could strike at any time. Tonight, tomorrow, next week. I have to be prepared."

"That's all?"

"That's all," he assured her.

She sighed and allowed her spine to sag slightly as tension faded. "All right."

"There is one other thing I wanted to talk to you about," Vaughn said.

"What's that?" Liz eyed him warily.

"We suspect that the killer will strike at Kimberley again within the next thirty-six hours. I intend to be here in the house with her every night. A deputy will be outside twenty-four hours a day, as usual. We're alert; we're expecting him: I'm certain that he won't get by us. But the fact remains that he has gotten through before. I can't ignore that."

"What are you trying to say, Vaughn?"

He cleared his throat. "I'm saying that I don't want you to stay here anymore." He saw stubbornness lower her brows and firm her lips. As she opened her mouth to argue, he held up his hand. "Look, what's the point in me naming you as Landon's guardian if you insist on placing yourself in needless danger. You've already been assaulted once. Your abilities didn't help you prevent that." He sighed, moderating the tone of his voice. "I need you safe. I don't want to be worrying about both you and Kimberley. I need to know that, if something *does* happen, you will be alive to take care of Landon. Do you understand?"

Liz sighed. "Yes. Yes, I do understand. I'll make other arrangements."

He squeezed her hands gently. "Thank you, Liz."

* * *

Storm clouds rolled in over the mountains, bringing early darkness. Liz drove away in the preternatural gloom leaving Vaughn and Kim to their evening meal together. The air outside was unnaturally still. Not a leaf stirred on the trees. Lightning charged the air with expectancy. The distant rumble of thunder, like the roll of drums in a circus act, foreshadowed the tension-filled moments to come. Kim started nervously as a particularly close flash wreaked momentary havoc with the electrical system. It sounded as though the unseasonably warm, dry weather was coming to an end.

As the low grumble of thunder vibrated the windows in their panes, Vaughn placed his hand over hers. "It'll be all right," he assured her.

"I know." But Kim was no longer thinking about the storm. Since the night that she'd tried to tell him that they should break off their growing relationship, they'd maintained an emotional distance. Now, as Vaughn's fingers drew gentle circles on the back of her hand, Kim realized just how much she'd missed the simple pleasure of his touch.

She supposed she should have been too terrified to think of anything but the need to preserve her own life and catch a killer in the process. She should have been anticipating all the possible means Coyd might have of getting to her and planning a means of preventing him. But she wasn't. She was thinking about Vaughn, and sex. With a brief flash of worry, she wondered if perhaps, after too many years of sexual frustration, she hadn't swung a little too far the other way on the pendulum. Was her preoccupation with sex, especially at a time like this, bordering on nymphomaniacal? An instant later, she didn't care.

What she did care about was getting Vaughn into bed without giving him the message that she was ready to consider a long-term relationship. She hadn't finished thinking about that, and until she had, she wasn't ready to risk any kind of a commitment. Withdrawing her hand gently from beneath Vaughn's stroking fingers, she pushed her dinner plate away and rose. Walking around the table until she stood behind Vaughn, she placed her hands on his shoulders.

"You're very tense," she said as she began to knead his muscles.

"Kimberley, what are you doing?" His deep bass voice caressed her senses.

"Helping you relax."

He cleared his throat. "And does this mean that you've thought about the conversation we had the other night?"

Kim hesitated briefly and then resumed massaging his shoulders as she tried to formulate a reply. Nothing particularly eloquent came to mind. "Not completely, no."

He grasped her hands, stopping the motion of her fingers, and pulled her around to face him. "Explain yourself, Kim."

Kim found it difficult to meet his intense golden gaze. "I enjoy being with you," she said.

He pulled her down onto his knee and, grasping her chin, forced her to meet his eyes. "In what sense, Kim?"

She hesitated. "In every sense."

"But you're still not willing to concede that you could love me someday."

"I can't. Don't you see that. It's like my love for a man is some kind of bad luck talisman or something. If I let myself love you, you'll be killed."

"And you think you can order love not to happen?"

Kim shook her head and looked down at her hands in her lap. "No. That's why I wanted us not to see each other for a while. But since that idea is impossible anyway, I don't see why we can't continue to enjoy each other's company."

"Ah, I see. So what you're telling me is that you're horny, and you would like me to, um, scratch the itch. But that, after all this is over, you'll probably never want to see me again."

Kim's eyes flew to his face in shock as she leapt up. "You don't need to be so vulgar! I don't see what you're problem is. I thought most men liked sex without ties."

A muscle leapt in Vaughn's jaw, and Kimberley realized just how furious he was as he rose to face her. "Initially, yes," he said in that ominously quiet voice he used when he was angry. "I suppose most men like to know that having sex with a woman once or twice is not going to result in protestations of undying love. But personally, after I've known a woman for a while, I like to know that there is at least a chance of some deeper emotional involvement."

Kim threw up her hands. "I'm sorry. I just can't give you that."

"You mean you won't."

"Fine," Kim bit off the word. "Have it your way. I won't."

"Then there's nothing more to say, is there?"

Kim sighed and rubbed at a sudden throbbing ache between her brows. Wow, she'd certainly carried that seduction off with the finesse of a master. "I guess not." Depressed, and unaccountably on the verge of tears, Kim began collecting the dinner dishes from the table.

Without comment, Vaughn began to help her. "I can handle this," she said. "Just go do whatever sheriff stuff it is you're supposed to be doing, Sheriff."

Lightning flashed and thunder rumbled adding to the tension in the air. "I wish it would rain and get it over with," Kim muttered to herself as Vaughn left the room. She'd always loved thunderstorms. But tonight it merely set her teeth on edge.

* * *

He'd fallen asleep. In some distant recess of the house, a clock struck one. The sound found an answering chord in his mind, propelling him back in time. Back to the boy he'd been.

The clock struck one. He winced. Now, she would come. He lay awake straining his ears to catch the sound of her footsteps. He couldn't risk sleeping. Not yet. It was worse when she found him asleep.

And then he heard it. The creak of the floorboard in the hall. His breath froze in his throat. She was coming. Straining his eyes in the thin moonlight that filtered in his window, he peered at the handle of his door. Oh God, it was turning. She had come to him again. Why? How did Vaughn always manage to escape her? God, he hated him for that. For leaving him alone to face her.

"Hello, darlin'." The whisper of her deep voice grated on his ears. "I've come to tuck you in."

He awoke with a start. Gulping great breaths of air to escape the suffocating dream, he peered into the unfamiliar darkness. Fuck! He'd allowed himself to fall asleep in a position that could have been very dangerous. He was becoming overconfident, and that confidence was breeding carelessness. Furious with himself, he squinted out from under the bed in the room where the so-called psychic slept. There would be no comfortable bed for him tonight. It was time for a little judicious self-discipline.

He suddenly realized he hadn't heard the psychic return. He frowned. Where was she? He was certain that, had she returned, he would have heard her. But just to make certain, he listened quietly for the sound of breathing before slowly crawling out from under the bed. She wasn't there. He shrugged. No matter. She didn't concern him anyway.

Cautiously, he walked across the room to the door. He cursed the rumble of thunder. It made it difficult to determine if there was any movement in the house. He listened silently for a few moments more. Nothing. It should be safe enough.

Opening his shirt, he removed the zip-lock bag. The surgical gloves he wore made his fingers less sensitive, but he was growing accustomed to working with them on. Patiently, he undid the bag and removed the contents before opening the door and stepping out of the room.

Within a few steps, he was able to see into the living room. On his right was the kitchen door. He was just about to proceed into the kitchen when a sixth sense made him hesitate. He scanned the darkened living room a second time and gasped in surprise. Quickly, silently, he hugged the wall. Somebody sat on the sofa in the dark. The realization startled him. Vaughn. It had to be him.

He hadn't expected Vaughn to stay the night when there was a deputy outside. Speculatively, he studied Vaughn's barely visible silhouette. He had seen Vaughn and Kimberley together enough to know they were sleeping with each other. So, since Vaughn had stayed the night, what the hell was he doing down here when he could have been upstairs fucking his brains out? Coyd turned his contemplative gaze toward the stairs. His lips twisted derisively. Maybe they'd had a lover's quarrel.

Of course that would never have stopped him from taking what he wanted. But Vaughn always had been too nice for his own good. Coyd gauged the distance to the kitchen door. Could he make it without Vaughn spotting the movement in the dark? No, he'd wait a few moments. Maybe Vaughn would leave the room.

Coyd leaned back against the wall and relaxed as he listened for the slightest sound of movement from the living room. A moment later it came. The slight rustle of clothing. Cautiously, he peered around the edge of the wall. Vaughn stood at the window, his back to him. Coyd grinned. Two steps, and he'd reached the door. A third, and he was in the kitchen. Slowly, carefully, he moved the door back into place without allowing it to swing and attract attention. Then, with bated breath, he listened. Silence.

Smiling, he moved slowly across the kitchen to the refrigerator. After making certain that everything was ready, he silently opened the refrigerator door, placed the contents of the plastic bag on the shelf and closed the door. There. Done. For someone who loved darkness, who knew how to become part of it, this kind of thing was always so easy. Almost too easy.

He smiled as he pictured the reaction to his little gift. His only regret was that he could so seldom see the response first hand.

* * *

It was dawn. The thunderclouds had rolled over, opening their bellies with a deluge of refreshing rain for the town. Probably not enough to lower forest fire hazard level though. Vaughn rubbed his eyes. They felt gritty from lack of sleep. He'd spent, virtually, the whole goddamn night sitting outside Kim's bedroom door, watching her sleep and thinking about relationships. About the one he'd shared with Doreen, about the now almost non-existent one he shared with Kimberley, and about the one he hoped to share with his son. Despite the hours of thought, he hadn't reached any illuminating conclusions.

Sighing, he rose to peer out the window at Deputy Hall's cruiser. Jordan sat resting his elbow on the ledge provided by the open driver's side window. Vaughn decided to make a pot of coffee and take some out to him.

Finished making the coffee, he opened the fridge to get some milk. That was when he saw it. A black rose. Beneath it laid a note. He donned gloves and, with infinite care, moved the rose and the poem to the surface of the counter top. He stood looking down at them, his eyes scanning the lines of poetry even as his hands clenched into fists.

O Earth, lie heavily upon her eyes;
Seal her sweet eyes weary of watching, Earth;
Lie close around her; leave no room for mirth
With its harsh laughter, nor for sound of sighs.
Darkness more clear than noonday holdeth her,
Silence more musical than any song;
Even her very heart has ceased to stir:
Until the morning of Eternity
Her rest shall not begin nor end, but be;

The last line was missing, but Vaughn knew it. *And when she wakes she will not think it long.* He remembered it. Although he couldn't remember the poet's name, he knew it was a poem from the collection that Anna had favored.

"Fuck!" He swore beneath his breath, slapping the counter in frustration. Then leaned back against the cupboard and tried to get his tired brain into gear. Kim! He raced out of the kitchen and took the steps two at a time. Except for a few minutes just prior to dawn, he'd sat outside her room all night. Still, there was a slight possibility that Coyd could have gotten by him in those few minutes.

As he reached her bedroom door and saw her wild mane of blonde hair, the rush of panic began to ebb. Leaning against the wall for a moment, he took a deep breath. Still, he needed to be certain that everything was all right. With his heart pounding like a drum, he silently entered her room and stood looking down at her. She was sleeping. Raking his fingers through his hair as he sighed with relief, Vaughn watched her for a moment. Then, he slowly tip-toed from the room to search the house.

A few minutes later, he was back in the kitchen. How had Coyd gotten in this time? Vaughn shook his head. The problem was that Lillooet Creek was a small town. Although most people locked their doors when they planned on being out, few, if any, locked their doors while they were home. And with a house this size, it would be relatively easy for a person to sneak in while the occupants were in another area of the house. Mind you, thus far locks had not seemed to provide any appreciable deterrent either. Coyd could have broken in through a window in this big old mausoleum of a house and run little risk of being heard, let alone caught.

Having a deputy stationed outside had not proven to be much of an advantage. Vaughn was almost positive that Coyd was approaching on foot, at night, from the rear of the house. That made him virtually invisible to the deputies. Short of having them walk a foot patrol around the house—which Coyd could easily avoid by simply waiting until the deputy was on the other side of the house—Vaughn didn't know how much more they could do. He needed a trained guard dog, but there just weren't any in Lillooet Creek.

Pouring two cups of coffee, Vaughn prepared to take them outside. He'd talk the situation over with Jordan. Somehow they had to come up with another means of protecting Kimberley. Before tonight.

* * *

What the fuck was going on? He stared at the empty cruiser in the driveway and then subjected the Bronco to the same perusal. It looked like Vaughn had changed his methods. Now that was irritating. But a challenge. He smiled mirthlessly in the darkness. He loved a challenge.

With narrowed eyes, he considered the brightly lit house. He could see Jordan Hall sitting in the living room. He couldn't see Vaughn, but from the way Jordan kept lifting his gaze to the right as he spoke, Coyd was fairly certain that Vaughn had positioned himself at the top of the stairs. From that vantage point, he would have a partial view of the living room, and a good view of Kimberley's bedroom door. Coyd lifted his gaze to Kimberley's window. It was dark. Was she asleep?

The thought angered him. She should be waiting for him. Did she think her sheriff boyfriend could protect her? Coyd thought he'd been most effective in exposing Vaughn for the inept fool that he was. Couldn't Kimberley see that? Oh, well, she'd see soon enough. For the moment he had to decide how to circumvent Vaughn's last moment change of tactics.

He fingered his weapons. He always carried his 9mm Beretta semiautomatic pistol, but he rarely used it except as a rather efficient club. He didn't like guns. To his way of thinking, it took no guts and even fewer brains to kill with a gun. His primary weapon, as always, was a hunting knife. Tonight that might have to change.

The problem was, he didn't have a silencer for the gun. Not that any of the silencers he'd ever tried had proven to be very effective anyway. A good one suppressed the blast noise to a certain degree, but he'd yet to find one that could diminish the sound to the soft hissing pop you heard in the movies. So what did he do now?

A brilliant flash of lightning caused the lights of the house to flicker. He frowned. Another storm. Lightning had the exasperating tendency of occurring when you least expected it. The last thing he needed was to be spotlighted in the open. He would have to be exceptionally careful in his planning. He hunkered down in the shadows to think.

A few minutes later, his plans were made. There was no help for it. He would have to alter his previous strategy to include Vaughn. He had really wanted to save Vaughn's punishment for last. To watch him writhe in the pain of his own incompetence as the death toll rose. But whether Vaughn died tonight or next month made no appreciable difference. So Kimberley and Vaughn would die together. He grinned. Lovers. In each other's arms.

Oh, yeah. That was good. Real good. Why the hell hadn't he planned it that way from the beginning? He could have prepared a suitable eulogy. He shrugged. Too late now.

The only thing left for him to do was to move his truck closer. The fact that there would now be two passengers instead of one necessitated a shorter distance. But since both deputies were inside the house, that shouldn't prove too difficult to accomplish.

* * *

For the second night in a row thunder rumbled and grumbled in the distance as clouds boiled over the mountain tops. Ray had found an old favorite to watch on television, and now sat with his arm around Liz as they watched *Backdraft* together. A large bowl of buttered popcorn sat half on his knee and half on hers. Yet despite the quality of the movie, Liz found it extremely difficult to keep her mind on it.

Something teased at the edge of her mind. Tantalizing, táunting, and then receding before she could grasp it. Could it have something to do with her conversation with Vaughn the previous evening? She was now godparent as well as grandparent to a child whose existence she had not even suspected. No. It was something else.

Ray lifted his hand from her shoulder to smooth back the hair from her brow as he looked into her face. "Is something wrong, Liz?"

She shrugged. "I think the weather is just making me a little jumpy."

"You sure?"

She smiled and patted his knee. "I'd tell you if I felt anything important needed my attention. You know that."

"Okay." Ray returned his attention to the television, and Liz attempted to follow suit. For a while, she even managed to become involved in the movie again. She reached for a handful of popcorn. And then suddenly, like an explosion of color within her brain, disjointed scenes began to flash in her mind. The popcorn flew from her hand. Distantly she heard Ray's voice, but she couldn't make out his words over the roaring in her head as picture after picture flashed and was replaced.

Blood dripped from painted red lips on a mirror. Vaughn lay in a pool of blood. Kimberley stood before a mirror. Behind her, in a doorway, stood the dark silhouette of a man. The blade of a large knife glittered. Kimberley, her eyes wide with terror, screaming a soundless scream. Lightning flashed and candles stuttered. Moving. Quickly now, running through trees. The cathedral. A procession of people in black carried a white coffin. A grandfather clock striking one o'clock.

"Liz! Answer me, Goddammit!" Slowly Liz managed to focus on Ray's worried face. "What is it?"

She leapt to her feet. "Vaughn. Kim." Her thoughts were in chaos. She couldn't form a complete sentence. She tried to take a deep breath but it was merely another gasp. Her body seemed to be demanding more oxygen than she could possibly give it. "We have to go. Now!"

CHAPTER 20

"Mississippi," Jordan said with a smile as he reached for his can of Coke. Noticing that it was empty, he grimaced and replaced it on the coffee table. He looked up at Vaughn's silent, thoughtful face. "You need more practice, Vaughn."

"Hmph," Vaughn snorted. "Ireland."

"Nope. You said that already."

"When?"

"After I said Tripoli."

Vaughn scowled. "Okay, Indian Ocean."

"N, huh? I'm just gonna grab another Coke while I think on that one." He rose and headed for the kitchen. "You want anything?"

Vaughn shook his head. "No, thanks. And make sure you prop that door open."

Jordan turned to look at him with raised brow. "You don't think you're being just a little paranoid?"

Vaughn looked solemnly down at him. "No."

Jordan shrugged. "Suit yourself." He picked up one of the end tables and used it to prop the kitchen door open. Then, looking up the stairs at Vaughn he said, "Nile."

"Euphrates," Vaughn shot back.

Jordan disappeared into the kitchen and reappeared a second later sipping on a fresh can of Coke. Stopping in the doorway, he leaned against the jamb and looked up. "S. That's easy. Stockh . . . ." A boom—louder, sharper-sounding that the thunder outside—echoed through the room. A shocked look appeared on Jordan's face at the same instant that a jagged red hole appeared in his neck. He tried to reach for it, but his hand never completed the distance.

"Jesus!" Vaughn grabbed his gun from one side of his belt and grabbed his cell phone with the other. "This is Garrett. I need backup and an ambulance up at the Tannas place. Now! You got that?" Thank God for speed dial. He began backing toward Kimberley's room.

He vaguely heard Ethel Wright's affirmative response as he reached the door to Kim's room. She met him there wearing jeans and a t-shirt. He realized with a sense of relief that she'd never prepared herself for bed. "Close this door. Lock it. You understand?"

He was thankful that she couldn't see Deputy Hall's body from this angle because, judging by the terror reflected in her eyes, hysteria hovered dangerously close to the surface. "Kim! Do it. Now!" he barked at her in a stage whisper.

She swallowed and nodded. "Be careful," she whispered as she closed the door. He heard her begin to shove something in front of it. Of course! The door had no lock. Shit! He waited until he was certain that the door was blocked.

Then he crept forward, gun at the ready, steadying the wrist of his gun hand with his other hand. Jordan lay in the kitchen doorway, unmoving. The kitchen light had been turned off. Vaughn descended the stairs, slowly, warily. The need to hurry, to render first aid to a friend who lay unmoving within mere feet of him, warred with the need for caution. Where was Coyd? The shot had come from inside the kitchen. Was he still there?

A shadowy form moved within the darkened room just beyond Jordan's body and, reflexively, Vaughn fired. An instant later, he ducked and hugged the wall as a bullet whined past him to lodge in the staircase. At least he knew now where Coyd was. He continued his descent, his breathing so loud in his own ears that he was certain Coyd could hear it. He had almost reached the base of the stairs when suddenly he heard a couple of steps and the slamming of the kitchen door. He frowned. What the hell was Coyd up to now?

Vaughn flicked a glance at the large living room windows. Was Coyd moving around to get a clearer shot? Vaughn hastily completed his descent of the stairs and stepped into the small hallway that lead toward the rear of the house. At least there, he would have the corner of a wall for protection. He waited. Nothing happened.

He noticed the growing puddle of blood beneath Jordan's head. To hell with this! He'd taken only two steps toward Jordan when somebody stepped from the kitchen. Instantly, his gun came up.

"Hi, Vaughn." Deputy Lewis, gun in hand, bent over Hall's body. How had he gotten here so swiftly? It wasn't possible unless he'd been right outside. And he'd had no reason to be right outside. Not in this area of town.

"What are you doing here?" Vaughn demanded.

Marty straightened and looked at him. He smiled. Why would he smile? "I'm your back-up," he said. He looked at Vaughn's extended weapon. "You going to shoot me, Sheriff?"

Vaughn didn't lower his weapon. "How'd you get here so quickly?"

Marty shrugged. "I was just at the bottom of the hill getting gas when I heard your call. It doesn't take long to travel half a mile when you have the pedal to the medal."

Vaughn watched Lewis as he weighed his response.

There was something bothering him about Deputy Martin Lewis. Something different. But he couldn't put his finger on it.

"Did you see anybody outside?"

Lewis frowned. "No. Thought I might have seen something for an instant there, but— nothing." He shrugged.

Vaughn nodded. How long would it take Lewis to drive up the hill and get into the house? Four minutes? Five? Had it been that long? He didn't think so. But he couldn't be certain. Why was he standing here mistrusting a deputy who'd been with the department for two years?

Ignoring the peculiar feeling of mistrust, he lowered his weapon. "How's Jordy?" he asked.

Marty shrugged as Vaughn joined him. "Alive. For the moment." Vaughn squatted to examine Jordan personally. Even as he did, he suddenly realized what was different about Deputy Martin Lewis. His eyes. Deputy Lewis had dark brown eyes. Today his eyes were a hazel green. Vaughn remembered those eyes shining from the thin face of a teenage kid. They were Coyd's eyes. Ah, crap!

He started to turn, grabbing for his gun even as he did, but it was too late. A thousand tiny pinpoints of light exploded in his mind. Everything went black.

* * *

Having heard Vaughn call the station, Coyd didn't bother wasting time. He'd neglected to consider the cell, an unforgiveable miscalculation. He was furious with himself. With no more time to squander, he took the stairs two at a time. Reaching Kimberley's room, he tried the door only to find something blocking it. Fuck!

He took a deep breath to control his breathing. "Ms. Tannas," he called. No answer. He choked on his impatience. "Ms. Tannas, it's Deputy Lewis. I have to get you out of here. Now!"

"Where's Vaughn?"

Inspiration struck. "He's downstairs fighting the fire, ma'am. The house is on fire. Hurry!" He thought he managed to inject a suitable expression of panic into his voice.

"Oh, my God!"

He listened with satisfaction to the scraping sound on the other side of the door as Kimberley moved something. The door opened. As Kimberley looked trustingly up into his face, his fist shot out clipping her on the jaw. She dropped like a stone.

Removing the duct tape from his pocket, he peeled off a strip for her mouth before securing her hands with it. That done, he threw her unceremoniously over his shoulder and quickly exited the house. He'd just finished placing Kimberley in the back of his Suburban and was turning back to get Vaughn when he saw headlights appear on the road barely seconds away.

"Fuck!" Slamming his fist against the roof of the truck, he hesitated a split second, staring longing toward the house, before jumping into the vehicle and gunning the motor. There was no time to take Vaughn. Since Vaughn now knew who he was, that meant that his future plans were probably completely unsalvageable. That infuriated him. As the truck bounced across the lawn and out onto the road, he recognized the man behind the wheel of the approaching cruiser. Ray.

How the hell had he gotten here so quickly? Ray's house was on the opposite side of town halfway up a mountain side. And Coyd knew for a fact that he'd been off duty.

Shit! He couldn't risk being followed. Pulling his Beretta, he fired. Three holes, in quick succession, appeared in the cruiser's grill. A fourth appeared in the windshield. By then, he was beside the car. He fired one more round into the car via the side window, and another at the rear tire. Then, he was by and racing down the mountain road. He felt reasonably confident that they'd have little chance of following him.

Ray might not have been hit, but it would take time for him to switch vehicles. Jordan was dead, or nearly so. Coyd felt a twinge of regret. He'd had nothing against Jordan. Oh, well. Like Skeeter, he'd gotten in the way. Killian was still recuperating at home in Crystal Falls at least 20 minutes away. Special Agent Stone was staying at the hotel and would not have heard the radio transmission. If Ethel even remembered to call him, it would take him too much time to get here for Coyd to be concerned. And Vaughn, although definitely alive, was out cold and would be for some time. All in all, he should be home free for the time being.

* * *

Kim stirred. There was a terrible roaring in her ears. A minute later pain stabbed demandingly at her as her elbow struck something. She felt herself rolling and tried to put out her hands to steady herself. Why couldn't she move her hands? Slowly, she opened her eyes.

It was dark. Extremely dark. Where was she? Lightning split the heavens. In the brief brilliant flash, Kimberley recognized the nature of her surroundings. She was in the back of a vehicle similar to Vaughn's Bronco, but larger. The truck hit a bump and jostled her painfully. Automatically, she cried out. The sound was strangely muffled. There was something over her mouth. She frowned. The last thing she remembered was—

Oh, Lord! There had been a noise, a blast like a gunshot. And then Vaughn had told her to lock herself into her room. Next, she'd heard more gunfire. Silence. Muffled voices, but not angry or threatening. Then there had been the knock on her door. She hadn't known what to do. Surely if it was Vaughn he would have identified himself. So she'd waited. A second later, Deputy Lewis had named himself. But as far as Kim knew, he hadn't even been there. Her fear made her suspicious. But when he'd said that there was a fire and that Vaughn was fighting it, his anxiety had sounded so genuine that she'd opened the door without further question. Then he'd struck her. She had seen his fist coming at her, but the half second it had taken to make that observation left no time for evading it.

Kim swallowed. She almost wished her memory had failed her this time. Reality was almost too horrible to face. Because Kim knew with bone-chilling certainty that she was now in the hands of the killer. And the killer was Deputy Martin Lewis. Deputy Lewis was Coyd!

Oh, God. What had he done to Vaughn? What if—? She refused to complete the thought. Right now, she had to concentrate on staying alive. She tugged experimentally at whatever bound her hands behind her back. She couldn't release it. Okay, so she wouldn't waste her strength trying to break the bonds. Vaughn or somebody would be looking for her even now. But she couldn't pin all her hopes on rescue. She'd have to use her wits to stay alive until help came. To do that, she'd have to delay Lewis in whatever plans he had for her. The best way to accomplish that was to escape. She'd try to get her bearings and hope that an opportunity to run would come later.

She strained her eyes, attempting to see what lay beyond the vehicle in the darkness. The flashes of lightning, growing ever more frequent now, lent a horrible nightmarish quality to the landscape. A thick forest of trees surrounded them. The eerie black foliage whipped in the rising wind as thunder rumbled overhead. And Kimberley closed her eyes in despair. How could she tell one forest of trees from another?

The vehicle jounced along for another few minutes and then took a sudden turn to the right onto an extremely narrow road. Tree branches scraped at the sides of the truck like skeletal fingers. Despite her determination to stay calm, to watch for an opportunity to escape, terror and despair clawed at her throat. She choked it back, hating herself for the tiny whimpering noise that escaped her. Closing her eyes, she took a deep breath. As she did, she remembered something her father had once told her on one of their camping trips. *If you encounter a bear, or any wild animal for that matter, you must never show fear. It only prompts an attack.* She didn't know if the advice was pertinent in this situation or not, but it was the only guidance she had.

The truck jerked to a stop. She heard the door slam and footsteps rustling through the brush along the driver's side. The rear door suddenly opened with a jerk, and a flashlight beam pinned her.

Coyd grasped her ankles and began dragging her from the vehicle. Rage and fear more potent than anything she'd ever felt gripped her. Despite the muffling effect of the tape over her mouth, she called him every vile name she'd ever heard as she kicked franticly trying to release his grasp on her legs. It was no use. Within seconds, he yanked her from the vehicle and stood her before him.

"Hello, darlin'," he said as he gently smoothed the hair back from her face. His tone taunted her. "It's party time." Lightning flashed in that instant and she clearly saw the grin on his face. A cold caricature of a smile, it reminded her of a beast baring its teeth. A frigid drop of rain, warmer by far than the icy fear that gripped her, struck her upturned face.

* * *

Silence, so complete it seemed unnatural, blanketed Liz. She lifted her head and slowly, painfully, opened her eyes. A sudden flash of brilliant light lanced through her brain spreading agony in its wake. A loud, vibrating rumble quickly followed. The storm. Still battling for comprehension, she pushed the air bag out of her face and looked out at the hood of the car. The metal buckled unnaturally where the vehicle had come to a sudden stop against the trunk of an enormous fir tree. An accident. She frowned. The last thing she remembered was Ray talking on the radio to Ethel Wright. Ray!

She almost blacked out again as she turned her head too swiftly. After blinking back the fog, she moved cautiously across the seat. Ray sprawled across the steering wheel.

"Ray?" She shook his shoulder. "Ray, answer me." A faint groan reached her. Grasping his shoulders more firmly, she tugged at him, trying to move him off the air bag and steering wheel. But Ray was a big man, and her first try failed. Sighing in frustration, she brushed in annoyance at her dripping nose and was surprised to see a dark streak stain her hand. Her nose was bleeding! The observation intensified her concern for Ray.

"Ray! Ray! Answer me this minute. Do you hear me?" Fear made her voice sharp as she prodded his shoulder.

"God*dammit*!" he grumbled as his hands found the steering wheel and he pushed himself back off of it. A loud pop followed by a strange hissing noise punctuated his profanity as something beneath the damaged hood of the car took on a life of its own.

Liz stared at the rising steam in apprehension. "Ray. Get out of the car." Moving quickly back across the seat to her own side of the car, she opened her door and crawled out. Then, with her vision blurring and her legs wobbling, she made her way around to the driver's door. It took her a full minute of fumbling with the handle before the stubborn catch released and the door opened. Glass fell on to her hand. She looked for evidence of bleeding on Ray, but it was too dark to tell for certain. "Are you hurt?"

"Of course, I'm hurt, woman," he barked. "Do you think I enjoy movin' this slow?"

She ignored his gruffness and began examining his

torso with her hands. "I mean are you shot?"

"No."

"Good. Then, come on." She grasped his arm and pulled. "We have to get up to the house."

He moved a foot out of the vehicle and tried unsuccessfully to lever himself out of the seat. "Jesus H. Christ!" he roared, as pain brought his temper to the fore.

"Quit bellowing like an old bull and get your ass out of that car. Do you hear me, Ray Cheney?"

He groaned. "Yeah. Yeah, I hear you."

After another concentrated effort, Ray was standing, albeit shakily. While he and Liz half supported, half leaned on each other, they made their way up the driveway to the house.

"Do you know who it was that shot at us?" she asked.

Ray shook his head. "No. I thought I recognized the vehicle for a second there, but—" He shook his head again. "No. I don't know."

They had entered the house via the open front door when the sound of the ambulance siren reached them. Liz only vaguely noted it because it was at that second that she saw the two bodies lying in front of the kitchen door.

"Vaughn?" She hadn't found him after all these years just to lose him again. She refused to believe that. Abandoning Ray at the doorway, she ran to her son. Holding panic at bay with an effort, she checked for a pulse. As she felt the slow steady beat beneath her fingertips, relief made her light-headed and she had to take a deep breath before examining him for injuries. Oh, Lord, there it was. Behind his left ear, just like in her vision, a small puddle of dark sticky blood colored the floor. Her throat closed.

She knew from the single glance she'd taken at Deputy Hall that he'd been shot. Now, she was afraid to look at Vaughn's injury. What if he'd been shot and had somehow managed to cling to life only to die later? She couldn't take that. But she had to know. With shaking fingers, she reached out to turn Vaughn's head slightly and inspect the wound. A minute later, her body sagged with relief. There was a large gash behind his ear, but no hole in his skull.

A sudden commotion at the door announced the entry of Dr. Harcourt and a couple of uniformed men carrying equipment. With surprise, Liz noted that Ray was now kneeling at Jordan Hall's side. "Who's first?" Harcourt demanded.

"Over here, Doc." Ray pointed solemnly at Jordan. He's got a faint pulse, but . . . ." He shrugged.

Liz watched dully as Ray turned and ascended the stairs. He was looking for Kim, but Kim wasn't here. Liz knew that. Dr. Harcourt and the technicians accompanying him, gently prodded her out of their way as they set to work.

A second later, Vaughn groaned. "Kim?" He opened his eyes, saw the man bending over him and reacted violently. "Kim," he bellowed as he shoved the medical technician. "Where's Kim?"

Desperate to make certain he didn't hurt himself, Liz raced to kneel at his side. "Be still, Vaughn." She held him, supporting his shoulders, as the technician tried once again to care for the wound on his head. "We'll find Kimberley." She sent a brief silent prayer to heaven.

"Jesus, he got her didn't he?" Vaughn stared anxiously into her face. "Lewis got her?"

Ray had come back down the stairs just in time to hear Vaughn's last question. "What do you mean?" Ray frowned as he knelt at Vaughn's side. "What's Lewis got to do with this?"

Vaughn shook his head slightly and stopped with a wince. "Marty. . . Martin Lewis is Coyd Davis. We lived together as foster kids for about eight years. And Coyd is the killer."

"How come you never told anybody this before?"

Vaughn swallowed before replying. "I didn't recognize him. Last time I saw him, he was a skinny fourteen-year-old kid with brown hair and green eyes. Besides, I thought he was dead."

Ray could not have looked more stunned if somebody had told him the earth was flat and he'd just walked off the edge. Then, slowly, realization dawned. "That bastard has been goin' around for two years pretending to be one of us, acting like a friend, when really he was laughing at us behind our backs." He watched the doctor and one of the technicians lifting Jordan onto a gurney and his face twisted with a rage so virulent that it frightened Liz. "When I catch that prick I'm goin' to—" He broke off apparently unable to come up with a suitable punishment. At least nothing that a sheriff's deputy could voice.

Ignoring Ray, the medical technician focused on Vaughn. "Come on, Sheriff," he said as he finished taping a dressing into place. "We have to get you to the hospital."

"Get your hands off of me! I'm not going to any goddamn hospital. I've got a job to do."

"Now, Sheriff—"

"Please," Liz interrupted the man. "Is he in any immediate danger?"

"No, ma'am. But that wound needs a couple of stitches and he probably has a mild concussion."

"Well, then, couldn't we come in later?"

"If you don't mind my saying so ma'am, it looks to me like you should all come in now." He stared momentarily at her face and Liz remembered that her nose had been bleeding. "But suit yourselves. I don't have time to argue." He shrugged and hastily followed the gurney.

"Does somebody want to tell me what the hell is going on?" The voice was Stone's. Vaughn looked up and saw him standing in the entrance.

Slowly, with Ray's help, he rose to his feet and faced the man at the door. "He got her," he said. "Coyd is the perp. And he's been living here as Deputy Martin Lewis for two years."

Stone's eyes grew distant for an instant. "I'd wondered—" His voice trailed off and his face hardened. "Okay." He stepped into the living room and began to pace the floor as Vaughn took a seat on the sofa. "This guy is living in the past, and you're our only link to his history, so we're going to have to dredge up some memories to help us. According to Liz, he does his killing in a place made up to resemble a church. He probably refers to it as the *cathedral*. Does that ring any bells with you?"

Vaughn frowned in concentration. "No."

"It doesn't provide a link to one of those poems or something? Anything that could give us a lead?"

Again Vaughn shook his head. Frustration ate at him. Kimberley was out there somewhere, alone with a killer. And his only chance of finding her lay in playing guessing games.

"Damn!" Stone said. "All right, then. Ray, can you drive?"

Ray frowned. "Of course, I can drive. What kind of a question is that?"

Stone shrugged. "You have a lump on your forehead." He waved a hand. "Never mind that. We need someone to search Lewis's place. Quickly but efficiently. It may yield something."

"On my way," Ray said as he walked out the door.

Stone turned back to Liz. "Okay, Liz. I know this will be extremely difficult for you at a time like this, but we need you to see if you can give us anything more to work with."

Liz stared at him. He didn't say it, but he didn't have to. Kimberley's life depended on whether or not she could get her unpredictable psychic ability to work on demand. The idea terrified her. "All right," she nodded. "Can we go into the kitchen? I feel more comfortable at a table."

"Certainly."

Stone paced the kitchen as Liz and Vaughn seated themselves. Vaughn struggled admirably to conceal his anxiety, but it was visible to Liz. She'd been reasonably sure before that Vaughn had fallen in love with Kim. Now, she was positive. That new certitude weighed heavily on her and she sent a silent prayer to heaven.

"Concentrate on the cathedral, if you can, Liz," Stone directed.

"All right." Clasping her hands on the table before her, Liz closed her eyes. An image of the room she'd seen the other day flickered in her mind, but it was supplied by memory rather than any psychic facility. Taking a deep breath, she cleared her mind and tried again. Seconds stretched into minutes. Nothing. She began to grow desperate. Tears escaped the corners of her eyes as she faced the possibility of failure.

"Liz." It was Stone's voice. She felt his hand cover hers. "Liz, you're trying too hard. Open your eyes."

Opening her eyes, she avoided Vaughn's gaze. What would she see there? Pain? Desperation? She didn't want to know.

"Do we have anything here that could provide a link to him?" Stone directed his question to Vaughn.

There was a moment of silence. "Yes!" Vaughn leapt up and retrieved something from the other side of the kitchen. "This," he said. "I found it in the fridge yesterday morning. Somehow I never got around to cataloguing it."

Liz looked down. She saw the note, but it was the withered black rose that drew her eye. Her body grew cold. If a flower can have an aura, then this one did. She didn't want to touch it. It was evil. But she had to. Kim's life depended on her.

Lifting her hand, she placed it over the sinister bloom and closed her eyes. The coldness intensified.

She felt as though she'd been encased in ice. Slowly, the iciness seeped deeper and deeper into her body. Blackness settled behind her eyelids like a curtain. She concentrated. The cathedral.

Tiny pinpoints of light flickered to life and gradually grew. The candles. "I have it," she whispered.

"Where is it? Can you see where it is?" Vaughn's anxious voice cut through the image. Liz frowned as she struggled to hold onto it.

She sensed rather than saw Stone make a sharp motion. Vaughn subsided. "Liz," Stone's voice soft and soothing, "Can you describe what you see?"

"It's the same as before."

"What about the walls? Can you see the walls?"

The walls. She sensed them there, just beyond the range of the candlelight. Why couldn't she see them? She needed more light. As if in answer to her need, there was a sudden increase in the intensity of the light. "They're stone," she said.

"Like a basement?"

She frowned, tried to bring the vision more clearly into focus. "No." She shook her head. "Not a basement. It's like—" Sighing in frustration, she tried to identify the type of location. She needed to see more. And again, as though someone or something responded to her need, the perimeters of the vision extended. Stalactites! Stalagmites! "It's a cave!" At her exclamation, the scene abruptly dissipated.

"A cave!" Vaughn leapt up and began pacing the floor.

"That means something to you?" Stone asked him.

"Yeah." He raked his fingers through his hair. "When we were kids, we found this cave. God, it was enormous. Not very big around, but the ceiling must have been at least thirty feet high." He suddenly stopped and looked at Stone with an unusual expression. "When we told Anna about it, she called it one of nature's cathedrals."

Stone nodded. "Can you find this place?"

"God, it's been years. But, yeah, I think so."

Ten minutes later, they were bouncing over mountain back roads in Vaughn's Bronco. "I received more information on Mike Drayton today," Stone shouted over the noise of the pelting rain.

Vaughn didn't take his eyes off the road. "What information?"

"Drayton isn't his name. His real name is Ed Bailey. He's made a career of armed robbery. Kills anybody who gets in his way. A real sweet guy. He escaped from prison almost three years ago. Unfortunately, when I went over to arrest him, he was gone. It looks like he might have lit out for less hostile climes. I've reported his recent whereabouts, however."

The wind careened around the vehicle like a howling banshee as it tore at the trees on either side of the narrow road. "Jesus!" Vaughn said as lightning flashed and thunder rumbled. Nature's turmoil echoed that of the vehicle's occupants.

CHAPTER 21

Kim shivered. Her summer T-shirt did nothing to protect her from the frigid temperature of the cavern. After bringing her into the cave and shoving her unceremoniously to the sandy floor, Lewis had taped her ankles together and proceeded to forget her existence. Thank God! But Kim knew it wouldn't last forever and, thus far, she'd seen no opportunity to affect an escape.

Despite her determination, tears seeped from the corners of her tightly closed eyes and moisture dripped from her nose. No matter how strong she tried to be, it seemed that fear always triumphed. She'd allowed fear to rule so much of her life, and she hadn't even recognized it. Fear was a chameleon. It transformed itself to suit each new situation. Vaughn had been right. Why hadn't she listened to him? Life was much too short to throw away a chance at happiness for the sake of fear. If only she'd recognized that while there was still time to tell him she loved him.

She loved him. The words burned into her brain. God, she'd been so stupid to think that she could control that most powerful of all emotions. She could no more control the force of love than she could control the weather.

For the first time in years, Kimberley prayed. Really prayed. She prayed that God would let her live long enough to tell Vaughn how sorry she was for being a fool. She prayed that she would have the opportunity to tell him she loved him. And she prayed that she would feel his arms around her just one more time.

Her throat convulsed, but the agony of suppressing her sobs was nothing compared to the pain in her chest. If her heart was only muscle and tissue, why was it breaking now? A clatter from another part of the cave made her jump, drawing her from her self-absorption. She struggled into a kneeling position as her eyes searched the cave for her captor.

Lewis, dressed now in white coveralls, hung his gun holster from a small rocky protrusion on the wall and turned back to the black leather bag. Extracting a number of articles from it, he laid them out on some kind of tray. Seeming thoroughly absorbed in his preparations, he picked up a knife.

As the light of a thousand candles refracted from the shiny blade into her eyes, Kim froze with terror. A sense of déjà vu swept through her like a drug, paralyzing her. She no longer saw the man who wielded the knife. The walls in her mind crumbled with the rapidity of a falling dominoes. And she saw.

She saw the night of her father's murder. There were four teenage boys, strangers. If only her father had given them the money from the till without argument, maybe he'd still be alive. But he had tried to deal with them like the recalcitrant children he thought they were. It hadn't worked.

They stalked her with the bloodied knife they'd used to kill her father. The leader, a young man with pale, celery-green eyes smiled at her menacingly. And then the bells for the pumps had rung. With one last glance at her, they'd run out the back.

She knew those eyes, had seen them only days ago in a face made slightly more fleshy by the passage of time, but easily recognizable. The face of Mike Drayton. Mike Drayton was her father's killer.

Why had the walls in her mind crumbled at a time like this? Why when her own life was in question? If she didn't get out of this alive, a murderer would never see justice for his crime. She had to escape! Somehow. . .

Kim's eyes swung back to the gun on the wall. And she wondered . . . .

Suddenly Lewis turned to face her. "Kimberley, darlin', it's time." His hazel-green eyes glowed with an unnatural light in the dimly lit cavern. They chilled her, terrified her more than any other aspect of him. They were the fanatical eyes of a madman. He raised gloved hands and took a step toward her. In one hand, he held a pair of battery operated clippers, in the other, the enormous knife.

Oh, God!

Lewis knelt before her, setting the clippers on the cavern floor nearby and Kim swallowed, jerked unrelentingly back to the present. Slowly, so slowly, he reached out with the hand that held the knife until Kim felt the cold, cold blade against her cheek. And then, with a yank, he removed the tape from her mouth. "There. That's better isn't it, darlin'."

As she licked her dry, stinging lips, he watched her, curiously, like a child watching a bug in a jar. "Why"— she hesitated, trying to banish the fear from her voice— "why are you doing this?"

He reared back. "Another one who does not remember the transgression. You wound me, Kimberley. Your obvious lack of remorse for being such a naughty, naughty girl, pains me deeply."

"What are you talking about?"

"Tut, tut, Kimberley." He touched the end of her nose with the cold point of the knife and Kimberley closed her eyes, leaning back on her heels as terror shot through her. "Protestations of innocence do not help your case. Your punishment is at hand."

He gripped the back of her neck with one hand to keep her from leaning any further away from him. She felt his warm breath on her face. Then, with agonizing slowness, he drew the flat of the knife down over her lips and chin, down the curve of her neck. Kim's pulse raced as apprehension lanced through her. Her breathing, made tremorous by her shivering, quickened. She swallowed and opened her eyes to face her tormentor.

He drew the knife over her chest and lingeringly inched it toward her left breast. Her nipples, tautened by cold and fear, attracted his lurid gaze. Dread momentarily paralyzed her. And then the instinct for self-preservation kicked in and hate rose like bile in her throat.

Revulsion gripped her so strongly that she thought she might vomit. Spontaneously, before she had time to consider her action, she gathered the saliva in her mouth and spit it into his face. "You pig!" she grated.

Fury twisted his features. He grabbed her cruelly by the hair and yanked her close until a scant inch separated their faces. "That will cost you, darlin'," he said with a smile. "But you're not the type of girl who learns from her mistakes. Are you, Kimberley?"

Tears stung her eyes from the pain in her scalp, where he pulled her hair, but she met his gaze squarely and refused to respond. His breath washed over her face. It smelled of peppermints. The incongruity of that struck her.

He released his grip on her so suddenly that she almost fell. Then, without warning, he placed the blade of the knife inside the neckline of her t-shirt and yanked. Kim felt the material separate. She tried to twist away, but she only managed to fall over on her side, becoming that much more vulnerable to him.

With two more slashes of the knife, he slit the garment completely.

Then, bending over her as she lay on her back at an awkward angle because her hands were still secured behind her, he prodded her chin with the point of the knife until she met his eyes. "I can do anything I want to you," he whispered. His maniacal gaze raked her exposed body before returning to her face. "Anything. And you can't stop me. You know that. Don't you, Kimberley?"

"You bastard!"

With an abrupt move he slit the small scrap of fabric hooking the cups of her bra together and exposed her quivering breasts. "You know that, don't you, Kimberley?" he repeated his question as he ran the flat of the cold blade over her right nipple.

Suddenly she saw what he wanted. He wanted her to admit that he was in control. And if she didn't. . . But she wasn't strong enough to deny him what he wanted. She loved life too much. She would do anything to buy a few more minutes. Finally, she swallowed. "Yes. Yes, I know that."

He smiled beatifically. "That's a girl. You see, you can learn." Then, grasping her arm, he yanked her back onto her knees and picked up the clippers. "Now, it's time for your punishment to begin."

Moving behind her, he shoved her head forward until her chin rested on her chest. Kimberley flinched as the drone of the clippers filled the chamber. Oh, God. Time was running out.

The clippers grazed her scalp in one long swipe from back to front. An enormous mass of thick blonde hair fell, brushing her arm before falling to the floor of the cave. A sob caught in her throat and she squeezed her eyes tightly shut to try to keep the tears from escaping. But it was no use. Silent tears tracked endlessly down her face as clump after clump of her thick, unruly blonde hair fell to the floor. Her head felt lighter by the second. He was almost finished. *Please, God, let me live.*

* * *

The trip seemed to take hours. In reality it was probably less that 45 minutes. Yet that time stretched into an eternity as Vaughn struggled desperately to remember half-forgotten details from a lifetime ago. After one wrong turn, Vaughn managed to find the trail that led to the old cave. Rain continued to pelt them unrelentingly, interfering with his vision. He almost missed the faint reflection of tail lights in the stygian gloom. The Bronco slid to a muddy halt just inches from the vehicle. "That's Lewis's suburban," Vaughn said. "This is it."

Stone nodded. "Let's go." As he grasped the door handle, he looked over his shoulder at Liz. "Stay here, Liz. Ray should be here shortly."

Vaughn had spoken to him by radio earlier to let him know where they were going. Ray was the only backup they had. Following Stone's gaze, he looked at Liz and was relieved to see her nod.

Vaughn made his way through the thick forest, blinking against the downpour as he tried to pick out landmarks he hadn't used in more than a decade. He felt Stone at his heels. About 30 yards farther on, he began to discern the rocky outcropping that contained the cave. He turned to Stone. "It's just up there." He pointed.

Stone appraised the cave entrance. It was about five or six feet above the forest floor. Access was facilitated by a rocky path. "Is there any way to get in there without him seeing us?"

Vaughn frowned. "Maybe, if he's not watching the entrance. Otherwise, no way."

Stone continued to study the area consideringly. "Okay. Let's play it by ear. The first thing we have to do is get up there."

Five minutes later, with icy rain pouring down on

them, Stone and Vaughn flattened themselves against the wet stone face of the outcropping. The entrance to the cave was on their right.

"You hear anything," Stone asked.

Vaughn shook his head and slowly looked into the entrance. He saw light flickering on the rear wall, but nothing more. The entrance was low and narrow, a short tunnel affect. No more than five feet high and four feet wide, it was about eight feet long. Gesturing to Stone, Vaughn moved into it. He removed his gun.

The sudden cessation of the pelting rain seemed to blanket him in silence. He was abruptly conscious of the noise of his own breathing, the sweat forming on his brow to mingle with the rain dripping from his hair, and the faint crunch of his feet on sandy, pulverized rock. Cautiously, he inched forward until he had a view of a portion of the cavern. Nothing—he still couldn't see or hear anything. God, he wasn't too late was he?

He inched further forward and peered cautiously around the edge of the entrance. That was when he saw him. Coyd, alias Martin Lewis, wearing baggy white disposable coveralls, stood with his back to the entrance as he worked intently at some task. Vaughn continued to watch for a moment, observing the details of the scene. The candles. The altar-like stone. The gun hanging to Coyd's left. Suddenly, Coyd shifted his stance slightly, and Vaughn saw what he was doing.

He was braiding hair. Blond hair. But Vaughn refused to consider what that might mean. He couldn't allow emotion to affect his thinking. Not yet. Swallowing, he gestured Stone closer. "Look," he whispered.

Stone cautiously peered around Vaughn. When his eyes met Vaughn's they were hard and solemn. He gestured with his head and mouthed, "Go."

Glancing around the corner again, he caught sight of a natural stone pillar and hastily slipped toward it. Reaching it, he took a deep breath before turning to study the cavern again. That was when he saw her. For an instant, even though he should have expected it, he froze. All her beautiful blonde hair was gone. The bastard had shaved her bald. His heart ached for her, for the fear she'd already suffered. But she was alive. His eyes drank in the sight of her. Her beautiful, tear-streaked face. The trickle of blood that tracked down her throat toward her naked breasts. And a vicious red mark on her left arm. God, he wanted to rip the bastard in two.

Abruptly he discovered that Kimberley's eyes were on him. Hastily, he raised a finger to his lips, signaling her silence. Then, looking back, he checked to make certain that Stone was in place. Stone, holding his 9mm Smith and Wesson at the ready, nodded his head.

But they had taken a second too long. Coyd turned back toward Kimberley with the completed braid in his hand, and saw Stone. Without a second's hesitation, he threw the knife in his hand and leapt toward the gun hanging beside him.

There was no time to see if the knife found its target. Vaughn jumped from behind the pillar. "Freeze, Coyd!"

Coyd froze, empty hands in the air. "Vaughn," he said. "So nice of you to drop in. I had wanted to bring you earlier, you know. I had something special planned for you and Kimberley. But Cheney arrived at a most inopportune time."

Vaughn ignored him. "Turn around! Slowly." He sensed Stone moving into the chamber.

As Coyd turned to face him and Vaughn saw the madness shining from his eyes, he wondered how the man had managed to fool so many people for so long. Sure he'd added bulk to his body by weightlifting; he'd dyed his hair, and worn contacts. But even if he hadn't been recognizable as Coyd, why hadn't Vaughn seen the insanity? Because he hadn't been looking for it or because, like cancer so often did, it remained undetectable until—

A sudden flash in Coyd's eyes made him tense. "On your knees," Vaughn ordered as he gestured with his weapon.

Coyd didn't move.

"Now!" Vaughn barked.

"Fuck you!" Coyd leapt to the side and grabbed the weapon in the holster on the wall.

"Drop it!" Vaughn ordered even as he fired a shot. He missed.

Coyd ignored the order, pivoting to face Vaughn and Stone. Before he could aim the weapon, he jerked as a bullet struck and penetrated his body. The blast from the gun echoed and re-echoed in the cave. Before the sound could die away, Coyd tried once again to bring his gun to bear. Another bullet struck him, and another. The echoes of the shots threatened to deafen the occupants of the cave. And then, almost convulsively, Coyd pulled the trigger of his pistol. A bullet wild and wide of the mark ricocheted from stone to stone. Two more shots were fired. Both found their mark, and Coyd fell. In all, five bullets from two different guns riddled his body. For a moment, Vaughn stared numbly at the body of the man who, at one time, had been his brother; who had been his deputy for more than two years.

Was it over? Really over?

Then, leaving Stone to check Coyd, Vaughn ran to Kimberley and wrapped her in his embrace. "Oh, God, honey. I was scared half to death."

She sniffled. "You think *you* were scared."

He ran his hand gently over her shorn head. "I'm sorry I didn't get here sooner."

She looked up into his face. "It'll grow," she whispered. "I'm just glad you got here."

He removed his shirt and draped it around her to conceal her naked breasts before he began working at the tape binding her wrists and ankles. "Can you stand?" he asked.

"I don't know. It think my legs are asleep." Grasping his arm, she halted him. "Vaughn there's something I have to say. Right now."

He nodded. "Sure, honey. You say anything you want."

"You were right." Kim swallowed. "Life is much too short to waste any of it on fear." She met his warm golden gaze and wondered how she could ever have been so blind. "I love you, Vaughn. With all my heart, I love you."

Vaughn couldn't help but be wary of her sudden declaration. It was a complete reversal. He picked up her small dirt-streaked hand and cradled it in his palm. "If those words are true, then I'll be a very happy man, Kimberley. I'm just not certain I should believe them yet."

"But—"

He placed a finger over her lips to silence her. "You say them to me again in a couple of days—when you don't have quite so much reason to think I'm the best thing to happen to you this side of heaven—and I'll believe you. Okay?"

Certain that her love for him must be shining from her eyes like a beacon, Kim chafed at his hesitancy. But she realized she'd given him reason to doubt her, so she agreed. "Okay."

At that moment, Liz and Ray appeared at the entrance. Liz took one look at Kimberley and took charge. "We've got to get you back to the Bronco or you'll freeze to death."

Vaughn lifted Kimberley in his arms and passed her to Ray. "You take good care of her."

Ray smiled. "Yes sir."

"Garrett, come here will you?" It was Stone.

Vaughn joined him as he knelt by Coyd. "Is he dead?"

Stone nodded. "Look at this." He passed Vaughn a slip of paper.

Worn and crumbling with age, it almost fell apart at his touch. He squinted to read it in the candlelight.

I am! yet what I am who cares, or knows?
My friends forsake me like a memory lost.
I am the self-consumer of my woes;
They rise and vanish, an oblivious host,
Shadows of life, whose very soul is lost.
And yet I am -- I live -- though I am toss'd

Into the nothingness of scorn and noise,
Into the living sea of waking dream,
Where there is neither sense of life, nor joys,
But the huge shipwreck of my own esteem
And all that's dear. Even those I loved the best
Are strange -- nay, they are stranger than the rest.

As he finished reading, he looked down on the face of the man he'd thought a friend and tried to see the tortured soul of the boy he'd known.

"Do you know it?" Stone asked.

Slowly, not taking his eyes from Coyd's face, Vaughn nodded. "Yeah. It's a poem written by a man imprisoned in an asylum. I wonder if there was some part of him that recognized his own insanity. Why else would he carry a poem like this around with him?"

Stone cursed. "These cases give me the creeps."

* * *

A week had passed. A warrant had been issued for the arrest of Ed Bailey alias Mike Drayton for the murder of Kimberley's father. Skeeter's and Coyd's funerals were over and Lillooet Creek was beginning to revert to normal. Jordan Hall would be residing in the local hospital for a couple of weeks more, but he would definitely live. Amazingly the bullet had passed through his neck without causing critical injury. As he remembered receiving the good news, Vaughn grinned. Ray and Liz had been at his side. After blinking in amazement, Ray had affirmed with the certainty of an expert that the *damn guy must have had horseshoes up his ass.* He'd received a clout from Liz for his vulgarity.

Vaughn shook his head in amazement as he reflected on the changes the last few weeks had wrought in his life. He'd found his mother, or rather she had been drawn to him. After the way Liz had helped to find Kim, he'd been forced to admit that his mother was psychic, although the admission still came with limitations. It still didn't mean he was willing to accept angels, or Atlanteans, or little green men.

In addition to a mother, he was gaining a stepfather. God, it was hard to believe that Ray Cheney, his deputy, was marrying his mother. And within a few days' time, he'd be meeting his half-sister, half-brother, two nephews and a niece. Life sure took some astounding twists at times.

Now he looked across the vehicle at the child car seat and smiled at his son. He was in the process of taking Landon home. For good. That topped the list of good changes in his life.

He sobered. The only blight on his happiness was Kimberley. She'd still not repeated the words she'd said to him that night a week ago. Although she'd stayed on with her aunt, and they'd seen each other for at least a few minutes every day, something was wrong. It wasn't that she wasn't attracted to him. Her eyes followed him constantly whenever he was around. He'd begun to wish that he hadn't closed the door on sex without the possibility of commitment. It was driving him crazy to know that she wanted him, sexually at least, as much as he wanted her. But he'd obviously been right to doubt her. She was still afraid of love. Damn, that hurt!

Turning into his driveway, he passed the lane of trees and slammed his foot on the brake so quickly that the Bronco rocked. There, in his driveway, was a small red Ford Focus. Swallowing, he looked for her. Where was she? Why had she come? He refused to allow hope to surface. Not again. Not yet.

Parking the Bronco, he walked around to the passenger side and released Landon from his car seat. Then, carrying his son in his arms, he walked around the corner to the deck. She was there, peering in a window, wearing the sexy little blonde wig she'd purchased at the hair salon.

A sense of déjà vu struck him. "What the hell do you think you're doing?" he barked, just as he had a few weeks ago.

On a squeal of startlement, she swung to face him, drinking in the sight of him. It seemed like an eternity since she'd seen him last. "I–I was just looking."

"Kim!" Landon announced, pointing a pudgy finger at her.

"Hello, sweetheart," she said. And then, as though drawn by a magnet, her eyes went back to Vaughn's face. She wanted to throw her arms around him and hold on to him for the rest of her life, but the expression on his face stopped her.

"Why are you here, Kimberley?" he asked. His face was tight and wary. Kim supposed she couldn't blame him.

"I'm here to tell you that I still think you're the best thing this side of heaven."

"What?" He was afraid to believe his ears.

She smiled and held out a piece of paper. "Read this."

Taking it from her, he read, but the words didn't make any sense. "What is this?"

"I've sold my interest in the business in Seattle," she said. "I love you and I'm staying."

Kim felt tension seep into her muscles as his face froze. His eyes scanned and recorded every detail of her expression.

Oh, my God! He'd never really said the words himself. Had she just made a terrible fool of herself?

"You"—she swallowed—"You do love me, don't you?" Her stomach churned with fear as her eyes searched his face. If he turned away from her now, she didn't know what she'd do.

Suddenly, he sighed. "Of course, I love you." Holding out his free arm to her, he said, "Come here."

Kim didn't wait for a second invitation. Resting her head on his chest, she wrapped her arms around his waist.

"I could wring your neck, you know," he said against the top of her head. "You put me through a week of hell. I thought you were having second thoughts."

"I was," she said. "Second, and third, and fourth. But every time I thought about it, the answer came up the same. I love you."

Vaughn closed his eyes and kissed her forehead. "And you're certain you're willing to be an instant wife and mother?" he asked.

Kimberley tilted her head back and looked up at him. "Do I understand you correctly? Are you—and your son—proposing to me?"

Vaughn looked down at her in surprise. Looked at his son, and then grinned. "Yeah," he said. "Yeah, I guess we are."

Kim rose on her toes to plant a kiss on his lips. Then, turning her head she brushed her lips across Landon's soft baby cheek. "I accept," she said. Standing on tiptoe so that she could speak directly into Vaughn's ear, she whispered, "Now, will you take me to bed?"

He laughed and looked down into her face. "You are becoming a very forward woman."

Kim frowned. "Does that mean yes?"

"Yes." Moving his son a little aside, he kissed her deeply, sensuously. Then, lifting his head, he looked down at her with his gaze of molten gold. "Let's go in the house."

THE END

BOOKS BY CHRISTINE MICHELS

Ascent to the Stars
Danger's Kiss
In Fugitive Arms
In Destiny's Arms
Beneath A Crimson Moon
Beyond Betrayal
A Season of Miracles
Undercover with the Enemy

AND CO-AUTHORED AS

SHARICE KENDYL

To Share A Sunset

ACCLAIM FOR
CHRISTINE MICHELS' NOVELS

UNDERCOVER WITH THE ENEMY

(Contemporary Romance)

"I was caught with the very first line ... A well-paced tale of secrets, deception, and family ties ..."

— *The Romance Journal*

A SEASON OF MIRACLES

(Contemporary Romance)
(Heart of Romance "Reader's Choice" Award Winner, 2nd place)

"Super story. Great plot, riveting emotion, danger, and suspense that compels you to turn the pages ... A gotta-read!"

— *Rendezvous*

BEYOND BETRAYAL

(Western Historical Romance)
(Colorado Romance Writers "Award of Excellence" Finalist)
(Heart of Romance "Reader's Choice" Award Finalist)

"An exciting journey to the Old West ... Ms. Michels spins a tale of love and betrayal with sophistication and style ... *Beyond Betrayal* is a treasure for romance fans and everyone else who appreciates the Old West."

— *Rendezvous*

BENEATH A CRIMSON MOON

(Futuristic Romance)

"An intelligent plot with a twist; strong, well-developed characters and a romance that is out of sight!"

— *The Literary Times*

IN DESTINY'S ARMS

(Futuristic Romance)

"Fans of futuristic romance will love Ms. Michels' newest creation! Her talent for creating fascinating new worlds is boundless!"

— *The Literary Times*

IN FUGITIVE ARMS

(Futuristic Romance)
(Heart of Romance Award Finalist)

Fantastic! If you've never read a futuristic romance, *In Fugitive Arms* will be a pleasant, addictive surprise!"

— *The Literary Times*

DANGER'S KISS

(Contemporary Romantic Suspense)
(Heart of Romance Award Winner)

Danger's Kiss is "a gripping and intense tale of a small town tormented by dark deeds and murderous secrets. A great read!"

— *Romantic Times*

ASCENT TO THE STARS

(Futuristic Romance)

"Christine Michels skillfully blends a totally realistic alien society with a beautifully believable romance that mixes into a superb novel."

— *Affaire de Coeur*

Dear Reader,

I hope you've enjoyed reading DANGER'S KISS. This was the third novel I wrote (my second solo novel following ASCENT TO THE STARS) and my first foray into the realm of romantic suspense. I thoroughly enjoyed writing this story and exploring the depths of the human psyche. What makes people with similar backgrounds choose divergent paths? How does tragedy affect us? And can meaningful relationships, even love, develop despite it all?

I always appreciate hearing from my readers. If you would like to contact me, please look me up on Facebook, follow me on Twitter, or write to me at one of the addresses that follow.

Best Wishes and Happy Reading!

Christine Michels

mailto:christinemichels@fastmail.net

ABOUT THE AUTHOR

Christine Michels lives with her family on the Canadian prairie in Southeastern Alberta.

You may write to her at:

Christine Michels
c/o Northern Fire Publishing
P.O. Box 153
Redcliff, AB.
Canada T0J 2P0
mailto: contact@nfirepublish.com

Follow Christine on Twitter:
@CMichelsAuthor
~~~
"Like" Christine on Facebook at:
http://www.facebook.com/Michels.Christine

Visit Christine at her webpage at:
http://www.christinemichels.com/

www.ingramcontent.com/pod-product-compliance
Lightning Source LLC
Chambersburg PA
CBHW071156250626
47159CB00001B/113